Praise for Karin Rit
And *The Silver* wep

"A tale of female oppression, p
Eolyn touches on issues that are
times both heartwarming and h
women about the ways in whic
them – but it does so in a way t

"The story's greatest triumph is Gastreich's prose, a consistent blend of lyrical verse and dark imagery....Lush, evocative descriptions carry readers through an unforgettable journey."

-Kirkus Reviews

"War propels the story forward, and the characters are at their best when the circumstances engulfing them are at their worst."

–Publishers Weekly

"A splendidly imagined tale that neatly sidesteps the stereotypical offerings relied on by much of the genre."

–Book Viral

"Wonderfully written, with vivid descriptions, engaging characters and a unique storyline."

–Libri Amori Miei

"I especially love that this trilogy has such intriguing women playing significant roles on both sides of the story."

–The White Sky Project

"Masterfully written."

–The Kindle Book Review

Also by Karin Rita Gastreich

Eolyn
Book One of The Silver Web

Sword of Shadows
Book Two of The Silver Web

Daughter of Aithne

Book Three of The Silver Web

Karin Rita Gastreich

ORB WEAVER PRESS

Daughter of Aithne
Book Three of The Silver Web
Copyright © 2017 by Karin Rita Gastreich

Cover art © 2017 by Thomas Vandenberg
Cover design © 2017 by Thomas Vandenberg

Trade Paperback ISBN-13 978-0-9972320-2-8

Orb Weaver Press
Kansas City, Missouri

For Mom and Dad

CHAPTER ONE

Eolyn of Moisehén

EOLYN SIGNALED HER COMPANIONS for silence. High above the woodland path, verdant branches creaked and groaned under a restless summer wind. Closing her eyes, she listened as the wind's whisper grew in strength. She strained to make sense of the voices of the forest, but all she heard was the cry of her dead mother carried inside their hollow wail.

You know the consequences! His power will be unstoppable.

Unsettled, Eolyn opened her eyes.

A mosaic of shadows cut through ancient oaks and moss-covered beeches. Leaves fluttered down from the canopy in a green-gold shower. The creatures of the forest, silenced by the sudden gust, began to move and chatter once more.

"What is it, Mama?"

Eolyn's daughter, Briana, looked up at her with wide, attentive eyes. The girl's cheeks were smudged with dirt; her dress torn by brambles. All that remained of Briana's careful plait was a wild splay of black curls. The disorder brought a smile to Eolyn's lips.

"Don't fret, Briana," she said. "It's only an afternoon chill."

"Maga Eolyn! Look at this." Several paces ahead, Mariel, a young maga warrior, studied the ground. Her ash-brown hair was neatly bound. Her hand rested on the hilt of a well-loved sword.

Eolyn followed Mariel's gaze to the dark earth, where a large cat had left its mark: four neat ovals forming a crown over a rounded triangle.

Awed, Eolyn bent and laid her hand over the print. Her fingers tingled with the animal's magic, fresh and undiluted.

"It's bigger than your hand!" Briana exclaimed.

"So it is," Eolyn said, intrigued. "No cats of this size reside in the South Woods. She must have wandered from the Paramen Mountains."

"A snow tiger?" Mariel's sun-darkened brow creased in doubt. "What would have driven her so far from home?"

"Perhaps we can speak with her and find out."

"Papa says the Mountain Warriors can shapeshift into Snow Tigers." Briana's voice sparked with excitement. "At the Battle of Aerunden, brave Sir Drostan turned into a bear and slew them by the hundreds!"

"Your father embellishes his tales of war," Eolyn replied. "Sir Drostan slew many snow tigers, but he did not—"

A movement in the shadows caught Eolyn's eye. She tightened the hold on her staff. The crystal head ignited in a steady hum.

"Get behind us, Briana," she said. "Stay close."

Eolyn did not fear snow tigers, but if one appeared, this would be Briana's first encounter with a large predator. A wild cat this far from her territory might be frightened, even hungry. The situation had to be handled with care.

An unnatural silence descended on the forest. Briana's breath was reduced to short, nervous gasps.

"Ground yourself, daughter," Eolyn said. "Remember what I've taught you."

"I'm trying, Mama."

Some twenty paces ahead, the bushes rustled. A tall, grim-faced man stepped into view, broad in the shoulders, with blue eyes and golden hair.

Eolyn lowered her staff, disappointed. "Lord Borten? For the love of the Gods!"

"Forgive us, my Lady Queen." He bowed. "It was not our intention to startle you."

Guards now showed themselves, and Eolyn heard other men-at-arms nearby.

Briana ran toward Borten and proffered a basket filled with fruits, herbs, and mushrooms. "Look what we found!"

Borten bent to greet the princess with a warm smile. "You

must tell me all your adventures when we've returned to camp."

"I've got stones in my pockets, too," Briana said. "Lots of them, of every color. And we almost saw a snow tiger!"

Borten's frown returned. He straightened. "It is late, my Lady Queen."

Eolyn nodded to Mariel, who took Briana's hand and walked ahead. Lord Borten strode next to the Queen, maintaining a stiff silence as men-at-arms fell in place around them.

Squirrels chased each other across the path and up a trunk, furry tails flicking in rhythm with their aggressive chatter. The trill of a Tenolin sparrow floated from somewhere beyond the trees, igniting a dull ache in Eolyn's chest. She paused, hoping to catch sight of the bird, but the notes faded into the distance.

Borten cleared his throat. "With all due respect, my Lady Queen, I do not understand—"

"We've been through this already, Lord Borten. If my daughter is to become a maga, then she must experience the truth of the forest, away from men-at-arms, away from anything that disturbs the magic of this place. That is why we come to Moehn. That is why we visit the South Woods every summer."

"It is not safe for you to go out alone."

"I did not claim it was safe. Only that it gives me peace."

Borten shook his head. His aroma of earth and leather wrapped around Eolyn like a well-worn cloak. She quelled the impulse to touch him.

"A snow tiger, for the love of the Gods," he muttered.

"We have nothing to fear from the creatures of this forest," Eolyn said. After a moment she added, "I had rather hoped you would focus your protective instincts on the Prince today."

"I assure you, he is well looked after."

"Exhausted, I imagine. He and your sons had invading armies to defeat this morning, and Thunder Trolls to slay."

"Is that so?" Borten's tone relaxed a shade.

"Eoghan has not played for a very long time. In the City, he can no longer indulge in Children's Magic. The friendship of your sons is the greatest treasure he has."

"Prince Eoghan is a noble youth. Thoughtful and strong of heart."

3

Eolyn cast Borten a sideways glance. "Strong of heart and quick of temper, like his father."

"True of purpose, I would say. He will make a fine king. One who inspires respect and loyalty."

Eolyn understood these words were meant as a compliment, but they troubled her nonetheless. A boy of ten summers, Eoghan was already imprisoned by his status. As soon as he could walk, they had taught him to kill. The brighter his flame of magic, the more they molded it to the bloody purpose of defending crown and kingdom.

The voice of her friend Adiana now returned as a murmur inside Eolyn's heart. *They will take him to the City and teach him the sordid ways of princes and kings.*

Eolyn shivered, despite the heat of her exertions and the warm summer afternoon. A strange magic had been let loose in the forest. All the warnings of the past were floating on the wind.

The trees thinned into a loose stand of spindly birch. Beyond that, tall grasses shone in golden hues under the afternoon light. The camp came into view, a village of large canvas tents. Overhead, banners snapped, bearing the new sigil of her husband's house: two dragons, one silver and one black, with tails intertwined.

Eolyn's footsteps slowed, dragged to a halt by the heartbreaking pull of the forest behind. There she remained, torn on the edge between the love she had chosen and the life she had left behind.

Weariness clutched at her spirit. Not the refreshing fatigue of a long day's walk, but a deeper exhaustion born of some vague burden that escaped her understanding.

"Is something amiss, my Lady Queen?"

Borten's question brought her gaze to him.

The lord's brow furrowed. He started as if to turn away but then remained, alert under Eolyn's scrutiny, his chest rising and falling in a steady rhythm. From one moment to the next, his mask of duty fractured, exposing subtle threads of shared memories.

Humble houses nestled against a sun-lit hill.

Borten's men vigilant upon a half-finished wall.

The laughter of Eolyn's students in her garden.

A shared glance.

4

A forgotten kiss.

"Mama!" Briana's cry shattered the exchange. "Look!"

High above the fields, a misplaced wisp of night swirled through the sky, growing larger as it approached.

A knot of trepidation took hold of Eolyn's gut.

"Briana," she said, "stay with the guards."

With Borten at her side, Eolyn hurried to where Mariel stood at the edge of the pasture.

"Those are not common ravens," she said, drawing her sword. "See the sparks of amber that dance on their wings?"

Borten shouted to the guards in the camp. Some came on foot, others on horse. The prince ran alongside them, half the size of the men who served his father, yet twice as fierce. One of the knights caught the boy and held him back. Eoghan kicked in indignation and demanded to be released.

The raptors dove, their wings beating with an aggressive cacophony of calls.

Faeom shamue!

Eolyn's ward parted the flock, forcing it back on itself.

The birds landed on the grass. Light flashed through them as they assumed human form. Staves raised and swords drawn, a party of dark-cloaked mages set sharp eyes on the Queen and her attendants.

Eolyn frowned when she recognized their leader. "High Mage Thelyn?"

Tall and elegant in bearing, Thelyn came forward and knelt at Eolyn's feet. His robes shimmered with the prism colors of a raven's wings. His neatly trimmed beard marked an angular face that defied the passage of time.

He proffered a note bearing the King's seal and said, "My Lady Queen. We are most relieved to find you well."

Eolyn accepted the missive, conscious of the tremor in her fingers. She broke the seal and unfolded the parchment.

A bitter mood impregnated his message. Akmael had written in his own hand, each pen stroke reflecting carefully controlled anger.

By order of Akmael, High Mage and King Moisehén, all Magas are to be stripped of their staves and arms, their magic bound, their persons returned to the City and confined to the Fortress of Vortingen until the King's Justice is served.

The words blurred in front of Eolyn's eyes. She blinked and read again.

"Rise, Thelyn, and tell me what this is about."

The wizard obeyed. "Princess Eliasara has been abducted."

"What?"

"Maga Ghemena stands accused of treason."

"*Our* Ghemena?"

"She and two other maga warriors slew half-a-dozen of the King's men and took the princess west by flight."

Cold horror gripped Eolyn's heart. "They took her to Roenfyn? They mean to wage war against us?"

"So we suspect."

"It's not true!" Mariel interjected. "It can't be. Ghemena would never—"

Thelyn silenced Mariel with a glare. "How is it, my Lady Queen, that your daughters in magic never seem to know when it is their place to speak?"

Eolyn lifted a hand to stall Mariel's impulse. The maga warrior gave a reluctant nod and stepped back.

"High Mage Thelyn," Eolyn said with forced calm, "what evidence is there against Ghemena?"

"The traces left by her magic are unmistakable. And there was a witness: The last man to perish by Ghemena's blade survived long enough to tell us what he saw." Thelyn's serpent-like gaze slid back to Mariel. "Why would a dying man, a faithful soldier of the King, lie?"

Eolyn drew a breath to steady her pulse. She assessed the number and disposition of the men who accompanied Thelyn. It would not be easy for them to overcome the maga warriors in her escort, but they would very likely succeed. Indeed, they might well use any resistance as an excuse to slay them all.

"Mariel," she said, "by the King's orders, you and the other maga warriors are to surrender your arms to Thelyn's company at once."

Mariel hesitated but laid down her sword.

The other maga warriors shifted on their feet, exchanging wary glances. A ring of metal unsheathed turned Eolyn's head.

6

"Betania," she said. "You, too, must lay down your weapon."

The fair-headed woman shook her head and leveled her blade at the mages in front of her. "I will not surrender my weapon to any of these men."

"Do as I say," Eolyn commanded.

"They deceive us!" Betania declared. "They would take our blades and destroy us all."

Fire tunneled up Eolyn's staff and lanced from its crystal head, knocking the sword out of the woman's grasp. Betania stared at her tutor in shock, cradling the singed hand against her chest.

"This is the will of our King," Eolyn said sternly. "And it is my will as well. You do not need metal to defend yourselves as magas. Have I not taught you this from the very first day of your apprenticeship? Lay down your weapons, I say! We will return to the King's City in peace."

Stunned silence descended on the magas. One by one, they set down their blades.

Eolyn's jaw clenched as she turned back to Thelyn. She despised the cold triumph she sensed in his aura, like a net of steel woven through dense shafts of purple and blue.

"The weapons of my warriors are entrusted to you, High Mage Thelyn, until we return to Moisehén," she said. "I will not, however, allow their staves to be surrendered or their magic to be bound."

"The command of our Lord King is clear, my Lady Queen," Thelyn replied smoothly.

"No woman here has committed a crime that merits such a measure. I will assume responsibility for their return to the City, and I will answer to the King for any decision I make contrary to his orders."

Thelyn bowed in deference. "With all due respect, my Lady Queen, I do not think it prudent to counter the King's will."

"My Lady Queen." Borten intervened. "High Mage Thelyn speaks wisely. Ghemena was one of your captains, and she did not act alone. Obedience will meet with the King's understanding and mercy. Disobedience, no matter how small, may breed mistrust."

Eolyn shot Borten a hard glance, her resentment tempered by the sober recognition that he spoke the truth. She had never been discrete in her objections to Princess Eliasara's confinement.

7

Indeed, she had argued on many occasions that the princess be reunited with her mother in Roenfyn. They would remember this in the King's City and use it against her.

She fingered the jewel at her throat, a silver web crafted by Akmael's mother and gifted to Eolyn years ago. With a whispered spell, the amulet could take her to the Mage King. She would have argument and debate, but perhaps no resolution. And if Akmael did not allow her to return? Briana, Eoghan, and all her daughters in magic would be left alone at the hands of these mages.

She had abandoned her own once before to go to Akmael. She would not take that risk again.

"Come." Eolyn beckoned Mariel and the other magas.

They gathered close and at her behest, linked hands, forming a tight circle.

"One of our own is accused of treason." Eolyn met the gaze of each woman as she spoke. "And the shadow of this crime has descended upon us all. We must trust the King's wisdom and obey his command. This is the oath we took, and it is the oath we will keep, as Daughters of Aithne and servants of the Crown. Once we have returned to the city, I will see your magic restored. And I promise you, by the breath of Dragon, that I will not allow it to be taken from you again."

Uncertainty, trepidation, and anger played across the women's faces. Eolyn feared some of them might never forgive this moment, but she also knew from hard experience they had no choice if they wished to survive.

I may not see a way to stop this, beloved daughters, but at least I can lessen your pain.

At Eolyn's bidding, they knelt, still holding hands, and closed their eyes.

Eolyn waited until her maga warriors breathed in unison. Then she intertwined her magic with theirs to sustain them, and sent tendrils of her spirit deep into the earth to feed her own power. Calling upon Dragon, she invoked an ancient spell for protection and courage. When at last she believed her daughters were ready, she nodded to High Mage Thelyn.

At his signal, the mages closed on them as a single dark tide. Each man took hold of a maga, one hand firm on the back of her neck, the other palm hard against her forehead. Their curse thundered through the circle.

Behnaum ukaht!

Screams pierced the air, the excruciating cries of women separated from their souls. Eolyn drew her daughters' agony hard into her own spirit, channeling their suffering toward the heart of the earth. Her lungs burned, her breath came in choked gasps. Just as her body was about to buckle, Thelyn set a firm hand upon her shoulder. The wizard's magic flowed around her spirit, cutting Eolyn off from her daughters and jolting her out of the trance.

"That was noble on your part, my Lady Queen," Thelyn said, hauling Eolyn to her feet. "Noble, but unnecessary. And dangerous."

Eolyn's knees trembled. Cold sweat broke out on her skin. Yet she could stand, and she felt magic flowing through her veins.

Mariel and the other magas lay spent upon the grass, their auras caught inside shadowy nets. Mages hovered over them, checking their pulse, the dilation of their eyes, the heat of their foreheads.

"You need not worry, my Lady Queen," Thelyn said. "The curse deals a harsh blow, but they will be well enough to travel by morning."

Disoriented, Eolyn wrenched herself away from the wizard and stumbled toward the forest, finding support against a young birch. Thelyn followed, maintaining a respectful but watchful distance.

Briana and Eoghan appeared at their mother's side. A troubled frown darkened the prince's brow, and Briana's cheeks were wet with tears. Eolyn clung to them, as if their presence could anchor her against this sudden tide of anguish.

"Why was I spared?" The words fell from her lips in a shaky whisper. "I, too, am a maga. Why did you not bind my magic?"

"My Lady Queen." Thelyn's voice registered only a hint of surprise. "You are not counted among those women. You are the chosen consort of our Lord and King. As such, you can always count on our protection."

CHAPTER TWO

Taesara of Roenfyn

TAESARA REMOVED THE LAST of the bandage from Berena's arm. A tug as it held to tender, rotting skin pulled a sharp breath from the bedridden woman.

"I am sorry, Berena," Taesara said. "I do not mean to hurt you."

Berena managed a black-gummed smile, one good eye sparkling in her bloated and misshapen face. The ward in which they sat was long, filled with quiet moans of the sick and dying. Shafts of light knifed through narrow windows, providing dim illumination for the diligent work of the Sisters of the Poor.

"I don't feel anything anymore, milady," Berena slurred. "Not on my skin, I don't. Just the pain of my ugliness, that's all I feel."

"You are not ugly." Taesara placed the bandage among other soiled linens in a basket at her feet. Taking a clean rag, she plunged it into a bucket of water scented with juniper needles and arogat root. "None of us are ugly before the Gods of Thunder."

Taesara took the stump of Berena's hand, her fingers long since fallen away, and held the arm steady as she bathed Berena from shoulder to wrist, cleansing scabs yellowed by blood and puss. Berena's affliction was a slow rot that had endured for years, forcing the woman to watch without hope or remedy as her body decayed.

"There you are wrong, milady," Berena said. "The Gods like their women beautiful. The only reason they make ugly ones is so they can appreciate the pretty ones all the more."

Taesara smiled at the jest. "The Mother of all my Sisters

teaches us that those visited by the plague of Catlan are the most blessed of all. The Gods have chosen you to suffer the trials of the Underworld in this life. Thus they purify your spirit, so you will not be ensnared by the slow decay of the Lost Souls when you pass from this world into the next."

A wet chortle escaped Berena's sagging lips. "She's a clever one, that Mother. Merciful too, and good at heart. But she's wrong. Wrong about the Gods, wrong about me, and wrong to make pretty ones like you waste their pretty lives on this ugly rot." Berena pointed with her chin down the length of the infirmary.

"She makes us do nothing. We are all here of our own accord. We follow her because we share her beliefs."

Taesara plunged the rag into water, refreshing its fragrance before she continued to wash Berena. She worked systematically, with a gentle skill founded on years of attending the worst miseries of the poor and destitute.

"You follow her because you're afraid," Berena said.

"Afraid?" Taesara glanced up, startled by the accusation. "I am not afraid, Berena. Certainly not of you or of the disease that haunts your body. You must forgive me if I have ever done anything to make you think otherwise."

"I ain't talking about the sickness." Her good eye glazed over, hard as crystal. "Thunder set his red eye on you, that's what I think. Then you got scared and ran away."

"I would never turn my back on—"

"Not that I'd blame a fine lady like you. It's always trouble when the Gods notice us. Look what happened when they noticed me."

"Thunder is a loving guardian to all our people, especially to the poor and the afflicted. I do not hide from him or the Gods he serves." Taesara lowered her voice. "But this I will confide in you, Berena: I loathe the men of this world. I abhor their desire, their rage, their lust for blood and power. I saw too much of men's truth when I was young and at their mercy. I wish no more of it. That is why I came here, and that is why I stay. Having lived in their company, I can say that you are not ugly, Berena. You are one of the most beautiful people I have ever known."

Berena blinked and drew a ragged breath. Scrunching her

11

deformed face, she looked away.

"I don't want a bath anymore," she said hoarsely. "I want to rest."

Taesara nodded and withdrew, taking the bucket of water and the basket of soiled linens with her. She walked along the row of beds in respectful silence, pausing only to inform one of the Sisters that Berena was ready for fresh bandages.

Outside the infirmary, the harsh sunlight caused Taesara to squint. She crossed the courtyard, stepping carefully through the gardens, and left the linens with women who tended the laundry in boiling cauldrons set over open fires.

The bucket of bath water she took to the kitchen, where it was mixed with the rest of the water collected from the infirmary that day. At the evening meal, the purest of the Sisters would cleanse their spirits in preparation for the Afterlife by drinking water used to bathe the sick.

Taesara was not allowed to participate in such sacred rites, because she had known a man and worse, a mage. It had not been her choice to lie in his bed, and she had taken no pleasure from her duty. Indeed, she had suffered what no mother should be forced to bear. Yet a lifetime of service would not atone for her sin, nor erase the stain he had left upon her soul.

"Our blessed Mother has sent for you," the head cook announced, taking the bucket from Taesara's hands. "She wants to see you as soon as you're finished with the baths."

Taesara greeted this news with an obedient nod.

She left the kitchen and climbed the narrow stairs that led to the Mother's study and a handful of chambers set aside for receiving guests from the outside world. The rest of the cloister was stark and modest, but here the chairs and tables were finely carved. Tapestries graced the walls with images of men and women called by Thunder during the long and difficult history of Taesara's people.

When she entered the study, a man standing at the window wheeled about and pinned Taesara with a stern gaze. His long face was framed by graying hair, his sage cloak richly embroidered with silver threads.

"My Lord Regent." Taesara sank to her knees, deeply troubled by this unannounced visit.

A rustle of skirts indicated the Mother's approach. The old woman laid a frail but steady hand on Taesara's shoulder. "If it pleases you, Lord Regent, I will take my leave now, so that you may speak with your niece."

Taesara looked up at the Mother with a mixture of hurt and trepidation. "Dear Mother, I have no family in this world, not since I—"

"Hush, my daughter." The Mother took Taesara's face in her hands and studied her with kind eyes. "I know the vows you took when you entered this place better than you. I do not doubt the devotion with which you have served the Gods as part of our community these many years. Your family has indeed been dead to you, but now Thunder wishes to call you back to the world of the living. Listen to your uncle, for he seeks to resurrect your heart from its grave. The news he bears will bring you much joy."

"But I don't want—"

"Know that whatever you decide, you have my blessing." The Mother kissed Taesara and left, closing the door quietly behind her.

Taesara lowered her gaze to the floor, burdened by a terrible uncertainty she had not felt in years.

Sylus Penamor, Lord Regent of Roenfyn, strode forward and extended a gloved hand to his niece. "Rise, Taesara."

She obeyed, stiffening as Penamor took her chin in hand and subjected her to cold inspection. After a moment, he shook his head. "Only the Sisters of the Poor could take a woman at the height of her flower and turn her into a dried-up weed."

Taesara bristled. "There is no place for vanity within these walls."

"Apparently not. They've made you skinny and sallow. Though it is nothing, I'll wager, that a bit of sun and some proper food cannot remedy. What are these rags they dress you in?"

She stepped away, clenching her jaw. "This is all I need. All anyone needs, to live at peace in this world."

Penamor snorted. "Indeed."

"Why are you here?"

"I've come to fetch you home."

"This is my home."

"This was your temporary refuge. A foul place, but one of your choosing. We were generous enough to let you stay, first your father and then I, as we put the outside world in order. Now it is time for you to return."

"I am not going back."

"Oh, but I think you will." Penamor spoke with an odd tone, at once menacing and full of promise. "War is at hand, and you will be the one to lead it."

Taesara forced a laugh. "You know I will have no part of that. Eliasara would die at their hands if we so much as—"

"They do not have Eliasara. We do."

Shadows flashed through Taesara's vision. She stumbled and caught hold of the back of a chair. A chasm opened inside her heart, swallowing the vines and trees with which she had concealed her love and pain during all these years. A bitter flood of anguish returned full force.

"Where is she?" Taesara did not look at her uncle, her mind consumed by the image of King Akmael's stony countenance, his dark intent, his merciless heart.

"About a day's ride from here. She has been asking for you."

"Is she…whole? Have they harmed her in any way?"

"Do you mean have they turned her into a witch? No. Eliasara is a true daughter of Roenfyn. She has remained faithful to her memory of you, and to the convictions of her people. And she is beautiful, Taesara, as lovely as you were at her age, with the same sweet smile and golden hair."

"She will not recognize me. She had only just begun to walk when we were separated."

"She will know who you are. That is enough. She wants a mother to love, and one who will love her. She needs you, Taesara."

Unable to endure the weight of the moment, Taesara sank to the floor.

"What is this unbearable work of the Gods?" she whispered. "How has such a thing come to pass?"

"That is an amusing story to tell." Penamor knelt at her side. The smell of leather and horse stung her senses. "The wizard Tzeremond often said the magas always betray their own, and once again, that old hawk's wisdom has proven true. The Witch Queen's

14

very own student, a maga warrior by the name of Ghemena, broke into Eliasara's prison with two of her companions. They slew the Mage King's guards and brought the Princess to Roenfyn, to me. Now the magas stand with us, ready to fight."

Fire surged through Taesara's veins.

"Who else?" she demanded. "Who else stands with Roenfyn?"

"Galia has agreed to support our cause, and messengers have been dispatched to Antaria. We await their response. We also have allies inside Moisehén: noble families whose loyalty I have cultivated in secret; mages who pretend to serve King Akmael; and others among the Witch Queen's own who are anxious to see the line of Mage Kings dissolved. This is our moment, Taesara. Your moment. To exact vengeance on the King of Moisehén and his villainous harlot, to kill their bastards, and to see your daughter and all her descendants claim the Crown of Vortingen."

Taesara straightened her back, withdrawing from her uncle's grasp and taking deep breaths as she tried to steady her pulse.

After a long moment, she leveled her gaze at him. "I don't care about any of that, Uncle. All I want is to see my daughter."

A smile of triumph touched his lips. "As well I knew you would."

CHAPTER THREE

Arrest

HEAVY OAK DOORS SWUNG INWARD. A cavernous space hung with bright banners greeted Eolyn. Courtiers hushed and turned to acknowledge their queen. Men and women in fine robes bowed, their jewels glinting in light that streamed through high windows.

Anchoring her spirit to the heart of the mountain, Eolyn began the long walk to the throne of her husband. Briana held her hand tight. Eoghan strode with a formality acquired in recent years, fingers resting upon the hilt of a sword gifted to him by his father.

Behind them came High Mage Thelyn and Lord Borten. On their heels followed Borten's young squire Markl, a long-time friend of Mariel's and occasional visitor to the court.

Mariel and the other magas had been separated from Eolyn at the castle gates and taken to dark cells beneath the fortress. Eolyn tried not to think about her daughters alone in the dungeons, lest her nerves unravel. Their future depended on her ability to manage this situation with patience, cunning, and no small amount of grace.

Robes rustled as the courtiers drew back to allow her passage. They kept their faces downcast while following the queen with furtive glances. Suspicion hung heavy in the air. Eolyn knew every word and gesture would be measured during the coming moments, as everyone present evaluated whether it was still prudent to call the queen their friend.

King Akmael maintained a stony countenance. No emotion, no hint of love, disappointment, anger, or relief showed upon his bearded face. He rose, however, and Eolyn drew courage from this gesture of respect.

Around the King stood the members of his Council, Mage Corey of East Selen among them. Years ago, when Eolyn had first entered this hall as a prisoner, Corey had been the only man to defend her. Now he stood in place of Tzeremond, the wizard who would have seen her burn, his hawk-like gaze not unlike that of his predecessor.

Eolyn stopped a few paces short of the dais and dropped on bended knee, dark red curls falling freely over her shoulders. She had left her hair unbound, knowing how much this would please Akmael. She had chosen an elegant gown that honored the colors of his house, deep purple embroidered with silver and black.

Beside her, young Eoghan gave a stiff bow. Princess Briana, however, ignored all protocol and sprang, laughing, into the Mage King's arms.

To Eolyn's relief, Akmael indulged the girl's impulse, lifting Briana high and holding her close.

"We had the most wonderful adventures, Papa," she said, "but it takes forever to get to the South Woods, and as soon as we arrived, you made us come back!"

"It is better this way, to have the family united."

Eolyn felt the heat of her husband's gaze as it came to rest upon her bowed head.

"Your mother's presence keeps me whole," he continued. "Has she not told you about the curse cast upon me when I was a boy?"

"No." Briana's voice sparked with curiosity.

"If I am parted from your mother for too long, I turn into an ogre." He embellished this with a fierce growl.

Briana squealed and kicked until he set her down. She ran laughing and took shelter behind Eolyn, who held steady in her bow.

Gentle amusement rippled through the hall, undercutting the tension.

"Mama told me that when you were young, you could travel to the South Woods in the blink of an eye," Briana said from behind Eolyn. "Is it true?"

"Yes."

"Will you teach me how?"

17

"Your mother is the guardian of that magic now. It is she who must teach you."

"But she won't. She says I'm not skilled enough yet."

"Then so say I."

Akmael stepped close. His aroma of polished stone and timeless magic washed over Eolyn. She felt the Spirit of the Forest stir within. She wanted to rise and wrap her arms around the man she loved, to feel once again the strength of his embrace, but she held her position as protocol demanded.

"Well met, Eoghan." Akmael addressed his son. "What news do you have for me?"

The prince responded in solemn tones. "My Lord King, you will be most pleased to know that Moehn continues to prosper under Lord Borten's stewardship, and his sons are becoming fine soldiers. The new tower at Falon's Ridge is well-manned and maintained. We did not have the opportunity to visit the fortifications along the eastern border, but Lord Borten assures me they are in order, and I trust his word."

"As do I," the King said. "Well met, Borten. I am happy that you decided to join the Queen's escort. I will have need of your wisdom and judgment in the days to come."

"I am, as always, at your service, my Lord King," Borten replied.

Eolyn sensed a hesitation in Akmael's stance, as if he had noticed something not entirely to his liking. Her heart stalled, and she risked a glance upward.

The King's black gaze had settled upon young Markl, Borten's ward and squire.

A lanky youth with a freckled face and a shock of brown hair, Markl was grandson to Makadias Felton and sole survivor of the house that ruled the province of Moehn before the Syrnte invasion. It was not unusual for Markl to accompany his guardian at court. Yet for some reason the boy's presence did not please Eolyn's husband.

Akmael looked as if he were about to say something, but then shook his head as if dismissing the thought.

"I would have a word alone with the Queen," he announced. "Eoghan, look after your sister. We will speak again come evening."

If the courtiers felt disappointment at being denied the spectacle of the first exchange between king and queen, they concealed it well. Everyone recessed behind the prince and princess. The Council members, led by Corey and Thelyn, were the last to depart.

The closing of the oak doors echoed through the great hall, and Akmael extended his hand. "Rise, Eolyn. Let me see you."

She lifted her eyes to his, uncertain as to what she might find.

Akmael's expression softened as he took her in. Love flared through his aura. He touched her hair, tracing its length with his fingers.

"Gods, how I've missed you." Wrapping her in his arms, Akmael set his lips upon Eolyn's.

She melted into the embrace, reaching up to intertwine her fingers with his dark hair, responding with a sigh of pleasure as his kisses coursed down her neck.

"My love," she whispered.

They sank as one to the unyielding floor. The lacings of Eolyn's bodice loosened at Akmael's touch, and he bent to taste the salt of her exposed flesh. Then he paused in his caress and simply gathered Eolyn close, holding her tight against his broad chest. With a muffled groan, he buried his face in her hair and inhaled.

They remained like that a long while, savoring the rhythm of their mingled breath, the pulse of their shared need. The many years of their love filled the silence with warmth and comfort. The spirit of the South Woods rose up around them, coalescing until Eolyn heard the chatter of its creatures, the laughter of its trees, and the roar of the Tarba River in springtime.

Eolyn took heart, and shifted inside Akmael's embrace to kiss him again.

"Shall I claim you now?" His breath tingled against her ear, igniting a shiver of desire. "While the court waits beyond closed doors?"

"I thought I would find you most angry, my Lord King. I have been sick with worry since your orders reached us in the highlands of Moehn."

"As well you should be," he murmured. "Sick with worry for the fate of my daughter and the treachery of your students. Sick

19

with worry for the armies now gathering under Sylus Penamor's command. But not for want of my love, Eolyn. Never for that."

Reluctantly, she extricated herself from his embrace. "Akmael, the magic of the magas must be restored at once."

"I cannot allow it."

The finality of his tone caught her off guard. "None of them would be party to this treason."

"Would you have said the same of Ghemena a fortnight ago?"

"No! I mean, yes…" Eolyn bit her lip. "I don't know. She has always been willful, but this…I don't understand. Why she would do such a thing?"

"Perhaps she thought she was acting on your behalf."

"I never incited her to—"

"I am not saying you did. Nonetheless, you have freely expressed your objections to almost every decision I have made regarding Eliasara. And you have argued on multiple occasions that the princess be returned to her mother. That could easily have been interpreted as a call to action."

"I do not regret what I've said. Eliasara is a girl, not a pawn."

"She is the daughter of a king."

"*Your* daughter."

"Yes, my daughter! My mistake. One for which we will all pay dearly in blood and in lives."

Eolyn bristled. *Not a mistake. A girl, innocent of the circumstances that led to the exile of her mother.*

As much as she longed to say this, Eolyn knew from experience that voicing the thought would get her nowhere.

"I gave Eliasara life," Akmael continued, "but I did not make her a pawn. She was born to this destiny. Now all those who long for the death of my son are gathering around her, thanks to the actions of your student. Why did Ghemena not accompany you to Moehn?"

The question came sharp, unexpected. Eolyn stiffened and withdrew. "Ghemena asked to be given leave."

"And you granted it without question?"

"Of course. She has always served me loyally. Why should I have doubted her now?"

"Because she has never missed the opportunity to return to the

South Woods."

Anger flared in Eolyn's veins. She stood, lacing her bodice. Akmael rose with her.

"Speak plainly, my Lord King. I will not be subject to this cat-and-mouse game. If you do not trust me, if you do not believe me, then say so."

"I trust your heart, Eolyn, but your heart has led you to ill-advised decisions in the past. For this reason, I am not always inclined to trust your judgment."

"For the love of the Gods, Akmael! I am not the confused and frightened girl I was when my brother took up arms against you."

"No, but you must understand the dilemma you have put me in."

"The dilemma *I* have put *you* in?"

"If you knew of Ghemena's plan and did not inform me, you were party to treason. If you did not know, then your authority over the magas is uncertain. Either way, the magas must remain bound and imprisoned until this conflict is resolved."

Eolyn blinked and stepped away.

Not even Thelyn had put it so bluntly.

"The magas have lived in peace in Moisehén for more than a decade." Her voice shook, and her hands were clenched. "You cannot let the action of one woman—"

"Three women. The blatantly treasonous act of three women, all devoted students of yours. They have brought war upon us, Eolyn. Who knows how many others among your followers support them?"

"The magas who remain in my service have done nothing to merit suspicion."

"All magas merit suspicion." Akmael hesitated at the look on her face. He let go a slow breath and softened his tone. "There is a history here that we have not yet overcome, Eolyn. You, of all people, must understand that. Too many of our subjects still remember the war against my father."

"And the purges that followed? The magas he slaughtered?"

"The violence that tore this kingdom apart," Akmael conceded. "Right or wrong, the magas were left with the blame. There are many who fear your power, Eolyn. They fear the

21

ambitions of all women of magic. We must manage this situation carefully, to protect you and your daughters. To see that justice is done."

"What Thelyn did to my magas on your orders was not just."

"A precautionary measure. Nothing more."

"You must give me your word—" Eolyn's voice broke. Was there nothing he would allow? No small concession she could demand? "At least promise me that none of my daughters will be mistreated during their confinement."

"Mistreated?"

"That they will not be…" Eolyn choked on her words. "That they will not be subject to the techniques once used by Tzeremond and his mages."

Realization washed over Akmael's features. He smiled and shook his head. "Come, Eolyn. The situation is not that grim. I assure you the days of Tzeremond will not return. We are at a momentary impasse to be endured until we determine whether this web of treachery ends with Ghemena or begins with her. If found innocent, your magas will be restored to their former positions. If any of them harbor treasonous hearts, it is better we find out now before further damage is done."

Eolyn nodded, though she found little comfort in his reassurance.

"I have had the rooms of the East Tower prepared for you," Akmael said.

"What?"

"I knew you would not be pleased," he hastened to add, "but I do this for your own protection."

"My protection?"

"There are no wards more powerful than those of the East Tower. You will stay there and the children with you."

"You would imprison me? The woman you love, your Queen?"

"Your magic will not be bound. You will be permitted visitors, and you will be allowed to leave the confines of the tower during daylight hours, but always in my company or in the company of guards appointed by me."

"You cannot ask this of me."

"Eolyn." He took her gently by the shoulders. "Do not close your eyes to the delicacy of our position. Half the court speculates it was your command that led Ghemena to deliver Eliasara to Roenfyn."

"You know I would never—"

"And I, seeing that my daughter has been stolen from me, wonder what is next in the minds of those who plot to bring down my house and reign. Will they attempt to kill my son? Will they try to take away my Queen? Because those two things would destroy me, Eolyn. Me and all the futures I have imagined."

Eolyn stared at Akmael in disbelief. A ghostly cry echoed through her heart, the forgotten lament of a woman betrayed.

"This is how it began, isn't it?" she whispered. "The confinement of your mother began just like this."

"Eolyn—"

"Your father wanted only to protect her, but he never allowed her to leave. In the end it made no difference. Kaie penetrated the wards and slew her. You remember, Akmael. You were there."

"My love—"

"You cannot lock me up in that place!"

"You will not be left alone as my mother was. Not tonight, not in any night to come."

Akmael pressed his lips to her forehead. Then he took the fine chain that suspended the Silver Web and lifted the jewel gently over Eolyn's head. He held the amulet in the palm of his hand, its delicate crystals glittering in the afternoon light.

"This magic can be used to penetrate the wards," he said.

"How?"

"That is for me to know." He set the silver chain around his own neck, slipping the amulet beneath his tunic. "I promise you, Eolyn, I will be with you in every moment I can."

"You secure your way into the East Tower while leaving me with no way out. At night you would use your mother's magic to come as a thief, a surreptitious lover, not openly as my king and husband. Why?"

Akmael nodded to the door that separated them from the courtiers outside. "Because they must believe my judgment is free from the influence of desire and love, free from any spells a maga

23

might cast."

"They are fools if they believe a maga can control the decisions of men. If we had such power, I assure you this world would be a very different sort of place."

"Fools they may be, but those fools hold my levies. Soon they must follow me into war. I cannot let them doubt me, not even for a moment."

"But you would let them doubt me?"

"The Gods did not appoint you to command them."

"No, Akmael. You did. You chose me to command at your side, to lead and to protect our people, to restore the ways of Aithne and Caradoc. You believed in this dream as much as I did. Or so I thought, until today."

A frown darkened his brow. "This situation will pass, my love. Your loyalty and the loyalty of your magas will be proven by your obedience. Do as I ask. Accept the protection of the East Tower. Let them see that you have no quarrel with me, and I give you my word, everything will soon be set right."

CHAPTER FOUR

Reunion

PENAMOR ORDERED THEIR PROCESSION to halt at a bend in the road near a wooded area. The Lord Regent dismounted and helped his niece to the grassy earth. Ladies who had once served Taesara met them in a chorus of joy, kissing her hands and cheeks. Their bright gowns and colorful jewels sparkled in the sun. One woman, her dark hair streaked by the passage of time, stood apart. Taesara recognized her and began to weep. She drew the stern lady into a lengthy embrace.

"Sonia, my loyal friend," she said. "I think I have missed you most of all."

Lady Sonia had accompanied Taesara to the land of the Mage King, proving a true and constant companion during the terrible years of Taesara's marriage.

"Your absence has been deeply felt," Sonia said, tenderness softening her otherwise bitter cast. "But now we are reunited, in joy and triumph."

Taesara pulled away and wiped the tears from her eyes. "Where is my daughter?"

"She waits for us at Adelrod." Penamor's terse response deflated Taesara's enthusiasm. The fortress was at least a half a day's ride away. "We will rest here but a little while, long enough for you to be bathed and properly dressed. And to eat before we continue."

Lady Sonia took Taesara's hand and led the princess, ringed by her ladies, into the adjacent wood. The women's chatter floated among the sun-dappled branches. Every footstep released a heady fragrance of herbs. A sense of buoyancy overtook Taesara's spirit, as if she were a spring flower tossed into a river and bobbing happily along with its current.

After a short walk, they arrived at a small glen where a misty cascade fed a pool of crystalline water. Taesara gasped in delight.

"My Lady Queen is pleased," Sonia curtsied with a gracious smile.

It felt odd to be addressed as queen again. Queen in the eyes of one kingdom, but not in the eyes of another. Queen for the purposes of her uncle, but not for the pleasure of her Gods.

The women assisted Taesara as she shed her worn russet gown. They protected her modesty with linen sheets while she stepped into the cool water. Cold wind rushed from the cascade, kissing Taesara's face with dew. She approached the waterfall in slow reverence and stepped into the center of the vigorous roar.

Water poured over her, cleansing away regrets and doubt. She welcomed the river's sensual embrace, opened her arms to its constant caress. For ten years she had washed with nothing but a small bowl of sullied water, once a week. Now the sheer excess ignited a flood of forgotten sensation.

Remembering the countless infirm she had tended, Taesara felt shame at this luxury, at her inability to deny this gratification, at the forbidden hope that she would never again confront extremes of poverty, disease, and denial.

After she finished bathing, the ladies brought a stunning robe of rose silk embroidered with sage leaves. They plaited her hair with flowers and pearls. With the women holding her train high above the damp earth, Taesara made her way back to Penamor's table.

All eyes turned when she emerged from the edge of the woodland. A hushed reverence settled upon the men as they bowed to greet her. When Penamor stood, Taesara knelt, savoring the soft rustle of her skirts, the way the fabric blossomed around her slim waist. She kept her eyes downcast until she saw the Regent's boots in front of her and felt his hand firm upon her shoulder. Rising at Penamor's behest, Taesara met the satisfaction in his eyes with her own glow of renewal.

"On your feet, all of you!" Penamor thundered, and his people obeyed. "This is Taesara, my niece. A true daughter of Roenfyn and

Princess of the House of my brother Lynos, may the Gods keep him safe in the Afterlife. She is the anointed Queen of Moisehén, mother to the Mage King's one true heir. You will love her as I love her; you will obey her as you obey me. We will fight, and some of us will die, that she may be restored to glory, and that her daughter Eliasara may wear the crown intended for her by the Gods."

"Victory to Taesara, Queen!" they shouted.

"Death to the Mage King!" Penamor roared. "Death to his wicked whore and their ugly bastards!"

This was met with the beating of swords upon shields, the bellowing calls of lords, and the shrill cries of ladies. Taesara, unsettled by the magnitude of their aggression, wanted to step away, but Penamor's grip held her in place.

"Come, Niece," the regent said when the shouts of his men had faded. "Let us go to meet your daughter."

The evening sun hung low, casting saffron rays across the land when they arrived at Adelrod, a modest yet sturdy fortress that rose over faded fields and scattered trees. Outside the walls a vast expanse of tents had been erected, overhung with banners of all the noble houses of Roenfyn.

A multitude came to meet them: soldiers and knights lifting arms in salute, noblemen in rich robes and ladies in silken veils, lackeys, servants, and commoners. Children ran unfettered among them.

Taesara recognized many faces from her father's court, though countless more were new and unknown. A path opened for the Regent among this sea of people, allowing them to ride through the gates of the castle and into the front courtyard. There, for the first time in a decade, Taesara set eyes on her daughter.

Eliasara stood on stone steps leading up to the main entrance, surrounded by guards, council members, and ladies of the court. They had dressed her petite figure in the royal colors of Moisehén and placed a silver circlet upon her fine golden hair. They had given her an ornamental breastplate and strapped a sword to her hip.

Taesara's throat constricted painfully at the sight of this stranger born of her own flesh, a girl of twelve summers poised to lead an army.

27

Fighting a persistent tremor in her hands, Taesara dismounted and approached the Princess of Moisehén. She saw her own uncertainty reflected in Eliasara's face, and took comfort in their shared apprehension.

"Daughter." She halted a few paces in front of Eliasara and extended her arms, an invitation toward embrace. "It is with the greatest love and joy that I receive you today. Come and live among your people. Be happy, for you are free."

Eliasara's lips quivered. In a burst of infantile need, she scurried down the stairs and sprang into her mother's arms. Taesara smoothed her daughter's hair and murmured words of encouragement. After a prudent wait, she took the girl's chin in hand and wiped away her tears, replacing them with kisses. Strong displays of emotion were permissible, even strategic, in certain moments; but too many tears on Eliasara's part might erode their people's faith in the strength of her heart.

Taesara looked to the company that surrounded them. "I would honor the valiant warriors who have returned my daughter to me. Where are they?"

Three women separated as one from the crowd. They wore burgundy cloaks and leggings. Their bearing was proud and self-assured.

The smallest watched Taesara with keen hazel eyes partially hidden beneath wisps of ash brown hair. There was something disturbingly familiar about this woman's diminutive stature and sharp gaze. She reminded Taesara of the legends of wood elves and other strange creatures that populated the treacherous forests of Galia.

"These are the maga warriors who have come to our aid," Penamor said.

The three women knelt at Taesara's feet.

"The fair-headed one is Nicola." Penamor nodded at each warrior in turn. "Her partner, with the dark curls, is Ireny. This one, small but fierce, as I'm sure you will discover, is called Ghemena."

Ghemena.

Taesara rolled the name on her tongue until its flavor crystallized into memory.

More than a memory; a sudden rush of excruciating pain.

28

In one swift movement, she claimed her daughter's sword and set its deadly point beneath Ghemena's chin. The onlookers gasped. Nicola and Ireny sprang to their feet and unsheathed their weapons.

Ghemena remained still as a viper about to strike. She met Taesara's gaze with narrowed eyes.

"Taesara," Penamor rebuked her quietly. "This is no way to reward the service of these women."

"I know what I do, uncle. I recognize this one. The last time I saw her she was a girl of nine summers. It was she who appeared in the streets of Moisehén by means of dark magic, casting a curse upon my womb and causing my unborn son to die in a river of blood. You must remember that day; you were there. She has ever been a servant of the Witch of Moehn. I know not by what trickery she seeks to call herself our friend now, but I will not have it. I would see her dead."

Not a single person stirred in the courtyard. Even the dogs had gone quiet.

Ghemena lifted one gloved hand and said to her companions, "Nicola, Ireny, lower your weapons."

The magas obeyed.

Taesara's grip on the sword tightened. All rage, all remorse that had consumed her after the loss of her son returned fresh and raw. Years ago, the Mage King's blind obsession for his peasant enchantress had left Taesara powerless to punish those responsible the prince's murder. But she was not powerless now, and it would be good to watch a maga die.

"Taesara." Penamor drew close to deliver his counsel. "Think about what you do. These women are a gift from the Gods. Already they have provided information about the Mage King and his army that might well turn the tide of the war. They have allies in Moisehén ready to act at our behest. Their services are not to be disposed of lightly."

Taesara clenched her jaw.

"Milady Queen," Ghemena said. "I remember the day your son died. I ask that you hear my story before you condemn me."

Taesara pressed the blade against Ghemena's pliant skin. "Very well, witch. Speak."

"Milady Queen, I was a frightened child back then, fleeing a

29

brutal invader. I had no way of knowing what curses might be unleashed with the invocation Maga Eolyn taught me. I have since come to recognize her many deceptions, and I share your anger and your thirst for justice. That's why my sisters and I delivered Princess Eliasara to you. That's why we have sworn an oath to her cause."

"The allegiance of a maga is meaningless."

"Taesara—"

"You know the legacy of our ancestors, Uncle! We cannot tolerate any practitioners of magic. Even if she tells the truth, even if we were to accept the services of these three women, they must burn along with all the others once Moisehén is ours."

Ghemena's gaze shifted to the ground.

Penamor cleared his throat. He lifted his arm to the onlookers, his smile one of an indulgent father. "As you can see, our Queen has been well-cloistered these past ten years."

Forced amusement rippled through the crowd.

Taesara faltered. Was it possible they had drifted so far from the path of Thunder? Did her people now condone magic?

She realized she had no understanding of the workings of Penamor's court or the dispositions of his subjects. Such ignorance could lead to disaster, if she were not careful.

"Forgive me, my Lord Regent," she said. "I spoke out of place. The destiny of the followers of Dragon will be for my daughter to decide, once she sits upon the throne of Moisehén. But this woman before us is a killer of princes. I cannot suffer her to live."

"You won't be able to slay her." The fair-headed maga spoke in a haughty tone. "She's too good for that."

"Nicola." Ghemena's rebuke was clear. She returned her gaze to Taesara. "Milady Queen, allow us to accompany you on this campaign, and you will see that true magas are not like the woman I once called my tutor. True magas don't succumb to selfish ambitions or seek crowns or marry kings. My sisters and I would see the balance of our ancestors restored, and the perverse reign of the Mage King ended. We long for the rule of your daughter."

"Why?"

"Because the practice of magic is forbidden to the Kings of Moisehén." Ghemena's hands curled into tight fists. "Akmael and his father violated this prohibition, and murdered all who opposed

30

them. Now Prince Eoghan follows their path. The line of Mage Kings must be terminated. Let me live long enough to achieve this task, Milady Queen. Once we have set your daughter on the throne, you may do with me as you please."

Taesara studied Ghemena, unconvinced.

"My Lady Queen, if I may be so bold." Sonia's tempered voice sounded in Taesara's ear. "I can vouch for the sincerity of Maga Ghemena. At the behest of your uncle, I have been in contact with her almost since the day we were banished from Moisehén. There is no dream closer to Ghemena's heart than the one you have just heard. She has assisted our cause in countless ways, including the safe return of your daughter. No one would question the justness of your decision if you were to take her life in this moment. But vengeance is often sweeter than justice. If you let Maga Ghemena live, vengeance is what you will have."

Vengeance is for the selfish and small-minded, the Good Mother would have said. *Forgiveness opens the path to a more just world.*

Taesara lowered her sword, uncertain whether she was choosing vengeance or forgiveness, or both.

"I have heard you, Ghemena of Moisehén," she said. "Rise, then, and join our campaign. May the Gods grant that you prove your worth."

31

CHAPTER FIVE

East Tower

EOLYN AND HER DAUGHTER, Briana, stood at a window of the East Tower watching the courtyard below, where Eoghan was at his evening lessons with Sir Gaeoryn and Lord Borten. Steady focus and a deep sense of duty marked the prince's every effort. His rapid progress in the arts of war filled Eolyn's heart with pride and trepidation.

Soon the gray stone walls of the fortress would be tinged with reddish hues of sunset. Eoghan would return to the East Tower, flushed from his exercise and filled with new questions about warrior magic. He would ask for yet another story of Caedmon and the war against the People of Thunder. For a few fleeting hours, the prince would become a child again, easy with his laughter, affectionate in his embrace.

Eolyn wondered whether Queen Briana had stood at this same window during her imprisonment, whether she had struggled with the same love and the same doubts as Akmael grew into the burden of being both mage and king.

"When will I start my lessons, Mama?"

"I would rather you not learn the sword at all," Eolyn replied tenderly, stroking her daughter's hair.

"But I'm to be a maga warrior." Briana kept her gaze intent upon her brother.

"If that be your calling, yes. You must remember, Briana, that the most powerful magas in history were not warriors at all."

"You're a maga warrior."

"I learned the ways of war at your father's request, in order to become a better queen. But war was not my first calling."

"I will be a queen, so it must be my destiny to be maga warrior too."

Eolyn gave her daughter a hug, though sadness touched her heart. From the time she had learned to walk, Briana had endeavored to keep up with her brother in all things, and the arts of war were no exception.

Indeed, most of the magas Eolyn had trained these last ten years, with the notable exception of the healer Jacquetta, had chosen the warrior's path. Perhaps this was inevitable, given the recent history of conflict and persecution. Yet Eolyn had hoped to leave a different legacy through her students, one of peace and respect for all living things; an order of magas dedicated to healing the earth and its people.

Perhaps Briana would yet choose a different path and become a true Daughter of Aithne. There was still time, after all, and hope.

Briana spun on her heels, interrupting Eolyn's thoughts.

"Uncle Corey!" she exclaimed, clapping her hands.

Turning in surprise, Eolyn saw the mage of East Selen in the doorway. He wore the dark green robes of his station and held a staff of polished walnut crowned by a crystal of malachite.

How long he had been watching them, Eolyn could not tell.

Undaunted by the appearance of the most powerful wizard in the kingdom, Briana darted away from her mother and ran headlong into Corey's embrace, wrapping her small arms around his neck and planting a kiss on his cheek.

"I have a gift for you, little Princess." Corey showed her his empty hand, front and back. With a graceful dance of the fingers, a long turquoise feather appeared in his grasp, eliciting a gasp of delight from Briana. "This is a tail feather from a Dragonmot of East Selen."

"You plucked it from a Dragonmot?"

"No, of course I did not pluck it. I found it at the foot of an oak. The males pluck out their own ornamental feathers, once the mating season ends. No use making a show if the females have lost interest."

"It's beautiful, Uncle Corey! Thank you. When will you take me to East Selen so I can see a Dragonmot for myself?"

"You just returned from the South Woods."

"Yes, and now I want to go to East Selen."

"You have a wandering heart, Briana," Corey said gravely. "That is not a healthy trait for a princess."

"But it's a fine trait for a maga. Mother says so."

"Does she?" Corey met Eolyn's eyes. "Wise words from a High Maga, perhaps not so much from a queen."

"When will you take us to East Selen?" Briana insisted.

"Perhaps we can celebrate Winter Solstice there," Corey said. "Much depends, of course, upon your mother."

Eolyn abandoned her place at the window. She kept her expression neutral, trying to hide the reluctance she felt in receiving him. "Welcome, Mage Corey."

"My Lady Queen." He bowed and touched her fingers to his forehead. "I am most pleased that you are safely returned to the City."

"Talia, Rhaella." Eolyn nodded to the ladies-in-waiting who had been sitting quietly in the room engaged in needlework. "Please take Briana for a walk through the gardens. These cramped quarters have made her restless."

"But I want to stay," Briana protested. "Uncle Corey just arrived, and I've so much to tell him."

"Mage Corey has requested a private audience with me, Briana."

"Is it about Mariel?"

"I don't know, my love. He has not told me."

"If it's about Mariel, then I want to stay."

"Briana." Corey knelt to meet the child's gaze.

Eolyn caught her breath at the vivid display of their shared heritage. Though Mage Corey was fair and Briana dark, they both had the silver-green eyes of East Selen.

"You must obey your mother," he said "You and I will have other opportunities to talk."

"When?"

"As soon as I've finished speaking with our Queen. I'll find you in the gardens, and we'll search for moon spiders and fire beetles."

"And you'll give me news of Mariel?"

"More than that. I have a secret message from her, just for you."

Briana grinned. She hugged him and departed. Eolyn's ladies fell into place behind the princess, along with the guards. The doors closed. The magic seal that protected the East Tower hissed into place.

Eolyn sat down and bade Mage Corey to do the same. For a long while, they regarded each other in silence. She wondered who Corey saw sitting in front of him: the peasant girl from Moehn or one of the dancers of his Circle? The maga in hiding, the famed healer, or the woman warrior? The queen, the mother, or the prisoner? She had walked so many paths since they first met in the highlands of Moehn, and he had known each of them all too intimately.

"I'll wager you never imagined the trap could be sprung so quickly," he said.

Eolyn bristled. "I have never doubted the swift cruelty of your mages."

"This trap was not ours to command."

Eolyn shifted in her seat. A thousand words stood poised upon her lips, of which only a handful could be chosen and delivered. Each conversation in the coming days had to be undertaken with great care, especially when it came to this mage. "Why did Thelyn come for us, and not you?"

"I was needed to track down the magas still residing in the City. Besides, Thelyn was the better mage for that task."

Mariel, she thought. *He would not have had the heart to bind Mariel.*

A small sign, perhaps, that he could yet be counted among her friends.

"I understand you are to oversee their interrogation," she said.

"It is true, my Lady Queen."

"I have expressed my concerns about this to the King. He assures me that you and your mages will not be permitted to—"

"My Lady Queen, if there is one thing you have learned in the years of our friendship, it is that I will do whatever must be done in the moment at hand, and I will harden my heart to see it through."

"That may be the case, Mage Corey. Yet I also know that words are your most effective tool. You have never resorted to violence to obtain what you require."

Corey let the statement hang in the air.

Eolyn averted her gaze, suddenly aware of the icy tension in her hands.

I, too, am being interrogated.

"You did not bring a scribe," she said quietly.

"What need have I for a scribe, my Lady Queen?" His tone softened. "We are, as of yet, simply conversing."

There was a time when Corey would have risked his life to protect her, but in the years since Eolyn's coronation, circumstances had changed. Corey had consolidated his power, and she had borne two children who carried the blood of his people. Eoghan and Briana could now continue the legacy of East Selen. Perhaps just this much had made her dispensable.

"I see Lord Borten returned with you from Moehn," Corey said.

Eolyn refused to flinch at this barb. "Borten wished to offer his services on the King's Council, now that we face war with Roenfyn."

"He has always been a loyal servant of the King."

"Yes, he has."

"And that ward of his…What is his name?"

As if Corey did not know. "Markl."

"Yes. What brings him to court?"

"Concern for Mariel, I believe."

"I doubt that would be his only motivation."

"Markl wishes to be sworn as a Knight of the King. Borten has decided to sponsor him."

"Markl? A knight?" The idea seemed to amuse Corey.

"Some might say he lacks discipline," Eolyn admitted.

"Some might say he's a liar and a thief."

"Lord Borten has been pleased with Markl's service," she countered. "He believes it will do the boy good to train with the King's men."

"It might, but *Sir* Markl? That's bound to sting for a boy who might have lorded over an entire province."

Impatience pricked in her blood. "I do not understand what Borten or his ward Markl have to do with the plight of my

36

daughters in magic."

Corey leaned close and invoked a sound ward. "I should not have to tell you this, Eolyn. You must find a way to send them both home, at once."

"With the drums of Roenfyn sounding over the Furma River? Akmael would never hear of it. He needs men like Borten at his side."

"Having Borten here will only complicate matters."

"How can you be so obstinate?"

"How can you be so obtuse?"

"For the love of the Gods, Corey! All of that happened a very long time ago."

"Eleven summers, to be precise."

"It was over before it began. Lord Borten is content with his lands, his lady, and his heirs. He has served our King and our people well. He thinks no more of me than I think of him."

"I assure you, Eolyn, once a man's heart has been lanced by you, he will never fully recover."

Eolyn averted her gaze. "Not all men are as you say."

"Borten may be a loyal subject, but the desire you once felt for each other can still destroy you both."

"Vile rumors abound in this place. My enemies need more than malicious gossip to turn my husband's ear. They need proof, and they cannot find proof where there's none to be had."

"Do not underestimate the cunning of the noble houses of Moisehén."

"The only person whose cunning I have underestimated is Ghemena."

Corey drew a breath as if to respond and then stopped himself.

Striking a fist softly against his chair, he rose and retreated a few paces, long fingers running through his fine blond hair. He paused to consider their surroundings with a furrowed brow.

Eolyn wondered whether he could hear the voice of his dead cousin, Briana of East Selen. He had spent time with her here, when he was but a child and she Kedehen's hard-won queen.

"Mariel, too," Corey said, his voice subdued. "She must be removed from this place. The sooner, the better."

Eolyn's heart contracted painfully, though she had known

37

these words were coming. One of Eolyn's first and most beloved students, Mariel was the only witness left from the days of the Syrnte invasion. If she fell into the wrong hands now, it could be disastrous for everyone. "I will send Mariel anywhere you recommend, Corey. Just set my magas free."

"The magas will not be freed. Not until this war has ended." Corey must have registered her stricken look, for he softened his tone. "Though perhaps in Mariel's case, an agreement can be reached. I will put some thought into how."

"Do you think Ghemena anticipated the consequences?" The words slipped from Eolyn's lips before she could consider them. Corey's alliances were forever difficult to decipher. To confide too much in him now was less than wise. Yet deep in her heart she felt that if she could not speak with him, she could not speak with anyone. She refused to let herself feel that alone.

Something akin to pity flickered across his face. "Yes, I have no doubt that she did."

"Ghemena was a child of five summers when we first met. Stubborn and quick-witted. Angry at everyone and everything. Yet I took her in. I saw her rage as a source of power; burning like an insatiable fire in her heart. She was my first daughter in magic, Corey. Everything began with her."

"Everything may well end with her, too."

"Why would she bring this upon me, upon her sisters?" Eolyn gestured to the confines of her chambers. "What transgression have we committed against her?"

"I doubt she holds any resentment toward her sisters. Perhaps she even regrets leaving them behind. You, on the other hand, are beyond forgiveness. You abandoned the dream of reviving women's magic in order to bind yourself to the Mage King."

"I abandoned nothing. Look at all we've accomplished these past years."

"Ghemena did not live through what was lost, and this makes it difficult for her to appreciate what has been recovered. She sees nothing in this fortress, Eolyn, save your subservience to Akmael."

"I am not subservient to him."

Corey arched his brow.

Eolyn gave an exasperated sigh. "Very well. I was not

subservient until now. And *now* would not have happened if it weren't for Ghemena's folly. I thought she would come to understand—"

"She is not the sort of girl who comes to understand. Ghemena has thrust us into the most precarious of situations, Eolyn. If the rift between you and Akmael should become serious—"

"This is not serious?"

"Not yet."

Corey had circled behind her. She could feel the heat of his gaze on her back.

"Does the King still favor you?" he asked.

Eolyn stiffened. "He visits as often as protocol allows, in the company of his guards or advisers."

"You know that is not what I mean."

Her throat went dry. An unwelcome sting invaded her eyes. "I cannot answer your question, Mage Corey. If I say yes, it may be used against my King. If I say no, it will be used against me."

"I ask out of concern for our people, Eolyn. It is a thin curtain that separates us from the Naether Demons."

"They are the least of my worries now."

"Perhaps they should be foremost in your mind."

"There is no evidence for what you and Thelyn believe, save vague and disparate references gleaned from your mysterious annals. The Naether Demons disappeared when we defeated the Syrnte, and the dark magic that drew them out of the Underworld ended when you slew Rishona."

"Yet the portals through which they traveled still exist. The union between you and the Mage King is what keeps those portals sealed shut."

"That is mere conjecture."

"The balance between men's and women's magic was restored when you and Akmael made your vows to each other. Any rift in your love places that balance in peril."

"Your speculations are wasted on me, Corey. Even if what you say is true, I am not the one upsetting the balance."

To this he did not respond.

Enthusiastic shouts drifted through the window. Eoghan and

his companions had heightened their swordplay, drinking up what was left of the day. On the West Tower, a baritone chorus marked the evening change of the guard. For ten years Eolyn had coexisted with this constant murmur of men and swords, of metal on stone. She missed the living breath of her beloved South Woods, the soft sway of ancient trees, the melodious lilt of rare birds. The ache of that absence had always accompanied her, but it was especially keen now when evening crept upon the city and seduced its people toward their darkest dreams.

Corey drew close. She sensed the heat of his presence behind her, his fingers hovering just above her hair. A tingle settled on the nape of her neck. The provocative sensation spread in subtle waves down her back as the threads of their magic intertwined.

The jewel on her arm stirred, an heirloom of East Selen gifted to her long ago by Akmael. The silver bracelet was etched in images of Dragon: winged serpent and river otter, spider and bear, squirrel and lynx, countless creatures blended into a single, timeless dream. For reasons Eolyn never quite understood, this symbol of her bond to the Clan of East Selen carried much greater weight with Mage Corey than her marriage to his cousin ever would.

The landscape of his home flickered in her mind: snow drifts and warm cottages, spiced wine and glowing hearths. A majestic forest silenced by winter's icy grip. Midnight visions drawn from the restless heart of the sleeping earth.

"You suggested we might celebrate Winter Solstice in East Selen this year." She bit her lip, wishing she had not said these words, regretting the nostalgia that invaded her voice.

The mage released her abruptly. He circled the chair to face her, his expression indecipherable. "Perhaps it will be so. I should go, my Lady Queen. Dusk is at hand, and the Princess expects me in the gardens."

"Briana will be most disappointed if you don't appear. This is the best time of day to find fire beetles." The quotidian nature of her remark brought a feeble sort of comfort, as if threads of the mundane could somehow mask this crisis. Eolyn glanced toward the fading light. She wondered what questions Corey would ask of her daughter.

"When will you and I speak again, Mage Corey?"

"In a few days' time, once I have had the opportunity to converse with your magas."

"I would like to be present when you meet with them."

"I assure you, there is no need." He bowed low in respect, his tone gracious but final. "We have everything well in hand."

CHAPTER SIX

Lady Sonia

TAESARA WATCHED ELIASARA SLEEP. The girl's fair hair splayed across the pillow. Her chest rose and fell in a quiet breath; the apparent peace of her dreams a stark contrast to the unsteady rhythm of the queen's own heart. Taesara blinked back the sting of tears, torn between the intense joy of this simple luxury and the seething rage at having been denied it for so long.

Her daughter's childhood had all but vanished. Taesara would never know the pleasure of watching Eliasara grow day to day, of doting on her every accomplishment, of waking her with a loving kiss, or putting her to sleep with stories of times long past. Indeed, she might never know the experience of having Eliasara call her *Mother.*

She bent to kiss Eliasara's forehead. The girl stirred but did not wake. Turning away from her mother's touch, she murmured her father's name. She snuggled deeper into the covers, a frown creasing her brow.

It had been no small task to subdue Eliasara's rage. The girl's eyes were swollen from the tears she had shed, her cheeks splotched as if with a fever.

"You must give her time." Sonia's quiet words beckoned Taesara from the bedside.

Drawing a deep breath, Taesara rose and stepped away.

Sonia offered a steaming cup of tea. Taesara accepted gratefully before taking a seat in front of the hearth. The midsummer's night carried an odd chill, and the bright yellow fire

42

did little to ward off the shiver that plagued her. Sonia's soothing brew tasted of mint and chamomile and other herbs unknown. Taesara drank deep and savored the warmth that settled in her belly.

"Let us pray to the Gods of Thunder that every night is not like tonight," she said.

In a rustle of skirts, Sonia took a place at her side. "Princess Eliasara has been under the Mage King's spell for a very long time. We cannot expect her to escape those shadows from one day to the next."

"But to speak of him so..." Taesara's heart contracted painfully. "She loves him, Sonia. She calls his bastards brother and sister. She even refers to that witch with affection and begs me to return her to them. I am her mother, Sonia! Ten years I have been denied her company. How could she ask such a thing of me?"

"You were patient with her today. She will remember that and learn to love you."

"Not as she loves her father and his whore."

"More than she loves them, and certainly more than she loves her uncle."

"Penamor." Taesara rolled her eyes. "Now there is a very difficult man to love."

"He has already struck her once."

"What?"

"When she asked — no, demanded that he send her home. All the court witnessed it. That is why Penamor retrieved you with such urgency. You are to build a bridge between the Regent and his great niece, and to reaffirm Eliasara's commitment to claiming her crown. If you do not succeed, then this whole endeavor will fail. Our people are wary of raising arms against a realm of magic. They will not attack Moisehén under a divided house."

"Perhaps it would be better that way."

"Would it?" Sonia took a quiet sip from her cup. The candles flickered under a passing breeze.

"No war, no bloodshed." Taesara repeated the words of the Good Mother. "No suffering, no strife. It is a simple recipe."

"Save for the fact that Eoghan and Eliasara will forever be pitted against each other by virtue of their heritage. If we do not kill that bastard prince now, then he will find a way to slay her. You cannot deny this. It is the way of kings; most especially the way of the Mage Kings."

Taesara glanced at her daughter's sleeping form.

"Do not worry," Sonia said as if reading her thoughts. "She will not wake."

"How can you be certain?"

"Secrets of an old woman." Sonia's dark hair was streaked with gray, and her hands had begun to spot with age. Her appearance would be judged unpleasant by most, with puffy cheeks and a small rat-like nose.

"Your family…" Taesara stumbled over her question, flustered that she could not recall in which province they lived. "They are well?"

Sonia expressed her gratitude with a slight nod. "We lost many in the war. Those who survived have taken up my father's land, and were generously rewarded by our Lord Regent with more."

"And you have not married?"

"With all due respect, my Lady Queen, who in this realm do you think would have me?" Sonia's hazel eyes glittered.

Taesara wondered whether that shadow of resentment had always been there, or if it were a new element of recent years. Nostalgia surged in her heart, a longing for the quiet faith of her sisters, a peace unfettered by cynicism or resentment. A world untouched by men.

"A woman as loyal and disciplined as you," Taesara said, "from a good family and with the favor of my uncle, would be an excellent match for many."

"Marriage would have meant abandoning you, my Lady Queen."

This surprised Taesara. "I freed you from my service when I joined the Sisters. Surely that was clear when we parted ways?"

"It was clear that you thought your journey had ended, my Lady Queen, but I have always believed otherwise."

"I am flattered by your loyalty, sweet Sonia, though I do not deserve it."

"You are the chosen vessel of Thunder, the instrument with which we will destroy the Mage King."

44

"Well." Amused for the first time since she left the Sisters, Taesara set her cup aside. "I hate to disappoint you, but I do not have that kind of power. We learned that lesson well enough, during my years as King Akmael's spouse."

"Eliasara will be the first queen of a new era, an era in which magic will be obliterated from the line of Vortingen. You will make this happen."

"Penamor will make that happen."

"Not without your help."

Taesara's gaze strayed to the fire. "Do you really trust the magas who brought her here, or did you merely want to avoid the scandal of me slitting Ghemena's throat in front of the entire court?"

A smile touched Sonia's lips. "A little of both. There are certain dreams we share."

"I don't trust any of them. I want them eliminated once we finish this war."

"I would advise against taking on such a task. All of Kedehen's men and all his mages could not eliminate the magas."

Taesara stiffened, retreating from her own anger.

To wish death upon so many is the worst of all wrongs, the Good Mother would have said.

"It will not be my decision in any case," she reminded herself, "or Eliasara's for that matter. My uncle will rule both kingdoms, when all is said and done."

Sonia merely swirled the tea in her cup.

"Has he been a good king?" A seemingly small question, but Taesara's skin prickled at the wary silence it inspired.

"He has established order and peace," Sonia replied at length. "After all these years, his eye is still fixed on restoring your honor. The people respect and fear him. More than this, we cannot ask."

"And my brother?" Taesara's voice broke, becoming a tiny echo inside the room.

Sonia frowned and set her cup aside. "We should save that conversation for tomorrow."

"I would know now. Is he well?"

"As well as can be expected under the circumstances."

"I want to see him."

"I doubt our Lord Regent will allow that. You are needed here with your daughter."

"Eliasara can accompany me." Taesara's breath came up short. A sudden weariness weighed upon her. Dizzy, she sat back in the chair and closed her eyes, keenly aware of the ache that had penetrated her limbs. She had become unaccustomed to the demands of court and travel.

Sonia's hand settled upon her shoulder, steady as the earth itself. "Your bed has been prepared, my Lady Queen. Rest now, with the peace of the Gods. There will be time enough to attend to all our troubles when you awake."

CHAPTER SEVEN

Ghemena

TASHA HEARS SHOUTS and heavy footsteps. The curtain of the litter is thrust aside. Torchlight blinds her. Instinct drives the girl to scramble away, but large, powerful hands stop her retreat. The soldiers cut the bonds around her ankles and haul her to her feet.

"What's happening?" Catarina whimpers, stirring from a drug-induced sleep. They pull her out of the litter and set her next to Tasha. She clutches Tasha's hand, nails digging into skin like a frightened bird. "Where's Mistress Adiana?"

Tasha dares not answer her friend, for fear the captors will cut out her tongue. The old hag has returned, the one who called herself priestess before she took Adiana away. She peers at them with shrewd, kohl-lined eyes. Rubies drip from her sagging earlobes. Her lips are a thin line in a crevassed face.

"The San'iloman requests your presence," she says. "A fine privilege for a pair of peasant girls like you. Be thankful for this night, as it will be your glory."

"We aren't peasants." Catarina lifts her small chin. "We're magas."

"Hush!" Tasha urges, but it's too late. The old priestess raises a hand to strike, but then hesitates. An odd smile curls her lips. Her eyes glitter like stone. Letting her arm drop at her side, the priestess nods to the guards, who prod the girls forward.

Torches light their way, beating back the hungry night. Up ahead, a luminous curtain of blue, purple, and red dances against the starless sky.

"It's beautiful," Catarina murmurs, gazing upward.

Her wonder is cut short by Mistress Adiana's cry. "Not them! Not them, I beg you. Take me instead."

Adiana's entreaty breaks open Tasha's awareness. Suddenly the girl sees the world as she has never seen it before, cut from crystal, hard and unyielding.

Catarina's body tenses like a fox caught in a trap. "Where is she? Where's Adiana?"

"Tasha! Catarina!" Adiana wails in the distance.

"We're here, Mistress!" Catarina bolts toward the voice, but the men catch her with ease. She claws and bites until they cuff her into silence.

Tasha's feet have rooted into the ground. Every sound, every sensation of the night reaches out to her.

I will never be here again, she thinks, and knows it to be true.

The San'iloman stands proud and tall before them. She spreads her arms in false affection. Ebony hair cascades over her pale shoulders. Her moon-white gown is spattered with blood.

Next to her, an armored man watches with pitiless eyes. Tasha recognizes him, and her heart contracts in fear. He is the general who beat Adiana until she bled. When Adiana refused to speak, he had thrown Tasha upon a table and…

No, she must not think about that. That did not happen. None of that happened at all.

"Stop!" Adiana's cries fade against the night. "For the love of the Gods, stop! You cannot permit this. Spare the girls. Take me instead."

"Silence that woman!" the general roars.

Adiana is heard no more.

Catarina collapses into a fit of weeping. The guards pick her up and lay her shaking body at the San'iloman's feet.

The old priestess takes Tasha's hand, and finding her compliant, leads the girl gently forward.

Beyond the glowing curtain, giant beasts rumble and purr. Their eyes are vacant pits set in unformed faces. Their ebony claws drip with blood.

The San'iloman's smile is quick and subtle as her knife. Tasha does not feel the cut that opens her throat. As her spirit descends into darkness, she remembers the songs of passage Maga Eolyn taught her. She tries to sing so her sisters might guide her to the Afterlife.

But the monsters find her first, and they do not let her escape. They claw open her chest and consume her innocent heart. They extract her magic in long glowing ribbons and devour it with ravenous pleasure. Terror consumes the last of Tasha's spirit, and she screams in anguish.

"Sisters! Why did you abandon me?"

GHEMENA JOLTED AWAKE, gasping for breath. A fiery knot of pain consumed her chest.

Nicola stirred and set a gentle hand upon Ghemena's back. "Are you all right?"

Ghemena shook off Nicola's concern and rose, unsheathing her knife. They had made their small camp outside the fortress, at a prudent distance from the levies of Roenfyn. The fire had dwindled to a pit of ash-covered coals. Torches lit the ramparts of Adelrod, and stars hung low over the landscape.

"Ireny's watch is almost over," Ghemena said.

The three maga warriors took turns providing support for Eliasara's guard, though Ireny was the only one Eliasara deigned to speak with. Indeed, if it had not been for Eliasara's trust in Ireny, the princess might not have followed them to Roenfyn at all.

"I will relieve Ireny soon," Nicola replied. "But the end of her watch is not what brought you out of your sleep."

"I don't like this land. It does not let me rest."

Ghemena had imagined Roenfyn a brighter place, with dense forests and fertile fields, but all they had seen were gloomy hills and faded grasslands. The damp earth of Roenfyn was impregnated with mold and rot, pockmarked by gray pools that reflected a colorless sky. During the day, mournful calls of wind pipers floated on the air. At night, the lonely yips of marsh dogs rose in the distance. Occasionally Ghemena sensed a low-pitched groan, as if some menace stirred deep inside the earth.

Nicola stood. "The people of Roenfyn say their kingdom was cursed by wizards of ancient times. After the war of Thunder and Dragon, the ancestors of Galia punished this land by trapping the breath of Dragon in a great crater that lies to the west. To this day, the smoking cavern feeds the region with poisoned rain."

"A mage invoking a volcano?" Ghemena's laugh had a harsh edge. "If only we had such power. I would use it well."

"You dreamed about her again, didn't you?" Nicola drew close. Her aroma of fresh grass and summer rain settled around Ghemena. "It's been a very long time since you've had that dream."

"Tasha," Ghemena said through clenched teeth. "Her name was Tasha."

"I have not forgotten your first sisters in magic, nor what

you've told me about them. But you should not carry such a burden of guilt. You were just a little girl back then."

Tears of anger stung Ghemena's eyes. So many years had passed, yet Tasha's absence still burned deep, a raw and hollow ache, as if she had died yesterday. "I should never have abandoned her. Why was I so stupid?"

"Your only fault was to trust Maga Eolyn in making your escape."

We must defend our kingdom, Eolyn had said when they were reunited. *We must put our gifts at the service of all our people.*

"Nothing could break the Mage King's hold over her then," Ghemena spat. "And nothing will break it now, save death itself."

"Their deaths will come soon enough." Nicola placed an arm around Ghemena's waist. "Is it true what Queen Taesara said? Did Maga Eolyn also send the curse that caused her miscarriage?"

"No, of course not."

Nicola stiffened. "You shouldn't let Taesara believe it, then. These people already blame the magas for every bit of rotten luck they have. I don't want them looking at us every time a woman miscarries."

"We will show by our example what it means to be a true maga, and they will lose their superstitions. Until then, the more reasons Taesara has to hate Eolyn, the better. There can be no room for mercy in this campaign."

"I'd be careful about wishing away Taesara's mercy. She spared you, after all."

"Only as a means to an end. I'll wager her tolerance of me lasts just as long as my usefulness in her eyes. We must cultivate that woman's friendship, Nicola. She must understand we serve her and her daughter before everyone else. Once we have their trust, we must see to it that they are the only ones left to rule our people."

"This endeavor grows more complicated with each passing day. There are Penamor's ambitions to worry about, not to mention the Galian wizards he's recruited to their cause. And now you've started speaking of the Mountain Queen."

"Taesara needs an ally to make sure the Galians do not overstay their welcome. Khelia can be that ally."

"Unless Khelia takes up Maga Eolyn's cause."

"She would never ally with the Mage King."

"Still. It's three armies to keep track of; three kingdoms with their own ambitions." Nicola sighed. "Sometimes I think we should have simply destroyed the Mage King's heirs ourselves."

"The kingdom would have collapsed, each noble family making its own claim and no one supporting Eliasara. Penamor is strong enough to subdue them all and set the princess securely on the throne. Once Eliasara's power is consolidated, we can eliminate him as well. It will be a long road, and a dangerous one. But it is the surest route to success."

Nicola intertwined her fingers with Ghemena's and pressed the maga warrior's hand over her heart. "What a complicated web you weave, sister."

Ghemena smiled. "With so many flies to catch, what choice do we have?"

They touched foreheads, seeking unity of breath and thought.

Frogs sang in a nearby pond. Crickets chirped beneath the damp grass.

Ghemena's and Nicola's spirits intertwined, connecting with each other and the sleeping earth. Ghemena savored the moment. Nicola's presence never failed to calm her restless spirit.

"As long as you don't entangle all of us as well," Nicola murmured.

"I won't. Remember our promise: Their lives for the lives of our sisters."

Nicola nodded and joined Ghemena in the reaffirmation of a vow made long ago.

Eolyn for Adiana.
Her children for Tasha and Catarina.
The Mage King for them all.

CHAPTER EIGHT

Petition

"I would like to visit my brother."

Taesara broached the topic at the evening meal, in full view of Penamor's court. Lords and ladies sat at long tables, satiating their appetites on roasted meats and stewed vegetables. Sweet wine and bitter ale flowed freely. This seemed a louder court, less disciplined than the one presided over by Taesara's father. Despite the noise, conversation paused for a heartbeat at Taesara's soft-spoken words.

"You may see him whenever you like." Penamor's shrewd gaze slid to his niece. "Though I would not recommend a visit now. He is much changed, and it may dishearten you."

Words and laughter resumed among the courtiers, though Taesara felt the needle prick of their surreptitious glances. Eliasara, claiming a lack of appetite, had begged to take her leave much earlier in the evening. The maga warrior, Ireny, had followed the princess, along with a special guard that accompanied Eliasara wherever she went.

First her father, now us. We are all Eliasara's gaolers.

"I have spent years among the suffering and the sick," Taesara said. "Even the most wretched of diseases cannot dishearten me now."

Penamor snapped a leg from the pheasant he was devouring. Juice glistened as it ran down his fingers. "None of those vile peasants were your own flesh and blood. None of them could drive a dagger through your heart by not recognizing you."

"Lady Sonia has informed me of his state."

"It is a tragedy, a boy so young and full of promise." Penamor

52

chewed as he spoke. Bits of meat flew with his words. "His descent after your father's death was precipitous, horrific. Some say it was the work of the Witch Queen."

A chill took hold of Taesara. "Is it possible that woman's magic can reach into the very heart of Roenfyn?"

Penamor shrugged. "All I know is the kingdom nearly fell apart because of your brother's madness. Be glad you were spared that mess."

"We were not spared, Uncle. The abbey suffered severe shortages of food and supplies. We were often overwhelmed by the injured and dispossessed who came to us for aid."

"I hope you did not waste your charity on traitors."

"We never asked on whose side they fought."

"You delight in your own piety, don't you, Taesara?"

She looked at him, startled. "Of course not, Uncle. It's just that the Good Mother always told us—"

"Enough of the Good Mother." The Lord Regent washed down his meat with a vigorous gulp of wine. "You're back in the real world now. The teachings of that dried-up old hag have no relevance here."

Taesara opened her mouth to object, but then stopped herself.

"May I see him?" she asked.

"We have a few days before the Galian army arrives. That would give you time, I suppose, to ride to Merolyn for a brief visit. I'll appoint your guard. Lady Sonia will accompany you."

"Thank you, Uncle."

"But your daughter stays here."

Taesara had expected this. Even so, her heart caved in.

"I thought that if Eliasara were to come with me, it would be a good opportunity for us to know each other better and to show her the land of our people."

"It would be an even better opportunity for thieves and traitors to kidnap the heiress to Moisehén and ransom her to the highest bidder."

"Merolyn is a peaceful region, and we will be accompanied by your guard."

"The only guard big enough to protect the Princess is the army I've assembled here. Besides, I need that girl with me when the

Galians arrive. Their prince is doubtless eager to see her attributes."

"Attributes?" Taesara puzzled over this word but a moment before drawing a sharp breath. "You are going to offer them Eliasara's hand?"

"They have not indicated whether they will seek a marriage contract, but we must anticipate the possibility."

"You cannot give my daughter to those wizards!"

Conversation at the tables stopped.

Penamor looked truly surprised.

"May I remind you, Niece, that Eliasara is first and foremost heiress to the Crown of Vortingen. She will do whatever duty requires in order to secure her claim."

"Marriage to a Galian prince would forfeit everything she struggles for. The kingdom would pass to their hands. What good would that do for her or for us?"

Penamor chuckled and addressed the watchful court. "My niece seems to have lost her instinct for subtlety."

Laughter rippled through the courtiers. They returned discretely to their own conversations.

"Taesara." Penamor lowered his voice. "I have said nothing about a wedding, only a contract. Contracts can be promised, rescinded, dangled about for years if necessary. All we need at this juncture is for the Galians to believe they have an opportunity. I'm prepared to indulge their whims, nothing more."

"This is a dangerous game you undertake, Uncle. The Galians have never had any love for our people. What will they do if they believe you have made false promises, if they have nothing to show at the end of this campaign for the blood and lives of their warriors?"

Penamor rolled his eyes. "Pray tell me, Taesara, why should I listen to your counsel now in matters of war and diplomacy? You have spent the last ten years as a hermit in a hovel."

"I do not presume to speak as a diplomat, Uncle, but I can speak as a mother. Eliasara should not be dangled about as a prize for the highest bidder. She is only a child."

"She's as old as you were when we first offered you to the Mage King."

"Years passed before those negotiations were completed. I was not sent to Moisehén until—"

"You have another bait in mind, then?" He leveled his gaze at her. "A union with an older woman, perhaps? Someone more experienced at bedding a wizard, though she is incapable of pleasing one?"

Taesara flinched and looked away. "There is no need for insults, Uncle."

"Then stop insulting me with your impertinence." He signaled a servant to refresh his wine. "I indulge you, Taesara, because you have been away from court a long time and because the teachings of those old spinsters have befuddled your mind. But even my patience can run thin. Remember that when you visit your brother."

At dawn the following day, Taesara bade her daughter a reluctant farewell.

Eliasara seemed little moved by her mother's departure. The princess's words were clipped and her embrace stiff. Her stony expression speared Taesara's heart, reminding her all too well of King Akmael's callous gaze.

Perhaps too much time has passed, she thought as she mounted and rode away. *Perhaps this distance cannot be breached.*

Outside the castle gates, flags fluttered high over the army's growing encampment. Men-at-arms clashed with each other in their morning drills, shouts of encouragement or derision flowing in easy rhythm with metal on metal, shield upon shield.

Taesara caught sight of two of the magas in their midst. The fair one, Nicola, watched in amusement as Ghemena took on a soldier almost twice her size. Ghemena moved with exceptional grace and speed, seeming to float above the ground at times before spinning like lightning beneath her opponent's feet. Every blow she landed met with roars of laughter from the soldiers gathered around their contest. Bets were being laid, and coins passed from hand to hand.

"My Lady Queen," Sonia prompted her quietly.

Taesara realized she had drawn to a halt. Penamor's guard was assembled around her, expectant.

"Wait here," she told Sonia. Nodding to her captain, she said, "Come with me."

55

By the time they reached the edge of the circle, the contest had ended. The burly man lay in the dust, disarmed and with Ghemena's blade at his throat.

Ghemena threw back her head in laughter before helping him to his feet. She clapped him on the back and then reenacted every moment of their encounter, showing all those assembled where the use of magic had given her the upper hand.

"You've got to remember everything I tell you." Her eagerness carried its own authority. "The Mage King's warriors are men like you, but they command magic like me. If I can best your strongest soldier with a few easy tricks, what hope have you against a host of mage warriors on the battlefield?"

The discourse was interrupted by recognition of Taesara's presence. The men dropped to their knees, leaving the maga standing and confused, until she turned and saw Taesara watching her.

"Milady Queen." Ghemena gave a deep bow of respect. Her cheeks were smudged with dirt, her fine brown hair matted with sweat.

"Maga Ghemena," Taesara said. "Is it my uncle's wish that you train our men?"

A wry smile curled Ghemena's lips. "That man challenged me, Milady Queen. I'm only making sure he learns from his mistake."

A chuckle rippled through the crowd.

Taesara had wanted to slit that slim throat just a few days prior, but now she found something compelling in Ghemena's defiance.

An idea occurred to her.

Folly, perhaps.

Or perhaps not.

"Tell me, Maga Ghemena, can you recognize a curse cast by one of your own?"

"One of my own?" She gestured to her companion. "You mean Nicola or Ireny?"

"Or any other maga. The Witch Queen of Moisehén, for example."

"What curse?"

"Madness."

"There are only a few curses in our tradition that cause

madness," Ghemena said. "The teachings of Aithne and Caradoc forbid almost all of them. A common exception is *Ahmad-melan*, which can be cast in battle to intensify the fears of our opponents."

"Can you recognize it?"

"Yes, of course. Any of us can. But the Witch Queen couldn't cast such a curse here."

"Why not?"

"*Ahmad-melan* is an intimate spell. It would unravel over such distances."

"I see." Taesara said. "Can you ride a horse, Maga Ghemena?"

The woman laughed. "I'd hardly be a warrior if I couldn't."

"Then you will ride with us to Merolyn."

"Merolyn?" Ghemena's eyes widened. "What's in Merolyn?"

"My brother, the King."

"And Princess Eliasara?"

"She remains here, under Penamor's protection."

Ghemena frowned and shook her head. "I beg your pardon, Milady Queen, but we are sworn to protect the Princess. We must stay close to her."

Taesara tapped impatiently upon the pommel of her saddle. "This is not a request, Maga Ghemena. But to ease your heart, your companions will remain here. Ireny and Nicola can share the duty you have sworn to my daughter while you accompany me. Surely you trust them with this task?"

Ghemena glanced toward Nicola, who gave a slight nod.

Ghemena grinned and bowed with a flourish. "Very well, Milady Queen. Let us be off to Merolyn."

CHAPTER NINE

Compromise

MAGE COREY ROSE along with the King and all his advisors as
Eolyn appeared in the doorway of the Council's chamber. The
Queen was flanked by guards and accompanied by two of her
ladies, Talia and Rhaella. Light slanting through the windows cast a
warm glow over Eolyn's features, deepening the reddish hue of her
hair and accentuating the curve of her face.

Time had done well by Eolyn, Corey observed. Over the years
she had shed the innocent look that had so charmed him when she
first wandered into his Circle. Now she bore the mature features of
a woman at the height of her splendor, High Maga and Queen of
Moisehén. A Mother of Kings.

*It's an unfortunate irony that in Moisehén, women at the height of their
splendor invariably ended up in the East Tower.*

"Welcome, my Lady Queen," the King said.

"Thank you, my Lord King, and the honored members of
this Council, for receiving me into your presence."

Eolyn bowed and took her place in an ornately carved chair at
the foot of a long oak table. She held her back erect. Her face was a
mask of perfect calm. Yet Corey could sense the shimmering
threads of her magic as they reached toward the heart of the
mountain. She was grounding her spirit, casting a ward to protect
herself from fear and anger, from any emotion that threatened to
cloud her mind and compromise her judgment.

In a rustle of robes and scraping of wood upon stone, the
Council members resumed their seats. Eolyn's ladies-in-waiting,
Talia and Rhaella, retreated to one of the long tapestry-covered

walls, where they remained standing.

Talia was a raven-haired beauty with a spray of freckles across a pert nose; Rhaella sharp-eyed with glorious auburn tresses that rivaled the queen's. These were but the latest in a long string of comely maidens placed strategically in Eolyn's service by rival families of Moisehén. Lords Herensen and Langerhaans, in particular, had been implacable in their attempts to seduce the Mage King with the daughters of their households. All their efforts, even the most admirable, had failed. Akmael was as single-minded in his devotion to Eolyn as Kedehen had been to Briana of East Selen.

"My Lady Queen." High Mage Thelyn opened the meeting with a voice as smooth as silk. "On behalf of the Council, let me express how grateful we are for your endorsement of our efforts in this most delicate matter. The heinous abduction of Princess Eliasara has brought grief to us all, not only for the loss of a beloved daughter of Moisehén, but because the crime was committed by our own sisters in magic."

Thelyn paused. For several heartbeats, the only sound was that of a scribe scratching pen upon paper.

Eolyn's gaze remained steady; her hands rested on her lap.

Pride flickered in Corey's heart at her display of impermeability. He had seen Eolyn in similar straits many years before: imprisoned by the Mage King and subject to the whims of his Council. She had been so young then, innocent with her emotions, vulnerable to unchecked anger and paralyzing fear.

Gods, it seems a lifetime ago.

"I share your outrage at the crimes committed against the Crown," Eolyn said at last, "and I stand with my most revered husband, our Lord and King, in his commitment to seeing justice done. Please High Mage Thelyn, let us begin."

Thelyn looked to Akmael, who nodded his approval. The mage drew a sheet from the stack at his side and read. "It is the finding of this Council that the Maga Warriors Ghemena of Moehn, Nicola of Selkynsen, and Ireny of Moisehén, are guilty of high treason. By order of Akmael, High Mage and King, and his consort Eolyn, High Maga and Queen, the three women herein named are to be apprehended and committed to the pyre. Any subject of Moisehén who delivers them to the King's justice or who provides proof of their deaths will be generously rewarded. Any subject who gives refuge or aid to these magas will be judged guilty of treason and hanged."

A scribe accepted the parchment from Thelyn and set it before the Mage King. Akmael signed the edict and placed the seal of Vortingen upon it. Then the scribe walked the length of the table and delivered the declaration to Eolyn.

All eyes settled upon the Queen.

High Mage Echior, new to their company as court physician and a long-time friend of Eolyn's, was red in the cheeks and fidgeting. Lord Herensen's horse-like face wore the same unrevealing expression of grim duty that he had mastered years before. A momentary wetting of the lips revealed Cramon Langerhaans's delight at seeing Eolyn cornered. Toward the end of the long table, Borten sat tight-lipped and tense, eyes shifting from Eolyn to the empty space in front of him.

Eolyn accepted the quill. Its feathery tip trembled almost imperceptibly in her hand. She studied the edict as if searching for an answer to an unspoken question.

One of the Council members stifled a cough.

"My Lady Queen," Akmael prompted. "Do you have any further questions regarding this condemnation?"

"No, my Lord King." Eolyn set her jaw. With a few quick strokes she engraved her name beneath Akmael's. Lifting her eyes to her husband, she returned the parchment to the scribe.

Thelyn drew the next edict from his stack and read again. "The Council recognizes that following the Syrnte invasion, our Lord King acted with wisdom and mercy when he reinstated, for all magas, the privilege of learning weaponry. This decision rested on the confidence that the maga warriors of Moisehén would use their craft to serve and protect our people, just as our Lady Queen did during the Syrnte invasion. This trust has been recklessly and grossly violated. By order of Akmael, High Mage and King, and his consort Eolyn, High Maga and Queen, from this day forward any maga found in use or possession of a weapon of war, or any maga who invokes wartime magic, will be apprehended, stripped of her powers, and burned on the pyre, a fate that befits all practitioners who violate the peace and security of our kingdom."

Again the edict was passed from Thelyn to Akmael, who set his signature and seal on the paper before having it presented to the Queen.

Eolyn paused once more, pen poised above the parchment, her breath coming a shade shorter than before. Then, without signing, she straightened and set the quill aside.

"My Lord King," she said, "there was another matter discussed in these days that I expected to have formalized in this morning's Council."

Lord Langerhaans sputtered. "You would question the protocol determined by our Lord King and the venerable members of his Council?"

"Cramon." Akmael lifted a hand to silence him. "Our Lady Queen may speak as freely as any person appointed to this table." He turned to his wife. "Everything is in order, Eolyn. No detail has been omitted. We will attend to the fate of the imprisoned magas forthwith."

Eolyn held her husband's eyes, tapping her fingers lightly on the table. "With all due respect, my Lord King, I would have a decision regarding the imprisoned magas before endorsing this edict."

Several members of the Council shifted uncomfortably. Murmurs were exchanged.

"You heard our Queen." Akmael's bark stilled the restless lords. "Do as she commands."

With a slight lift of his brow, Thelyn leaned forward and drew a third sheet from the stack. "We continue to the matter of the magas currently bound and imprisoned under our Lord King's most prudent command. Their names are recorded herein. All of them will remain confined to dungeons of Vortingen—"

"My Lord King," Eolyn said, "this is not what we agreed."

Akmael regarded his Queen with a steady gaze. "Eolyn, the Council reached its decision last night."

"In my absence?"

"Your prudent advice was taken into account, as was all the other evidence brought against the magas."

"We spoke of this at length." Eolyn scanned the faces of all those present. "All of us at this table, or do you not remember?

61

High Mage Corey's interrogations produced nothing that indicates any of these magas had prior knowledge of Ghemena's plans, or that they in any way support this treason. These women have remained faithful to my Lord King and to the people of Moisehén from the moment they accepted the path of Aithne. They should be set free."

Thelyn set down the edict and steepled his fingers, casting a hooded glance at Corey.

Corey leaned forward. "My Lady Queen, please understand, the Council is most sympathetic to your interpretation of the evidence. We respect the love you bear for your daughters in magic, but as the venerable Mage Tzeremond was known to say, love shrouds judgment like a mist in the night."

"My judgment is not compromised."

"The judgment of any *doyenne* would be compromised under such lamentable circumstances. We are one at heart with you, my Lady Queen. Many of us have daughters and granddaughters whom we have loved and raised, guiding them from a state of innocence into the harsh cruelties of this dishonest world."

Corey embellished his words with a generous sweep of the arm that elicited grim nods across the table.

"Our daughters are a reflection of our hopes for a better future," he continued. "Yet by the same token, all of us understand what must be done when a beloved daughter threatens to bring shame upon our household. Our discipline must be strict, our punishment swift, no matter how much it burdens us to see them suffer."

Something broke behind Eolyn's expression. She blinked and glanced away.

"My Lady Queen." Thelyn spoke in conciliatory tones. "The Council's decision was made with great care and comes with the assurance that the magas will not be mistreated for the duration of their confinement."

"Confining them is mistreating them."

"Eolyn." Akmael's tone signaled an end to the discussion. "The decision has been made. All the magas will remain imprisoned, save for the healer Jacquetta and the maga warrior Mariel, who received not only your endorsement but the support of key members of this Council. Jacquetta, because she has eschewed warrior magic from the first day of her apprenticeship, will be released to the custody of High Mage Echior. Mariel, because of her longstanding and impeccable service to the Crown, will be removed from the City and placed under the care of Lord Borten's household in Moehn. They are expected to heed the restrictions we have placed on all magas, and they will be punished accordingly if they disobey."

Eolyn's shoulders tensed. Corey imaged her hands curling into fists beneath the table. He would have surrendered all of East Selen for a touch of Syrnte magic just then, that he might speak to Eolyn's heart and remind her that this was a great concession they had achieved. More than they could have hoped for a few days ago, when talk of torture, retribution, and pyres ran rampant through the halls of Vortingen.

Akmael signed and sealed the third edict, and it was set before Eolyn.

She stared at both parchments, immobile as a stone effigy in one of the castle gardens.

"Eolyn, please." The King's tone softened. "This is all in the best interests of our people."

Without raising her eyes to him, she reached for the quill. Twice she signed her name, in rapid succession.

As the scribe retrieved the edicts, she looked away. Corey sensed her instinct to run, to escape the castle in the form of Hawk and seek refuge in the distant and quiet maze of the South Woods. Yet here she remained, struggling to reinforce her mask of honor and compliance as everyone gauged through his own lens how much ground the Queen had lost in this swift and vicious game.

"If there is nothing more to discuss on these matters," she said through tight lips, "perhaps it would please my Lord King to turn the Council's attention back to the very pressing problem of the forces amassing against us in Roenfyn."

Akmael rose, and everyone with him. He strode the length of the table to Eolyn's side, drew her into his embrace, and kissed her on the forehead. "It would please me, my Lady Queen. We have much to discuss. I will have the guards see you safely back to the East Tower."

"I intend to stay."

"You have done enough for one day."

"Enough?"

"Eolyn—"

"Our latest emissaries inform us that Roenfyn has secured the support of the Galian wizards," she said. "We know very little of Galian magic, save what has been preserved in the annals of the Royal Library and what has been revealed to me by my brother's sword, Kel'Barú."

"That weapon is an object of treacherous wizardry," Langerhaans said. "It should be confiscated at once."

"Kel'Barú served us faithfully against the Syrnte," Eolyn replied. "It could reveal much about the threats to come, if we but listen to its song."

"A Galian sword cannot be trusted any more than a maga."

"Enough!" Akmael's rebuke thundered across the table. "You overstep your bounds, Langerhaans. Justice has been served today by this Council. When peace is restored to our kingdom, the magas' power will be reinstated and our Lady Queen will, by my leave, continue her very noble work of weaving the magic of Aithne back into this land. The age of the Maga Warriors has ended, once and for all, but the rebirth of the Magas has only just begun. Anyone who speaks ill of our Lady Queen's sisters or their legacy will meet with my wrath."

Langerhaans lowered his head. "Forgive me, my Lord King. It was not my intention to offend."

Eolyn placed her hand on Akmael's arm. "Let me stay. I can help, just as I did when we faced Prince Mechnes and Queen Rishona."

The King kissed her hand. "Thank you, Eolyn, but it will not be necessary. Tibald, see our Lady Queen safely back to the East Tower."

The guard stepped forward, along with Eolyn's ladies-in-waiting.

Eolyn searched Akmael's face in a final, wordless plea. When he did not yield, a shadow appeared in her aura. The ebony thread pulsed inside her light, gathering strength from the landscape of color through which it snaked, until it reached the place where

Eolyn's aura merged with the King's. There it came to rest, coiled like a serpent in wait, a thin but palpable barrier between them; the stark breath of the Underworld ready to deliver its strike.

Corey's grip on his staff tightened. Trepidation crept into his heart, coupled with the incongruous taste of cold satisfaction.

Eolyn lowered her gaze and bowed.

"As you wish, my Lord King." She delivered her words without passion, icy as the northern forests on Midwinter's Eve. "I am, and have always been, your loyal servant."

CHAPTER TEN

A Conversation between Mages

CATCHING DUST IN SPECKS OF GOLD, afternoon light streamed through high windows and illuminated tall desks where robed men worked. The scratch of quills dominated a silence broken by occasional discrete murmurs and the quiet rasp of pumice over parchment.

It was here, in the Royal Library, that Mage Corey found some of the aromas he most enjoyed: the scent of old scrolls and cracked leather bindings, of dusty shelves and polished oak, of vinegary ink and dry chalk. Beneath it all, Corey heard the compelling hum of intense thought, an unending search for truth, and the fleeting illusion of understanding.

Drawing a random tome from a nearby table, Corey took a place at one of the desks, greeting the mage next to him with a brief nod. He opened the book and leafed slowly through its pages, paying only cursory attention to the elaborate illustrations and fine calligraphy while taking mental note of who was present in the library and who was not.

After a prudent period of time had elapsed, he let his gaze come to rest at the far end of the hall, where High Mage Thelyn was engaged in attending the petition of a fellow mage.

With an almost imperceptible glance toward Corey, Thelyn finished his discussion and proceeded to clear the library of scribes, mages, and apprentices. He did not rush, but wove patiently through rows of desks stacked with books, speaking with each man in turn, assigning or suggesting tasks that would take them elsewhere.

In the end, only a handful of High Mages remained, all members of Thelyn's inner circle. These he dismissed without explanation. They departed quietly, staves in hand, arms laden with books and sheaves of parchment.

Behind them, Thelyn closed the entryway and sealed it with a simple but powerful ward. He then turned to Corey, who now examined the tome laid open on the podium next to him. There was a peculiar essence woven into to the ancient vellum, of dry leaves and wet loam, of twisted oaks and heavy spring showers, of womanly passion and motherly love.

"This is from the Queen's personal library," Corey said in surprise.

"Very astute, my friend," Thelyn replied. "As always."

"She granted you permission to transcribe it?"

"Would you object if she hadn't?"

Corey shrugged. "Perhaps."

"I must admit, I have been most tempted in recent days to break the wards of Maga Eolyn's valuable collection and confiscate whatever should please us. It would be a propitious moment to do so. But like you, I suspect our Lady Queen will weather this storm as she has so many others. And like you, when she does I intend to be counted among her friends."

"And if she does not survive this latest onslaught?"

A smile touched Thelyn's lips. "Then her library will come into my possession in any case, and I will honor her desire to see the knowledge of her sisters preserved."

"What did she ask from you in return for the opportunity to transcribe this work?"

Thelyn arched his brow. "Not everyone bargains as you do, Corey. Our good Lady Queen wants nothing more than to ensure that the knowledge of her revered sisters is preserved through as many avenues as possible. She asked me to assist her in the task. Indeed, this is not the only volume she has lent to us in recent months."

Corey rolled his eyes. "Gods, she will never learn. Why she has come to grant you even a modicum of trust is beyond my understanding."

"Perhaps my gifts of persuasion are better than yours."

"I think not."

"Then perhaps it is because I have not yet betrayed anyone she loves."

Corey shook off the sting of Thelyn's remark. "You should return the favor, whether she asked it of you or not. It is the mark of an honest mage."

Amusement sparked in Thelyn's black eyes. "What would you have me do, my old and honest friend?"

"Lend her something of the royal collection, a set of volumes equivalent to what she gave you."

"Equivalent?"

"Annals that never would have been placed in the hands of a maga during Tzeremond's time."

"That could be anything." Thelyn scanned the shelves that surrounded them, many sagging under their burden of books. "Indeed, that would be everything. What work do you have in mind?"

"Haern's chronology of Galian warfare."

"I see." Thelyn tapped his chin thoughtfully. "Very well. It is a fair enough trade, and I daresay it will be useful to place it in her hands. Perhaps she will see something the Council does not, and use the discrete gifts of her magic to bring that wisdom to the attention of the King."

"I also want her to have the third volume of Eranon's journeys into the Underworld."

"That would be—"

"And Tyrendel's history of the Naether Demons."

"—less wise. Maga Eolyn read what we found of Tyrendel in Tzeremond's library, back when the Syrnte were ravaging Moehn and marching on Rhiemsaven. I doubt she wishes to read it again, though I will not stand in her way if she commands it. As for Eranon, I would not entrust that work to anyone but a select few among our own mages. Indeed, not many beyond you know it exists."

"She may be in need of his knowledge, Thelyn."

The mage looked at him in curiosity. "Why?"

Corey considered his answer, then drew a breath and said, "The portal is opening up again."

Thelyn eyed him in doubt. "You're certain?"

"I saw it today, at the Council meeting. Eolyn's aura has been breached. It is a slight fracture, but a fracture nonetheless."

"And the King?"

"Unfortunately, I cannot read his colors with nearly as much certainty."

"We should inform him."

"All he would do is increase Eolyn's guard and render more stringent the terms of her confinement. That would enhance the bitterness of this situation, giving the Underworld an even greater foothold on her spirit."

"This is not just about the Queen. The risk extends to our King as well. Both of them should be warned."

Corey paused to consider his friend's advice. "Very well. Allow me to speak with the Queen first. She, I think, would be the best person to bring this matter to the King's attention."

"Would she, knowing the consequences?"

Corey nodded. "I believe she would. She has always tried to act in the best interests of our people."

"And if she chooses to remain silent?"

"Then you and I will speak again, and decide on the best course of action."

Thelyn nodded. "I would say a bargain has been reached."

"Splendid. Now if you would be so kind, old friend: I cannot depart until I have in hand all the volumes requested by our Lady Queen."

CHAPTER ELEVEN

Fatigue

MAGE COREY'S ARRIVAL was announced shortly after the evening meal.

Eolyn wanted to turn him away, but under the circumstances it seemed less than prudent to snub the highest ranking mage in the kingdom. Besides, Briana's bright eyes and Eoghan's happy grin proved too much for her troubled heart to refuse. The prince and princess adored their uncle from East Selen. They took delight in all his mischievous tricks and adventurous stories. Despite her own misgivings, Eolyn could not deny her children the pleasure of his visit, especially now, when what little happiness they could invent was fast disintegrating inside these walls.

"Papa says we have to stay in the East Tower until the war is over." Briana took the liberty of climbing into Corey's lap as he sat down. "He says it's to keep us safe, but I don't believe that for a moment."

"Are you saying Father is a liar?" Eoghan's indignant frown brought a pang of nostalgia to Eolyn's heart. By the Gods, he was the image of Akmael as a boy. "Father is a king. Kings do not lie. To suggest otherwise is treason."

"I didn't call Father a liar! I'm only saying it doesn't make sense. If Father wants us to be safe, he should send us to East Selen, or even better to the South Woods. That's the safest place in the world. Mother hid in the South Woods for ten whole years when she was a little girl."

Corey's glance met Eolyn's as he pressed his lips against Briana's dark hair. "Ten long years in which the kingdom

70

languished for want of our Lady Queen's beauty."

Heat rose to Eolyn's cheeks, and she looked away. The remark was unusually candid for Mage Corey. Invasive in its intimacy.

"You must convince Father to send us to the South Woods, Uncle Corey," Briana was saying. "And you should come, too. We can all hide together until Roenfyn is defeated and all the bad magas are eliminated."

"Briana," Eolyn rebuked her sharply. "You must not wish death upon your own sisters."

The princess shrugged. "I can't call them my sisters any more if they are traitors. None of us can. That's what Lady Rhaella says. She says we must be very careful whom we call our sisters now, because the magas have once again proved a treacherous lot, just as they did under Kedehen."

Corey's eyes turned leaden. "What else has Lady Rhaella told you, Briana?"

The princess frowned and studied her hands. After a moment of concentration, she succeeded in invoking a small butterfly of light over her fingertips. "I've done it, Mother! Look. I made a butterfly all by myself."

"Briana." Corey gathered the spark in his palm and sent it fluttering toward the window, where its colors faded into the night. "Answer my question."

"She doesn't say much else. She tries to, but Lady Talia and the others tell her to hush and watch her tongue. And then they see me looking at them, and Lady Talia says—" Briana assumed the affected tone of a noblewoman from Selkynsen. "—surely you do not mean to speak ill of our good Lady Queen, who is herself a maga trained in the honored tradition of Aithne. And Lady Rhaella says, of course not, who would ever think such a thing? But then later she whispers — and I hear her whispering, even if she thinks I do not – that once not so long ago, everyone thought that Ghemena was good and loyal, and look how wrong we were about her, and about the magas who followed her. And if we were wrong about them, who knows what other magas might turn out to be bad, and who knows just how bad they have been?"

Icy dread shivered down Eolyn's spine.

"Lady Rhaella is fomenting sedition," Eoghan said.

"It is just talk," Corey replied. "And woman's talk at that."

"The lies of a woman cut deeper than any knife."

"Eoghan!" Eolyn checked her tone then sighed. Never had she needed to scold her children more than inside this tower. "That is a deplorable saying, and you are not to repeat it."

"You should have the Lady Rhaella arrested, Mother," the prince insisted. "Or at the very least, sent back to New Linfeln in disgrace."

"It is the King who makes these decisions at the moment," Corey reminded him, "not our good Lady Queen."

"Then we must speak to the King," Eoghan said.

"I will speak to him at the earliest opportunity." Corey set his silver-green eyes on Eolyn. "If it would please our Lady Queen that I intervene on her behalf."

Eolyn gave a brief shake of her head. "Thank you, Mage Corey. But I will speak to Lady Rhaella myself, and to the King if necessary."

"With all due respect, my Lady Queen, it would be better if you maintain a prudent distance on this matter. As a daughter of the house of Cramon Langerhaans, Lady Rhaella must be handled with utmost care."

Bile surged in Eolyn's throat. She rose abruptly and paced the room, restless with fury and frustration kept under tight rein for too long.

Retreating to a nearby window, she gripped its stony ledge, knuckles turning white as she took in the cool night air with deep and desperate gulps.

Eoghan drew close and placed a warm hand over hers.

"Mother," he said softly, "it will be all right. Everything is going to sort itself out. All the traitors will be caught and the reputation of the magas restored. Then we will leave this tower freely and without fear of any danger. Father will make it so."

Had young Prince Akmael said the same to Briana of East Selen, when he stood as a boy at her side?

Had Briana suffered the same suffocating terror that death would claim her in this place, that she would never see the forest or freedom again?

"Mother." Eoghan squeezed her hand gently.

72

Eolyn drew the night air deep into her lungs and willed her pulse to slow. When she turned around, she saw Mage Corey watching them with his serpent-like gaze, her beloved daughter ensconced in his arms.

Nothing has changed since the day you and I first met, she realized.

Always she had been under Corey's watch.

Always she had lived in fear of his betrayal.

She asked herself now if there were any step she had taken — any decision made over her life — that had not in some way been sanctioned by him.

His was a world of surreptitious movement and hidden agreements, of maneuvers unknown to her. The higher she had risen, the tighter the tendrils of Corey's power had grown, weaving like a slitherwort vine through the fabric of her fate.

She feared him because of this; but she also needed him — more, she suspected, than he would ever need her. Corey could simply walk away from her if it pleased him, his indecipherable path undisturbed by her absence.

You would not look back if the ravens fell upon me. You would feel no remorse as they tore at my flesh and plucked out my eyes.

Corey drew a pensive breath and as if privy to her silent accusation, averted his gaze.

"This conversation has grown tedious," he said, setting Briana aside. "I came here for some diversion tonight, to escape my worries and forget the burdens of this long day. I will not go away unsatisfied. Shall we have a story, Briana and Eoghan?"

Briana clapped her hands. "Oh yes, Uncle Corey!"

"What would you like to hear?"

"Aithne and Caradoc!" Briana exclaimed.

"Caedmon on the battle field," Eoghan countered.

"The doomed heart of Lithia."

"The adventures of brave Sir Drostan."

"All of it!" cried Briana, jumping up and down. "I want to hear it all."

Corey laughed and touched her chin. "No, little Princess. You must choose just one. One for each of you, and then you will both go to bed."

"But Uncle Corey--"

"That is my final word. This has been a trying day for all of us. Your mother is weary." He looked at Eolyn, a rare spark of sympathy in his eyes. "And so, quite frankly, am I."

Later that night, Eolyn lingered at her children's bedside, entranced by their sleeping faces under the flickering candlelight. She envied their peace during the midnight hours, when the caravan of her doubts began its long winding journey through the ever more anxious landscape of her mind.

Even in sleep, Eolyn could no longer find rest. In every dream the plight of her students mingled with the death of her mother. Flames licked at Kaie's tattered dress, heat crisped her skin, a crown of fire burst over her fair head. Screams of agony and defeat, of terror and remorse, danced inside a terrible light. Then Kaie would reach toward Eolyn with blackened arms, and the faces of all her dead sisters would melt off her skull.

Why? Kaie wailed. *Why do you betray us?*

Tears sprang to Eolyn's eyes, though they did not fall. So much loss and persecution. A generation of women massacred, a host of families destroyed, yet somehow she had managed to forgive them all. She had fallen in love with a prince, the heir to this bloody legacy. She had made his allies her own. She had welcomed the pleasure of his embrace and given him a son.

All this because she believed in the promise of love, in the possibility of renewal.

Perhaps a people so torn by war and violence can never be renewed.

Letting go a quiet sigh, Eolyn planted a tender kiss on each of her children's foreheads, adjusted the covers, and rose.

Circling the room, she ran her fingers over the cool stone walls, searching for tiny fissures in the wards that held them captive. Though she was not ready to desert her King, Eolyn refused to be held any longer against her will. Every ward had a seam, every spell a counter spell. Once she found a way to unravel this net of magic, she could seek out Mariel and Jacquetta and speak with them. She would visit her imprisoned magas and give them comfort in the never ending darkness of the dungeons of Vortingen.

Perhaps she would even find a way to set them free.

Passing from the children's room into the antechamber, Eolyn continued her search, but to no avail. In places, the fabric of spells waxed or waned, but never did it yield even a hairline crack.

The fire on the hearth hissed and sputtered.

Eolyn watched the glowing coals, reluctant to return to her own room though her muscles ached with exhaustion. She fingered a stack of books left by Corey, curious as to their content but too tired to sit down and open them just yet.

I meant to speak with you about this today, he had said, *but it can wait. Rest, Eolyn. There will be time to attend to all our troubles on the morrow.*

Indeed, time was all she had left in this dismal tower, and even that ran out at the end of each day.

There was nothing left to do now save retire to the bedchamber.

"Sweet Aithne, grant me wisdom," she whispered. "Dragon, give me strength and resolve."

Akmael was waiting for her, just as she expected, spirited into her chambers by the magic of the silver web. He stood at the foot of her bed, studying the Galian sword Kel'Barú. The long silver-white blade gave off a wary hum.

"Have you come to confiscate my brother's weapon, my Lord King?" she asked.

He set his dark gaze upon her. Just this much made Eolyn catch her breath, igniting desire in her heart. "No, my love. The Galian blade protects you like no other. It will always be at your side."

"But I am a maga, Akmael. By your own edict, I can no longer bear arms."

"You are my queen."

"I am a maga first. It has always been that way, in their eyes and in my heart."

He set the weapon aside, closed the distance between them, and took her chin gently in hand. "You did well today. I thank you for that. I know this has not been easy for you."

"Yes, I did well today." She stepped away, irritated. "I signed a death warrant for my daughters in magic. I struck down the privileges of all magas. I surrendered my powers to the Council. And here I am: a prisoner in the East Tower still. I would say I've done very well indeed, though by what measure, I cannot imagine."

"Eolyn—"

"Do not patronize me, Akmael! Not in this of all moments. I left behind the dreams of my youth to be the woman — the ruler — you asked me to be. I ignored the warnings of my *Doyenne* and the pleading of my students. Indeed, I ignored the very truth of history. For ten years I have governed this country faithfully, lovingly, even happily, at your side. Now everything I have built is being torn to the ground."

"Your work is not being undone. Did the Council not grant your most important petitions? Jacquetta and Mariel have been set free. As for the rest of the magas, their status will be restored as soon as we have determined—"

"Whether I, too, am guilty of treason?"

He paused, a troubled look on his face. "You are not so accused."

"Don't play me for a fool. Even our children can see you have imprisoned me. My own daughter wonders whether I betrayed our people."

"I will speak to Briana and explain the reasons for your confinement."

"You will speak to her about nothing. Too many people are speaking to her already, filling her mind with lies and suppositions. I cannot bear it, Akmael. I cannot bear to see my children poisoned against me."

"I swear to you, Eolyn, I will put a stop to this slander."

"*This* is slander!" She gestured angrily at the room. "If you wish to put a stop to it, then set me free."

"You are protected here, and free to go whenever and wherever prudence allows."

"A prudent king would take me into battle at his side, just as you did when we faced the Syrnte invasion."

"I almost lost you because of that foolishness. You and our unborn son."

"I won that war, or have you forgotten? I slew Prince Mechnes as he stood over you on the battle field. I saved this kingdom from enslavement, and when everyone thought our King beyond hope, I brought you back from the grip of the Underworld."

Akmael's expression softened. He stepped close and gathered

her into his arms.

"So it was." His lips touched hers, then grazed her ear. "May your magic always call me home."

Eolyn's resolve wavered under the potency of her love's embrace; always new and yet ever familiar, a spark that refused to be extinguished no matter how vicious the storm. Every fiber of her body yearned to respond, to accept the full promise of his pleasures. She allowed Akmael to loosen her bodice, shivered as his ardent lips explored her throat and descended to her bared shoulders. Her breasts escaped their confines and rose of their own volition, desperate for the sweet flame of their shared desire.

"Akmael," she murmured in protest.

He lifted Eolyn off her feet and carried her to the bed.

"Akmael, please—"

Still he persisted, every caress more demanding than the last, oblivious to the subtle change in her tone, to the fact that she no longer returned his ardor.

"For the love of the Gods, stop!"

The walls of Eolyn's prison wavered. For a brief moment she saw in Akmael the boy she once knew, startled and uncertain in the face of her defiance.

Averting her gaze, Eolyn withdrew from his embrace. Her heart contracted painfully at the sudden absence of his touch.

"Forgive me, my Lord King," she said. "I am weary, and I cannot do this. I cannot make love to you in this place."

Akmael stepped away, confusion plain upon his brow. "Of course, my love. Let us rest, then. It has been a long day."

"No." She shook her head. "I will not sleep with you at my side. Not like this. Not as your prisoner."

"You are not my prisoner."

"Just go!" The words flew from her lips, swift and sure as daggers. "Gods help me, I cannot bear to be in your presence!"

Akmael stared at her, stunned. Then his chest rose and fell in quiet resignation. Stepping back, he picked up his cloak and set it about his shoulders.

Eolyn's spirit buckled under the onslaught unbearable sorrow.

"Forgive me," she whispered.

"There is nothing to forgive."

"When this is over and all doubt has been swept away..." Eolyn faltered, uncertain what she was trying to say. Her eyes began to burn. She gathered the loose fabric of her dress and covered her naked torso.

"I do not doubt you, Eolyn," he said quietly. "I love you. I have always loved you, and I always will. Perhaps it is difficult for you to understand because I...I do not like to speak to you of such things, but when I was a boy I watched women with your gifts, mere girls, even, tortured at the hands of my father's mages and burnt on the pyre. I have sworn to myself a thousand times I would never let such horror touch you. But ours are a difficult people and now with everything that's happened, I...I have to protect you, Eolyn. This is the only way I know how."

Eolyn covered her face with her hands. Tears streamed hot down her cheeks.

"Set me free," she begged. "Our magic will die here if you do not set me free."

Akmael did not respond. He drew forth the silver web and let it dangle from his grasp. The tiny crystals caught sparks of candlelight as he spun the amulet. With a brief, whispered spell, he vanished from her sight.

Candles flickered under a sudden breeze, filling the space he left behind with a somber dance of shadows.

CHAPTER TWELVE

Madness

WHEN SHE WAS A YOUNG GIRL, Taesara had spent summers with her parents and siblings at Merolyn. Though the surrounding terrain seemed dull and lifeless to the eyes of many, she had always found comfort in the muted tones of its marshes; in the quiet rustle of wind through tall brown sedges. During autumn and spring, migratory waterfowl would settle over open pools, resting briefly between their winter and summer homes.

The last time she had visited Merolyn, Taesara was a girl of fifteen summers, filled with dreams and fears of her pending marriage to the Mage King, of the formidable crown she would wear, and of the mysterious traditions of Moisehén. Kahrl was a toddler waddling at her side, his hand clasped tightly to hers, his chubby face bright with laughter. Together they had walked to the edge of the waters, where they spied on brightly colored Fanferen ducks and snow-white winter geese.

When she had explained that she was leaving and why, little Kahrl had cried.

The clay-colored tower was just as she remembered: dull and flattened in aspect, like the landscape itself. Taesara rode through the arched entryway at a brisk pace then reined in her steed. Her men-at-arms circled around her. Her escort was modest, yet it outnumbered the servants and guards who appeared to greet them. As she dismounted, a young man in simple but well-tailored clothes stepped forward and dropped to his knees in reverence. All his companions followed suit.

"Hail, Taesara," he said, "Princess of Roenfyn and Queen of

Moisehén."

Taesara extended her hand, allowing him to touch her fingers to his forehead before she bade him to rise.

"I was told Lord Claredon has been charged with the guardianship of my brother," she said. "Where is he?"

A sheepish look crossed the young man's face. "My apologies, my Lady Queen, but I am Lord Claredon. His son, that is. My good father perished during the Battle of Lendhill, defending our King against the usurpers."

"I see. I am very sorry for your loss and grateful for your family's faithful service to our King…" Taesara studied him, looking for a recognizable thread from her past. After a moment she said tentatively, "Thomen?"

He grinned and bowed. "Yes, my Lady Queen."

"You are not as I remember you." She could not help but smile. The last time she had seen Thomen, he was a mud-splattered boy of ten summers.

"I should hope not." He gestured to a young lady behind him, beckoning her forward. "This is my wife, the good Lady Myella. And our two little girls, Rebekah and Katelyn."

They were cut from the same stone, Thomen and Myella, with straight dark hair and honest brown eyes. Their girls offered Taesara precious smiles and bouquets of fragrant wildflowers.

"Welcome, my Lady Queen," Myella said. "Ours is a humble home, but we do our best. I hope you will find everything here to your liking."

"I believe I will, Myella."

"You must be weary from your long journey. We have food and drink prepared."

"No. Not for me, thank you. Not until later. See that my companions are fed and their horses tended, Lady Myella. Thomen, I would have you take me at once to the King."

Myella cast a nervous glance toward her husband.

"In truth, my Lady Queen," she said, "we had hoped to speak with you first."

"Myella." The warning beneath Thomen's breath was clear.

"But someone must tell her," the young woman insisted. "Our Lord Regent does not provide nearly enough resources to—"

"We will have time to discuss these concerns later." Thomen bowed in deference to Taesara. "If our Lady Queen deems it necessary."

Myella pursed her lips and nodded.

Troubled by this curious exchange, Taesara called upon Lady Sonia and Ghemena to follow her, along with two of her guards. She remembered well the narrow winding stairwells of the castle and the cool touch of the sandstone walls. Despite the comfort she found in this familiarity, a sense of dread haunted each step that brought them closer to her brother's chambers.

At the entryway, Thomen paused and cleared his throat. "If I may be so bold, my Lady Queen. I know that you have not been in the presence of our Lord King for many years—"

"No more words, Thomen. Let me see him first."

The door creaked on its hinges, and Taesara stepped into her brother's quarters.

Thin shafts of light penetrated drawn curtains. The smell of burning herbs and strong tinctures suffocated her senses. A rustle of fabric and scuffling against the floor startled Taesara. She had the fleeting fear of rats underfoot, but as her eyes adjusted she saw the source of movement and sound. Several healers surrounded the King and hovered over a long table lit by yellow candles. Their tonsured heads identified them as Brothers of Waking Thunder, an old and wealthy sect that for centuries had served the Kings of Roenfyn.

"Dear Brothers," Thomen said, "Queen Taesara has arrived."

At once they parted from Kahrl, like the wings of a crow unfolding. Amid their kneeling figures Taesara saw her brother, shriveled and listless in a cushioned chair. He did not move. He did not speak. His breath rattled through hollow lungs.

"Open the curtains," she said.

"My Lady Queen," one of the brothers replied. "For a sickness of this sort, strong light is not recommended. The effects of such a shock—"

"Open them, I say!"

Thomen hastened to see her will done. The others reluctantly followed suit. Daylight flooded the King's quarters. The curtains were worn and patched, the tapestries faded. Only the most essential furnishings remained: a bed, a table, a few simple chairs. To one of these they had secured Kahrl with straps of leather. He did not respond to the sun's brilliance but looked unseeing into the space before him, his mouth slack and drooling.

Taesara drew a sharp breath. "Why do you have tied him up like that? He is not a prisoner. He is your King!"

"He cannot hold himself upright, my Lady Queen," Thomen said quietly. "If they did not use the tethers, he would double over and be unable to breathe."

"And the seizures, my Lady Queen," one of the brothers added. "They come without warning, and are of such violence that he bruises himself if he is not secured."

Overcome with nausea, Taesara turned her back on them and retreated to the doorway, one hand clutching her abdomen, the other grasping the wall for support.

"My Lady Queen." Sonia appeared at her side and laid a comforting hand upon her arm. "This is too much for you to bear. Your Lord Uncle suspected it would be, and I warned you as well. Come and eat. Rest from your long journey, and then let us leave this place. There is nothing to be done here; your brother is lost to the curse that was placed upon him years ago."

"Do not say that." Taesara spoke between gritted teeth.

"We have a greater task ahead of us in Moisehén."

"Silence!"

Sonia flinched and stepped away.

Recovering her composure, Taesara looked again upon her brother.

"You," she said to one of her guards, "unbind the King and bring him with me."

The brothers murmured in protest.

"And you," she instructed the other man-at-arms, "bring his chair and those awful leather straps."

"Where are you taking him?" one of the brothers demanded.

"I am taking him to see the sun and to look upon the sea."

"You cannot do this!"

"What is your name?" she shot back. "Who are you to question the Queen's will and wisdom?"

The brother retreated a step. He was an older man with a

curved spine and a muskrat-like face. Streaks of gray ran through his black hair. "I am Father Wilhem, my Lady Queen. I have overseen the care of the King for many years now."

"And has his condition improved under your attentions?"

"He is alive."

She snorted. "You call this living?"

"It is more than we could have hoped for when the sickness took hold."

"Then your capacity for hope is piteously small." She nodded toward Ghemena. "This woman is in my service. She is a maga of Moisehén, trained in the tradition of Aithne."

Gasps spread through the room. The brothers made the sign of Thunder to protect themselves.

"She will remain here with you, Father Wilhelm, and you will tell her everything that you have done for our King from the moment he was entrusted to your care."

"My Lady Queen," Sonia intervened, "I do not think it wise to allow this woman to—"

"Enough, Sonia. Go see that my quarters are prepared."

The lady stiffened and with a brief bow, departed.

"Ghemena," Taesara said. "Do you understand what is expected of you?"

The maga warrior stepped forward. "Yes, my Lady Queen."

"My Lady Queen," said Father Wilhem, "with all due respect, it would be dangerous to share our knowledge with this witch."

"What danger can there be in sharing a knowledge as useless as yours, Father Wilhem?"

While he struggled to invent a response, Taesara nodded to Ghemena. "You have vowed to put your gifts to our service. I would see that oath realized today. I want to know what ails him, what they have done to help him, and why it has not worked. I want to know how he can be cured."

"Yes, my Lady Queen."

She nodded to her guards. "Bring the King with me."

They followed Taesara up long, winding stairs to emerge on the crenelated southern wall, which afforded a view to the hazy rim of the Sea of Rabeln. The sun had sunk low on the horizon and cast a reddish-gold sheen over the vast marshes. Wind blew from the southwest, constant and true, carrying the sulfur-hued scent of Galia.

Taesara instructed the guards to set the King in his chair, and took it upon herself to gently strap his shoulders and head so he could look out toward the happy fields where they had played as children. His hair was thin and limp, his skin gray and clammy. Removing her cloak, she covered his emaciated legs and knelt at his side. The guards retreated a respectful distance as she laid her hand over his.

"Kahrl." She searched his vacant eyes. "I am Taesara, your sister. Princess of Roenfyn and Queen of Moisehén. I have come to bring you back from the darkness."

There was no twitch of life from his hands, no spark of recognition in his face.

"Hear me, Kahrl," she pleaded. "See me. Now."

Still he did not respond.

Resting a weary head upon her brother's lap, Taesara surrendered to grief and wept.

The sun was a blood-red slit on the western horizon when Thomen appeared and asked in compliant tones whether they might have leave to return the King to his chambers to feed him, bathe him, and put him to bed for the night.

Too exhausted to argue, Taesara allowed them carry Kahrl away while she lingered on the ramparts. As much as she felt an obligation to tend personally to her brother, she was unable to face the dank interior of the castle just yet.

Ribbons of purple and saffron streaked across the sky. Stars began to glimmer in the firmament. Guards lit torches along the wall. Still Taesara did not abandon her watch, though the night grew chilly and her muscles ached.

Lady Sonia appeared with a handful of servants who set up a chair and table, upon which they laid out a simple meal of bread, sausage, and hot tea.

"The Lady Myella asks if there is anything our Lady Queen requires." Sonia poured a steaming cup and set it on the table. She wrapped a warm cloak around Taesara's shoulders.

Taesara merely shook her head and sent them away.

Setting her hands upon the parapet, Taesara looked out over

the land that had once belonged to her father, an endless expanse of muddy bogs shrouded in white mist. The waxing moon peered through translucent clouds. The yips of marsh dogs rose to meet its ephemeral light. This place was her home and held its own mysterious beauty. But in the end, the sodden earth of Roenfyn had yielded little for the noble families who ruled over it for so many centuries. No wonder they coveted the rich and fertile fields of Moisehén. No wonder they longed for the Mage King's precious mines and dense forests.

Taesara sighed and sat at the table where she picked at her food until the stars called her attention once again. Perhaps somewhere in their pure light she could find an answer, a glimpse past this cruel world into the place of hope that she once knew. She envisioned herself playing across the fields with her siblings, arriving late for the evening meal fevered with laughter and joy, immune to the half-hearted rebukes of their loving parents.

"Were they all empty promises?" she murmured. "Was everything they said nothing but cruel indulgence of a child's dreams?"

"What promises, Milady Queen?"

Taesara sprang to her feet, sending the cup clattering to the floor and spilling hot liquid across the flagstones.

"Show yourself," she demanded.

The maga warrior, Ghemena, stepped into a pool of light cast by a nearby torch.

"How dare you approach me without announcing your presence." Taesara hoped her rage and indignation hid the fear that had shaken her to the core.

"I didn't mean to startle you, Milady Queen. In fact, I was thinking not to disturb you at all, but then you asked that question and I became curious. I thought maybe you and I heard similar promises. When we were children, that is."

"Do not distract me with your witch's riddles." Taesara rubbed damp palms against her skirt and looked to the men stationed along the wall. "Did the guards not see you?"

"I'm a maga warrior. We're trained to pass unseen."

"You are not to pass by me unseen, ever again."

"As you wish, Milady Queen."

Taesara did not expect such instant capitulation. She studied Ghemena with suspicion, fists clenched at her side. "Well out with it, then. What do you have to report?"

"You wanted to know if your brother—"

"Our King."

"If our King is a victim of *Ahmad-melan,* and I'm here to tell you I do not believe he is. *Ahmad-melan* is a temporary madness. It can't last years like that. I mean, the scars it leaves may last a lifetime, but for a person to lose all awareness of the world around him…that wouldn't make sense. A victim of *Ahmad-melan* is still connected to this world; it's just that he doesn't see the world as it is. He sees it as he fears it to be."

"So my brother is not under a curse?"

"No. Well, not that curse, at any rate. There's always *Ahmad-dur.* Or something similar."

"*Ahmad-dur?*" Every curse named by a maga sounded fouler than the last.

"That's the curse that was used to banish the Naether Demons in ancient times. The same one that was invoked by Master Tzeremond against my tutor, the one you call the Witch Queen, during the Battle of Aerunden. The spirit is tethered to the living body and then cast into the Underworld. Because of the tether, the victim can't cross into the Afterlife; because of the curse he can't return to his body. So he languishes in darkness, until he fades into nothing. Or worse, until he's consumed by the Lost Souls or the Naether Demons."

"Yes." Recognition blossomed in Taesara's heart, followed by hope. "Yes, I remember that story. The Mage King brought the witch back from the Underworld. That means this curse can be reversed by someone with the proper knowledge. You perhaps, or your companions."

Ghemena shook her head. "I'm sorry, Milady Queen, but even if one of us were familiar with the teachings of Master Eranon and others who have made the journey in the land of the dead, even if the Mage King himself taught us how, we wouldn't be able to save your brother."

"Why not?"

"The men who serve your uncle tell me the King has

86

languished in this state for almost seven years. Maga Eolyn's spirit was recovered because only moments had passed between the casting of the curse and the Mage King's decision to go after her. Her spirit hadn't yet forgotten the world of the living; it hadn't begun to fade. Your brother, on the other hand—"

"Our King."

"The King, he's been gone too long. If *Ahmad-dur* is what took him..." Ghemena broke off and looked away. "If *Ahmad-dur* is what took him, then there is no hope."

Taesara turned from the maga and pressed her hands upon the cold stone wall. Night shrouded the sodden plains of Merolyn, black as the shadows that consumed her heart. What false piety had compelled her to abandon her young brother to this brutal world? Why was she not at his side when this malaise attacked his spirit and chaos consumed the kingdom?

"Milady Queen." Ghemena spoke softly behind her. "I speak of curses because that's what you asked about. But the truth is I don't think he's under a curse. At least, not a curse in the tradition of Moisehén."

"Why would you say that?"

"Well, it's what I mentioned before. These are intimate curses, *Ahmad-dur*, *Ahmad-melan*...There are no magas or mages among your people who could've gotten close enough to the King to cast them."

"Perhaps a maga crept unseen into our lands."

"Perhaps." Ghemena chewed her lower lip, uncertainty furrowing her features. "But there are other tricks that could accomplish the same malaise."

"Speak plainly, Maga Ghemena."

"Do you trust these Brothers of Waking Thunder?"

"They have served our Kings for generations."

"Well, their medicine is strange and contradictory. They use some herbs that might alleviate your brother's — I mean, the King's — ailment, but other herbs that must needs enhance it."

A cold knot took hold of Taesara's stomach. "What herbs?"

"Carobane. Nightshade. Fennelswort. All of these used in small portions are effective sleeping potions and pain killers, but larger doses over a long period—"

"Can cause madness, paralysis, even death."

Ghemena's eyes widened in surprise. "How do you know this?"

"I learned something of herbs and healing during my years among the sisters."

The maga warrior grinned. "In Moisehén, we call that Simple Magic. It makes you a maga, you know. In our eyes."

"I did not bring you here to suffer your insults."

"None intended, Milady Queen."

"Who else have you spoken to about this?"

"No one."

"You are to maintain silence on this matter," Taesara said. "You will not share what you have told me with anyone."

"I understand, Milady Queen."

"Nor will you reveal to anyone that I command knowledge of herbs and medicine. Can I trust you with this?"

"Yes, Milady Queen."

Taesara eyed her doubtfully. "We shall see. There is one more task I would give to you, Ghemena. I would have you watch for me."

"Watch what?"

"Everything. You say there are none like you among us, and yet you claim magas can pass unseen."

Ghemena wrinkled her nose. "If there's a practitioner behind all of this, he is almost certainly a mage. Mages are much more likely to do something nasty like this."

"Mage or maga, I do not care. If you suspect anyone at my uncle's court of practicing magic, I am to be informed at once. I and no one else."

"It will be as you wish, Milady Queen."

"Very well. You are dismissed, Ghemena. We will speak again on the morrow."

Ghemena remained, shifting on her feet. "If I may ask one more question, Milady Queen?"

Taesara quelled her impatience. "Make it quick."

"If the King's your brother, why is your uncle Regent and not you?"

Taesara glanced around to see who was within earshot. "Is it not obvious? I am a woman."

"But there's precedent in all the northern kingdoms for a woman to command as regent. And anyone who knows their history can see women make far better rulers than the men who come before or after."

"Watch your tongue, Ghemena, lest it guide you back into treason."

"I'm just saying you could've been regent, and a good one at that. I can see it in your eyes, in the set of your shoulders, in the way everyone watches you at your uncle's court. People would follow a woman like you. All you'd have to do is—"

"Enough! I dismissed you. Now go."

Ghemena set her jaw. She bowed and slipped back into the shadows.

Unsettled, Taesara bent to retrieve her cup. With shaking hands, she refilled the vessel, but found the tea had turned cold and bitter.

Disgusted, she threw the cup over the wall and into the darkness beyond.

My uncle is Regent because he is ambitious and cunning.

Anger rose in her blood.

Anger, frustration, and a renewed sense of self-loathing.

I, on the other hand, am a coward and a fool.

CHAPTER THIRTEEN

Mariel and Markl

"Aren't planning to fly away, are you?"

Mariel jumped, startled to hear Markl at her side. Unkempt brown hair shrouded his dark, mischievous gaze.

"Gods, don't sneak up on me like that." She glanced around her new prison, comfortable and well-lit, though sparse in its furnishings. A pang of guilt clutched at her heart as she remembered her sisters still trapped in the dungeons below. "How did you get in here?"

Mariel had not heard the creak of the door or the sound of his steps over the freshly strewn rushes.

Markl shrugged. "I may be the squire of the great Lord Borten, but I'm still as good a thief as there ever was. I go wherever I please, whenever I please."

"You found a hidden entrance?"

"Maybe I did. Maybe I didn't."

He produced two apples from his tunic and offered one to her. She accepted the gift with a smile. The fruit was crisp and tart, a burst of sweet flavor on her tongue.

"I'm here to escort you, Milady Mariel," Markl announced with an exaggerated bow. "Out of this city and back home to Moehn."

"You? My escort?"

"You're surprised?" He leaned close and peered out the window. Markl's tunic was freshly washed and smelled of alomint. "We've got quite a mummer's show in the courtyards this morning. I can see why you were distracted. Men shouting, servants running about, and ho! There's Prince Eoghan at his lessons. He's growing into a handsome boy, that Eoghan. A little young for you, I'd say, but that sort of thing doesn't stop a maga, does it?"

She elbowed him in the ribs.

"Ow! No insult meant, milady. I'm just sayin'…no wonder you didn't hear me come in."

"I wasn't watching him."

"Who were you watching, then? Sir Gaeoryn? Young Lord Meryth? It better not be Lord Borten, as he is doubly taken."

"For the love of the Gods, Markl. Not every woman you know is pining away after some man."

"I hope not. Unless, of course, they're pining away after me."

"I didn't hear you because all my senses are dulled. That's what happens when one's magic is bound. It's like someone put a bucket over my head." And a leash around her throat. Every time she reached for her magic the tether tightened. Painfully.

Markl scanned the ample courtyards and lush gardens enclosed by the stone walls of Vortingen. "Ah-hah! I see the comedy that had you so distracted. Mage Corey over there in the northern gardens, casting his spell on Lady Rhaella."

Mariel would have abandoned him in a huff, were she allowed to leave the room. Instead she turned on her heel and paced a circle, before sitting on a stool and taking a fierce bite out of her apple.

Markl sat next to her. "You're still sweet on him, aren't you?"

"Mage Corey is the least of my concerns." Though it was true she had been watching him, curious as to the nature of his interest in Lady Rhaella. "And I'm not sweet on him. Not in the way you think."

"You're sweet on him in the only way it matters."

"That's not true. Corey and I…" She searched for the words to explain. "We are mage and maga. The Spirit of the Forest calls us at times, that's all."

"The Spirit of the Forest?" He threw his head back in a mocking laugh. "That's a fine excuse you magas have invented. What if I were to tell you the Spirit of the Forest calls me too?"

"I would say that is a fine and healthy thing."

"Then I hear the Spirit of the Forest every night, Mariel. She whispers your name in my ear and says we are meant for each

91

other."

Laughter burst from Mariel's lips.

"That wasn't meant as a joke."

"Oh, Markl." Mariel struggled to catch her breath. "It's not what you say; it's how you say it."

"Does that mean you want me too?"

"No!" She laughed again and took his hand. "I mean, I like you, but no. You have a fine sense of humor, though. It seems forever since I've laughed."

The squire shook his head and rose. "A man has bad luck indeed, if he has no luck with a maga."

He swaggered a few steps away to lean against the wall, where he watched her with hooded eyes while munching on his apple.

"So you're to be sent back to Moehn," he said, "to wander free on the highlands."

"Not free, not entirely. I'll be under vigilance, and my magic will remain bound. Still, Borten and Corey say it's for the best."

"But you don't want to go?"

Mariel shook her head. She glanced back at the window.

"Because of Mage Corey?"

"Oh, Gods, no." She rolled her eyes. "Not for him. For Maga Eolyn, and for all my sisters. I do not wish be parted from them now, even though I am not allowed to see them. For my King as well, and for my people. I hope these terrible suspicions will pass, and soon, so that he will let us bear arms again and fight at his side against the usurpers from Roenfyn."

A low whistle hissed through Markl's teeth. "You're a noble one, aren't you? I don't understand you maga warriors. War is a nasty business, and you've an easy way out of it just by being a woman. Yet you insist on learning swords and spears and wartime magic. Seems more than a little foolish to me."

"Being a woman doesn't spare me from war. I learned that well enough when I was a girl."

The terror and tragedy of the Syrnte invasion still burned deep inside. Renate beheaded, Adiana enslaved, Tasha and Catarina slaughtered in blood sacrifice. And Sirena, Mariel's sweet, beloved Sirena. The image of her friend's fair figure, torn open by a Naether Demon, her heart pulsing in the clutches of its ebony claws, haunted Mariel's nightmares to this day. She shuddered and pushed the thought deeper into the recesses of her mind.

"There is no escape from war," she said. "The next time that door opens to release its bloodthirsty monsters, I prefer to confront them well-armed."

Markl shrugged and threw his apple core into the coals on the hearth. The apple popped and steamed, blackened edges curling into flame.

"Well," he said. "This has been a lovely conversation, Sir Mariel, but I have my orders and my orders are to depart with you for Moehn today. Already we are off to a late start, thanks to some confusion regarding your escort. That and a momentary, shall we say, distraction with one of the kitchen girls. I'd rather slip away now before Borten notices we haven't yet left."

"Is it Borten you are trying to avoid or that kitchen girl?"

"Both could be equally unpleasant at this point."

"I asked Sir Borten to make a petition for me," Mariel said. "Do you have any word on that?"

"No. What petition?"

"I want to see Maga Eolyn, I mean, our Lady Queen, before we depart."

Markl frowned and shook his head. "Haven't heard a thing about it."

"Well, then, perhaps we should wait. Give him a little more time."

"Borten isn't thinking about you or your petitions, Mariel. The King wants the army to march in three days' time, so loyal Borten is tending to his orders. You're being packed off to Moehn because the sooner you're out of the way the better."

"But he said—"

"You'll be waiting a long time if you expect Borten to honor a request from you. You'll be waiting until this war is over."

"He knows how important this is to me," Mariel insisted. "I don't want to go without saying good-bye."

Markl sat close and put an arm around her shoulders. The gesture should have been comforting, but it filled her with unease. Why was he trying so hard to talk her out of this?

"Come on, Mariel," he said. "You don't want to linger in this

93

place. Everyone here is in a foul mood. It'll be fun to go home again. When we get to Moehn, we'll have a pint or two at Olleo's Tavern. We'll talk about the old days when you were an innocent young maga and I a child-thief who ruled the alleyways of Moehn. And we'll dance, we will. And sing a bit. And go riding through the fields; maybe even visit those forests you can't ever get enough of."

"You won't have time for all that. I imagine Borten wants every able-bodied man from Moehn back here to assist the King. Your orders must include an immediate return."

"Pah." He dismissed her words with a wave of his hand. "I'm not coming back here."

She studied him, puzzled. "You're serious?"

"I don't care about Borten or the King. Not when you and I can be alone in the highlands, following the sweet call of *aen-lasati*."

Laughter bubbled through Mariel's chest. She had always liked Markl, even when he was an unruly boy running half-wild through the streets of Moehn. For a moment, she was tempted to heed his advice.

"We'll be in Moehn soon enough," she said nonetheless. "But before we depart, I must speak with the Queen."

Markl scowled and griped all the way to the East Tower. They had no writ from the King, he said, and no proof of Borten's petition on her behalf. Without either they would never be allowed into the Queen's presence, as she was under strict confinement and hardly had the authority to admit her own guests, especially if that guest were a maga.

His pessimism seeped into Mariel's spirit until she, too, half expected she would be bound and sent back to the dungeons if she so much as appeared at the foot of the East Tower. Yet she held steady in her course and her intentions. She would not be swayed from this one desire.

By the time they arrived at the first barrier of guards, Markl had sunk into a petulant mood. The squire hung back, forcing Mariel to approach the mage warriors alone, grim-faced men with whom she had trained. At their head stood Rennert, bear-like in aspect, with a history of battles written across his broad face. Blood rushed to Mariel's cheeks under Rennert's steely-eyed gaze. She felt like a child in his presence, a fool to have even considered

94

breaching this prison the Mage King had erected around her tutor.

"If I may, good sir." She quelled the tremor in her voice. "I have come for an audience with the Queen."

"She expects you?" Rennert barked.

"I'm not certain," Mariel admitted, "though a petition was sent. Perhaps if you could advise her that I am here?"

Rennert looked her up and down before his expression broke, not so much into a smile, but into a more relaxed version of that dependable scowl. "You always were too honest for your own good, Mariel."

She blinked. "I beg your pardon?"

He nodded toward the stairs. "Go on, then. I'm sure she'll be pleased to see you."

Mariel looked from him to the others, bewildered. "Is this a jest?"

"You think me funny?" Rennert's growl sent her back a step. He nodded to one of his companions. "Accompany her."

The man moved to obey, but Mariel's feet remained rooted to the ground, unable to resist the force of her own doubt.

"A few days locked up, and already you've become an impertinent wench." Rennert's words came sharp, though amusement flickered across his face.

"I'm sorry, Sir Rennert, I just thought—"

"That'd we'd turn our back on you?"

"No, but after what Ghemena and the others did, I rather expected—"

"You ain't like that traitorous witch. All spit and ire that woman, but you, you're a steady flame all right, and we haven't forgotten. The men were glad when the King released you. Think you should know that. Wish you were coming to Roenfyn with us, too. Gods know we'd be better off for it if you did."

Mariel stared at him in astonishment. Any hint of praise from Rennert was rare, a declaration like this near impossible. During the years of her training, Mariel had suffered greatly under his endless and scathing criticisms. Yet she always believed she had grown into a better warrior because of him. It moved her deeply to discover he believed the same.

"Thank you, Rennert."

He shrugged and glanced away. "Just don't forget I said it, 'cause I won't be saying it again."

Mariel nodded and started up the stairs, pace quickening with a sudden lightness of heart.

"What about me?" Markl's whine echoed behind her. To the maga's secret relief, Rennert did not let him pass.

Eolyn received Mariel's sudden entrance with a cry of joy. She wrapped her arms around Mariel and kissed her face while murmuring thanks to the Gods.

Reluctantly, the young maga extracted herself from Eolyn's embrace. She bowed as protocol demanded, aware of the arched gazes of the Queen's ladies and the hooded interest of her guards.

With a quick command, Maga Eolyn sent everyone away.

"They haven't hurt you?" Eolyn set her hands on Mariel's shoulders, eyes flicking over the maga's person and aura. Worry and gratitude played across Eolyn's features, neither emotion gaining ground against the other.

"No. Not since they bound our magic. I have been treated with as much dignity as the situation allows."

"And the others?"

"I do not know." Mariel's disappointment showed in her voice. She had hoped Maga Eolyn would have information about her sisters, and it troubled her to discover otherwise. "They kept us in separate cells. No one speaks to me of them, not even Mage Corey or Borten."

"Oh, Mariel," Eolyn whispered. "Can you ever forgive me?"

"Forgive?" The question surprised her. "There's nothing to forgive. Indeed, Borten says if it wasn't for your intervention, I'd still be in prison."

"I should have told you to run when we had the chance."

Mariel shook her head. "It wouldn't have made any difference. They came prepared to hunt us down. I understand that now."

A frown furrowed Eolyn's brow. She guided Mariel to a divan near the windows and invoked a sound ward about them. "Lord Borten told me the King had given you permission to visit the East Tower before leaving."

"He did? But Markl said—"

"We do not have much time, Mariel. There are mages who

96

monitor this tower day and night. They will detect my sound ward soon, and will begin to unravel it at once."

"Surely their magic is no match for yours."

"A stronger ward, or one more subtly crafted, would resist their counter spells," Eolyn acknowledged, "but in this much I prefer to let them believe they still have the upper hand."

Mariel smiled. "That seems a game more suited to Mage Corey than to you, Maga Eolyn."

"It would seem the East Tower teaches the same lessons to all its guests. Mariel, I want you to know it is my express wish that you return to Moehn."

"But I thought Lord Borten decided—"

"I instructed Borten to submit the petition, and counseled the King to approve it."

"I would rather stay here," Mariel replied, confused.

"I know." Eolyn took Mariel's hands in hers. "It breaks my heart to be separated from you, Mariel. After the Syrnte invasion, I promised myself I would never let this happen again. But these circumstances..." The maga turned her focus inward, burdened by some difficult thought. "These circumstances I did not anticipate, though if I am to be honest with myself, I should have seen all of this coming a long time ago."

"None of us anticipated that Ghemena would ever—"

"I do not speak of Ghemena." Eolyn's expression hardened, like stone cut by flame. "I speak of the people of Moisehén, their fickle moods and their fierce jealousies. Ghemena was their excuse, but if they did not have her they would have found someone or something else, some other reason to imprison us once more."

This uncharacteristic display of pessimism disconcerted Mariel. "You think this is not going to end? That not even the King will protect us anymore?"

"I don't know," Eolyn's tone softened. "But I have made my choice, Mariel. I will stand by the man I love, and I will protect my children no matter what bitter end awaits me. You, however, still have your life and all its magic ahead of you. You have chosen the path of Aithne. I wish for you to continue in her steps."

"I won't get much farther with my magic bound."

"You forget we have friends in Moehn. Echior has sent

instructions on my behalf to Mage Taenler. Your magic is to be restored once you are delivered into Lady Vinelia's care."

"Restored?" Hope leapt in Mariel's heart.

"After that, you may remain as a guest in Borten's household, but you must be vigilant. If the tide turns against us further, if Roenfyn wins this war or the purges are renewed, you are to take refuge in the South Woods. Do not return until the Gods make this land safe for the magas once again."

"I see." Mariel remembered Eolyn's childhood home, the humble cottage of Doyenne Ghemena nestled inside the farthest reaches of that ancient forest. She loved its peace and tranquility, but she had never imagined she might one day take refuge there, just as her own tutor had done.

The thought was more than sobering.

"This is not the end." Eolyn continued, as if sensing Mariel's distress. "This is simply another beginning. Now is your time. I have given you everything I can as your Doyenne; it is up to the Gods to teach you the rest. In the highlands of Moehn, there are women destined to walk the path of magic with you. Find your sisters, and keep them close. Teach them the ways of Aithne and Caradoc. Together you can weather this storm and preserve the traditions of our people. You are our future, Mariel. You always have been."

Tears blurred Mariel's vision. Was Maga Eolyn saying good-bye forever? A thousand questions crowded into her mind, but when she opened her mouth to speak, Eolyn hushed her with a sudden lift of the hand.

The Queen tensed like a doe catching the scent of a predator. Mariel heard a long sustained hiss, followed by a subtle ripping, as if a length of fine fabric were being torn asunder. The ward that masked their conversation had been breached.

"It is growing late." Eolyn stood, bidding Mariel to rise. "I imagine your escort is waiting."

"Maga Eolyn, I—" Mariel's words broke into a choked sob.

She had not come prepared to assume the burden of the worst possible future. How could Maga Eolyn send her off like this? How could she, a woman of humble origins, ever hope to carry this magnificent heritage forward, all on her own?

"Everything you did for me," Mariel whispered. "This life that you gave us...I would be lost. I would be lost, Maga Eolyn, if it weren't for you."

Eolyn regarded her with an expression of intense joy and unbearable pain. For a moment, she clenched her hands into tight fists. Then she wrapped her arms around Mariel in a crushing embrace.

"You are wrong, Mariel," she murmured. "It is I who would be lost without you. Lost, and never found again. Remember what I have taught you. Trust in the will of Dragon. May the Gods keep you safe in their love and magic. May they show you the way to a better future."

CHAPTER FOURTEEN

Betrayal

AROUND MID-AFTERNOON, Markl reined in his horse and instructed everyone in Mariel's escort to dismount at a large ramshackle inn along the Furma River. It seemed a popular watering hole for travelers between the King's City and Rhiemsaven. Mummers and gamblers, merchants and thieves, musicians and prostitutes spilled from the dim interior onto tables set up at the river's edge. Even at this hour of the day, the air was filled with chatter and shouts, laughter and song.

Mariel had never been fond of seedy taverns like this one. Her spirit was much more at home in the open, wind-blown highlands of Moehn. The interior of the inn reeked of stale ale and fried pork, of flea-bitten dogs and soiled clothes, of human sweat and hidden sex. She insisted on finding a table outside, and Markl, fortunately, had agreed.

While Mariel held a place, Markl went for some ale. He brought back two wooden mugs and set one down in front of her. The maga warrior wrapped her hands around the cool drink with gratitude.

"What about the guards?" she asked. "Surely they are thirsty as well?"

"What guards?"

Mariel glanced toward a tree nearby, where just moments before the men of her escort had been resting in the shade and keeping a hawk's eye on her.

"Where'd they all go?" she said, surprised.

"No need for you to feel like a prisoner at your meals." Markl's

100

eyes darted over the crowd, as was his custom. At a glance, he could tell the sharp-witted from the fools, the killers from the cowards, and the virtuous from the wanton.

"They're only half a dozen of them. Feels more like a scouting expedition than a true escort."

"You'd rather have thirty men watching over you?"

"Well, no. I just thought this would be different, that's all."

She had not recognized any of the men-at-arms that accompanied them. Not that she knew all the soldiers in the kingdom, but Mariel had imagined the escort might include some of the King's guard, or at least the men who served Borten.

Then again, both King and Lord needed their best warriors for other purposes right now.

"Don't worry." Markl pinned her with a sharp gaze. "I'm not letting you out of my sight."

"No, I suppose you aren't." She took another swig from her ale, refreshing with its bittersweet bite. "How many servants did you seduce this time, Markl, during our short stay in the City?"

He puffed up his chest and counted on his fingers. "I reckon I nabbed a different girl every day this time. They're easy pickings for a handsome youth of noble blood."

"And you've no scruples about that?"

"Should I?"

"It's not very honest."

"What's dishonest about my noble blood?"

"Not your ancestry; the way you use it to cajole them."

"I don't say anything more than the truth. They make their own choices. Besides, nothing's more honest than a good squeeze. I thought magas understood that. That's what your great traditions are about, aren't they? The High Ceremony of Bel-Aethne, the sacred offerings of Winter Solstice?"

"That's not the same."

"Bah!" He waved away her indignation. "You're just jealous."

"I'm not jealous. Those girls are given so few options in life, and they have illusions too, you know. They might think you care for them, that you intend to give them a better life in exchange for their favors."

"I do care for them, after my own fashion."

101

Mariel gave him a withering stare.

He folded his arms. "If you've got something to say, you'd best say it now."

"It's just...Well, it's not so much about the girls, Markl. Though that does upset me. But mostly, it's you. You're always so scattered with everything. Like an overactive puppy."

He rolled his eyes. "Now I understand why magas never marry. You're nags, the lot of you. You'd make nasty wives."

"I'm not a nag," Mariel snapped. "Gods, Markl. You're the one who asked me to speak plainly. We've known each other a long time, and I like you, but you've always seemed distracted somehow, whether it's with weapons, girls, the demands of your lord—"

"My lord?"

"Or just day to day tasks. You don't seem to know what you want from life, or from yourself."

His expression hardened, and his gaze settled on his mug. "I know what I want. I want the world returned to us as it was. Before the Syrnte invaded, before my family was massacred and all our lands lost."

Mariel caught her breath, embarrassed by her own callousness. Markl had lost everything when he was a boy. Why had it not occurred to her that beneath that cynical, carefree exterior lurked a world of pain as deep as her own? She reached forward and laid her hand upon his. "I'm sorry, Markl. Truly I am. I wasn't thinking when I said all that."

He shrugged. "Doesn't matter. What I want doesn't exist. Not in this ugly world. So I just do like everyone else. I take the bright spots where I can."

A scuffle at a neighboring table interrupted their conversation. Two men rose to confront each other. Fists pounded on tables and then smashed into flesh. Objects took flight, and Mariel ducked as a cup whisked past her head. The tavern's henchmen sprang on the brawlers and dragged them away, aided by laughter and shouts from the customers.

When the noise settled down, Mariel grinned.

"I despise these places," she said, "but I admit, it's rather refreshing to see a brawl."

"Is it?" Markl cast her a sideways glance. His eyes glinted like shards of glass.

Uneasiness crept into her heart.

"Everything would have been different, wouldn't it have?" she said. "If it weren't for the Syrnte invasion, all of us would still live in the highlands of Moehn. Maga Eolyn would have her *Aekelahr*, and you the lands of your family. Sirena would still be alive, and we would be healers and herbalists, nothing more. I might never have become a warrior. It's hard to imagine now, having Sirena at my side instead of a sword."

"We were going to marry Maga Eolyn's girls, the gang and I," Markl said. "We each had our favorites picked out. Of course, we were going to ravish all of you first. But after having our fun, we intended to do the honorable thing."

Mariel laughed. "You, do the honorable thing?"

"That so hard to imagine?"

"No, I suppose not," she conceded. "Who was your favorite?"

"Sirena." His eyes misted over. "No offense to you, of course, but she was my favorite. The prettiest of them all."

"She was the prettiest of us all." Mariel took another long drought from her beer, leaving the mug nearly empty. "One of the truest friends I've ever had. I miss her still."

When she set the mug down, the ground wavered.

"Sometimes I wish…" Mariel's stomach lurched. She gasped and clutched at the table. Instinctively she reached for magic that could ground her, only to be choked off by that excruciating, invisible tether.

Markl was at her side in an instant. "Whoa there! You all right?"

"I don't know." A cold sweat broke out on her skin. "I feel ill."

"Come on." He helped her up, but Mariel's knees buckled. She had to lean against him for support.

"Gods." She tried to make light of it, though her stomach convulsed and her breath came in labored gasps. "First my magic, now my strength. There'll be nothing left by the time we get to Moehn."

"Maybe they've got an empty bed where you can lie down for a bit. I'm afraid I let you drink too much."

"But I only had one."

Markl half dragged, half carried her away from the river. Faces loomed and receded. Laughter and taunts rang in her head.

"Ho, there! Looks like the little lady's had her first taste of Parson's ale."

"Deadly poison, that."

"Better let her sleep it off on the table over here. Over here, I say!"

"Markl." Mariel's voice was reduced to a hoarse croak. "Get me out of here, please."

Strengthening his grip, the squire carried Mariel away from the lecherous catcalls and weaving faces.

"I think I'm going to pass out."

"Keep breathing."

Markl helped her find purchase against a side wall of the tavern, shaded by trees and an adjacent building. The place smelled of horse manure, rotting fruit, and human waste, but at least it was away from the crowd. He leaned close, holding her up and smoothing the hair off her face. She could feel the heat of his body.

"Sirena may have been the prettiest," he said, "but I've learned to like you too, you know. Learned to like you a lot."

His lips brushed hers.

Mariel jerked away. "Don't! Not now."

"Would you have married me?"

"What?" The question confused her.

"If we had grown up in Moehn, if I were the lord I was meant to be, would you have married me?"

"Stop talking nonsense."

"Would you have at least wanted to?"

"Magas don't marry!"

"Your tutor married the King."

"That was different." Mariel struggled for breath between words. "Exceptional. Necessary."

"Well, if you wouldn't marry, perhaps if I were a grand lord you'd at least consent to…?" His traced her throat and neckline, letting his hand come to rest on her breast.

"Get your hands off me." She tried to slap him away, but her limbs were numb. "This is a silly conversation, Markl. I'm tired, and

I'm ill. I need a place to rest."

Markl released her.

Mariel slipped downward, unable to find purchase on the wall, dragged body and soul toward some deep, dark pit. Shadows overtook her vision.

Markl's laughter echoed after her, taunting and cruel.

"You give all the wrong answers, Mariel," he said. "Then again, I suppose there wouldn't have been a right answer. Not today. Not anymore."

CHAPTER FIFTEEN

Baedon

MARIEL AWOKE GROGGY, sitting upright in a hard wooden chair. Rough-woven twine bound her hands and feet.

Spitting a foul taste from her mouth, she studied her surroundings, a dimly-lit room adorned by empty and rotting shelves. The stone walls were blackened and damp. One small window had been set high and shuttered tight. Sounds of people seeped into the room as if from a great distance, and the musty breath of the Furma River penetrated her senses.

How long had she been out?

Where had they taken her?

"Markl." Anger outstripped her trepidation. Whatever his game she despised it, and she vowed to make him pay. "Show yourself."

A shadow in one of the corners shifted, and a bent and twisted figure detached from the wall. He was cloaked and hooded, with an ebony staff in his bony hand.

"Mariel." He spoke as if dragging her name over gravel. "Loyal student of Maga Eolyn, part of a new generation of women warriors. I am most pleased to meet you."

The man removed his hood, revealing a wizened face. Thin gray hair sprouted in short tufts from his balding head. One eye was clouded and unfocused, but the other sharp as a dagger. Gaze fixed on Mariel, he tapped at the door with his staff.

The door opened on oiled hinges. A young man appeared, portly and of unimpressive stature, with rat-like eyes sunk into a flaccid face. He closed the door behind him and bolted it.

106

The old man took a seat opposite Mariel. He studied her as if she were some fascinating creature dredged from the depths of the river. He nodded to the young one, who brought forward a table, lit a candle, and laid out sheet of paper next to an elegant quill.

"My name is Baedon," the wizard said. "I suspect you have heard of me."

"No, I have not."

His chuckle was low, tempered with a note of humble resignation. "The greatest servants of Dragon are always least remembered, their quiet and enduring work forgotten by the keepers of history, who honor only the most insipid seekers of glory. I was one of the great mages of my generation. I fought at Kedehen's side against the magas. I was the right hand of the noble wizard Tzeremond, and the architect of the purge that should have cleansed us forever of the magas and their vile magic."

"Our magic is not vile. We are the Daughters of Aithne, the chosen ones of Dragon. Keepers of the most sacred traditions of Moisehén."

"You were young when the maga took control of you, Mariel, and you were misled. It would be heartless of me to hold this against you. In truth, I believe that you are capable of recognizing the deceptions you have suffered, and turning from your misguided ways. I believe that today you will be redeemed."

Mariel drew a shallow breath, beating back the wisp of fear that wrapped around her heart. "Where is Markl?"

"He keeps watch nearby to ensure that we are not interrupted. Do not judge your friend too harshly, young maga. He brought you to us on the understanding that we would return you whole, a promise that I intend to keep."

"Why, then, do you have me bound?"

"So that you will listen to me." His lizard-like smile made her skin crawl. "I am an old man, Mariel, and my appearance does not, shall we say, warm the heart."

"Speak then, and let me go."

Baedon leaned back in his chair, good eye disconnecting from the present as he drifted into a lengthy silence. "This is about your tutor, Eolyn, the one who calls herself Queen and High Maga, though she is nothing more than a harlot and a witch."

"You would do well not to insult my *Doyenne*."

"What fine reflexes you have, Mariel. How accustomed you are to coming to her defense. But you need not fear speaking the truth in this place. I have set this cellar aside as a refuge for both of us, and protected it with formidable wards. Here, we can share the truth, you and I. That is all I want from you, Mariel. The truth."

He drew the sheet of paper from its resting place. Mariel saw words written across its face. The calligraphy, of high quality and laid out in meticulous rows, looked disturbingly like her own handwriting.

"What is that?" she asked warily.

"There are so few witnesses left from those precious weeks before the maga at last ensnared the Mage King. Your companion, Ghemena, might have cooperated with me, but now she has committed open treason. Who would trust her word? Mage Corey could be moved to act, but as much as I have contemplated that path, I have yet to see how to make it in his interests to do so. Borten, of course, has the most to lose in this whole affair. He would never speak unless the King himself demanded it, and then only under the most compelling circumstances.

"So I am left with you, Mariel. Only you. At first I thought perhaps the Gods had forsaken me, but I realize now that this is a truly wondrous turn of events. Of all the players in this insidious game, you are the only one whose noble spirit has never been questioned. The only servant of the Mage King without a single blemish on her reputation. Everyone respects you, Mariel. Everyone will believe you."

Mariel's pulse quickened. She focused her breath and grounded her spirit as best she could, but the tether that held her magic burned against her throat, impeding her effort.

"This conversation is without merit, Master Baedon," she said. "A waste of your time and mine. I have no truth to give that has not already been spoken. Even if I did, I would not confess it to you."

"There you are wrong, Mariel. You hold the truth in your heart." He pointed a crooked finger at her chest. "And you will commit to it by signing this paper. The only question that remains is how much persuasion you will require."

Mariel's nose stung with a metallic scent. The room wavered. Her eyes began to water. "I know what you are trying to do. The spell you cast will not work."

"Oh, but it will. Your tutor may have told you of *Ahmad-melan*, but I am quite certain she never prepared you to confront a mage as skilled in its nuances as I. Even if she had, with your magic bound..." He let his words hang in the air as he traced the line of her cheek.

She flinched and spat in his face.

A smile touched Baedon's lips. He produced a clean rag and wiped away her insult. "I must admit, I find a rather seductive pleasure in your impulse to resist. Do you know who the last maga was that I interrogated?"

"I do not care to know anything about you or what you have done."

"Your tutor's mother, the warrior Kaie."

The full horror of her situation crystallized in Mariel's mind. Kaie had offered the last and greatest resistance to Kedehen's ambitions. If this mage had broken her, he could not be surpassed in cruelty.

"That seems a long time ago," Baedon continued. "Little more than a lost dream from a grander, more enlightened age. My circumstances were not as mean as all this, but Kaie had a formidable will. She held a stubborn silence during the long, agonizing road to capitulation. But she was vanquished in the end. We acquired what we needed from her, and more.

"We searched for her daughter, Eolyn, but the girl could not be found. Then she was found, but she could not be had. Already she had seduced my liege, and to this day Prince Akmael flounders in the shadows that she invokes. But now, destiny has finally turned in our favor. I have been waiting, Mariel. Waiting and watching. For the right moment, for the appropriate circumstances. The actions taken by your sister Ghemena have at last driven a wedge between the King and his whore. The time has come to break their bond once and for all, and to lead my Liege back into the light."

"You cannot succeed in this. They will see that I was tortured. They will know any confession I make is false."

The wizard clucked his tongue. "Young Mariel, my methods

are not as crude as all that. High Mages do not bruise, cut, or maim during our interrogations. Indeed, we leave no scars at all."

Baedon leaned close and blew into Mariel's face, clouding her senses with the dust of rue, bitterwort, and nightshade mushrooms.

"At least," he murmured, "not in places that anyone else can see."

CHAPTER SIXTEEN

Cry for Help

SNOW TUMBLES FROM THE SKY and blows harsh across the forests of East Selen; tiny crystalline daggers that could strip a man of his skin.

Corey, sitting comfortably in his quarters, listens to the howling wind outside. Wine warms his stomach and soothes restless thoughts. The fire burns low, its golden flames a small but sure defense against midwinter's onslaught. The mage has known many difficult winters, but the frigid descent of this storm seems the breath of death itself. He hears the fury of his ancestors inside its screams; imagines them beating upon the shutters and clawing at the roof.

They have not forgotten, he thinks.

Neither have I.

A shiver runs through the mage. He adjusts the cloak around his shoulders and becomes cognizant of a new sound inside the wind: An animal caught in the storm scratches desperately at the window.

Puzzled and curious, Corey rises to open the shutters. Snow bursts into the room. A bundle of white fur lands at his feet. Winter Fox shakes the damp from her coat. She stretches and then paces a small circle, ears flattened and tail tucked between her legs. She does not look at him, but Corey recognizes the dark depths of those eyes and the sharp colors of her aura. For a moment he is tempted to throw her back into the storm, but voices on the wind urge otherwise.

He closes the shutters and nods at the hearth.

"Warm yourself," he says, "if it pleases you."

Her ears perk up, though her movement remains timid. She approaches the fire and sits before the flame, curling a fluffy tail around nimble feet.

Corey pours a second cup of wine and takes a place beside her. He scratches the fox's ears and strokes the soft, creamy fur on her back. She presses her damp snout into his palm.

"You," he murmurs. "Here."

Two words, filled with mystery and promise.

A shiver of light passes through her. The skin of Winter Fox is shed and a woman kneels before him. Her nudity is beautiful to behold, but Corey sets his cloak about her shoulders to ward off the winter chill.

There is deep magic at work here, a power awakened from the very heart of East Selen, a spell cultivated during one distant, brutal night and then kept dormant all these years since his people perished.

Corey touches the maga's cheek, lets the silky strands of her hair brush the back of his fingers. His heart buckles under the weight of his desire, hidden for so long he hardly recognizes its bittersweet essence as his own.

"I should not be here," she whispers without meeting his gaze. "I should not want this."

Corey closes his eyes and presses his lips against her forehead. The faces of all those who perished flow through his mind, their loss and pain redeemed in this moment of tenderness.

"You honor me with your presence, Daughter of Aithne," he says.

And that should be enough.

It should be enough simply to see her here.

A prudent man would ask for nothing more.

A prudent man would send her away.

Corey draws the maga close instead.

She shifts under his touch and melts into his embrace.

His lips find hers, and they become one with each other, invoking the pleasure of the Gods as the storm renews its fury outside.

COREY JUMPED OUT OF SLEEP, knife in hand. With a quick spell he ignited the candles in his room.

Illumination chased back the shadows. A summer breeze drifted through the curtained window. The squall of fighting cats echoed from a nearby roof and was suddenly silenced.

Her breath lingered upon his lips.

I should not be here. I should not want this.

Unsettled, Corey rose. He refreshed his face with water from the basin.

A knock sounded at the door.

"Come."

A servant poked his head into the room. "Forgive the late

hour, Mage Corey. There is a young man at the back entrance who insists on seeing you."

"Does he have a name?"

"He calls himself Markl, ward and squire of Lord Borten."

Corey gave a derisive snort. "Markl is halfway to Moehn by now. Give the weasel a piece of stale bread and tell him to return to the beggar's alley from whence he came."

The man shifted uncomfortably on his feet. "I don't know, sir. The boy says it's urgent. If you could see the look of him—"

"You heard me. Get rid of the waif! Call on the guards if you require assistance. I will not be bothered at this hour."

"Yes, Mage Corey."

The man withdrew.

Corey sealed the door behind him with a ward.

When the servant's footsteps had faded, the mage retrieved his medicine belt and snatched up a clay amulet kept safe among his sacred stones. Then he called upon the shape of Screech Owl and flew silently out the window.

As he alighted on the roof over the servants' entrance, a guard was giving Markl a back-handed cuff. The boy stumbled under the blow. The kitchen door slammed shut in his face.

"Please!" Markl pounded on the door and cried to the darkened windows. "Please, Mage Corey. I need your help."

Silence reigned over the Mages' Quarter, though Corey's sharp ears detected a quiet rustle of human movement in an adjacent home, followed by the more subtle skitter of a juicy mouse down below. He made note of who among his neighbors might have witnessed this untimely visit, and what they might have heard.

The boy paced in dark below, striking fists against shuttered windows. When no one responded, he retreated on foot in defeat.

Corey spread his wings and took off in pursuit.

Following Markl's winding path, the mage flitted from shelter to shelter, concealing himself beneath overhanging roofs and in shallow windowsills. Markl did not return to the castle, but wandered through the streets until a pattern of rough circles emerged, each narrower than the last. Eventually the squire slowed to a stop in a crooked alley in one of the most miserable districts of the city. There he sank against a rotting wall and remained hunched in filth, arms folded, head hanging over his knees.

Corey descended from the high roofs, alighted next to Markl, and resumed his human form. Before the boy realized what was happening, Corey gripped his throat and thrust him against the wall.

He waited a moment while the boy choked and writhed. Then he said in low, even tones, "I am going to release you, Markl. When I do, you will not run. Nor will you make any noise, not even to catch your breath. Do as I say or I will burn the skin off your face."

Markl ceased struggling and nodded, eyes wide with terror.

"Why did you seek me out?" Corey asked, releasing him.

The boy coughed and sputtered. "Mariel...Mariel is in trouble."

"What happened?"

"They took her and brought her back to the city. They've had her forever. In there." Markl nodded down the alley.

"Who?"

"An old man and a boy."

"How much did they pay you for giving her to them?"

"Pay me? They didn't pay me!"

"Do not play me for a fool."

"I swear to the Gods! I received nothing."

"Save a promise, perhaps? A man destroyed for treason, a province ripe for the taking. Why did you seek me out instead of Lord Borten?"

"I couldn't..." Markl faltered and looked away.

"You couldn't face the man you intend to betray?"

"It's a wizard that's got her, I tell you! Borten wouldn't be a match for that old man, but you can help. I know you can. That's why I came to you."

Corey struck Markl hard in the face. "That is for your lies and for your foolish ambition."

"They said they wouldn't hurt her!" Markl spat blood from his mouth.

"Show me where she is."

The building, well inside the beggar's district, was little more than a mass of blackened timbers. The structure hung precariously over a foundation that dated back to the time of the first Kings of Vortingen, an immutable heart of stone that had likely seen the rise and fall of countless houses. Corey detected the reddish glow of wards that protected the cellar, formidable in their magic, but nothing that he could not overcome.

"What kind of trap is this, Markl?"

"It's not a trap. She's in there. I swear she is."

Corey immobilized Markl with a curse. Then he bound the boy's hands and feet for good measure. "I should have had you eliminated a long time ago, Markl."

"Eliminated? I never did anything to—"

"You are dangerous and a fool. That's all the excuse I needed. But here's the sad irony: I spared you because I could well imagine our Lady Queen's horror at the mere thought of terminating your pathetic existence. Do you understand what that means, Markl? You are alive today thanks to the very woman you seek to destroy."

"That witch sired a bastard," he retorted. "She means to put him on the throne."

Corey dipped a rag into the sludge at their feet and stuffed it into the boy's mouth. "Repeat those words and you will hang."

Markl would hang no matter what, but there was no point telling the boy that just yet.

"You will not move from this place until I return," Corey said.

Markl nodded, eyes tearing from the noxious smell of his gag.

Calling upon the shape of Rat, Corey scuttled through mud and shadows to the edge of the building. He found a hole in its fragile carcass and slipped inside.

Smells of rot and decay attacked his snout, but he caught a wisp of Mariel's perfume of fresh grass and summer flowers, muted beneath an icy sheet of torture and terror. The mage followed her essence through the maze of timbers until he came to a door that emanated an incongruous odor of fresh pine. A sliver of yellow light penetrated its base.

Corey paused and groomed himself. Muffled sounds of Mariel's suffering pricked his ears. Every moment she remained with these men pushed her closer toward a precipice of no return. Yet to interrupt them could mean Corey's own capture – not a risk he was inclined to take.

The door opened without warning and flooded the narrow corridor with light.

Corey let go a startled squeak and skittered further into the shadows, heart pounding inside his small furry chest.

The silhouette of a mage filled the doorway, tall though bent at the spine, long staff in hand and a hood concealing his features. The sound of Mariel's weeping spilled onto the floor and pooled around his feet like a crimson mist.

"Well done, my lad." He spoke with the voice of an old and patient man, a voice Corey recognized with sudden dread.

Baedon.

The wizard's aura shone sharp as ever, woven with bronze threads of cunning, anger, and conviction. Corey had studied magic under Baedon and understood the man's power all too well. Direct confrontation was not advisable, in part because of the attention it would draw, but more importantly because Corey was likely to lose.

"Entertain yourself until I return," Baedon said, "but remember: no marks and no bruises. We will have further need of her before this is over."

The door to Mariel's prison closed, casting everything once more into darkness.

Baedon walked away in a quiet sway of woolen robes.

Corey remained immobile, clicking his teeth and flicking his tail, glancing after Baedon, then toward the door that separated him from Mariel.

To understand Baedon's intent, Corey had to follow the man now.

Yet that would mean abandoning the young maga.

Curse it all.

He waited until Baedon's essence faded in the distance and then resumed his human form, releasing the full force of his magic. The door splintered under the impact. Shards of wood exploded into the room, revealing a young mage with beady eyes set in a flaccid face, his robes hiked up to reveal the rolling fat of his thighs.

Faeom dumae, Corey thundered.

The mage was flung against the wall. His skull cracked upon the ancient stone. His eyes rolled back into his head, and he sank limp to the floor, a trail of blood marking his descent.

Kneeling beside Mariel, Corey undid the bindings that cut into her ankles and wrists. The maga slumped forward.

Mariel's eyes shivered in their sockets, locked in battle against some nightmare of Baedon's making. Her skin burned, and her clothes were damp with sweat.

"Mariel," Corey said. "Hear me."

She wailed and beat against his breast.

"Mariel." Corey caught her fists and held her fast. "I am Corey of the Clan of East Selen, High Mage and friend to your *Doyenne*, Eolyn. I have come to guide you out of the darkness. Hear me and see me, now."

Rivulets of sweat streamed down her temples. Her eyes dilated and then focused for a fleeting moment.

"Corey?" she whispered.

He tore the clay amulet from his neck and broke it open, releasing a cloud of copper powder in her face. "Breathe, Mariel. Breathe deeply."

She coughed and wheezed, head shooting back with the sting of the dust. Rising, Corey took a stance behind her, one hand firm upon her feverish forehead, the other spread over her pounding chest. Grounding his spirit deep in the earth, he focused all his strength on pulling the curse out by its roots.

Ehekahtu

Naeom denae daum

Erenahm rehoernem ehekaht

Benauhm enem

Mariel keeled over and vomited copious bile. The fever broke, and she trembled uncontrollably. Corey hastily removed his cloak and wrapped it around her.

"Mariel, listen."

"Leave me!" she cried.

"I am going to unbind your magic."

"No." She tried to push him away. "Leave me. I am not worthy."

"Few are more worthy than you."

Her eyes settled on him, muted green beneath her agony, like grass cloaked inside a venomous mist. "You don't know what I have done."

"It does not matter. You must have your power back if I am to get you out of here."

"Corey, please. I want to die."

"Breathe, Mariel. Just breathe."

She obeyed. Corey grasped the tether that held her magic and loosened it with a quiet spell. Light surged through Mariel's aura, and she clung to him, gasping for breath. Color returned to her face and fingertips.

"Can you shape shift, Mariel?" He was wary of pushing her too hard too fast, but only the Gods knew how long Baedon would stay away.

"I don't know…There are shadows everywhere."

"Allow me to transform you."

She shook her head.

"They have brought you back to the City," Corey insisted. "We cannot risk anyone recognizing you."

"No animal spirit will accept me now."

"Let the Gods be the judge of that."

"Maga Eolyn said one should never shape shift when—"

"I understand the risks." More than Mariel would ever know. "All you must do is receive my magic and stay in touch with your spirit. Can you do that?"

She glanced around the room, eyes pausing over the limp body of the boy. "Where is the other one?"

"Awaiting my wrath." Corey pulled the maga to her feet. "Do you trust me, Mariel?"

She nodded.

He set his lips upon her forehead.

Ehekahtu, naeom habei.

The maga collapsed into herself, assuming the shape of Rabbit. Not one of the bold hares of the northern plains, but a quiet creature from the highlands of Moehn, with mottled fur and placid but alert eyes.

Tucking Mariel into the crook of his arm, Corey retrieved his cloak as well as that of the fallen apprentice, and left the cellar. He crept through the dark corridor and onto the street. Dawn was beginning to break. Conscious of the hour, Corey found Markl and untied him. The boy retched as Corey hauled him to his feet.

"What's this?" Markl asked when Corey placed the rabbit in his arms.

"All that's left of Mariel, thanks to you."

"Gods. You're joking, right?"

Corey threw the apprentice's cloak around Markl's shoulders. He fastened the clasp and covered the boy's face with the wide hood. "It will take powerful magic to bring her back. Do you know the residence of High Mage Echior?"

"The court physician? Yes, I know where he lives."

"Take her there by an indirect route. Enter through the back door as you tried to do with me. Do not tell them I sent you. Speak only to Echior, and give Mariel only to him."

"What about you?"

"I will be watching you, Markl. If you ignore my instructions or fail to deliver the maga safely, I will see to it that you suffer a slow and painful death."

"I understand, Mage Corey."

"Do you?" Corey knifed him with a glance.

The boy flushed and looked away.

"I am not finished with you, Markl. You have yet to atone for your transgressions."

Markl cleared his throat and nodded.

"Go on, then," Corey said. "I will follow."

As Markl departed, Corey turned to the dilapidated house.

Ehekaht naemu, he murmured.

With an ear-splitting crack, one of the rotted pillars broke, causing the entire structure to crumble in a cloud of dust.

CHAPTER SEVENTEEN

Dancing Upon a Knife

THEY SPENT THE BETTER PART of the day trying to retrieve Mariel. Long and terrible hours passed while Corey feared he might lose the young maga, just as he had lost Eolyn's friend, Adiana, during the Syrnte invasion. To his intense relief, Mariel at last returned to her human form, whole but unconscious. As Corey and Echior laid her out on the bed, she convulsed under the remnants of the curse.

Echior sent for Jacquetta, who appeared shortly, auburn hair loosely tied with a strip of bright ribbon. She cried out and rushed to her sister's side. Enfolding Mariel's hand in hers, Jacquetta examined the maga's pulse, her breath, the dilation of her eyes.

"I've never seen Mariel so pale," Jacquetta said, "and she's as cold as ice. What happened?"

"*Ahmad-melan*," Echior replied.

"Worse than *Ahmad-melan*," Corey said. "This is the beginnings of possession, Jacquetta. The emptying of a maga's soul, the extraction of all magic through curses and violence until her power is consumed by the attacking mage."

"Maga Eolyn had spoken of this practice," Jacquetta said. "I thought it too awful to be true."

Echior shook his head. "That practice should have died with Tzeremond. There is no place for such malevolence among the Sons of Caradoc."

"There you are wrong, old friend," Corey said. "History has shown there is room aplenty for whatever malevolence we care to assume."

"Who did this?" Jacquetta asked.

120

"An ally of Tzeremond," Corey replied. "A wizard of great power. He was known to us as Baedon."

"Baedon?" Echior's blue eyes widened in astonishment. "I thought that old bastard died in the Battle of Aerunden."

"As did we all." Corey released a weary sigh. "I sent two mages to follow Mariel's escort in secret, but I never expected they might confront an enemy as formidable as this. They are dead now, or hiding under Baedon's wing."

Jacquetta laid another woolen blanket over Mariel and tucked the edges around her unconscious form. "Can she be healed?"

"I caught them early in their sport," Corey said, "and they were in no rush to complete the task. That will work in her favor. Mariel is strong, but healing after an assault like this takes patience and skill. In the meantime, we must make certain they do not find her again."

"She can stay here," Echior said. "I will cast the necessary wards to hide her. With your help, Corey, they can be made nearly impenetrable. Jacquetta will attend Mariel day and night. Since she is not allowed to leave the premises, no one will inquire about her absence at court."

"I was counting on Jacquetta's help," Corey replied, "and on yours, Echior."

The old mage nodded. "Jacquetta, we need abundant supplies of winter sage, rosemary, camomine rust spores, white albanett, and nightberry candles. And send for water, fresh spring water, at once."

"Yes, Mage Echior." The maga hastened to obey.

"And Jacquetta." Corey's voice stopped her at the door. "Be discreet."

"Of course, Mage Corey. I understand." Jacquetta closed the door behind her.

Corey turned his attention to Markl. Bound hand and foot once more, the boy cowered in a corner.

"What shall we do with you, Markl?" Corey did not bother to hide the menace in his voice. "What would be just penance for the crimes you have committed?"

"I swear to the Gods, they said they wouldn't hurt her! I wouldn't have taken her to them if I'd known."

Sinister magic stirred in Corey's veins. He hauled Markl up by the shoulders and set his palm against the boy's chest. "You knew very well what they intended, Markl. What you did not anticipate was how her suffering would make you feel."

A curse fell from Corey's lips, one he had not invoked since the earliest years of his apprenticeship under Tzeremond. Scalding heat flowed from the mage's hand into Markl's chest. The boy's eyes widened in terror and agony. He wheezed, choked, and began to convulse.

"Do you know what that is, burning inside of you, Markl?" Corey murmured with icy calm. "That's your heart. Pity you should discover you have one this late in the game."

Echior approached and laid a hand on Corey's shoulder. "Leave him be, old friend. He's just a boy and a fool."

"It hurts, doesn't it, Markl?" Corey said. "To feel your flesh cooking inside of you. Yet I assure you it does not hurt nearly as much as what they did to her."

"Corey," Echior insisted. "I do not want to start the day with a corpse in my home."

The mage released the squire, who crumpled with hoarse gasps to the floor. The stench of singed flesh tainted the room.

"You needn't worry, Echior. Today is not Markl's day to die. I would have you keep him here, though. Bound and gagged, and out of sight."

"Whatever you say, old friend."

Corey returned to Mariel and took her icy hand in his. "I have to disappear for the time being."

It sobered Corey to speak these words. Over the years, he had used almost every strategy imaginable to ensure his own survival. Yet until now, he had always managed to avoid the most desperate measure of all: self-imposed exile.

"Maga Eolyn should be informed of what's happened," Echior replied, "as well as the King. If these men are preying upon the magas—"

"Baedon and his allies do not do this out of hunger for magic. There is a more ambitious plan afoot here, one that may bring ruin upon the House of Vortingen. If my suspicions are correct, my own life may well hang in the balance."

"And you value your life above theirs?"

A bold affront, especially from Echior.

"I must decipher this web of treachery in order to properly contend with it," Corey replied. "I cannot do that unless the enemies of Moisehén believe they are still in command of the game."

Echior let his gaze settle upon Mariel. "I think they are in command."

"Not for long."

"Your confidence betrays you, Corey. You have lived your life dancing from one impossible risk to another. Someday, you will stumble into the chasm you allowed to open up and perish inside its depths. You and everyone else you manage to drag down with you."

Corey clucked his tongue. "I never knew you to be such a pessimist. Let us hope you are wrong, Echior. And if you are right, let us hope that today is not the day my luck is destined to end."

"We must tell the King."

"I will tell the King," Corey said impatiently. "But first I will speak with Markl, to see what he knows about Baedon and his allies. Can you provide me a place where I might converse with the boy in private?"

The portly mage cleared his throat. He glanced around as if the walls might be listening, despite the many wards they had erected. "This is a nasty business."

"Necessary, Echior. Nothing more than necessary."

The old healer wrung his hands. "Very well, Corey. I'll make sure the hallways are empty and help you get the boy into the cellar. Keep it quiet, though. And keep it clean."

CHAPTER EIGHTEEN

Ahmad-melan

IN THE DAYS FOLLOWING EOLYN'S last meeting with the Council, she refused all of Akmael's invitations. She did not dine with him, join him for afternoon walks through the garden, or appear upon the western ramparts at sunset. Akmael's daytime visits to the Tower were greeted with stiff formality. His Queen was always respectful and obedient, but never loving. At night, she did not receive him at all.

The sudden chill in their relationship had been noted by servants, guards, and nobles alike; indeed by the entire court.

Akmael had endured Eolyn's physical absence on countless occasions during the long and tortuous journey of their love, but never had he confronted this complete and painful withdrawal of all intimacy. The absence of Eolyn's affection haunted him like the shadows of the Lost Souls, gnawing at his heart and draining his magic. He felt distracted and weary, aged before his time.

This, too, will pass, he reassured himself, taking a seat at the long oak table that dominated the Council chamber. *Once Roenfyn is defeated and this latest plot against the throne put to rest, once the magas are restored to their place, I will win back Eolyn's heart.*

Servants set out wine and lit candles.

The setting sun cast auburn light through the windows. The whinny of horses and calls of men floated from the courtyard below. Outside the city walls, torches flickered to life over a vast camp where levies had gathered under the banners of Moisehén and Selen. On the table in front of him, a stack of missives awaited the King's attention.

Akmael nodded to his scribe. The young mage took a seat nearby and readied his quill.

Akmael's focus returned as he read and responded to each report. His muscles tensed, and his pulse synchronized with the heart of the mountain, a predatory awareness that often came to him on the eve of battle. He felt the spirit of his ancestors alive within, a great stone dragon ready to tear loose from its foundations and consume all enemies in smoke and fire.

Tomorrow, they would march west to Riemshaven to unite with the forces Lord Borten had summoned from Moehn. From there, Akmael's army would continue toward Selkynsen in hopes of meeting the enemy before they laid siege to that bright city.

We will achieve victory. I will see my son's throne secured, even if it costs my own life.

Akmael had learned long ago to honor his mortality. In war, death could come to anyone, even a king. Yet the prospect of not returning from the battlefield had never weighed on him as it did now. The shadow of the Underworld hovered close, teasing the edges of his vision, mocking him like a cold knife at his back.

If only Eolyn would grant me one more night before our departure.

If only he could have some assurance of her love.

He dictated a response for each of his captains, congratulating them on their efforts, issuing further instructions, and reassuring them that reinforcements would soon be at hand.

The young scribe, though competent, proved a poor substitute for Eolyn. Akmael missed her thoughtful gaze and gentle wisdom, the unfailing astuteness of her advice, the tenderness of her hand upon his.

How could the absence of one person be so starkly and indelibly felt?

Having finished with the reports from Selkynsen, Akmael turned to the next set of letters, decidedly less ponderous in size. A piece of folded paper bearing a nondescript seal slipped from the stack. Akmael moved to return it to its place and then paused, his attention caught by a familiar magic that pricked at his fingers, feminine in quality, though he could not place its origin.

Puzzled, Akmael broke the seal, releasing a strange metallic scent. He unfolded the note and recognized the script of Eolyn's student, Mariel, woven through with shivering threads of remorse.

My Lord King, Mariel began. *I pray to the Gods that this letter reaches you despite the many who would see it destroyed.*

A tremor took hold of Akmael's hands.

...I write in haste and repentance, aware that I have guarded the truth for too long...

Dread coalesced in shadowy fingers around his heart, and instinct told him he should stop reading. Yet he did not.

...So it is with grievous heart that I, Mariel, High Maga and Warrior of Moehn, do affirm that eleven summers ago, in the days before the Syrnte invasion, I participated in ancient rites urged upon me by my guardian, the Maga Eolyn, who bade me and my sister Sirena, now deceased, to bring to her a knight of our guard called Borten, that she might use him for her own pleasures...

Akmael's vision wavered. His heart slowed to a stop.

...and there under the second moon of Bel-Aethne, we prepared the King's knight as was our way, with wine and song and sensual delights. When the fire of his manhood burned bright, Maga Eolyn came to us and embraced him with her own flesh, letting the Spirit of the Forest consume them until she cried to the heavens, "Your son, my Lord! Your son shall be king!"

The letter crumpled inside his fist.

"My Lord King?"

Akmael glanced up, startled to see the scribe still present. The young man's brow was furrowed.

"Is it ill news, my Lord King?"

Abruptly Akmael stood, wood scraping harsh against stone as he shoved away from the table. "Leave me."

The mage hastened to obey. Servants and guards soon followed.

Restless as a caged wolf, Akmael paced the confines of the room alone, footsteps echoing against the floor. He paused in front of the hearth and held the letter over its glowing coals.

Burn it.

A single hot breath from those hungry flames would convert Mariel's confession and all its reprehensible accusations to ash.

Burn it now.

Akmael released the note.

A draft caught the sheet of paper. It drifted away from the fire and came to rest at his feet.

Mariel's words stared up at him, shouting their silent message, impossible to believe and yet feeding a single doubt that had already lodged in his heart like a blistering thorn.

What if she spoke the truth?

Borten had served two years as captain of Eolyn's guard in the highlands of Moehn, at a time when Akmael had been occupied with his young and difficult wife, Taesara, and the consolidation of his new reign.

What man would not have fallen in love with Eolyn?

And what maga would refuse the desire of a man?

Akmael covered his ears, trying to shut out the voice of his dead tutor Tzeremond, whose warnings crowded into his memory like the strident cries of a crow.

Incapable of loyalty they are, beyond all discipline or control.

Five years of war they brought upon Moisehén, turning our people against each other, cursing us with division and bloodshed, burning fields, ravaging towns, leaving homeless orphans in their wake. And for what purpose? To keep your father from wearing the crown appointed to him by the Gods!

"We ended all that," Akmael said sharply. "We rose above the wars of the past and started a new future. Eolyn would never—"

Have I not taught you their cunning knows no bounds? Tzeremond materialized at Akmael's side, amber eyes aglow beneath his darkened hood, bony hand gripping a rowan staff. *Have I not told you they creep like velvet-toned vipers beneath our very feet? What a fool's heart you have! This is their final revenge. They have won their war with the illusion of love. They are ending your line with a bastard prince.*

"No!" Akmael's voice broke over the word. "She came to me of her own free will, surrendered her magic without reservation or regret."

Tzeremond's laugh was mocking and cruel. *A maga does not surrender her magic. She must be imprisoned, or she must be killed. It is that simple.*

"No!" Akmael roared.

Tzeremond melted away.

"It is not as you say..."

A knock at the door startled Akmael out of his deliberations.

"Enter," he said.

127

The scribe appeared and glanced around the room. "My Lord King, I thought…Did you call, my Lord King?"

"Yes. I would see my Queen. Send for the servants, and advise the guards." Akmael retrieved the letter and tucked it inside his doublet. "I want every messenger who has arrived in the last three days found and placed under guard."

"As you wish, my Lord King."

"Send word to Lord Borten that…" Akmael frowned, remembering he had given Borten leave to visit the Queen that very evening. Was it possible that even now they were..?

Stop it, you fool! You've known Eolyn's heart since she was a girl, what she sacrificed to be at your side. Do not allow that letter to blind you. It holds nothing but lies.

"Send for High Mage Thelyn and Corey of East Selen at once."

The scribe bowed and took his leave.

Night was spreading its heavy grip over the castle as Akmael departed the royal chambers, his personal guard assembled around him. A part of him was gladdened by the need for this visit, despite its grim purpose. He longed for Eolyn's refreshing presence, for the way her spirit always kept darkness at bay.

Curse them all for forcing this distance between us!

Anger surged at the endless and malicious intrigues of his court. For the love of the Gods, there was a war to fight! Why this new treachery against the woman he loved? And why now?

The letter burned against Akmael's chest, hissing and spitting like the torches ensconced along the corridors. An acrid sting assaulted his senses. Akmael wheezed and coughed, pausing to recover his balance.

In that moment, he recognized what was happening: the metallic aroma, the irrational thoughts, the fever rising in his veins.

Ahmad melan.

Dread took hold of Akmael. The hallway lengthened and narrowed; the walls closed in with crushing intensity.

Ehekahtu, faeom. Ehekahtu, naemu!

But his invocation came too late. The ward failed. The taste of metal and blood exploded on his tongue. The earth opened beneath his feet. Akmael struggled against the suffocating descent, but fell helpless toward the abyss. The calls of his men tumbled after him and then faded beyond awareness.

He landed in a void, a place so black he could not see his hand before his face.

Tzeremond's whisper returned to his ear. *Serpents they are, deceivers and harlots all. If you cannot believe the words delivered to your hands, then believe what I show you now.*

A breeze struck Akmael's face, the smell of moss and loam interlaced with the scent of desire. He rose as if in a dream. A quiet wood materialized around him. His feet fell silent upon wet grass. His fingers passed over rough, cool bark. As he rounded a large tree, Eolyn and her lover came into view.

Eolyn's skin glowed beneath the moon's pure and tenuous light. Dark hair cascaded over bare shoulders and breasts. Her head was thrown back as she straddled the knight who served her needs.

Agony ripped through Akmael. He cried out, but Eolyn paid no heed, consumed as she was by ecstasy. Every moan of pleasure cut a jagged path through Akmael's spirit. He tried to avert his gaze, but some unseen force paralyzed him, making him bear witness to every hungry thrust until Borten's feral groans filled the moonlit grove and Eolyn laughed in triumph.

Your son, my Lord! she cried. *Your son shall be King.*

The forest faded.

The fortress of Vortingen materialized around him.

Akmael found himself on the floor, shaking with fury. The bitter vision settled in his gut, assuming the hard shape of truth.

He had been there, had he not?

He had seen it all.

The guards bent forward to assist their King, but he shoved them aside in anger. Struggling to his feet, Akmael found his balance and adjusted his cloak. Then he continued toward the chambers of his errant queen, his gait gaining strength to match the murderous fever in his heart.

CHAPTER NINETEEN

Rage

LORD BORTEN'S EVENING VISIT brought a welcome respite from the gloom of the East Tower. For brief moments, the East Tower seemed to disappear, and they sat overlooking the highlands of Moehn once more, its wind-swept hills and ancient woods, its dark earth and fragrant crops. Eolyn reveled in the simple topics of their conversation: the turn of the weather, the promise of an abundant harvest, the recent birth of Borten's fourth son.

"I am so happy for you and Vinelia!" Eolyn exclaimed. "And I wish we could have been there to greet the child! Had the King not called me home, I would have stayed and helped with the delivery. Indeed, it was very gracious of Vinelia to allow you to accompany me with the baby about to arrive."

Borten gave a wry smile. "If it were up to Vinelia, she would have left the child bearing to me and accompanied you herself. She did not want you to be alone."

The declaration warmed Eolyn's heart. A daughter of Lord Herensen's household, Vinelia had been Eolyn's first lady-in-waiting. She had worked tirelessly to teach Eolyn the traditions and complexities of court, a service that left Eolyn forever indebted to her. They had become good friends by the time Herensen offered the young woman's hand to Borten, a match the humble knight would not have dreamed of soliciting. Yet Herensen had recognized a rising star in the new patriarch of Moehn, and was quick to cement an alliance that might prove beneficial for his own family.

The patriarch of Selkynsen had always been clever that way.

"You're letting me win!" Briana's rebuke cut through Eolyn's thoughts.

The princess was attacking her brother with a wooden sword recently gifted to her by Akmael.

"You shouldn't do that, Eoghan," Briana scolded. "I won't ever learn anything about swordplay if you let me win."

"You don't need to learn swordplay." Mild annoyance colored Eoghan's tone. "Princesses aren't required to go into battle."

"Mama went into battle, and I'm going to be a maga warrior just like her." Briana embellished her declaration with vigorous swipes through the air. "I'm going to vanquish our enemies in a single stroke, just as she did in the Battle of Rhiemsaven. I will defend Moisehén unto my death."

Eoghan sat down and blew a stray lock of hair from his face. "You won't be here to defend Moisehén. Father will find a prince worthy of your station and send you away to marry him. You can defend that kingdom as your own if you like, at your husband's side. But mostly you'll bear his children. That'll fill your time and occupy your magic well enough."

A frown creased Briana's brow. "That's not true. Father would never send me to another kingdom. Mama, tell him it's not true."

Eolyn's smile faded.

She wanted with all her heart to keep Briana in Moisehén, but Akmael was already considering the alliances he could forge with his daughter's marriage. Several southern kingdoms had been brought to his attention. Even the possibility of a Syrnte suitor had been mentioned. Eolyn had objected hotly to this. She would not tolerate sending her daughter to a place ruled by men like Prince Mechnes. In the end, Akmael had ceded to her arguments, but on the general question of Briana's union with the royal house of another realm, he would not be dissuaded.

Briana's shoulders deflated as she took in her mother's silence. She dropped her wooden sword and ran to Eolyn, seeking refuge in her embrace. "You must tell Papa not to send me away."

Eolyn held her daughter tight. "Not everything is in my hands, Briana."

"He'll listen to you. I know he will."

Eolyn blinked at the sting of Briana's misplaced faith. What had she done, sentencing her own daughter to this existence?

Briana was meant to be a true maga, free to follow the path of her heart.

"You will be a maga and a warrior," Eolyn spoke with more confidence than she felt. "If this is what you want and if the Gods will it. As to where your path as a woman and princess will lead, it is far too early to tell."

"My path cannot lead to another kingdom!" Briana cried. "My place is here, with you and Eoghan and Father."

"For many years to come." Eolyn kissed Briana's forehead. "May the Gods grant that those years extend into a lifetime."

The evening shadows had deepened by now, and Eolyn, realizing the hour, told her children it was time for bed.

After Eoghan and Briana took their reluctant leave, conversation with Borten turned to the coming war. His account of the levies summoned made it clear that Akmael was assembling an army even greater than the one that had met the Syrnte invasion.

His voice rang with pride when he described the extent of his own troops from Moehn. In ten short years, this man had transformed an impoverished province into a force to be reckoned with. Eolyn felt glad for Borten and the happiness he had found. She was glad for her husband as well, that he would have this able warrior at his side when he met Roenfyn in battle.

The candles were burning low when at last Borten rose to take his leave.

"With your permission, my Lady Queen," he said. "The King commands we march at dawn, and there is much yet to be done."

"You would abandon my company so soon?" The words slipped out before Eolyn could consider them.

She glanced away, a flush rising to her cheeks. Their conversation had kept her distracted from the pain of Akmael's absence. After Borten left, there would be only the silence of her aching heart.

What if Akmael does not come tonight? What if he does not return from this war? What if we lose this last opportunity to share our love?

"I am certain the King will arrive shortly to provide a company much more worthy than my own," Borten said quietly.

"Of course." She rose, agitated by his tone. "Let us say farewell, then. Not a day shall pass when I do not make my invocation to the Gods, asking them to keep all of you safe and grant our people victory."

"Thank you, my Lady Queen." Borten bowed and touched her fingers to his forehead.

As he turned to depart, the hairs on the back of Eolyn's neck pricked. She had a fleeting premonition of danger, like a deer that had caught the scent of wolves.

"Lord Borten."

He stopped and looked back at her, his gaze expectant.

She hesitated, uncertain what she had meant to say.

Then the doors to the chamber crashed open, and the Mage King stormed into their presence, face ablaze with fury. Akmael's gaze flicked from Eolyn to Borten and back again. With a thunderous curse, he sent Borten flying into the stone wall.

Lady Talia screamed.

Eolyn rushed forward and caught Akmael's arm.

"My love!" she cried. "What has happened?"

Akmael struck Eolyn with a back-handed blow that sent her sprawling to the ground.

She lay stunned, clinging to the stone floor, unable to comprehend what had just happened. Her ears rang. Her face throbbed with pain. As her head cleared, she heard the sound of fists pounding into flesh. When at last the room came back into focus, Borten lay limp at Akmael's feet. He had not raised a hand against the King, not even to defend his life.

"Akmael, stop!" Eolyn pleaded. "You'll kill him."

The Mage King froze, broad back turned to her, fists clenched tight and stained with blood.

"Would that break your heart, Eolyn?" he asked.

Icy dread ran down Eolyn's spine. *That is not the voice of the man I love.*

He let go a dry, bitter laugh. "No, I suppose it would not. After all, a maga's heart cannot be broken."

"Akmael—"

Again he kicked Borten. Eolyn flinched at the sickening crunch of bones.

"Get this traitor out of my sight!" He shouted to the guards that hovered in the doorway. "I do not want to see him again, until

133

he is on the gallows."

The men dragged Borten's unconscious body away, confusion plain upon their faces.

Akmael strode to Eolyn, caught her arm in a bruising grip, and hauled her to her feet.

"Do you love him?" he roared.

Undone by terror, Eolyn stared at her husband speechless, hands flailing as she struggled to loosen his hold.

"Do you love him?" he repeated, each syllable cold and deliberate.

"Mama?" Briana's frightened whimper cut between them.

The girl stood at the doorway to the children's bedroom. She clung to her brother, who watched the King with wary eyes, small sword in hand.

"What's happening, Mama?" Briana asked.

Something faltered behind Akmael's expression. He released Eolyn and paced the room like a rabid wolf caught in a pit.

Eolyn's magic coalesced around the presence of her children. She straightened her shoulders and smoothed her dress, wiped the blood from her lips. Anchoring her spirit to the mountain core, she sent a silent invocation to Dragon for protection and strength.

"Eoghan," she said, forcing calm into her voice, "take your sister and go back to your room. Do not return until I call for you."

"But Mama—"

"Do as I say."

Eoghan cast a suspicious glance toward his father, tightening his grip on the sword.

"Eoghan, please," Eolyn insisted. "It will be all right. Leave us now. I must speak with your father. Alone."

A frown furrowed Eoghan's dark brow, but the boy retreated and took Briana with him.

"You must speak with his father." Akmael mimicked her with disdain. "Tell me who his father is, Eolyn. I want to hear it from your own lips."

Rage was billowing through Akmael's aura. His eyes were dilated, one of them plagued by a twitch. Eolyn had seen this curse once long ago, in the face of her brother, Ernan, moments before he tried to kill her.

The curse of Ahmad-melan.
My love, who did this to you?

"Do you even know the father?" Akmael sneered. "It is said a maga loses count of her lovers."

"Akmael," she said, "I am Eolyn, High Maga and Queen of Moisehén. I have loved you since I was a girl, and have served you as your faithful queen the last ten—"

"Don't."

"I am here to bring you back from the darkness."

"Silence!"

"See me. Now."

"No more of your witch's spells!" He took hold of Eolyn's throat.

Terror surged anew, scattering her magic like seeds of grain.

"See me, Akmael," she pleaded in choked gasps. "For the love of our Gods, by the will of Dragon, see me for who I am."

"I see you," he growled. "You will deceive me no more. *Behnaum ukaht!*"

Akmael's curse screamed through Eolyn's spirit, a savage vortex that robbed her of breath and awareness. Flung away from Akmael, she tumbled through darkness and hit the stone floor at his feet.

Her skin shivered with icy sweat. She gasped for air and grasped at the space in front of her. Her limbs felt numb and weak, her body heavy as a corpse. Her vision cleared, yet even so she was blinded. All color had been sucked from the world, its aura of magic silenced, its threads of power cut off from her reach.

My magic! She realized in despair. *He has bound my magic.*

She heard the heartbreaking howl of a wolf separated from his mate.

"Eolyn!" Akmael cried to the heavens, as if she were lost to him. Dead. "Eolyn…"

His pain and desolation twisted around her own, billowing into a monstrous shadow that consumed them both.

Candles sputtered and gutted out.

Silence filled the chamber, heavy and ominous.

Eolyn remained frozen on the floor, not daring to move for fear Akmael might take her life as well as her magic. He stood over

135

her, consumed by *Ahmad-melan*, running fingers through his damp hair, gazing about the room as if trying to remember what it was that he sought.

Then his eyes settled on Talia and Rhaella, and his muscles tensed like a predator hot upon new prey.

Talia let go a frightened sob and sidled toward the doorway.

"My Lady Queen," she said. "Forgive me, I beg you—"

"There is nothing to forgive," Eolyn said. "Go, both of you. Find High Mage Thelyn or Corey or Echior. Any of them. All of them. Tell them to come here at once."

Talia fled the room, but Rhaella paid no heed to her Queen, choosing instead to meet the King's murderous approach. She put a sway into her hips and allowed him to back her against the wall.

"What is your name?" Akmael pressed close and fingered a lock of her auburn hair.

"Rhaella, my Lord King. Of House Langerhaans."

He traced her throat, let one hand come to rest upon the curve of her breast. "Are you a whore like your Lady Queen, Rhaella?"

"No, my Lord King," she said. "I am a virtuous woman from an honorable family."

Akmael loosened Rhaella's bodice. She did not resist, but lifted her lip to his, inviting his hunger.

Tears blurred Eolyn's vision.

"Not this, Akmael," she whispered. "I beg you, not this."

Akmael paused, a cloud passing over his features.

He stiffened and shut his eyes, then opened them again.

Gathering Rhaella's face in his hands, he said, "This feeling that binds our hearts is a gift. To deny it would be an insult to the Gods."

Eolyn drew a sharp breath. The curse had taken Akmael to another place, another time that he now experienced anew: A night lived long ago, with her and her alone, in the ancient forests of East Selen.

A sob escaped his throat. "Come back with me!"

He buried his face in Rhaella's auburn tresses, shoulders shaking under the force of his sorrow.

"As your prisoner?" Eolyn murmured.

"As my queen."

Then the Mage King lifted Eolyn's lady-in-waiting against the wall.

Rhaella wrapped herself around him, keeping her haughty gaze fixed on the queen as Akmael claimed her with increasing vigor.

Eolyn turned away, unable to face the unrelenting truth of her own prophecy.

Don't you see, Akmael? It is the same thing.

A wasteland of pain took hold of her, as if Akmael had drawn his sword and cut open her heart, the heart she had entrusted to him, to keep or destroy as he pleased.

She could not bear to watch them, but nor could she shut out the sounds of their savage display. At last they finished, the King releasing himself inside of Rhaella with a feral groan. Silken skirts rustled as he lowered her to the ground.

"Come back with me," he said again, his voice hoarse.

Rhaella smiled and kissed the Mage King's hand. Then she led him away, face radiant with triumph, laughter running under her breath.

Behind them, the heavy doors to the East Tower slammed shut, the hiss of its many wards sealing off all hope of escape.

CHAPTER TWENTY

Trapped

EOLYN RECOGNIZED THIS PLACE of eternal night, where air stood still and death penetrated the soul. She remembered its seductive peace, how its cloak of darkness enveloped one with the promise of oblivion. Regret flowed from her soul like a river unleashed, spreading in snaky tendrils over a barren landscape, igniting the insatiable thirst of the Lost Souls.

Beyond the shadowy horizon a deeper hunger stirred, a malevolent need born aloft on an eerily triumphant howl.

Naether Demons.

They are coming...

"Mama!" Briana's voice echoed through the darkness.

Eolyn became aware of someone weeping, a woman crushed by heartbreak and loss. The sobs moved her to pity, yet she refused to draw near or call out. She wanted no part of that world, no taste of its awful truths.

"Mama." A small arm wrapped around Eolyn's neck. Soft fingers brushed awkwardly at wet cheeks. "Mama, don't cry."

Eolyn moaned out loud, jolted into the waking world by the touch of her daughter. Pain wracked her body and sent spasms through her limbs.

Eoghan caught his mother's shaking hands and placed them around a warm cup, holding her steady inside his grip. "Drink this, Mother."

He lifted the cup to her lips, a simple brew of mint and chamomile, infused with the healing power of her children's love.

Eolyn let the elixir warm her throat and felt her vision clear as the tea settled in her stomach. She coughed, sputtered, and drank again. Briana clung tight, head buried in Eolyn's shoulder. Eoghan stood close by with fists clenched, jaw working in hard doubt.

"Why would he say that?" Eoghan asked. "Why would he ask who my father is? Does he not know? Does he not know I am his son?"

Eolyn put a resolute stop to her own tears. She rose to her knees and set firm hands upon Eoghan's shoulders.

"Listen to me, Eoghan Prince of Vortingen." Her voice cut fierce, her gaze was unyielding. "You are the true born heir of Akmael son of Kedehen, in whose veins runs the blood of a thousand kings. You carry the sacred seed of Vortingen, delivered into my womb by the man I love on the night appointed by the Gods. Nothing that came to pass here today, no amount of lies told or curses cast by our enemies, can ever change that. Remember this. Remember it always. Never doubt who you are or where you came from."

"But Father doubts," Briana said.

"Father is under a spell," Eolyn said sharply. "A powerful curse that renders him unable to see the world as it is."

"Who could do such a thing?" Eoghan asked. "He is the Mage King! No one should have such power over him."

"I don't know, Eoghan. But I intend to find out."

Eolyn glanced around their prison. The pain in her muscles was unbearable. Exhaustion and grief were taking its toll. She felt too overwrought to think straight, but her children needed her and she could not fail them.

"We must leave this place," she said.

"How?" Briana asked.

Eolyn rose and stumbled on weakened limbs toward the door. She pounded her fists against the carved oak.

"Tibald!" she cried. "Any of the guards, hear me! I must speak with the High Mages at once."

No one responded.

"He will have told them your commands are not to be heeded," Eoghan said grimly.

Eolyn sank to the floor, despair surging once more in her breast.

"We need an ally," she murmured. "Someone who can get both of you out of this fortress and take you to safety as soon as possible."

"Uncle Corey will help," Briana said.

"Perhaps." Unless the mage were behind this somehow, or poised to benefit by it. "I just hope Talia is able to find someone and bring them here. The longer we wait, the more precarious our situation becomes."

"Even if we find a way out of the tower," Eoghan said, "where will we go?"

"I don't know. Deep into Moehn, perhaps. Past the South Woods. High into the Paramen Mountains."

"We are going to see the Mountain People?" Briana's tone brightened a shade.

"Khelia was my friend once. Perhaps she will grant you refuge now."

"Grant us refuge?" A tremor ran beneath Eoghan's voice. "What about you, Mama? You have to come, too."

"I can't abandon your father. I must release him from this curse and help find the people who did this."

"And if he tries to kill you?"

Eolyn caught her son's gaze. Fear and anger smoldered in his eyes.

What fate has befallen us, that my son should feel compelled to ask such a thing about his own father?

"That will not happen." She spoke with more certainty than she felt. "Someone will be here soon to break the curse and rectify everything that has gone wrong on this night. Until then, we must rest and regain our strength. I want both of you in my room with me."

Eolyn rose. Together, they retreated to the bedchamber, where she bolted the door. Eoghan hid his sword carefully beneath a pillow. Eolyn laid Kel'Barú at her side. The Galian blade emitted a low and gentle hum, incongruous with the moment at hand but comforting nonetheless.

Briana curled inside Eolyn's embrace. Tears streamed down the girl's cheeks. Eolyn stroked her daughter's hair and sang softly, a wordless tune that interwove with Kel'Barú's deeper resonance.

140

Slowly Briana's sobs faded. At last her breath fell into rhythm with the lullaby, and the girl surrendered to troubled dreams.

Only then did Eolyn whisper, "How much did Briana see?"

Eoghan lay staring at the ceiling, hands folded behind his head.

"I kept her away as you asked," he said. Then after a moment, he added, "It was not what we saw. It was what we heard."

A storm of emotions twisted through Eoghan's aura, though he managed to hide everything beneath the stony face he had inherited from his father.

"What was the curse they cast?" he asked.

"*Ahmad-melan.*" Eolyn struggled to keep her voice steady. *I must show Eoghan strength and calm. No matter what happens, I must help him keep faith.* "It is a wartime curse. You will learn it, once you are granted a staff of High Magic."

"There is no counter-spell, no ward that can keep it away?"

"There are wards, but generally they are only invoked during battle, when one expects such an attack."

"And once cast, the curse cannot be broken?"

"Your father was ensnared by formidable magic. My powers…" Eolyn stifled a sob, feeling as if broken glass had lodged inside her chest. "Forgive me, Eoghan. I succumbed too quickly to my fear. I could not find a way to call him back."

Eoghan regarded her with a troubled expression. "If you were unable to bring him back, then no one can."

"That's not true. Thelyn or Corey or one of the other High Mages might be able to accomplish what I could not."

"If you are right, if they can break the curse, Father will understand what has happened and take action before we are attacked again." Hope crept into Eoghan's voice.

Eolyn's hand drifted to her eyes as she tried to put her thoughts in order.

Even if the curse is broken, where will that leave us?

Akmael's brutal attack could not be undone. The violence perpetrated against her, in front of the children, would haunt Eolyn for the rest of her life.

"Mother?" Eoghan said. "When the curse is broken, Father will remember what happened and set everything right?"

Eolyn regarded her son, aware of his need for comfort and

141

reassurance. She reached out and stroked his fine brown hair. "The Gods of Dragon will show us the way forward, Eoghan. For now, you must rest. I will wake you when help arrives."

She suspected he would not sleep, but Eoghan turned on his side and closed his eyes.

Eolyn adjusted the pillows at her back. A wary calm had descended upon the chamber. She prayed it would not be broken before help appeared.

Someone.

Anyone.

Wrapping her hand around the hilt of Kel'Barú, Eolyn kept her eyes trained on the doorway, alert to the muffled sounds of the fortress beyond.

CHAPTER TWENTY-ONE

Demons Unleashed

Wolf pads through the midnight forest, head slung low as he sniffs at loam and leaves. Aromas fill his senses: sweet herbs and fertile earth, acrid urine and smoky bark, rotting wood and sprouting seeds, all enveloped in a cloud of fragrant pine.

He pauses at the flesh-warm scent of Deer. His muscles tense. His ears perk, attuned to the whisper of leaves above, to the scratching of moles beneath the soil.

A doe passed through this place not long ago. A fawn followed her, perhaps two.

Wolf quickens his pace. Moonlight slips through the high branches, offering slivers of pale illumination. Gnarled roots threaten his progress, but he knows this woodland and he moves with confidence across the rugged terrain.

Their scent grows stronger, spreading over the foliage in a wide swath of musky fur and fresh scat, with an occasional hint of warm milk.

Wolf's mouth waters at the anticipation of blood breaking upon his tongue. He slows and stops; listens for movement, breath, some stirring in the night. Deer and her young are close, very close. All he needs is one whimper, one faltering hoof, to reveal their location.

A crash nearby startles him. He crouches, alert, tail tucked low.

Barks and growls reverberate through the woods, the snapping of jaws, the tearing of claws into flesh.

Just ahead, Deer springs into motion, clearing a large bush and fleeing the disturbance. Her young follow fast on her heels.

The hunt is lost, but curiosity pulls Wolf in another direction, toward the sounds of struggle. He expects to find two of his own kind grappling beneath the midnight moon, but when he arrives at the clearing, their wolf forms have been shed. A man and a woman argue with sharp tones and angry gestures, as if the fate of the world depended on this moment.

Wolf cannot tear his eyes from the man. He recognizes the set of the jaw, the heat of that gaze, the dark tresses that frame a young and earnest face.

Akmael.

The name surges as a growl in his throat.

They are one, this Akmael and he. Wolf's heart is pulled toward his human form. He sees the woman through the man's eyes. He knows the future of magic lives in her heart, that she carries his own salvation. Here lies a prize no King of Vortingen has ever mastered: Love.

A mage must learn to love. She can show him how.

"You have allowed your abilities to be twisted to foul ends," the woman says. "Dragon did not grant us these powers to invoke fear or take advantage of those weaker than ourselves."

"That may be the case," Akmael replies, "but your question about the third night of Bel-Aethne...That did not arise out of concern for the proper interpretation and practice of magic, did it?"

The woman hesitates. Heat flushes her cheeks. "There is no place for jealousy in the heart of a maga."

He takes her into his arms and sets his lips upon hers.

Wolf feels the woman as if she were his own, her aroma of honey and wood, the silky caress of her hair, the delicate contours of face and throat. Their magic intertwines, forest and stone, life and death, eternity captured in one moment of vibrant hope. His breath falls hot on her skin. The smell of blood running through her veins intoxicates his senses. She has ignited an unfamiliar hunger, a deep and aching need he fears will never be met. He sinks to his knees and covers her hands with kisses.

"Come back to the City with me." He does not hide the desperation in his voice, the fear that his spirit will descend into utter darkness if she refuses. "Come back with me, Eolyn."

Sadness dims her aura. "As your prisoner?"

"As my queen."

The maga pulls her hands gently out of his grasp and steps away.

"Don't you see, Akmael? It is the same thing."

Fading into the midnight forest, she becomes one with the shadows. Only her voice remains, wrapping splinter-filled threads around his breaking heart.

AKMAEL LURCHED OUT OF BED and stumbled into darkness. Spasms wracked his body. Pain pounded through his skull. Just as he reached the wash basin, vomit spewed forth, burning his tongue and leaving his throat raw.

Sagging against the table, he wiped the spittle off his lips. Icy sweat broke out across his skin.

"Eolyn."

He clung to her name, a sliver of light among shadows. Grief snaked around his heart. Every muscle was knotted with dread.

"My Lord King?"

Akmael started at the sound of her voice, odd in its tonality. Languid. Haughty. Triumphant.

He stared at his hands, forcing them into focus. Hands bred for war, for death.

I have destroyed something tonight. Something that cannot be replaced.

Nightmares danced before his eyes. Rage and violence, brutal release. A chase through the moonlit woods, Eolyn within his grasp, the taste of fur upon his tongue, the yield of flesh beneath his fangs.

What has happened?

Time spun out of his grasp.

Everything is just beginning.

Or had it all just come to an end?

"My Lord King." Impatience tinged the woman's tone.

Akmael could not see her face, but he heard her stretch like a satiated cat.

"Will you not come back to bed?"

His beloved Eolyn had not returned to the City. She had stayed with her brother to fight their war against him.

Two wars.

One as enemies, the other as allies.

Distance and death. Love and fulfillment.

Daughters and a son.

One precious son.

Akmael's shaking hand found the pitcher. He poured a cool torrent over his head, let the water wet his beard, trickle down his neck and chest. The room solidified, but his magic was fractured, scattered beyond reach.

It is a curse. Dark wizardry clouds my awareness.

"Who are you?" he demanded. His voice sounded hoarse and distant. His breath condensed on wintry air.

"Rhaella, my Lord King, of House Langerhaans."

"By what witchcraft have you come here?"

"No witchcraft, my Lord King." A strange light illuminated her, like a candle caught behind fog. She shivered and pulled a sheet around her bare shoulders. "You broke the spell of the only witch who held power over us. You destroyed her and granted me the honor of your intimacy."

"Destroyed?" Horror gripped him, and he remembered.

Eolyn at my feet, shattered like fine crystal.

Remorse crushed his chest, robbing him of all breath. The room blurred. The fog thickened behind Rhaella and reached toward her with misty tendrils.

"What have I done?" Akmael gasped.

Rhaella's responded with an ear-piercing scream.

The mist coalesced and a Naether Demon materialized beside her. Its amorphous face contorted into a howl of insatiable hunger. With ebony-claws, the beast caught Rhaella and tore her open from throat to sternum. Blood sprayed over the bed posts.

Reeling from shock, Akmael called for his staff and sword, but the instruments did not respond. As he watched, paralyzed, the Naether Demon scooped Rhaella's heart from her chest and stuffed it, dripping, into the vacuous maw on its formless face.

Then the empty pits of its eyes settled on the Mage King. It rocked on long limbs, glowing like a pale jade moon. A hungry purr rumbled across the room. With a cry of timeless rage, the Naether Demon leapt toward Akmael, bloody claws extended.

EOLYN JOLTED AWAKE, berating herself for having fallen asleep.

"Eoghan?" she said, heart pounding. "Briana?"

In an instant the prince sat up, sword in hand. He nudged his sister.

"What is it?" Briana said, sleepy and disoriented.

Eolyn invoked a spell to light the candles, only to be choked back by the noose that bound her magic.

"Eoghan, light the candles, will you? No. Wait."

Kel'Barú's hum had grown ominous. Eolyn adjusted her grip on the hilt and rose. The stone floor felt icy against her bare feet, despite the warm summer night. Sounds of alarm echoed through the wards that protected them, accompanied by unearthly screams.

It can't be.

Eolyn peered cautiously through the drawn curtains at her window. Glowing shapes of Naether Demons swarmed the castle grounds, emerging from darkened windows, climbing the walls, springing along the battlements. Shouts of consternation echoed across the fortress of Vortingen. Trumpets called the men to arms. Flames of mage warriors began to light up the night; the smell of sulfur and blood filled the air.

Horror spread its gelid fingers through Eolyn's veins. "Gods help us."

"What is it, Mama?" Briana's voice was now taut and alert.

Eolyn scanned the room, but found nothing out of place. There was no blurring of her vision, no tell-tale mist that heralded the escape of these monsters from their Underworld prison.

Perhaps the wards of the East Tower were protecting them, or perhaps the Naether Demons could not find a maga whose magic had been bound. Whatever was keeping them away, every instinct told Eolyn the barrier would not last long.

"Eoghan, Briana, come with me."

They followed her to the receiving room, the heart of the East Tower, the place where its magic coalesced in a single vibrant thread that extended to the roots of Vortingen's mountain.

Cries of battle penetrated the heavy oak doors as guards made a desperate attempt to defend the Queen and her children. Frost began to build around the door frame. A virescent mist crept through cracks in the wood.

Swiftly, with one eye on the door, Eolyn gathered winter sage, white albanet, and nightshade mushrooms from the herbs she kept in the tower.

"Briana," she said. "Take these and mark a circle in front of the hearth big enough for all of us to stand inside. Eoghan, help me with the torches. We need more light."

The prince and princess obeyed quickly and without protest.

A thunderous crash sounded against the door. Eolyn spun, sword in hand, but to her relief the wards held.

When the circle was marked and the torches lit, Eolyn gathered her beloved children close. She knelt to meet their gaze, keeping her voice and demeanor calm, though terror had taken hold of her heart.

If the Gods sacrifice anyone tonight, let it be me and not my children.

"I cannot cast a circle," she said, "not with my magic bound. So I will teach you the spell, and I need you to cast it together. Anchor your spirits to the mountain. Combine your magic to make it as strong as you possibly can."

Again the creatures of the Underworld flung themselves against the door. The impact sent a tremor through the stone floor.

"It's Papa, isn't it?" Briana cried. "He's turned into an ogre and he's going to kill us all!"

Eolyn took Briana's face in her hands. "Listen to me. Your father loves you and he will soon be here to protect you. But until then, we must defend ourselves against these monsters. They are called Naether Demons, and they are among the oldest enemies of Moisehén. They hunger for our magic, and on this night they have escaped their Underworld prison."

"But Papa said Sir Drostan slew them all!" Briana protested.

"This is no time to debate your father's stories. We are facing our first battle as a family. You must have all your senses open, all your spirit focused on the task at hand. Do you understand?"

Briana pursed her lips and nodded.

"Good. Now listen to me."

Eolyn took their hands and gave them the sacred verse, pronouncing each intonation with care. When she felt certain they understood, she bade Briana and Eoghan to repeat the spell in unison. To Eolyn's intense relief, the herbs ignited, enveloping them in a curtain of translucent fire and fragrant smoke.

Eolyn stood, Kel'Barú ready in her grip. The door shuddered under every impact. Splinters began to show on its face. Claws scraped at the wood in rabid fury.

"Whatever happens," Eolyn said to her children, "you must do exactly as I say."

AKMAEL DOVE SIDEWAYS as the Naether Demon reared over him. One ebony claw caught his thigh and ripped it open. He tumbled across the floor and rose on shaky feet. Blood ran hot down his leg. Neither staff nor sword responded to his calls. His magic wavered like grass in the wind, weakened by the curse they had cast upon him.

Again the Naether Demon charged, head slung low, its unearthly howl ringing in Akmael's ears. It caught the King and flung him against the stone wall.

Stunned, Akmael shuddered to the ground. Stars shot through his vision as he tried to find purchase with his hands. He heard the beast draw near, a purr of satisfaction rumbling through its broad shoulders.

"Drostan," he murmured in a desperate petition to his deceased mentor. "Help me."

The Naether Demon caught Akmael by the throat and pinned him against the wall. Vacuous eyes loomed in Akmael's face. The demon's breath smelled of rot and frozen wastes.

Choking inside the Naether Demon's grip, Akmael closed his eyes and sought to connect his pulse to the heart of the mountain. Summoning what power he could, he called once more for his staff. To his relief, the smooth oak found his grip. Its crystal head ignited in the white fire of Aithne.

Faeom dumae.

Thunder exploded from the staff. The Naether Demon howled. Releasing its prey, the demon stumbled back, pawing at the air in front of it.

Akmael found his sword just as the creature charged again. The Naether Demon reared up, towering over the King. Akmael lunged forward and drove the sword deep into its belly. The blade sank not into flesh but into a viscous, glowing fluid that released a thick black sludge. With a thunderous roar, the creature swiped at Akmael, but the claws missed their mark.

Dropping on all fours the Naether Demon retreated.

Akmael backed away, struggling to maintain his breath and balance.

The demon's body heaved. Shadows flowed from its wounds. Yet the empty black pits of its eyes remained fixed on the Mage King. It began to circle its prey once more.

Akmael adjusted his grip on sword and staff. Pain burned through his thigh. Spasms threatened to offset his balance. Every breath came labored. He tried to call his men, but his voice was reduced to a hoarse whisper. Sounds of terror and death echoed throughout the fortress. His men were besieged, his queen and children in danger.

I am the one who brought this upon us, he thought in bitter shame. *I, the Mage King, unable to resist a wizard's curse.*

The thought of Eolyn, alone and unprotected, spurred Akmael's rage. He sprang forward, blade connecting with the beast and cleaving a black gash from shoulder to sternum. The Naether Demon swung its good arm, slashing deep into Akmael's torso and releasing a river of blood.

Akmael staggered away. The pit of the Underworld invaded his entrails. Cold tides of death began to course through his limbs, and he understood, in the way every warrior understands when his moment has come, that he would not live past this night.

His spirit looked out across the wastes of the dead, and he heard his tutor's voice.

Dismember them with steel. Sir Drostan said. *Burn the remains.*

Releasing the staff, the Mage King took his sword in both hands. The Naether Demon lumbered forward and struck again, but Akmael's blade found its mark and severed the forearm.

Naeom anthae!

White hot flame burst from Akmael's palm and caught the ebony-clawed paw as it fell to the ground.

The Naether Demon's blood-curdling scream brought the King to his knees. Akmael swung blindly, furiously as the beast scrambled toward him again. By the grace of the Gods, another limb fell. Crippled and moaning, the demon dragged itself away, seeking refuge in the shadows.

Akmael rose and with a vicious cry rushed forward. Each strike came bolder than the last, eliciting agonized cries as the Naether Demon was hacked apart. At last the creature fell silent, its amorphous flesh converted into burning lumps.

The room spun. Sounds of the living faded from Akmael's awareness. Exhausted, he fell to his knees.

Eolyn.

Groping through the shadows, the Mage King found his staff. Slowly he stood and made his way to the bed, where he tore the soiled linen and bound strips around his lacerated torso.

The remains of his vanquished enemy littered the floor like jade colored coals. Outside the battle continued, marked by throaty roars and screams of anguish.

Torches flickered down the hallway. Galison and two others burst into the room, their bodies lacerated, their faces covered with blood and soot. "My Lord King!"

"Where is the rest of my guard?" Akmael demanded.

Galison shook his head. "Dead, my Lord King. We are all that is left of the night watch."

Convulsions wracked Akmael as he retrieved the sword from where it lay. Galison rushed forward to steady him. Akmael leaned on his captain with labored gasps, fighting off the excruciating pain that ripped through his entrails. Already his makeshift bandages were soaked with blood.

"My Queen!" His voice broke. "Where is Eolyn?"

"We have no word of her, my Lord King. The East Tower is besieged. No one has been able to get through."

Akmael withdrew from Galison and steadied his stance. Beyond his chambers he heard the cries of men and beasts locked in battle.

Shadows interrupted his vision. The voices of his ancestors called, but he refused to surrender to their embrace.

Not until Eolyn is safe.

"To the East Tower," he said. "May the Gods have mercy on us all."

THE HEAVY OAK DOOR SHUDDERED beneath another blow, hinges groaning against the strain.

Eolyn drew a deep breath. She bent to kiss and embrace both her children. Then she took up her sword and stepped resolutely outside of the circle.

"Mama!" Briana grasped Eolyn's skirt.

"Let me go, Briana."

"But Mama—"

"You must let me go if I am to protect you."

"You said we are not to leave the circle!"

"You and your brother are not to leave the circle. The Gods have other plans for me. Eoghan, take your sister's hand."

Pain caught in Eolyn's throat as she watched them, so small yet so brave.

Sweet Gods of Aithne, if you intend to call me home on this night, I beg you: spare them the horror of witnessing my death.

"Keep her safe, Eoghan. Do not let go of each other's magic. If I tell you to run, you must run. Do not look back."

Eolyn crept along the wall toward the failing door and pressed herself flat against the stone wall next to the frame.

Each impact reverberated against her back. Gripping the hilt with both hands, she held Kel'Barú ready and closed her eyes. The hum of the Galian weapon penetrated her fingers, extending through her arms and chest. She heard cries of the many who had fallen under its attack and felt the spirit of death wrap around her.

Show me what to do. Show me how to defeat my enemy.

The door shattered into a thousand splinters. An icy mist spilled into the room.

Wait, Kel'Barú whispered.

A Naether Demon lumbered through the fog, followed by another. They passed Eolyn without seeing her and paused, heads turning as if to scan their surroundings.

She noted wariness in their aspect, inspired by the torch light perhaps, or by the ward her children had cast. Kel'Barú had fallen silent, its glow subdued.

The Naether Demons separated and approached the children, heads lowered in a feline crouch. Eolyn stepped toward them, only to be halted by Kel'Barú.

Wait.

She stifled a cry as the Naether Demons crashed against the barrier erected by her children. The tenuous wall of flame wavered but did not break. The Naether Demons stumbled back and let go a mournful howl.

Then a third Naether Demon passed through the ruined doorway.

Eolyn sucked in her breath and pressed herself flat against the wall. The demon's heaving bulk rippled past her, its attention fixed on the children.

Now.

Eolyn lunged forward, dragging her sword across the back of

the demon and releasing a river of black sludge. The creature spun around and struck with its forearm. Eolyn found herself suspended in the air before she hit the stone floor. Bruised and winded, she sprang to her feet. Kel'Barú remained steady in her hand, the Naether Demon's black blood dripping from its blade.

"Mother, don't!" Eoghan cried.

"Stay where you are!"

The Naether Demon charged.

Eolyn leapt out of its path, but not soon enough to avoid another blow that sent her sprawling to the ground. Rolling onto her back, she set Kel'Barú between her and the beast. The sword penetrated the demon's throat as it leapt upon her, reducing its unearthly scream to a pathetic gurgle.

The Naether Demon grasped at the blade, trying to dislodge it but succeeding only in slicing open its paws. Eolyn held Kel'Barú steady, driving the Galian blade deeper even as she tried to push the beast off, its body holding her down not so much by earthly weight, but with a cold, suffocating void.

At last the flailing of its limbs ceased.

Gasping, Eolyn dragged herself out from underneath the icy mass of flesh. She struggled to her feet, head aching, muscles bruised. A tremor invaded her legs. Instinctively, she tried to anchor her spirit to the heart of the mountain, only to gag as the tether cast by Akmael tightened around her throat.

The other two beasts ceased their attack on Eoghan and Briana, turning instead toward Eolyn.

A fourth demon padded into the room, ebony claws clicking against the stone floor, vacuous eyes settling upon her.

"Sweet Gods of Dragon," she murmured, centering her weight and readying her sword. "Help me."

The three of them sprang at once.

A desperate dance of instinct took hold of Eolyn. Kel'Barú's whisper fused with her, body and mind. Its song echoed through her spirit, prompting her counters and leading her attacks. Furiously she struck at ancient enemies, unknown yet superimposed upon the formless faces of the Naether Demons. The silver-white blade flashed like lightning against a starless night, painting ribbons of black over jade-colored flesh, eliciting howls of rage and pain. Even so, the Naether Demon's ebony claws found her, slicing open gown and flesh, leaving wounds that burned on her face, arms, and legs.

At last one of the demons fell, long limbs converted to formless stumps by the merciless bite of Kel'Barú. Eolyn sagged against the stone wall as the Naether Demon collapsed. Her breath came in hoarse, painful gasps. Her legs quivered with exhaustion.

The remaining Naether Demons watched her from a few paces away, swaying on long limbs, purrs of satisfaction shuddering through her shoulders.

They understand how little fight I have left.

Eolyn drew a deep breath and raised Kel'Barú, supporting herself along the wall as she edged away from the children. Nothing would disrupt their ward faster than watching her die, and Eolyn knew with grim certainty that she would soon face her end.

"Eoghan," she said, "when I engage them again, take your sister and run from this place. Do not look back. Find your way to the gardens and stay high in the trees until dawn."

"I will not abandon you!"

"Do as I say!" Her words came sharp and ragged. Tears stung her eyes. "Do not disobey me in this of all moments. Your survival depends on it."

The beasts snorted, a hollow slurping sound, as they tracked her movement with lowered heads. Eolyn's attention was so fixed on their approach, she did not see the stray piece of wood that entangled her feet. Her ankle gave way. She lost her balance. The Naether Demons sprang.

Pain shot through Eolyn's torso as one of them pounded her into the floor. Its ear-piercing howl obliterated her senses. Then she saw its claw, black as the abyss of the Underworld, descend toward her chest. Terrified cries of the children echoed through her awareness.

"Run!" she cried.

Small sword in hand, Eoghan charged her attackers from behind. They spun on the boy and struck him with the fury of a winter storm. Eoghan fell back and hit the floor hard. Knocked from his grasp, the sword clattered out of reach.

Shadows filled Eolyn's vision. Her heart constricted. She could no longer breathe.

The Naether Demon took hold of her son by the ankle and lifted him high, claws scoring the flesh of his small chest.

"No!" Eolyn cried.

Wind roared through the tower windows. A raptor swooped down among them. Light flashed through the Midnight Owl. Wings and feathers twisted into the shape of a man. With staff in hand, he let go a thunderous curse.

The Naether Demon dropped the boy. Rising to her feet, Eolyn drove Kel'Barú deep into the beast, twisting and dragging the blade through its torso, bracing against the creature's anguished howl.

Naeom anthae! the mage cried.

Fire, white and pure, sprung from the crystal head of the mage's staff and pummeled the other demon into the wall. When the flame was spent, the beast lay crumpled on the floor, wheezing.

Eolyn strode forward, hacked off its head, and dismembered the body. The pieces melted into a thin gray mist that hovered over the floor. As Eolyn watched, the ghostly flesh faded. She became aware of the stinging welts that covered her body, of the sweat and blood that drenched her gown. An uncontrollable tremor took hold of her limbs.

Akmael approached from behind and placed his cloak around Eolyn's shoulders. She spun ready to surrender to the strength of her love's embrace, only to step back in astonishment.

"Corey?" she said, bewildered.

The mage took in her shocked expression and gave a slight shrug of resignation. "I'll never understand why you are so surprised every time I come to your aid," he said.

Briana rushed out of the ward and sprang into her uncle's arms. He covered her face with kisses before setting the princess down. Then he helped Eoghan to his feet, checking the prince for bruises and searching for signs of concussion. Satisfied the boy was unharmed, Corey turned back to Eolyn.

"Are you well?" he asked.

"As well as can be expected."

Corey eyes narrowed. "Not well, I would say. Someone has bound your magic. Why?"

Eolyn's knees buckled under the crushing weight of all the

heartbreak and terror she had suffered on this night.

Corey caught her fall. "What is it? Eolyn, what has happened?"

"Akmael." Sobs broke through her words. The memory of her husband's brutality returned full force. "He came…enraged, and I couldn't…and the children…Oh, Gods, Corey! Everything is falling apart."

Corey gathered her to his chest and held her until the shaking ceased. Then he pressed his lips against her hair.

"Not everything is lost," he murmured. "We are alive, aren't we? And where there is life, there is always hope."

His fingers slipped to the nape of her neck. She relaxed at his touch, drawn to the familiarity of his magic, to his aroma of ancient forests and winter winds.

Corey whispered a spell in Eolyn's ear, and at his invocation, the sadness receded. Color, light, and sound rushed back into her awareness. In one brilliant breath, the fullness of her magic returned.

Disconcerted, she withdrew from his embrace. "I'm not sure that was a good idea."

Corey rolled his eyes. "You are a wellspring of gratitude this evening, my Lady Queen."

"I am not ungrateful. What I mean is that my magic may be a liability. The Naether Demons had to break through the wards to get in here. It wasn't like the last time, when they simply found me wherever I was. Perhaps having my magic bound kept them at bay."

Corey studied her, a thoughtful look on his face. "You may be right, but I do not want to waste a single breath releasing your magic should we run into them again. We need to be ready. The Naether Demons are not finished with us yet."

The spell of this brief respite lifted. Shouts, explosions, and cries of agony could still be heard throughout the fortress.

"Where is the King?" she asked. "Why did he not come?"

"I do not know. You and the children were my first concern. A crime against the crown, perhaps, but one for which I am confident that I have earned your pardon. Did Akmael break your staff as well?"

"No."

"Then bring it, and the Galian sword. We will need them

both."

They left the tower chambers together. The cold mist of the Naether Demons shrouded everything. The corridors were littered with bodies, men and women with limbs missing or twisted at odd angles, breasts torn open and emptied, entrails spilling from their guts. The carnage made Eolyn's stomach turn. She bade Briana to look away, but Corey objected.

"Let her look upon this," he said. "Let her never forget what our enemies can do to us."

They crept down darkened stairs, picking their way over corpses. Sounds of battle still raged elsewhere, but here all was quiet and cloaked in death.

Corey paused at a place where the narrow stairwell opened into a large corridor. He peered carefully down the darkened passageway, then hushed them back into the shadows. Eolyn clung to her children, all of them frozen in silence. The sound of claws scraping against stone echoed down the passageway. A shaft of faint emerald light slipped toward the stairwell. Eolyn held her breath until the light faded again.

"Now," Corey whispered. "Hurry!"

They followed him across the corridor and through a servant's entrance. Corey invoked a soft glow in the crystal head of his staff, illuminating another silent stairwell.

"Why can't they find me?" Eolyn whispered. "Why do they not come directly to us, as they did before?"

"Perhaps the breach in your soul can no longer accommodate their passage."

"But why?"

Corey paused. "How do we close the portals to the Underworld, Maga Eolyn?"

"By planting new life, by covering our battlefields with trees and wildflowers. But the portal I carried wasn't like that. The breach was a part of my aura, my soul."

"Yet you have in recent years brought new life into the world. A son and a daughter, each planted by the seed of a mage. Perhaps that was enough to heal the wound."

"If you are right," Eolyn said, "that would mean Akmael is safe too. When he became a father, the shadow that plagued his aura

157

would also have been erased."

Corey glanced at her in the dim light. Eolyn noted a subtle hardening of his expression. "I do not know whether this magic works in the same way for a man. Instinct tells me it does not."

"Then we must find him."

"We have a greater task at hand."

"What task could possibly be greater?"

"In the time it takes to track down your beloved King, the Naether Demons will have finished off what few men-at-arms are left in this castle." Corey's words were colored with anger and impatience. "We must send those beasts back to where they came from at once. Everything else is secondary."

Eolyn frowned, the specter of defeat returning to her spirit.

"But we don't know how," she said.

"I know how." Corey took her hand, urging her to follow. "I have not been entirely idle these past ten years."

CHAPTER TWENTY-TWO

Reprieve

EOLYN, COREY, AND THE CHILDREN emerged into one of the inner courtyards. Aromas of night blossoms and fresh leaves kept away the stench of decay that had penetrated the stronghold. The sky was clear, the bright stars indifferent to the rage and suffering below.

Corey found a tall beech and lifted Briana onto a branch. "Up you go, little Princess. You too, my Lord Prince."

"I would stay and fight," Eoghan objected.

"You must protect your sister," Corey said. "Climb as high as you can. If we do not return, you are to remain hidden in these branches until dawn."

Eoghan stiffened and looked to his mother.

"Mage Corey is right, my love," Eolyn said.

"But I—"

"This is a threat that only High Magic can counter. You do not yet have the skills to confront these creatures."

Eoghan clenched his fists, his expression locked between anger and uncertainty. Then without warning, he flung his arms around his mother.

"What if they tear you to pieces?" he cried.

Eolyn give him a gentle kiss. "Hush, my brave Prince."

"I assure you, my Lord Prince," Corey said, "I have every intention of surviving this night."

"I can't let you face them alone!"

"My beloved son," Eolyn said. "You must not fear. Do as Corey says. Entrust your spirit to the protection of the trees."

He choked back a sob. "I'll never forgive myself if—"

"Eoghan, you know the nature of our duty. If I should be called home on this night, you must remember what your father told you: The end of our time will mark the beginning of yours. It has always been so."

"No!"

"Release me, sweet Prince." She kissed him again. "Dragon is calling me to defend our people."

Eoghan tightened his grip for a moment and then tore away. Wiping tears from his cheeks, he caught hold of a branch and swung up next to his sister. Then he continued higher, disappearing into the dense foliage without looking back.

"Come, Briana." His call came sharp and impatient.

The princess bit her lip, regarding Corey and her mother with a hard frown. Then she turned to the mage and said, "You are not to allow any harm to come to my mother, Uncle Corey. If she does not return safe and whole, you will answer to me. And I will show you no mercy."

With that, she followed her brother.

Corey smiled. "Your daughter has a special magic, Eolyn, that she can warm my heart on such a cold and treacherous night."

He took Eolyn's hand and led her toward the heart of the garden. Despite the late hour, fire beetles and moon spiders had ignited their glow. They spread over the garden, forming a net of ephemeral light that muted the sounds of battle beyond.

"They protect this place," Eolyn realized in wonder.

"As best they can. Their efforts will come to naught if the Naether Demons finish their task on the battlements and in the corridors of this castle."

"What do you intend to do, Corey?"

They arrived at the center of the courtyard, where the moon's light was reflected in a broad circle of small white stones. Corey studied the sky and garden before setting his gaze upon Eolyn.

"We are going to cast an old and forgotten spell," he said. "An illusion that I hope will send them back to the bowels of the Underworld."

"What illusion?"

"I cannot reveal the details."

"Gods, Corey! Your secrets will be the death of us all. Why

haven't you spoken about this before? We could have been prepared for a night such as this."

"Tzeremond always said a well-kept secret is the path to a secure future."

"And you have dedicated your life to proving him right?"

"In this much, I suppose I have."

"Where did you find this magic we are about to invoke?"

"Well-hidden among the annals of the Master's library. If we live past this night, I will gladly share it with you. Fascinating reading, really. It's evident from Tzeremond's notes that the existence of this curse ignited a great conflict in his heart."

"How so?"

"Because this curse requires the willing participation of a High Maga, a woman practitioner who is confident in her power and position. This was one of many pieces of history that could have unraveled Kedehen's campaign to eliminate the magas altogether."

"Well. That explains why Tzeremond kept it hidden, but you?"

Corey frowned and glanced away. He let go a slow breath. "Perhaps I was nurturing a feeble hope that we would never have to use it."

Shrill howls of the Naether Demons cut through their conversation, malevolent triumph rising over terror and destitution.

"We should not delay any longer," Eolyn said.

"I could not agree with you more, my Lady Queen."

Corey took a stance at the center of the circle, invoked the power of Dragon, and anchored his spirit to the heart of the mountain. From there he walked east thirteen paces and planted his staff in the ground at the circle's edge, marking the direction to his place of birth in East Selen.

Eolyn repeated the invocation, setting her own staff firmly into the ground at the southern border of the stone circle. The crystal head of her staff ignited in a low hum, connecting to the source of her power in the distant South Woods.

Eolyn felt the awareness of the castle turn inward, malevolent hunger focusing on the garden where they stood.

The cries of the Naether Demons paused.

The leaves of the garden shivered.

"They sense our magic," she whispered.

161

"Come." Corey held out his hand. "We must act now."

Mage and maga met at the center of the circle, invoking a curtain of purple fire that rose along the rim.

"Give me your sword," Corey said.

Eolyn recoiled on instinct. "I don't think Kel'Barú—"

"The Galian weapon understands what needs to be done. Grant me the sword, Eolyn."

Reluctantly she unsheathed Kel'Barú and proffered it to Mage Corey. The silver-white blade glowed with the tenuous light of the moon. Corey took the hilt in both hands and strode toward the northwest edge of the circle, the direction of the wastes of Faernvorn.

Naeom avignaes sahtue.

He drove the blade into the ground, setting off a tremor deep inside the earth. Liquid flame flowed from blade, weaving copper ribbons through the violet curtain. Eolyn felt a sudden pull beneath her feet, so strong she lost her balance. Corey caught her elbow and held her steady, positioning himself behind her at the circle's center.

One by one, the Naether Demons were abandoning the battle. They began clamoring down the walls, a swarm of glowing bodies with vacuous eyes drawn toward the light of the garden.

Fear rattled Eolyn's resolve.

"There are so many!" she said. "How can there be so many?"

"Focus, Eolyn. Connect with me."

"What if they find the children?"

"They won't. They've eyes for nothing but us now."

She rested her hands upon Corey's, their palms lifted toward the heavens. It was a strange embrace, at once formal and intimate. The jewel on Eolyn's arm, the silver serpent of East Selen, came to life, weaving toward her hand and intertwining her wrist and his. Corey's breath fell warm upon her ear.

"This curse will ask much of us," he said.

Eolyn's heart skipped a beat. She swallowed and said, "Corey, before we begin, there's something I have to tell—"

"We've no time left for conversation. Whatever happens, do not deny me your magic. Repeat my invocation. You will not understand the words, but it does not matter. Let the magic take you where it will. I will manage the rest."

Eolyn nodded and pressed her back against his chest.

The Naether Demons had advanced to the edge of the garden. Purrs rumbled through their glowing bodies. The beasts crouched low and sniffed at the trees and bushes, seemingly shy of crossing the barrier of fire beetles and moon spiders.

Corey began his invocation, uttering words in a language that Eolyn did not recognize, guttural yet strangely melodic. Closing her eyes, the maga focused on the sound and rhythm of Corey's voice until the verse began to fall from her own lips, somehow familiar in its foreign lilt, haunting and beautiful, filled with timeless longing.

Corey's fingers shifted, and sparks shimmered over Eolyn's skin. A pulse of magic ignited between them, drawing Eolyn toward lands unexplored. Ancient forests rose above her, towering black firs cloaked by wintry skies. Crystalline waters cut through landscapes scorched under the breath of Dragon. Generations of mages and magas chanted, danced, worshiped, and died. Eolyn recognized each face though she knew them not. She walked through places lost in time yet alive in her memory, and remembered dreams kept hidden in the labyrinth of her heart.

The black forest melted away, and the South Woods appeared, enveloping her with a mossy cloak. Golden light sliced through lush summer trees. The air buzzed with insects and birds; cool mud squished between her toes. Lynx slipped among the shadows, leading Eolyn on a winding path through dense stands of trees. Rounding a large trunk, she came upon Doyenne Ghemena, bent with age, gray eyes set in a deeply lined face, gnarled hands clutching a rosewood staff. The old maga's aura resonated joy and sorrow.

You are bound by the craft to serve them, she said. *No matter what they have done to us in the past, no matter what they may do to you in the future. When their hour of need arrives, you must respond.*

Eolyn's tutor faded away. Behind her, the Tarba River materialized, water rushing high over its rocky bed. Akmael stood on the far banks, a boy cloaked and crowned as king. His face was shadowed by mourning.

Eolyn called out to him, but no words fell from her lips. Akmael lifted his hand and pointed at the heavens, toward a source of light that illuminated their world.

163

Kel'Barú came into focus against the starlit night, its blade a shaft of obsidian that freed itself from the earth and rose to eclipse the moon. The landscape was cast in darkness. Night's shadow spread its wings over the earth.

Sweet aromas of the castle garden returned to Eolyn's senses, mingled with the stench of approaching death. She heard the Naether Demons, a lumbering herd not more than a few paces away, and opened her eyes.

Beyond the curtain of light, they watched her with vacuous eyes. Their maws worked in anxious hunger. They crouched on glowing limbs and waited.

The ground shifted beneath Eolyn's feet.

Uncertainty shook her voice. "Corey?"

His lips grazed her temple. "Forgive me, Eolyn."

Kel'Barú plunged into Eolyn's breast. The Galian sword tore open her sternum, releasing the river that was her soul. Eolyn fell and flowed into the chasm that yawned at her feet, her spirit a roiling current of sorrow, betrayal, terror, and disbelief.

The Naether Demons leapt after her, limbs outstretched and claws extended, faces contorted in a discordant roar. Together they descended in a swirling vortex of light and shadow. Claws caught Eolyn's skirt, jaws snapped at her face. Desperately she tried to invoke a ward, but the fabric of her magic had been unraveled, its strands held tight in Corey's distant grasp.

The abyss of the Underworld loomed below, cold and silent, patient with its final embrace. Eolyn's descent slowed as if caught by a viscous substance, and then stopped altogether. The Naether Demons pooled around her. Eternal night swallowed the maga's screams. Her kicks fell impotent against jade-colored flesh. Ebony claws immobilized her limbs and scored her spirit. Snarls sounded harsh inside her ears. Tendrils of fog reached through the mass of demons, latching onto wrists and ankles, snaking tight around her throat, choking away the last of her magic.

Eolyn felt the sudden violent pull of the life left behind, its triumphs and sorrows, its passions and disappointments, its sensual beauty and unfulfilled love. The voices of family, friends, allies, and enemies rose and then fell in a single tragic note of farewell. Then all heartache, all awareness, all hope was consumed by the void.

CHAPTER TWENTY-THREE

Death

SOFT BLADES OF GRASS spread in a fragrant carpet, muted colors pushing back the shadows of the night. Trees groaned as they took shape beneath the stars. Branches creaked and leaves rustled in a gathering wind.

A solitary owl gave a quiet hoot.

Air returned to Eolyn's lungs in a sudden painful rush. She gasped and then gagged, doubled over on her knees. Corey had his arms wrapped tight around her, lips pressed against her hair.

Fighting a wave of nausea, Eolyn shoved him away. She clutched at her breast, finding herself whole and unharmed. Violent fury guided her to where Kel'Barú lay discarded on the ground. She rose, shaking, to her feet and leveled the blade at Corey.

He lifted his hands in a gesture of appeasement. "Eolyn—"

"Do not speak to me!" She called the staff to her, but it did not respond. Infuriated, Eolyn retrieved it by hand, her sword still trained on the mage.

"It was the only way," he said.

"I am going to kill you, Mage Corey, just as I should have done a long ago."

"It is not in your interests to slay me. Even if it were, you do not have the strength to do so right now."

The garden wavered. Eolyn's knees threatened to give way. "I am sick beyond reason of your treacherous games."

"You cannot accuse me of treachery, not in this."

"Curse you, Corey!" she cried. "Let me live or let me die, but stop using me as your pawn!"

165

Corey set his lips in a thin line. "As you wish, my Lady Queen."

Eolyn's awareness opened to the world around them. The howls of the Naether Demons had been silenced. The cries of battle and chaos had faded into an uneasy peace, punctuated by moans of injured men and distant shouts of consternation.

Her children were calling.

Abandoning Mage Corey, Eolyn rushed toward Briana and Eoghan, dropping sword and staff as she found them. Their loving embrace melted into hers; their sweet aroma filled her heart with joy and relief. She showered their faces with kisses.

"Alive!" she exclaimed. "Thank the Gods you are both alive and whole."

Then Akmael's voice sounded upon her ear.

Eolyn.

She looked up, aware of the dark magic that still wove through the night. Her breath tripped over a terrible premonition.

Come quickly my love.

Rising, Eolyn sheathed her sword and gathered her staff. Trying to subdue the tremor that had invaded her spirit anew, she took Briana's hand and nodded to her son. "Come. We must find your father at once."

They made their way through torch-lit passageways littered with the fallen. Remains of Naether Demons glowed in the dark, releasing an icy mist as they melted away. The survivors had begun the grim task of sorting the living from the dead, of returning some sense of order to the ruin left behind. They bowed tight-lipped as Eolyn and the children passed. Confusion and despair weighed heavy over their auras.

Eolyn came upon Akmael in one of the broad corridors that looked over the courtyards below. They had laid him out on a table. His chest and legs were covered with a blood-soaked cloth. Several men-at-arms were gathered close, some leaning on each other, makeshift bandages wrapped around their wounds.

Upon Eolyn's appearance, their anxious murmurs ceased. They greeted her on bended knee, somber and respectful in their silence. Only Mage Echior did not kneel, intent as he was upon attending the King.

Upon seeing the man she loved, Eolyn felt a crushing weight inside her chest. A cry must have escaped her lips, for Echior paused in his examination and lifted his face to her. A frown crossed his brow. He averted his gaze and shook his head.

Briana's wail pierced the room. Her outpouring of grief was quickly muffled by Eoghan's firm embrace. The prince's gaze did not waver from his father. He kept his chin lifted, the force of his emotions hidden behind the stony mask of Vortingen.

Eolyn willed her numbed limbs into motion. The King's guard drew back as she stepped close. She brushed blood-matted hair off Akmael's pale and drawn face.

At her bidding, Echior lifted the bloodied sheet, revealing the horrific extent of Akmael's wounds. The Naether Demons had torn deep into his flesh, ripping open limbs and torso. The organs of his midsection had been exposed. His skin had turned a sickly gray. No trace of his aura remained.

"My Lady Queen, if I may..." Echior beckoned with a lift of his hand. She placed her fingers in his palm, let him guide her touch to Akmael's breast. The flesh here was still whole and unscathed, his skin so cold it burned.

"What is this?" Eolyn withdrew in fear. "What dark power has left him so?"

"I don't know, my Lady Queen," Echior confessed. "Whatever the spell, I suspect it kept the Naether Demons from consuming his heart, and in so doing, foiled the worst of their ambitions."

"Might it have saved him?" Her voice sank into a hopeful whisper. "Might he yet live inside this shell of ice?"

"I can find no pulse, no breath, no flicker of his aura. He has been like this since we found him. Every instinct tells me he is lost to us. Yet until we understand this magic, I humbly suggest we delay the final rites."

Eolyn nodded. Grasping at this wisp of hope she took Akmael's stiffened hand and bent to kiss him. "Return to us, my love. Do not let this be the end."

Akmael's fingers twitched. His body jerked and convulsed. Air rushed into his lungs, harsh and hollow, like a man coming up from the bottom of a river.

Soldiers gasped and stepped back, some drawing their swords.

The King's iron grip immobilized Eolyn. She watched in fear and awe as Akmael's breathing eased and his eyes opened. He focused on Eolyn and murmured her name.

Laughter mingled with the sob that escaped her lips. "Akmael, thank the Gods! We all thought—"

"No." The gravity of his tone sank into her like a stone thrown in a dark well. "No, Eolyn."

Akmael's body remained stiff, his grip cold as ice. He did not turn his head but looked upon her with gray and glassy eyes. "Three times I have used your magic to return from the world of the dead. The Gods will not allow me to remain on this side any longer."

She shook her head in denial. "I don't understand. What are you saying?"

"Eolyn, where is my son?"

"I am here, Father." Eoghan hastened to his father's side. He laid a hand on Akmael's shoulder.

"Eoghan," Akmael's voice was hoarse. "You are my one and only son, a true Prince of Vortingen. I leave you with the crown of my fathers, and charge you with this task: Find the ones who did this to us. Find them and eliminate them."

"I will see it done, Father."

"Akmael, please. You mustn't—"

"The Princess," Akmael said. "Where is Briana?"

"Here, my Lord King." Corey stepped forward, Briana in his arms. The girl set a wary gaze upon Akmael's animated corpse and retreated to the mage's embrace with frightened sobs.

Akmael's eyes grew damp. His voice thickened with emotion. "Daughter of East Selen, do not be afraid. Everything is as it should be. Find her a worthy companion, Eolyn. An honorable man of good lineage. If her husband should ever mistreat her, he will meet with my wrath in the Afterlife."

"My love, do not speak like this." Desperation rose in Eolyn's voice.

"I would ask your forgiveness, but there can be no forgiveness for this. Only atonement."

"Akmael, don't!" Her sorrow was giving way to anger. "We can reverse this. We will bring you back."

Tightening his grip, the King raised his voice as best he could and said, "Who stands witness to the last words of Akmael, Son of Kedehen and King of the line of Vortingen?"

"I do." Eoghan's voice shook, though his stance was firm and his expression resolute.

"As do I," Corey said.

"And I." Echior stepped close.

Every man in the room followed suit, declaring himself present and kneeling in attentive silence.

"This woman who stands at my side," Akmael said, "Eolyn, High Maga of Moisehén, is your true and rightful queen. I chose her to wear the Crown of Vortingen and to bear my children, a duty that she has fulfilled with great love and unflinching loyalty. Anyone who claims otherwise is guilty of treason and shall be hanged."

Akmael paused and closed his eyes. The tenuous spark that held him to the living world wavered.

"No one is more worthy than she," he continued with labored breath. "No one more capable of leading our people in the difficult times to come. She will rule in my stead, she and no one else, until my son Eoghan comes of age. This is the final command of your sovereign King."

Silence followed. A handful of men shifted their weight in uncertainty.

"So it shall be," Mage Corey said.

"So it shall be," the others repeated in an uneven chorus.

Akmael released a weary sigh. "Now go. Leave us, all of you. I would spend these last moments alone with my Queen."

They departed, Corey and the children the last to go, Briana weeping inconsolably.

Eolyn drew close, warming Akmael's lips with her own. "Your life has not ended. We will find a way to nurse the strength back into your body, just as we did at Rhiemsaven."

A smile spread, tight and unnatural, across his ashen face. "I was not truly dead then, Eolyn."

"You are not dead now!"

His smile faded, and his eyes clouded. "Eolyn...I could have stayed in your world, in that little cottage in the South Woods. I could have grown old with you, a hermit and a mage."

"Stay now," she begged. "Stay with me."

169

"Instead I brought you into my world. Forgive me."

"There is nothing to forgive."

"I took you out of your home and delivered you to this place of treachery and death. I brought our love to ruin."

"No!" A sob broke through her words. Eolyn wiped her tears away in frustration, struggling to find her voice.

"Eolyn," he whispered. "I have seen my father's home. I have stepped over the threshold of the place he prepared for me."

Akmael's grip on her hand was fading, the frost on his skin dissolving into a soft white mist.

"No." Eolyn pulled the sheet back over his chest with shaking fingers. "That was just a dream, Akmael. You see? The warmth is returning to your body. The battle is over, and now I will nurse you back to health."

"I hear his voice. I cannot delay any longer, but I will not stay with him. Eolyn, I am returning to the woods where you and I first met. There, I will prepare a place for us, a place where your magic can flourish."

"For the love of the Gods, Akmael, I can't—"

"Promise you will look for me when your time comes. I will be waiting by the river. Promise we will be together again, like we were before."

"I promise." Tears blurred her vision. "Anything you ask, Akmael, just don't—"

A smile passed over his features. "I love you, Eolyn. Always."

Then Akmael, anointed King of the line of Vortingen, released his last breath and let go of his true love's hand.

Eolyn gasped as a part of her fell away with him, becoming one with Akmael in death even as she remained in this world, bewildered, body and soul, by sudden, inexplicable loss.

She bent to kiss him, but found his lips cold and unresponsive.

"Come back," she whispered. "Please, Akmael. Come back."

He did not respond.

Laying her head upon her husband's chest, she waited for his quiet breath, for the familiar beat of his heart, for the strength of his embrace, but all she found was the silence of the dead.

Grief rose like a shadow at her back, choking off all light, knifing her heart with bitter despair, clawing out her spirit in long ragged shreds.

A long, terrible wail tore through her chest.

Set adrift in a sea of destruction, Eolyn clung to Akmael's corpse and wept without respite until dawn.

Chapter Twenty-Four

Alone

LADY TALIA MURMURED WORDS of comfort as she drew Eolyn away from Akmael.

The maga did not resist, emptied out as she was by anguish. As Talia led her from the room, mages gathered like a living shroud around her husband, chanting somber spells. They lit candles of nightberry and winter sage. Soon they would begin preparing his body for the final rites.

Giving no thought to bearing or dignity, Eolyn leaned on Talia for support. Her legs shook beneath her. Faces of people blurred as they passed. Talia led Eolyn not to the East Tower, but to her true apartments, located not far from Akmael's own. There, attendants removed Eolyn's shredded clothes, cleaned her wounds, and drew a fresh bath. They dressed her in plain gray silks, combed and plaited her hair, and served her breakfast.

Eolyn did not eat but stared unseeing out the southern windows. The day had dawned as colorless as her heart.

"My Lady Queen."

Eolyn started at Talia's gentle touch upon her elbow. The lady retreated a step and bowed in deference.

"High Mage Thelyn humbly requests the honor of your presence in the King's chambers," she said.

Thelyn.

Eolyn let go a long, inward sigh. Even death and tragedy could not stop politics. The mage undoubtedly waited with whatever remained of the Council. She would have to face them and assume command of this disaster.

The sooner, the better.

She focused on the room around her. "Where are my children?"

"The Prince and Princess are resting in their chambers, under the care of Mage Corey."

A cold knot took hold of her stomach. Akmael's breath had hardly stilled, and already the Mage of East Selen was casting his shadow over the King's heirs.

Rising on unsteady feet, Eolyn allowed Talia to cover her face with a veil of mourning. The maga retrieved her staff. As she exited the chambers, a small guard assembled around her.

Many of the bodies had already been carried off. Servants knelt on the floor, scrubbing away stains of blood. They paused in their efforts and touched their fingers to their foreheads as Eolyn passed.

"Long live the Queen," they said. "Long live Prince Eoghan."

But their voices were subdued and their expressions grim.

Eolyn kept her chin lifted and back erect. It seemed a perverse game, this show of strength so soon after the fall of her King and the evisceration of her spirit. Her body felt like a hollow shell. She held her staff, but she could not feel its hum. The water crystal had dulled; its image of Dragon was clouded. Eolyn could hardly remember a time when her magic did not mingle with Akmael's. He had always been a part of her journey as a maga. Indeed, he was the one who first revealed the true nature of her gifts.

As Eolyn entered the King's chambers, everyone went down on bended knee. She allowed the weight of their homage to linger, making note of who was present. Corey knelt beside Thelyn, his fair head bowed, his eyes fixed on the floor.

"Rise, all of you," Eolyn said, "and join me in the mourning of our King."

Thelyn stepped forward, took her hand, and touched her fingers to his forehead. "Words cannot express the depth of my grief at this terrible tragedy, my Lady Queen."

"We grieve as one people and one kingdom, Mage Thelyn," Eolyn replied. "Mage Corey, I was told that you were looking after the Prince and the Princess."

"They wait in their chambers, my Lady Queen. Guards have been assigned to their protection, and Mage Echior accompanies

173

them to attend to any need that may arise. I trust this arrangement is to your liking?"

"Yes," she reluctantly admitted. There were few men she trusted more than Mage Echior. Corey, of course, would know that.

"The Prince and Princess have been asking for you," he said.

"I will go to them as soon as we are finished here. What word does the Council have for me? What course of action do you recommend?"

"Our priority is cleansing this fortress." Thelyn said. "We must locate as many portals as possible and make certain they are sealed before nightfall. I have put our mages to this task, but the King's bedchamber cannot be breached until my Lady Queen and I have entered it first."

Every fiber of Eolyn's body revolted at the thought. "I've never heard of such a protocol."

Thelyn frowned and glanced away. "With all due respect, my Lady Queen, you have never witnessed the death of a king."

"But I don't understand why—"

"Please, my Lady Queen. Certain customs must be adhered to, especially in times like these."

Eolyn bit her lip and quelled the rise of bile in her stomach. "Very well. Let us proceed, then, Mage Thelyn. I would get this over with and go to my children."

Nothing could have prepared Eolyn for what awaited them. The furniture had been overturned, adornments shattered. The bed canopy sagged over splintered posts. Blood was spattered everywhere. A putrid mix of sweat and sex, of sulfur and vomit, of fear and decay assaulted Eolyn's senses.

Rhaella's corpse lay upon blood-soaked sheets. Her sternum was torn open; her eyes stared in blank horror. Already flies had found their way into the chamber and buzzed over her body.

Shadows passed before Eolyn's eyes, and she lost her balance.

Thelyn caught her elbow. "My Lady Queen."

"I cannot stay in this place." She wrenched herself away, heart pounding as she stumbled toward the doorway.

"Please, my Lady Queen." Thelyn halted her retreat. "It is only for a little while."

"Enough with your insistence! My magic is spent! I am of no

use to you here."

"If you leave, those outside will take it to mean they are free to enter. We cannot allow that to happen. There is something I must find first."

"Find?"

"Yes. A letter, or so I've been told."

"I don't understand."

"Nor do I. Not entirely."

Eolyn gagged as the stench caught in her throat. Thelyn produced a clean white cloth from his sleeve.

"Please, my Lady Queen, use this."

The silk was scented with mint and sage. Eolyn accepted it and placed it over her mouth and nose.

Thelyn led her to a chair and sat her down. "It is only for a little while, my Lady Queen, until I finish the task appointed to me."

"At least cover the body," she whispered, tears stinging her eyes.

Thelyn nodded and pulled a sheet over Rhaella's remains.

Tying a length of silk over his own mouth and nose, he began a meticulous search of the room. He poked cautiously at fallen objects and discarded robes with his staff, gaze sharp and shoulders tense, as if he half expected a serpent to appear.

His progress proved slow and tedious. Eolyn, unable to take in the sight of Akmael's ruined bedchamber, stared out the windows and at the landscape beyond. Her heart contracted painfully.

Oh, Akmael. Why did the Gods allow it to end like this?

"It seems you and Mage Corey have had an altercation," Thelyn said.

"What?" Eolyn looked at him, perplexed.

Thelyn continued sifting through the debris at his feet. He spoke in casual tones, as if commenting on the weather. "I noticed the flare in your aura when you set eyes on him just now. And Corey carries a curious shadow on his shoulders. If I did not know that man as well as I do, I would say he is struggling under a burden of shame."

Eolyn rolled her eyes. Under any other circumstances, she might have been amused. "Corey is not a man of regrets."

"Perhaps I am overstepping my bounds in saying so, my Lady Queen, but this is not the moment to antagonize Mage Corey."

"You think *I* antagonized *him*?"

"There were many witnesses to the King's final words, but your situation is still precarious, as is that of your children. More so now, with the royal family of Roenfyn ready to assert its claim." Thelyn's emphasis on *royal* was subtle but clear. "Corey holds sway over nearly half the kingdom, and he understands how to coerce the rest."

"You tell me nothing I do not already know, Mage Thelyn."

"I am glad to hear it. Grief can cloud our judgment, but of course, my Lady Queen is not new to tragedy or loss. I trust you will make wise decisions, as you have in the past, in spite of everything that has happened. Ah!" He froze, eyes alight with curiosity. "I believe I have found our prize."

Eolyn followed Thelyn's gaze to the floor. A curious slip of paper was pinned under the base of his staff.

Thelyn wrapped his hand in a length of black silk and bent to retrieve the crumpled sheet.

From his robes, he produced a small bowl carved from graystone, which he placed on a table near the window before setting the piece of paper inside.

"What is that?" Eolyn asked.

Thelyn cast a ward around the note. "A confession, my Lady Queen. A letter written by your own Mariel that describes in detail your infidelities with Lord Borten."

"Infidelities with Borten? Mariel would not have written such lies!"

"Not willingly. Look, my Lady Queen. Do you see the smoke?"

A shadowy wisp rose from the paper, curling back on itself when it hit the ward.

"That is *Ahmad-melan*," Thelyn said.

"Infused into a letter? I didn't know such a thing was possible."

"Only a mage of the highest order can trap a curse of this potency with pen and ink. This is the work of Baedon, a wizard of the old guard, friend and ally to your dead enemy, Tzeremond. He

176

was my tutor once." The thought seemed to amuse Thelyn. "Corey's as well."

"This is what drove Akmael mad," Eolyn realized. *The deepest fears of a king unleashed.* "Where is Mariel? What did Baedon do to her?"

"Mariel is safe, resting under the care of her sister Jacquetta in the residence of High Mage Echior."

"I must go to her as soon as possible. And her torturers?"

"We have not found Baedon. Markl, who delivered Mariel to the old wizard, has a new home in the dungeons of Vortingen."

"Markl? But he was her friend!"

"For some, friendship counts for little when weighed against ambition. Cramon Langerhaans will join the boy soon. Markl named Langerhaans as an accomplice of Baedon. Him and his hapless niece, Rhaella. It turns out your lady-in-waiting knew of this letter and its pending delivery. She had specific instructions regarding to how to respond to the King's fury. I gather she played her part to perfection."

Thelyn's glance strayed toward the bed, his expression one of cold indifference. "Rhaella always was too blatant in her ambitions. I suppose there's a lesson in her fate for all of us."

"No one deserves to die like that."

"You are kind to think so, my Lady Queen."

Eolyn felt as if her mind were in a fog. The horror of all this was simply too deep to grasp.

"We must keep the letter as evidence of Baedon's treasonous intent," Thelyn was saying. "At the same time, we must destroy it."

"Because anyone who reads this letter may also succumb to its spell," Eolyn said. "They will believe Mariel's words and accuse me of treason, and my children of being bastards."

Thelyn smiled. "Corey sometimes despairs of your ability to survive this game, but I have never doubted your grasp of the obvious or your instinct for subtlety. And if I may be so bold, my Lady Queen, you have a talent for keeping your head about you even when the world seems to be falling apart."

Ehekaht, he murmured. *Rehoernem anthae.*

The white fire of Aithne flowed from Thelyn's palm in a thin stream, penetrating the ward and igniting the letter. The paper unfolded like a rose inside a slow purple flame.

Heksue.

Abruptly the fire was extinguished.

Thelyn put the ashes and bits of paper onto a piece of black silk. He folded the cloth carefully while casting another ward.

"There, you see," he said. "The incriminating words are gone, but evidence of Baedon's curse remains."

Eolyn looked up at him, uncertain how to interpret the gift he had just given her.

"Thank you," she said. "Thank you for doing this."

"You owe me no debt of gratitude, my Lady Queen. I consider this a personal favor for an old friend. I will settle accounts with him when the time comes."

"Oh." She understood at once to whom he referred. Would Mage Corey expect something from her in return, or was this an effort to atone for his transgressions?

"I think we have lingered long enough," Thelyn said, offering Eolyn his hand. As she rose, he added, "I found something else that I believe is yours."

Thelyn opened her palm and laid the Silver Web upon it. Eolyn stared at the jewel that had bound her and Akmael since they were children. Its shimmer had dulled, its crystals shied away from the light. Her hands trembled as she closed her fist around the jewel and clutched it to her breast.

No amount of magic will ever bring us together again.

Grief washed over her anew. Tears begged to be released, but Eolyn forced them back, conscious of her place, of the attendants that waited outside, of the new role she must assume for her people.

Wordlessly she hung the silver chain around her neck, letting the amulet come to rest over her heart. With a nod to Thelyn, she continued toward the Council chamber, her spirit cloaked in darkness, her world transformed into night.

Chapter Twenty-Five

Duty

Taesara stood over her brother as he slept. Afternoon light cut through the windows, illuminating his moon-spun hair. It calmed her to see him like this, his withered form covered by soft woolen blankets, his breath steady and deep.

Sisters of the Poor moved about them in quiet murmurs and rustling skirts. They ground fragrant herbs in mortars and heated water over the fire in small pots. They burned sweet incense and prayed beside candles. The quiet rituals made Taesara's heart ache for the home she once knew among them.

The door opened on oiled hinges and the Good Mother appeared, her deeply lined face framed by a charcoal gray veil. Her only vanity was a string of wooden prayer beads that clicked as she walked. The old woman approached the King, laid a spotted hand upon his head, and gave a quiet blessing.

Then she signaled the others to depart. They obeyed with quick and reverent bows. Only when the door closed behind the last of them did the Good Mother address Taesara.

"I hope you are satisfied with the arrangements we have made?"

"I am. Thank you, Good Mother, for allowing some of the sisters to take up residence here. I know this decision was not without risk."

"We could hardly turn you away, though it was impulsive, on your part, to send the Brothers packing without word or warning."

"I assure you my uncle will be informed, and I will see to it he understands."

"I would have thought you'd have sent word to him by now."

"There's been no time."

The Good Mother lifted her brow. "There is always time for that which we deem important."

"I will tell Penamor myself. I need him to understand I made this decision out of love for my brother, nothing more."

"He may see that your motivations are pure, Taesara, but it will anger him for you to have acted on your own."

"All the more reason to delay his knowing."

"Why so much defiance toward your uncle?" The old woman circled the bed and took a place beside Taesara. "Why so much sadness when your daughter has been set free and returned to your family? You should not be brooding over the fate of your brother. Nothing can be done about that now. Thunder has a different destiny in mind for you."

"Destiny, it would seem, is the swiftest path to misery. I lived in happiness and peace among the Sisters. I'd give anything to return."

"Your time with us was a refuge, nothing more. You were always a guest in our halls. You must have known that, deep inside."

Frustration stung Taesara's eyes. "I do not belong with the Sisters. I do not belong in court. Where, then, do I belong?"

"At your daughter's side."

"Eliasara does not know me! And if I am to be honest with myself, I no longer recognize her. It pains me to be around her, Good Mother. She loves the man who humiliated me. She calls him *Father*, even as she looks upon me with suspicious eyes. What kind of family can we be if we share nothing, no history, no memories, no path in this world?"

"Your path will be made by walking it with her."

"Then I would walk with her to my home among the Sisters."

"If the Gods intended you to finish your days as a bride of Thunder, they would not have sent you to the bed of the Mage King. They would not have blessed you with a daughter by his seed. Eliasara is the key to a new future. She can unite our kingdoms and put an end to the misguided ways of Moisehén."

"I daresay you've been sharing wine with Lady Sonia."

The old woman smiled. "Lady Sonia is a wise soul, and a good friend to you."

"That she is." Taesara let go a quiet sigh. "During the years I was gone, my uncle swept away his rivals and claimed everything for his own. Perhaps he did it to keep the peace, but sometimes I wonder to what lengths he would go in his quest for power."

"Speak plainly, child. Our bond is not one for mysteries and riddles."

Taesara nodded to her brother. "Do you think Penamor would have done something like this?"

The Good Mother made the sign of Thunder over her forehead. "You would accuse the Lord Regent of witchcraft?"

"No, not him." Taesara spoke quickly, lest she lose courage before the words formed on her tongue. "I doubt Penamor knows a spell from his backside, but what would keep him from using someone who does?"

"Honor," the Good Mother said. "Respect for the traditions of our people. Your uncle may be a hard man, but he is not without scruples."

"I know my uncle as well as I know my brother. Kahrl was a gentle soul. He would have never led us into battle against an enemy as formidable as Moisehén. He would have let this whole conflict die a quiet death. My uncle, on the other hand, has wanted this war from the day the Mage King cast me out."

"Perhaps that is why the Gods punished your brother and gave Sylus Penamor the throne."

"Punish my brother? Why would the Gods destroy a humble prince and cast their favor on a ruthless lord?"

"Ruthless men are sometimes the better weapon."

Taesara looked at her in surprise. "You are the one who is always saying we must turn from the path of war."

"From the path of *unnecessary* war, my child. This conflict with the followers of Dragon is not of our making. It has been with us since the beginning of time. You and your uncle have been called to a noble cause, a war that could put an end to the line of Mage Kings and to the tradition of magic that taints their people."

"It all sounds glorious, Good Mother, but what if you are wrong? What if Penamor's only cause is the expansion of his own

181

power? He could discard me and my daughter, just as he discarded my brother. After Moisehén is won and the crown is in Penamor's hands, what use will we be to him?"

The Good Mother took Taesara's hands in firmly hers. "As useful as you make yourself, Taesara. Take up the mantle the Gods have placed in your path. Stand firm by your uncle, support his campaign on behalf of your daughter. Do this, and neither he nor the Gods who have appointed him will find reason to discard you."

Despite the Good Mother's insistence that she return to her uncle, Taesara lingered in Merolyn a few days longer. By the time she returned to Adelrod, Penamor and his army had already departed. Taesara was informed that the Lord Regent now marched toward Moisehén in the company of his Galian allies, and with Eliasara in tow.

A strange panic took hold of Taesara at the thought of her daughter alone. She hastened eastward with her escort. Each day they set out well before dawn and traveled as late as summer twilight would allow.

The army had left a large swath of cleared fields and desolated farms in its wake. Moved by the plight of peasants they encountered along the way, Taesara offered them what coin she could, but her small purse proved woefully inadequate and was soon emptied of its meager contents.

At last, one afternoon, they crested a ridge to behold a sea of tents spread over a grassy plain. Clouds blown by gusting winds cast ephemeral shadows over the camp. Bold flags displayed verdant mountains spewing golden fire into a sapphire sea, the colors and sigil of Galia.

Urging her horse forward, Taesara led her company in a wide arc that avoided the Galian tents altogether. They entered the camp under flags of Roenfyn, where they were greeted by trumpet blasts and shouts of welcome.

Penamor emerged from his pavilion, face beaming and arms spread wide. Behind him the war council appeared, grim-faced men who met Taesara's gaze with nods of respect.

Penamor strode forward to greet his niece. Taking firm hold of Taesara's waist, he pulled her from the mount and whirled her around in a dance as improvised as it was vulgar.

"Dead!" Penamor roared, triumphant. "He's dead, my beautiful niece! The Mage King has fallen."

Taesara stopped in her tracks. "What?"

"Killed by those beasts from the Underworld."

"Akmael was slain by a Naether Demon?"

"Gods, Taesara, you look as if you've just lost a lover. Yes, the prince who used you, humiliated you, and sent you away as if you were a common harlot is dead, by the justice of the Gods."

Taesara stared at her uncle in shock.

He was the father of my daughter.

Remorse filled her, a surprising and deep sense of loss. As many fates as she had wished upon the Mage King, never once had she imagined him dead. How could a man so indomitable be gone from this world?

"They say the Witch Queen herself summoned the Naether Demons to kill him," Penamor was saying.

"That makes no sense. Why would she want him dead?"

"Because she's a fool and a wench! She'll be on the pyre within a month, now that she's alone. But not before she sees her bastards' bodies thrown to the wolves and their heads mounted on spikes."

Taesara glanced around, a knot tightening in her chest. "Where is my daughter?"

"In her tent. She's been in a foul mood ever since you left, and she's gotten worse since word arrived of the Mage King's demise. Go see her, Taesara. Someone needs to talk some sense into that girl."

"The customs of Moisehén demand twelve days of mourning," Taesara said. "We must honor this, for Eliasara and her people."

"We are Eliasara's people now, and we will mourn no one. In three days' time, we cross the Furma River and begin our siege of Selkynsen."

"If they mourn their king, they will not have time to prepare."

"Precisely, my dear niece. Moisehén is ours for the taking. Go, find your daughter and bid her to rejoice."

Taesara bowed and took her leave. She walked to Eliasara's quarters in a daze, barely acknowledging the courtiers and soldiers who greeted her along the way.

Inside the tent, Eliasara was flung across the bed, her face buried in a pillow. The maga warrior Ireny sat next to her, stroking the girl's hair and murmuring words of comfort. Upon Taesara's entrance, Ireny stood and bowed.

Taesara gave a quiet signal to Ireny and the servants, and they departed in silence. Then she took a hesitant seat on the bed.

"My beloved daughter," she said quietly. "I am so sorry."

"You are sorry for nothing!" Eliasara cried. "You rejoice just as Penamor does."

"That is not true."

"You have no right to speak to me about this! He meant nothing to you."

He gave me you. Taesara bit her lip, desperately wanting to speak these words, but unable to expose her heart. *That makes him everything.*

"I hate you," Eliasara said. "I hate Penamor. I hate everyone in this forsaken kingdom."

"This kingdom is your inheritance. Your uncle, our Lord Regent, makes a great effort on your behalf. Whether you like him or not, you owe him your respect."

"I wouldn't care if he were emperor of the world! I owe him nothing. I want to go back to my family. I should be with them. I need to be with them now."

"We are your family."

"Stop insulting me!"

The words knifed Taesara. She struggled to steady her voice. "Please, Eliasara. I only try to comfort you. Truly I want what is best for you. I am your mother, after all."

"What sort of mother abandons her daughter when she is just a babe?"

Taesara drew a sharp breath, stunned into momentary silence. When she managed to speak again, her voice was subdued. "Surely you know I had no choice in that."

"There is always a choice! That's what Maga Eolyn says."

"That witch you feel so much fondness for has never been banished by a king. Indeed, it was she who—"

"Stop it! I won't listen to your lies." She sank into renewed sobs. Terrible wails shuddered through her shoulders. "Dead!

Father is dead. And you and Penamor laugh and dance about it. You keep me prisoner here and tell me I must put Maga Eolyn on a pyre, and my brother's and sister's heads on spikes. But I won't do it! I swear to the Gods I won't. I can't wage war against a people who have only ever been kind to me."

"They locked you in a tower," Taesara replied between gritted teeth. "Do you call that kindness?"

"I was not locked up! Father increased my guard when the war ended in Roenfyn. He said until the threat was understood, I had to be kept safe. Now I know what he wanted to protect me from."

A thorn lodged in the pit of Taesara's stomach.

"Before that, I could do anything I wanted," Eliasara continued. "We'd go north for picnics on the river, or to Selkynsen for Summer Solstice. We'd spend winter in East Selen and spring in the highlands of Moehn. Nobody ever said to me 'Lead this army' or 'Put your brother's head on a spike.' Nobody let the servants lace up my dress until I couldn't breathe or told me I had to sit next to some stranger and let him touch me whether I liked it or not."

Taesara's heart stopped cold. "Who has touched you?"

"No one has. And no one will, especially not him. I hate him, too. He's *old*. And ugly."

"Of whom do you speak?"

"The Galian Prince." Eliasara spat. "Penamor says I must be nice to him, but I am not going to be nice to anyone. Not until I am returned to my people."

Taesara rose abruptly and paced the room. Was this what she came back for? To endure her daughter's hatred? To see Eliasara wedded against her will? What could she possibly offer after so many years of silence and separation? What power would she ever have to protect Eliasara from the twisted games of this world?

Taesara paused to meet her daughter's gaze, and saw a poignant reflection of her own youth. Hope, need, and fear wrestled across Eliasara's tear-stained countenance. Taesara had looked to her mother in much the same way on the day they announced her betrothal to the Mage King. She had wanted words of comfort, a kind embrace, steady reassurance that this imposing destiny would be a happy one.

Bear him a son, was all her mother had said, *or you will have no*

185

future.

Drawing a quiet breath, Taesara returned to her daughter's side and set one hand over hers.

"I am glad, Eliasara, that you lived well with your brother and sister, and with your father, during the time you were together. You must guard all those memories like a treasure in your heart, for each happy moment of childhood is a jewel that will never be crafted again. But I cannot let you succumb to the illusion that everything would have remained the same had you stayed in Moisehén. We are bound by our heritage, you, me, your father, and your brother. Whether you like it or not, your blood gives you a superior claim to the throne of Vortingen."

"I don't want the throne of Vortingen."

"It does not matter what you want. This burden was given to you by the Gods, and you have no choice but to accept it. Deep in your heart, you must know this. And your brother knows it too."

Eliasara sank into troubled silence. She studied the space in front of her. "Ireny said the same thing."

"Of course she did. Do you think the magas risked death and exile on a whim? They knew your only chance for survival was with us."

"Everyone is trying to push me into war against my brother, but I love Eoghan! We grew up together. He's always been kind to me."

"You remember Prince Eoghan as kind and loving, but they have trained him to be the Mage King, a killer of men, a destroyer of all rivals."

"He's just a boy."

"On the day his father died, Eoghan became a man. And you, Eliasara, are now a woman. By virtue of your blood, you are your brother's enemy. It is better that you assume that destiny here, among your mother's people and with an army at your command. Had you been in Moisehén the night your father died, nothing could have saved you."

"Don't you dare make such an accusation! Eoghan would never have hurt me. He is not a monster. He's my brother."

"Worse than a monster, he is a king. Before your father's corpse turned cold, you would have perished, misused and murdered by assassins under your brother's command. This family and these people whom you hate so much saved you from that fate. You owe them respect for everything they sacrificed to set you free."

"But I—"

"Listen to me: If you wish to survive, you must move forward and assume the crown that is rightfully yours. Claim Moisehén, Eliasara. Claim it now, or you will have no future."

CHAPTER TWENTY-SIX

Prince of Galia

STARS SPARKLED IN THE FIRMAMENT as Sylus Penamor convened his court to celebrate Taesara's return. Rows of bright torches illuminated fresh-hewn tables laden with spiced meats and savory vegetables. Wine and laughter flowed freely; bawdy jokes and boasts of a victory not yet won saturated the air. Girls with inviting smiles and shrewd eyes crowded in shadowy corners, ready to offer their wares to the man with the fattest purse.

Taesara had thought to shield her daughter from such lewd revelry, but this was war in all its grotesque splendor. The sooner Eliasara understood the nature of the men who served her, the better.

A sound of horns followed by the beat of drums hushed the festive atmosphere. Smiles faded beneath wary glances. Men set down their wine. Hands drifted to hilts of knives and swords.

Undaunted by the tension, Penamor stood and spread his arms to welcome an entourage of bright flags and rhythmic movement. The warriors of Galia had arrived.

Eliasara took Taesara's hand in a tight grip.

"That's him," the girl whispered. "That's the Prince of Galia."

Taesara followed her daughter's gaze to a richly dressed man who walked amid drummers and dancers. His bearing was proud, his expression warm and jovial. His fluid gait marked the rhythm of the drums.

He is neither old nor ugly, Taesara observed with surprise.

Unless, of course, she were to count herself as old. The Galian Prince could not have been more than a few years her senior. He had a broad face with dark eyes and skin the color of tilled earth. Sapphire robes cloaked his massive frame, raw somehow beneath the soft fabric. The image of him naked, all sinew and hard muscle, invaded Taesara's thoughts. A flush rose to her cheeks, and she looked away, embarrassed.

Penamor and the prince embraced each other like brothers.

Fighting her own reluctance, Taesara bade her daughter to rise. "Come, Eliasara. We must follow your uncle's example and greet our guest."

Eliasara dragged behind her mother.

Penamor received their approach with a broad smile. "Prince Savegre, you remember my great-niece, Eliasara."

Protocol demanded that Eliasara step forward, but she remained, sullen, at her mother's side.

A smile illuminated the prince's dark face. He knelt before the princess.

"You are beautiful even when you are sad." Savegre's accent was rich and deep, the consonants soft, yet each syllable emphatic.

Tears slipped from Eliasara's eyes.

"Eliasara." Taesara regretted the cruelty of her rebuke, but there was nothing to be done for it. Crying was unacceptable when greeting a guest.

"No." Savegre touched the girl's cheek. "You must not stop this water. This water feeds the fire of life."

He drew his hand back, a single tear poised on his finger. The courtiers gasped as fire flared from the water and coalesced into a sphere of smoky crystal.

"My gift to you, Princess Eliasara," Savegre said, "to help you in your time of mourning."

Wonder washed away Eliasara's sorrow. She touched the crystal, and then took it into her hands. "What is it?"

"A window to help you see the ones you love."

"I can see them, even if they are far away?"

Savegre nodded.

"Even if they are dead?"

"Sometimes, but you must be careful and use this with an open heart. You may not always like what you see."

"How does it work?"

189

"Eliasara." Taesara did not hide her consternation. "You cannot accept this gift."

"Why not?"

"It is an object of magic."

"It is harmless, I assure you," Savegre said. "A child's toy."

"With all due respect, Prince Savegre, these devices may be harmless in the eyes of your people, but they were rejected by our ancestors long ago, a noble tradition that we strive to uphold."

Savegre rose to his full and imposing height. He set his hands upon his belt, an iridescent mix of green and gold, and regarded her with narrowed eyes.

Taesara did not waver under his inspection.

Penamor cleared his throat. "Prince Savegre, this is Eliasara's mother, Taesara, Princess of Roenfyn and Queen of Moisehén."

"This much I have deduced," Savegre said.

"You must have patience with her. She has spent years among the Sisters of the Poor and emerged quite…rigid in her ways."

Savegre laughed and leaned forward, catching Taesara's hand in his. He kissed her fingers, warm lips lingering upon cool skin. "This is a great honor for me, Taesara of Roenfyn. Our people have heard many stories of your generosity and good will."

Flustered, Taesara withdrew from his touch. "And my people have heard many stories of your magic and military prowess. We are most grateful that you have joined us to defend my daughter's cause, yet I pray you do not misinterpret our intentions. We need your help against the Witch Queen, but we cannot be asked to adopt your ways and beliefs."

"Of course." Savegre nodded in deference and extended a hand toward the crystal sphere that Eliasara held. "Forgive me, Princess, but we must respect the wishes of your mother."

Eliasara stepped away and gave her mother a pleading look. "Please, Mother. Let me keep it. I want to see Father."

Penamor rolled his eyes.

"Beloved daughter," Taesara said, "our ancestors teach us that magic is never what it appears to be. Spells we expect to make us happy bring sadness; curses intended to bring ruin to our enemies grant them triumph. So it is with this device. You believe seeing your father inside that sphere will make you happy, but you will

190

soon find otherwise."

"I did not say it would make me happy."

"Yet you believe it will."

Eliasara's lower lip pushed out in a frown. She stared into the misty glass.

"There is a better way to see your father," Taesara insisted.

"What way?"

"You can tell me about him."

"Tell you?"

"Yes, as many stories as you like, whenever you like."

In truth, Taesara did not know whether she could bear hearing happy tales of Eliasara's childhood with the Mage King and his harlot. But if Eliasara did not share this with her mother, to whom else could she turn?

"Every time you speak of your father," Taesara continued, "you will see him in your heart. This is the way we are meant to keep our loved ones close when they have passed into the next world; this is the gift given to us by the Gods of Thunder."

Eliasara's doubtful frown persisted, but she surrendered the smoky crystal to Prince Savegre.

"We will find another gift worthy of the Princess," he said.

The crystal vanished inside Savegre's grasp. In its place a pendant appeared, a dragon wrought in silver with great wings and fierce amber eyes, suspended on a purple ribbon.

"This, I think, is more suitable?"

He directed the question to Taesara, who found herself at a loss for words. She did not approve of any object created through magic, and gifts from this man seemed particularly suspect.

"With all due respect, Prince Savegre, I think it would be better not to—"

"The gift is lovely." Penamor snatched the pendant and proceeded to tie it around Eliasara's throat, his movements so harsh Taesara feared he might choke the girl. "The sigil of Eliasara's house and the symbol of her heritage. This is a jewel that will carry you to victory, Princess. Tell our guest you are grateful."

Eliasara looked at the floor as she spoke. "I am most grateful, Prince Savegre."

Savegre nodded and turned to his attendants. At a snap of his

191

fingers, a dark-skinned girl appeared. Head bowed, she knelt before Taesara and proffered a bolt of fabric, a stunning sheer silk woven in multiple shades of blue and silver.

"I was told the Queen of Moisehén has eyes the color of the sunlit sea," Savegre said. "I think this is a good match."

Entranced, Taesara laid her hand upon the fabric, finding it soft and inviting to the touch. The Good Mother's words echoed through her thoughts.

The temptation of magic begins with a whisper.

Yet this was not magic, it was merely a bolt of fabric, much like any she had seen from the exotic shores of Antaria or the distant realm of the Syrnte. Surely there would be no harm in accepting it?

"My Lady Queen is pleased?" Savegre asked.

Taesara met his gaze. She felt a pause in her heart; a keen, sunlit awareness of *him*.

"This is a most generous gift, Prince Savegre," she murmured. "Thank you."

CHAPTER TWENTY-SEVEN

Queen of Moisehén

THE BREATH OF DRAGON spread in tongues of turquoise and gold, igniting the wood in a pulsating orange glow. Aromas of charred beech, alder, and ash mingled in the billowing smoke. Woven among them was the stench of seared flesh and singed hair. Eyes, hands, muscle, bone, and heart all converted to black dust floating on the wind. His body, the landscape of their love, so familiar it had become a part of Eolyn's own, was surrendered to the unrelenting will of the Gods.

Heat scalded Eolyn's face and burned her eyes. Emptiness ruled her heart and drew her inexorably toward the flames. All she desired was to become one with Akmael and let the fury of Dragon consume her pain; to leave this world and return to the haven of their youth, forgetting all that was left behind.

"My Lady Queen?" Mage Echior touched her elbow.

Eolyn blinked, startled back into the present moment. The memory of Akmael's pyre vanished, replaced by the spacious room that was the meeting place of his—no, *her* Council.

A humid breeze filtered through the windows, stirring up the fragrance of freshly laid rushes. Light cut across the long oak table. With each passing cloud, the illumination faded and then intensified.

Members of the Council watched her, their expressions expectant. She glanced down at the three sheets of paper they had laid in front of her. Each warrant carried a single name.

Markl.

Langerhaans.

Baedon.

Eolyn rose abruptly, chair scraping against stone.

Mages and noblemen hastened to follow suit. They stood in silence while she paced a small circle. After several heartbeats, she paused and rested her hands on the back of her chair. "This meeting is adjourned."

Voices clamored in protest.

But my Lady Queen,

We need a decision.

— urgent matters —

— we cannot delay —

"I said you are dismissed!" Her reprimand silenced them. "No one understands better than I the immediacy of the threat we face. But every life in this kingdom is sacred, and the decision to end even one of those lives must be met with due deliberation."

High Mage Thelyn cleared his throat. "The Council has deliberated, my Lady Queen. Long hours, already."

"And I have heard your recommendations. Now I bid you to leave so that I may consider them. You will know my decision in due time."

Tense silence followed. Thelyn kept his discerning gaze fixed upon Eolyn while the other men shifted on their feet, exchanging looks of consternation. Then with a brief bow, the High Mage departed, an example reluctantly followed by everyone else.

Everyone save Mage Corey.

"My Lady Queen," Corey said as the tide of movement flowed around him. "May I have a word in private?"

Eolyn would have sent him away were it not for Thelyn, who paused in the doorway to look back at them. Something in his expression made her hesitate. A warning, perhaps. Or a plea.

She nodded to Corey and signaled the guards and servants to leave. As soon as the doors closed behind them, Corey invoked a sound ward.

"With all due respect, Eolyn, you are being a fool."

"Don't start with me, Corey."

"Those men must die."

"I am a maga, not a murderer."

"This is not murder. This is execution, on indisputable grounds of treason."

"I do not want to begin this my son's reign with blood on my hands."

"I hardly see how you have a choice."

"Magas always have a choice. Magas, and more so queens."

"You are neither maga nor queen now. You are a King of Moisehén. You must act the part or those vultures will tear you to shreds. You know the malicious rumors spreading through these halls: that you summoned the Naether Demons; that you desired the King slain; that you reanimated his corpse with dark magic in order to secure your power."

"*Why?*" Rage broke through her reserve. "Why do they say these things, when I have always been a good and loyal queen, attentive to my subjects, obedient to my husband? For years Akmael and I guided this kingdom in harmony. We gave them peace and prosperity unlike anything seen since the reign of Urien. I *loved* Akmael. I gave up everything to be with him, and now they say I wanted him dead? So I could bear this curse they call a crown?"

Corey softened his tone. "They say these things because they fear you. You are a maga. Worse, a commoner who has risen to unprecedented power. Many among the noble families of Moisehén need no other reason to despise you."

"If I turn away from blood and vengeance, I can show them they have nothing to fear."

"A king cannot fail in the delivery of justice."

"What of the mercy Akmael showed when he received the Crown of his father? He spared Borten even though Kedehen fell under the man's spear. He spared me, when by law I should have burned. Even you were spared, Corey, in spite of your treachery."

"Akmael was a prince secure in his claim to the throne. And he had much to gain from granting each of us our lives. What would you gain, Eolyn, from sparing these men?"

"It's not about gain. What is the purpose in killing them now? Baedon is old and withered." They had found the ancient wizard in one of the castle corridors, injured and disoriented, babbling his guilt and betraying accomplices. "Weary and repentant. You said so yourself."

"Baedon repents because he managed to kill the King instead

195

of you. He had no idea what he would unleash by breaking the magic that bound you to Akmael. Had he foreseen this, I assure you he would have found another way to achieve his ends."

"Still, he is near enough to death without me pushing him over the edge. And Markl! Gods, Corey. I watched him grow up. In so many ways, he is still a boy."

"Markl delivered Mariel to her torturers. He betrayed the man who raised him as his own son. He sought to have you executed and your children banished. If he is old enough to commit these crimes, he is old enough to assume the consequences."

Eolyn withdrew, seeking refuge from Corey's unyielding logic. Her feet came to a halt at one of the southern windows. Below, the city bustled with activity, and the Furma sparkled under the midday sun. A blue-green smudge on the southern horizon marked the rise of the Taeschel Mountains, the border of her home in Moehn.

The world was full of life, sound, and movement, its pulse unabated by the absence of her King. Only she felt frozen in the midst of an indecipherable maze of choices, unable to move forward from the moment Akmael left, incapable of comprehending her place without him.

"This was not what I was meant to be," she murmured. "I intended to bring magic back into this world, magic and joy and life. Now they give me the Crown and ask me to kill and kill and kill again. I cannot do it, Corey. I will not."

She heard the rustle of robes at his approach. "They did not give you the crown, Eolyn. That was Akmael's choice, a choice he made because he trusted you to see his will done."

A shiver ran through her shoulders.

Find them, Akmael had said. *Eliminate them.*

"I should never have come here," she murmured. "I should have stayed where I belonged in Moehn."

Corey drew a quiet breath and shook his head. "We are none of us the mages we had hoped to be."

She looked at him, startled by the confession. "What sort of mage did you hope to be?"

He returned her gaze, his eyes twin reflections of an ever-changing yet constantly familiar spirit. "A mage of East Selen, of course. Not the place, mind you. The people. The forest-bound

196

community that I knew as a boy. But like you, I saw my childhood consumed in flames. Like you, I was spared by a king and brought to this city half prisoner, half guest, to learn their games of intrigue and power."

"A game you play very well."

"I play to survive. This is the talent the Gods gave me when Briana of East Selen took my hand and pulled me out of the fire. I make use of their gift not so much because I enjoy it, but because part of me still believes our efforts somehow serve a larger purpose. Even if the shape and meaning of that purpose continues to elude me."

Tightness invaded Eolyn's belly. She bit her lip and looked away. "I don't know why I still listen to you."

"You listen because I speak the truth."

"You always betray the ones closest to you."

"When have I betrayed you?"

"Most recently? The night the Naether Demons attacked."

"That was not betrayal."

"For the love of the Gods, Corey!"

"I wanted to warn you, Eolyn, but to do so would have destroyed the illusion."

"That was no illusion."

"Eolyn—"

"I would have handed over my life freely! I would have surrendered all that I am to those beasts had I known it would save our people. Why did you not trust me enough to tell me the risk we were taking?"

"I had no intention of losing you!"

Eolyn took a step back, thrown off guard by the intensity of his response.

Uncertainty invaded Corey's expression. He frowned and averted his gaze.

"I am not ungrateful for what you did," she said quietly. "I owe you the lives of my children, and of everyone else who survived that night. But I..."

Her chest tightened, cutting short her breath. Her hand went to the Silver Web that hung at her throat.

I need to know if I can trust you.

Turning her back on Corey, Eolyn went to the table and laid her hand on the death warrants. "Signing these will change little. Those who wish to see me destroyed will not be dissuaded from their hatred."

"The message sent by these executions will be understood." Corey moved to join her. "And other actions can be taken to quell any lingering argument."

"There have been no other actions discussed by the Council."

"Not everything is under the purview of the Council. Baedon, Langerhaans, and Markl are but three connections in a web of intrigue that may stretch halfway across the kingdom. We cannot hope to bring all the players to trial and execution; indeed it would be counterproductive to do so. But we can strike in subtle and strategic ways. We can give them pause before they dare oppose us again."

"What are you proposing, Corey? Burn a few villages? Massacre families in my name?"

"No." Amusement colored his tone. "Though I admit the thought is tempting. It would be a sweet vengeance. But you know me, Eolyn. I have long preferred quiet actions and words of weight. I merely intend to make it clear to all parties that loyalty to you is in their own best interests."

Her heart slowed a beat. "Akmael would have never condoned—"

"Akmael learned to rule from his father. Few understand better than you to what lengths Kedehen went to secure his throne. His son would have done no differently — indeed, *did* no differently — when the need arose."

Eolyn closed her eyes, a thin defense against this harsh truth. "Do you never grow weary of the game, Corey?"

"I don't allow myself to grow weary. Nor should you, especially not now. Weariness is a sure path to destruction." Corey stepped close, his voice low and earnest. "One way or another, I intend to secure this kingdom for you and for your children. But my task will be made much easier if you grant me the heads of those three traitors."

"Why do you do this?" She met his gaze, wary of the answer. "Why would you defend me and my own against all of them?"

Surprise crossed his face. Then he smiled and shook his head. "You know why, Eolyn. I told you why years ago. You give me hope. And hope is something very much worth defending, don't you think?"

CHAPTER TWENTY-EIGHT

War Dance

TAESARA STEPPED OUT OF HER TENT, a soft woolen shawl draped around her shoulders, her breath a faint cloud upon warm lips. Drums sounded over the Galian camp, a deep and haunting rhythm that echoed the pulse of the earth under the midnight moon.

Guards shifted, ready for her command. The maga warrior Ireny stood among them. Their uneasy stance was but a small reflection of the skittish mood that had overtaken her uncle's army. Taesara had yet to understand how the warriors of Galia and Roenfyn would ever cooperate with each other on the battlefield. Of course, that was Penamor's problem to solve.

Though if he did not solve it, she and her daughter would suffer the consequences.

"As you were," Taesara said to her men-at-arms. "I only stepped outside to hear the music."

"With all due respect, my Lady Queen," one of them said. "That is not music."

Yet the melody was pleasing to Taesara's ear. It brought back memories of the days when Mage Corey's musicians came from faraway lands to entertain at King Akmael's court.

In recent days, during their tedious advance toward Moisehén, Taesara had learned that music came as naturally to Galians as breathing. They sang as they marched and chanted when they set up tents. Even their strange language was punctuated with rhythm and pitch.

At sunset, while the men of Roenfyn settled into drinks, gambling, and the weary company of ragged whores, the Galian warriors gathered inside a circle of fire and danced under star-filled heavens. Savegre insisted this state of constant celebration pleased their Gods.

A movement at Taesara's side distracted her. She looked down to see her daughter. "Why do you not sleep?"

Eliasara stiffened. "Why don't you?"

Taesara couldn't help but smile. She bent to kiss her daughter's hair. "Do you like their music?"

"I don't know," Eliasara admitted. "It's so different from anything I've heard, and yet it reminds me of home."

Home. The word pierced Taesara every time Eliasara used it. She wondered if the princess would ever consider being with her mother *home.*

"We should go watch," Eliasara said. "Prince Savegre has invited us, after all."

"I thought you did not like the Galian Prince."

"I don't. But I find their music intriguing. I want to see them dance."

Taesara contemplated her young daughter's face, lovely and pale under the light of the moon, eyes glinting with a now-familiar mix of need and defiance.

"If my daughter, Princess of Roenfyn and Heiress to the Throne of Moisehén, wants to see the Galian wizards dance," she said, "then we shall see them dance."

Taesara had their horses readied, and they departed in the company of her guards. Stars shone silent overhead. The song of crickets and frogs filled the shadows. The horses exchanged quiet, playful snorts as they approached the line of torches that marked the border between the two encampments, their slow plod matching the careful pace of deeper drums. Taesara thought it curious that as Roenfyn's men grew wary under the shadow of Galia, their beasts of burden had become ever more at ease.

Only when she heard the cautionary challenge of Galian guards did Taesara experience a sudden surge of doubt. She reined in her steed and lifted a hand to halt her escort.

From their position, she could see the central fire towering over the Galian camp, like an ancient fir set to flame. A dense crowd of warriors surrounded it, brandishing weapons and fists.

Feet pounded the ground. Cries pierced the night.

What was I thinking?

"You said something, my Lady Queen?"

Taesara turned to her captain, who watched her with an expectant gaze.

"I must have misunderstood Prince Savegre's invitation," she said. "This is obviously a ceremony in which we have no place. Let us return the pavilion now."

"But Mother—"

"The decision is made, Eliasara. I will speak with Savegre on the morrow to arrange a more appropriate hour for our visit."

Just as she turned to depart, a rush of shadows closed in around them. Taesara let go a startled cry. Galian guards caught her horse's bridle and separated Queen from daughter. In a heartbeat, they had surrounded Taesara's guard. Horses reared and swords were unsheathed, but the blades tumbled from her men's grasp in flashes of blinding light.

When Taesara's vision cleared, her captain's face was transformed into a mask of terror. He clutched at his sword arm, gloved fist smoking against his chest.

"They burned my blade!" he cried. "Set it on fire inside my grasp."

Taesara subdued her horror and hardened her gaze. "You should not have drawn your weapon, Sir Bevel. You or any of your men."

"But my Lady Queen—"

"The Galians are our friends, guests of our King and Regent."

Bevel set his jaw and lowered his gaze.

Taesara turned to the warriors that surrounded them. "Who here is your captain? I would speak with Prince Savegre."

Bodies shifted. A path opened, and a tall, aged man with angular features appeared. He bowed in respect.

Taesara recognized those ferret-like eyes. This person accompanied Prince Savegre at all times. He was said to be Savegre's closest friend, his most trusted advisor. For what seemed an eternal moment, his name escaped her memory. Then it returned in a quiet breath, like the moon revealed by a passing cloud.

"Urales," Taesara said. "Lord Urales, please inform Prince

202

Savegre that my daughter and I have decided to accept his invitation. We would be most pleased if he were to receive us into his presence, though we will understand, of course, if the hour has grown too late."

A smile touched Urales's thin lips. "My Lady Queen, time has no meaning for a wizard of Galia. Our Prince expects you, now and always. Please, follow me."

They were taken to a long table set on a terrace high above the sea of movement. Below them, a wide circle of torches illuminated a writhing mass of half-naked bodies. Drummers beat upon their instruments. Onlookers chanted over drinks. The place smelled of sweat and flesh and something deeper, feral and dangerous.

Five small bonfires had been set around the tallest blaze at the center, where Taesara caught sight of Prince Savegre. His muscular torso gleamed in the light of the flames. He stretched his arms toward the fire, exuding an aura of indomitable magic, as if he held power over the towering flames. Every chant uttered by Savegre was taken up by his people, repeated, varied, broken into pieces and then reassembled to give birth to new melodies while they danced.

Trepidation crept into Taesara's veins. More than a dance, she realized, this was a drill. Aggression marked every graceful movement. Men and women challenged each other, advancing and retreating. Their wooden staves met in a staccato of blows. Warriors leapt into the air and spun so fast their bodies became a blur, yet they landed in perfect balance. Despite the lavish moves, every pause was fully grounded, every focus absolute. When Savegre cut short his song and joined the fight, the extraordinary skill of the other warriors paled under his mastery.

No army could hold its own against such fierce solidarity. If they should ever turn against Roenfyn...

She glanced at her daughter. Eliasara stared at the flames, mesmerized by the Galian ritual.

We are all brought under his spell.

A servant showed them their seats. Wine was poured and offered to Taesara. She accepted the cup with a slight tremor in her hands. Closing her eyes, she sipped at her drink and tried to shut out the noise and rhythm, the smell of heated flesh. But the drums of Galia would not be stilled. Their devious rhythm crept into her pulse. The scent of blood and desire invaded her nostrils. The taste of *him* blossomed upon her tongue.

Unsettled, Taesara rose. The cup slipped from her hands, spilling wine in all directions. One of the servants came running with a cloth. The dark-haired girl knelt and wiped furiously at the blood-red stain that spread over Taesara's gown.

"I am so sorry, my Lady Queen," she said. "Please forgive."

Savegre's angry baritone cut between them. "Nyella!"

The girl glanced up, startled. She scuttled backwards and prostrated herself on the floor.

Taesara's eyes met Savegre's before drifting inadvertently to his bare chest. Fighting the sting of tears, she looked away. The wine had left an ugly mark. An entire panel of the skirt would need to be replaced. Yet the true stain had penetrated much deeper than her pastel brocade. The real blight had taken root inside her soul. In that moment, Taesara understood, with grim finality, that no amount of penance would ever make this shadow go away.

She swallowed, but her throat was dry. "Prince Savegre, the girl is not to blame. I am weary, and my cup slipped from my grasp. I fear I have insulted this ceremony with my clumsiness. Thank you for having us. My daughter and I will be on our way."

"On your way?" He spread his broad hands in a supplicating gesture. Servants appeared to wipe his torso clean and cover him with a fresh robe. "But you have just arrived!"

"We arrived late, my Prince." She stumbled over her words, feeling short of breath and dizzy. "I must think of my daughter—"

"But I want to stay, Mother." Eliasara's eyes were bright and pleading. "Just a little longer, please? I want to learn the Galian dance."

"This is not a dance that can be learned in one night, Princess." Savegre bent to meet her gaze and pointed to the fires below. "Those soldiers began studying *Kel'Meynú* when they were little children. By the time they were your age, most had already mastered the heart of fire."

"But I can learn a little can't I? I am not so prideful that I would think to master it, but I can learn a little."

Savegre straightened and studied her with narrowed eyes. He clapped his hands. "Nyella."

204

The servant rose to her feet.

"Take the Princess and show her what you know of the dance."

Nyella was of a similar height to Eliasara, though more muscular in build. With a broad smile and quick bow, she took Eliasara's hand.

"Prince Savegre, I must object," Taesara said.

The girls paused in their retreat.

"To this you will not object," Savegre replied. "The Princess will learn the Galian dance while I show my Lady Queen Galian hospitality."

"With all due respect, Prince Savegre, I cannot allow my daughter to engage in any activity associated with magic."

"No harm will come to the Princess. On that you have my word."

The word of a wizard is but false play.

As if sensing her doubt, Savegre stepped close, his rich aroma inspiring images of warm summer nights. "I would share the cup of truth with my allies from Roenfyn, but I have seen that truth is a bitter brew for you and your people."

Taesara bristled. "You know nothing of me or my people."

"I did not bring my army here to fight for a deceitful regent and an evasive queen. If you wish to ensure Galia's support in securing your daughter's future, then you will stay and we will speak."

All movement and laughter at the table halted. The air became heavy with expectation.

Ireny stepped forward. "My Lady Queen, I will accompany the Princess and answer for her safety."

Eliasara cast a hopeful glance from Ireny to Taesara. "There, you see, Mother? Please let us go. It's only for a little while."

Taesara clenched her jaw, uncertain what troubled her about the sight of these three young women and the simple desire that united them.

It is only a dance.

"Go," she said quietly, "but you must return the moment I call for you."

Eliasara and her new companion ran off, Ireny close behind.

Taesara watched them go, heart battling the onslaught of fear and uncertainty.

She realized the rest of her guard had drifted away. She caught sight of them at the edge of the dance. Some sang their own clumsy songs, others drank with increasing abandon. Women of Galia, sleek warriors with cat-like gazes, refilled their cups and invited their embrace.

"I must call my men back to order," she said.

"Them?" Savegre pointed toward the revelers with his chin. "Let them enjoy. Soon many will die for your daughter, will they not? We will give them this night, with its Galian wine and Galian pleasures, that they may remember us in the land of the Gods."

"I cannot allow it."

"This is my camp, not yours."

Savegre gestured toward her seat.

Reluctantly, she accepted.

Platters of food were set before them. Prince Savegre devoured the savory fare with passion, tearing meat from bone, sinking his teeth into fleshy fruits, washing everything down with generous gulps of wine.

Taesara was offered whatever she desired. Under Savegre's insistence she did her best to eat, but her appetite had fled and she was soon reduced to picking at her food.

Savegre did not speak with her as promised, but instead bantered with his courtiers in the strange tongue of Galia. His every declaration was met with ribald laughter and bold responses, their exchange of taunts not unlike the dance below, rhythmic in nature, light-hearted yet undercut by an element of challenge.

They spar even with their words, and respect each other all the more for it.

Taesara let her attention drift from the unintelligible jokes. She searched for her daughter in the crowd below. Eliasara bounced on her feet at the edge of the dance. Laughter bubbled from the princess's lips as she and Ireny tried to imitate Nyella's graceful and strong moves. Warmth blossomed in Taesara's heart at the sight of their nascent friendship.

"Why does your uncle want me to marry that little girl?" Savegre's challenge cut through the fleeting sense of peace.

"You find my daughter unworthy?"

"Not unworthy. Young."

"I assure you, the Lord Regent means no insult. The value of Eliasara's inheritance is undisputed. And it is customary, among our people, for girls to be betrothed before they flower."

"True men do not take children into their bed."

"The consummation of a marriage does not always happen at the time the contract is signed."

"Yet this is what many expect. Is that not so?"

Taesara stiffened and glanced away. "It is the husband's right. More often than not, undertaking the act on the wedding night serves both houses. Once the marriage is consummated, there is little risk of breaking the arrangement."

"Your marriage to the Mage King was consummated, no? Yet here you are, and he with another bride."

"He rules a different land, with different customs."

"A true man does not bring little girls into his bed. A true man requires a woman, one whose beauty is shaped not by youth but by the experience of her years."

The sound of laughter and music receded beneath the intensity of Savegre's presence. Taesara met his gaze. Her voice faded to a whisper. "You speak as if you know such a woman."

Savegre nodded toward where her daughter played. "Such a woman gave me Nyella."

"Nyella is your *daughter*?"

"Do you not see the likeness?" He struck a fist on his chest, his grin pleasing and wide. "She is beautiful and strong, like me."

"Yet you let her serve at the table, clean up our messes, even prostrate herself in front of you."

"If she is to rule, she must first serve. So it has been with all the kings and queens of Galia."

"What about her mother? Where is she?"

"She passed from this world on the day Nyella was born."

"Oh." Taesara shifted uncomfortably. "I am sorry. I did not know."

"Why do you know so little?" There was no rebuke in his voice, only puzzlement.

"I beg your pardon?"

"Ten years you served among your Sisters, now you have

returned to be queen. You should know every truth within your reach."

"Then tell me the truth of why you are here. My daughter's hand would give you sovereignty over three kingdoms. If you do not want her, then why bother to help us?"

Savegre sat back in his chair, satisfaction filling his face. "That is the Galian way. You have a doubt. You ask a question. I honor your courage with the truth. I come because the one you call Witch Queen has something that belongs to us."

"What thing?"

Savegre placed a hand on Taesara's shoulder as he refilled their wine. Taesara quelled the impulse to shrink from his touch.

"You are not as your uncle, Queen Taesara," he said. "You are made of waters from a different spring."

"Give me your answer."

"Maga Eolyn wields a Galian instrument, a sorcerer's weapon."

"Weapon?" Threads of memory coalesced in Taesara's mind. "You mean her brother's sword?"

"Not her brother's. Never his."

"But she has had that blade for years. Why would you seek it out now, in this fashion? Why did you not go to her before?"

Amusement flickered behind Savegre's eyes. He picked up his wine and saluted her. "I begin to understand, Queen Taesara. You know much, yet you do you not wish your knowledge to be recognized. Is this how the women of your kingdom survive, by hiding what they see?"

"Answer my question, Prince Savegre."

Savegre grinned and beckoned her to draw close. Against her better judgment, she obeyed. His palm felt rough against her cheek. Her skin tingled as the tips of his fingers came to rest at the nape of her neck. His breath fell warm upon her ear, and for what seemed an eternity, he held her like this, until a wave of subtle pleasure passed down her spine.

The tension in Taesara's muscles released. She closed her eyes and saw the restless mountains of Galia, their verdant forests, their hearts of fire. Her lips parted, and she drew a quiet breath.

"I will honor you with the truth, Taesara," Savegre murmured. "But not on this night."

CHAPTER TWENTY-NINE

Fury

GHEMENA'S FEET POUNDED into the solid earth. Rage fueled her speed. Hot wind blew at her back. Cold memory nipped at her heels. Though the landscape grew darker as she fled, she did not slow until her lungs threatened to burst and tears of anger blurred her vision.

"Curse them all!" she cried and sent an orange flame into a nearby tree. Leaves burst into fire, twigs curled in charred crisps. Ghemena fell to her knees before the blazing pyre, face bathed in its purifying heat.

Nicola came up breathless behind her. "Gods, Ghemena. What has gotten into you?"

"Did you not see them? Did you not see him casting his spell on her?"

"That?" Nicola nodded toward the Galian encampment from which they had come and shrugged. "He'll have little effect, I can assure you. Taesara's as cold a maid as I've ever seen. Truth be told, I rather hope he melts that crust of ice. Perhaps some of his fire will warm her to this war."

"Listen to you! It's no wonder our enslavement to men is without end. The Mage King was eliminated in one stroke, yet before we can celebrate his demise that Galian Prince appears. And Taesara already a fool trapped inside his grasp. We have traded one tyrant for another."

Nicola frowned. "I'm not sure I agree, Ghemena. Ireny seems quite taken by the Galians, by their women warriors and their knowledge of Primitive Magic. I'm inclined to like them, too. The

Galians have shown nothing but respect for us since we arrived. Certainly we are more at home among them than with the people of Roenfyn, don't you think?"

"I feel at home among no one." Ghemena snatched up a rock and threw it at the burning tree. "We are about to lose everything we have fought for. Taesara will become the puppet of that wizard, just as Eolyn became the Mage King's."

"I love you, Ghemena, but you are always inclined to see the worst of any situation, especially when it comes to men. Think about what you are saying. Can you really imagine Taesara seduced by a Galian wizard? There may be a nascent attraction, but that means little. Taesara is deeply entrenched in her mistrust of all practitioners. She is wary enough of you, the woman who delivered her daughter to safety. Why would she be at all inclined to listen to him, when he's done nothing to prove his loyalty to her interests?"

"Because women are fools when it comes to men." Ghemena spat. "We cannot risk losing this struggle to the ambitions of a Galian wizard. We must depart for the Paramen Mountains. Tonight. We must convince Queen Khelia to support our cause."

"Penamor has not given us leave to act as his ambassadors, and Taesara wants no more practitioners joining this war."

"This is not their war! It is ours. The Mountain Queen can help us win against Moisehén, and once victory is achieved, she can ensure the Galians return home."

Nicola let go a quiet sigh. "Very well, Ghemena. You are still our captain. Certainly there can be little to lose by asking her."

Ghemena gave a curt nod and started back toward their camp. Nicola hastened to match her purposeful stride.

"You will go with me," Ghemena said. "Ireny stays here, to make sure nothing disastrous happens between Taesara and the Galian wizard while we're gone."

"What would you have her do? Hide every night under Taesara's bed? Castrate the Galian Prince if he gets too close?"

"Ireny can seduce Taesara herself, for all I care. Whatever it takes to keep Savegre away from our queen. I will not have all our plans ruined by another wizard."

Chapter Thirty

Shadows

Jacquetta flung herself into Eolyn's arms. Eolyn enveloped her beloved student in a tight embrace. Tears of gratitude stung her eyes as she inhaled Jacquetta's aroma of warm hearths and evening spice. The Gods had taken much the night of the Naether Demons' attack, but at least they had allowed her sisters in magic to survive.

Jacquetta pulled away, smiling. "They said you would come. I did not believe it, with war at hand and a crown on your head. Our simple affairs are hardly worthy of your attention now."

Eolyn touched the girl's cheek with affection. "Nothing is more worthy of my attention than my sisters in magic."

Jacquetta slipped her arm into Eolyn's and guided her down the narrow entry hall. The guards moved to follow, but Eolyn signaled them to remain. She did not want the peace of Echior's residence disturbed by their heavy gait and hissing metal.

"I see Mage Echior has taken good care of you," Eolyn said.

"He has been most kind through this entire ordeal. My magic was released the moment your orders were delivered."

"And Mariel?"

"Recovering. Mage Echior insists we must have patience, but I am worried. Shadows have penetrated her aura. And she is visited by terrible visions."

"Dreams?"

"No, true visions. She saw the Naether Demons when they attacked; cried out in her sleep that they were swarming the castle. We thought she had gone mad under the effects of *Ahmad-melan*, but then we heard the alarms from the fortress. Mage Corey departed at once. He told us to alert everyone in the Mages' Quarter, which we did, although we weren't fast enough. Not to prevent all of this. Oh, Maga Eolyn! So many lives lost, and our beloved King taken from us as well."

"We did all that we could, Jacquetta."

"It was not enough. And Lord Borten? How is he?"

"Recovering, as well. I have sent for his wife, Lady Vinelia, so that she might attend to him and assist with other matters here in the city."

"I look forward to seeing her. It will be better for Borten with Vinelia at his side. Mage Echior says Sir Borten may walk again, but that he will never fight."

"His absence will be deeply felt when we march toward Roenfyn."

"They say he sent more than one Naether Demon to the Underworld before he fell."

Eolyn paused in her gait. "Who told you that?"

"Why, everyone. The whole quarter is abuzz with stories of his bravery."

"I see…What else is being said about Lord Borten on that night?"

Jacquetta glanced away. She fingered the blue ribbon woven through her auburn tresses. "There are other rumors, of course, but they are foul and foolish. No one believes them."

Eolyn nodded and beckoned Jacquetta to continue their walk. She understood at once who had sown the seeds of this rumor, hiding truth with confusion through subtle hints and meaningful conversation. The task would have been easy enough. As far as Eolyn was aware, the only surviving witness to Akmael's rage against Borten was Talia. And if there had been any doubts as to Talia's capacity for discretion…

A shiver ran through Eolyn. She refused to follow that thought.

Never trust the royals, her tutor had once told her. *They make their beds out of lies.*

And now I sleep among them.

"Here we are," Jacquetta said.

The young maga opened the door, revealing a spacious room

with simple furnishings. Light streamed through windows, illuminating Mariel where she lay. Her eyes were closed, her expression peaceful. Her dark hair had been gathered into a single braid.

At her side sat Corey, engrossed in a tome on his lap. The image moved Eolyn. She remembered how Corey had kept vigil at her bedside like this, years ago when she was recovering from the Battle of Aerunden.

"Mage Corey," Jacquetta prompted.

He looked up as if startled by their presence. Then he rose, set aside his book, and bowed. "My Lady Queen."

"I had not expected to find you here, Mage Corey," Eolyn said.

"I was just about to take my leave."

"But I thought you were staying for the evening meal!" Jacquetta said in protest.

A smile touched Corey's lips. "Not on this day. I have a thousand tasks awaiting my attention in the fortress, as our Lady Queen well knows. I will return tomorrow, however, and check on our ward once again."

Corey took Eolyn's hand and touched her fingers to his forehead. Then he departed, Jacquetta closing the door softly behind him.

Eolyn took a seat on the bed next to Mariel. Shadowy threads twisted through the maga's aura, writhing like tiny snakes. Taking the girl's hand in hers, Eolyn sent magic in gentle waves toward Mariel's spirit.

"Wake, my daughter," she murmured. "The world of the living calls you, and your sisters would hear your voice."

With a sharp intake of breath, Mariel opened her eyes. She looked at Eolyn and let go a wretched sob. Eolyn gathered the young maga in her arms, stroked her hair, and kissed her forehead.

"Hush," she said.

Mariel jolted out of the embrace. "I will not hush! I will never hush again."

The venom in her reaction caught Eolyn off guard.

"As you wish, Mariel," she said. "I do not seek to silence you, only to comfort you."

"When can I watch them die?"

Eolyn drew a quiet breath. "Jacquetta, leave us alone for a moment please."

The young healer nodded and withdrew from the room. When she had closed the door, Eolyn turned back to Mariel.

"Their deaths will not make you whole, Mariel. You need sun and music and laughter. Most of all, you need the forest."

"You won't do it, will you?" Mariel pinned her with an accusatory stare. "You won't kill them, not even after this. Ghemena was right. You're a coward."

"I have faced the Naether Demons and survived the Underworld. I slew Prince Mechnes of the Syrnte in the Battle of Rhiemsaven. Do not call me a coward."

"You should have slain him sooner!"

Mariel's bitter rebuke cut deep.

Eolyn closed her eyes and rubbed her forehead, weary of the weight her own failures. "Killing those men now will not undo what has been done."

"No, but it will give us place of strength inside this parade of shadows."

"It saddens me to hear you say such things."

"To speak the truth? To look at this life for what it is? Darkness and betrayal, betrayal followed by darkness, until we are all consumed by hatred and death!"

Poison was flowing from the open wound in Mariel's soul. Its bitter bite threatened Eolyn's own resolve. She invoked a quiet spell for protection, directing the toxic stream toward the earth.

"Life and beauty still abounds," she said, "though it seems far away at times. My dream for you has not ended, Mariel. I would still have you return to the South Woods."

"Not until I watch them die."

"They will pay for their crimes, I promise you."

"When?"

"On the morrow."

Mariel blinked. "They'll be executed?"

"I signed the warrants this morning."

"You did?" Doubt, relief, and trepidation filled Mariel's expression.

"It is what my Lord King would have wanted," Eolyn said.

"Each of them will perish in the manner recommended by my Council. This will be the last act of my husband's reign, but you must understand: their suffering will not heal you. Aithne teaches us that healing comes from renewed life, not continued death."

"You and your platitudes. I used to believe all of those useless words."

"Those words brought your magic to life."

"My magic brought Baedon's curse upon me. Don't you see, Maga Eolyn? Nothing is the same, now. Nothing will ever be the same again."

Eolyn held her silence. In truth, she could not argue. As much as she wanted to comfort Mariel, she, too, struggled with a deep sense of betrayal, of having been abandoned by the Gods. She burned for revenge as fiercely as Mariel. She longed to submit to its blind fury, though she stifled this desire, striving with every breath to conserve some sense of compassion and most of all, prudence.

"I want to attend the executions," Mariel said.

"I will not stop you, if that is what you want. But I counsel against it."

Mariel stared at her, perplexed. "How can you be so cold about all of this?"

"Cold?" The question caught Eolyn by surprise. How could she be perceived as cold, when her heart burned in torment?

"Do you have no desire to see them eliminated? Do you not despise them for how they mocked you, for what they took from you, from all of us?"

A hairline crack snaked through the dam that held back Eolyn's anger and grief. She clenched her fists and clung to her tutor's words for protection. "Aithne teaches us—"

"Curse Aithne and her useless platitudes! Baedon destroyed hundreds of women like you and me! He even possessed your mother!"

Eolyn blinked as if she had been slapped in the face. Her voice fell to a whisper. "What?"

"He told me himself. He possessed your mother, Kaie. He was the one who made her betray you and all your family. He said her suffering was sweet, and that her magic was the richest he had ever tasted."

215

The fissure in Eolyn's soul tore open. She stood abruptly and withdrew from Mariel. Fury and pain, fear and uncertainty, battled for control of her heart. Above this churning sea of emotions reared the head of a terrible beast. Its limbs stretched wide to trap the unrest; its countenance was the grim reflection of absolute power. Eolyn longed to surrender to its dark embrace.

I am their King now. I can do anything to them that I want.

Akmael's ghost rose beside her. His hand came to rest, heavy on her shoulder. The ephemeral touch deepened her pain and yet steadied her resolve. She drew a long breath and opened her heart to her liege's presence, allowing his warrior spirit to become one with her own.

When Eolyn returned to Mariel's side, Akmael's mask of stone had slipped over her features.

"Sleep, my daughter," she said, taking the girl's hand and kissing her forehead. "Rest with the peace of the Gods, for tomorrow our enemies will perish."

CHAPTER THIRTY-ONE

Distraction

IN THE EVENINGS, SAVEGRE liked to hold Taesara's image in the palm of his hand, as a play of light trapped inside smoky crystal. Shadows defined her high cheekbones. Cerulean eyes shone in her fair face. Fine strands of hair, pale as the rare white sands of Galia, escaped her elegant braids.

He found it curious that she did not smile, save in rare moments when she looked upon her sleeping daughter. Even then the truce of her heart was fleeting. It faded like the light of a winter's day, faltering under the weight of her many burdens.

At times, Taesara's brow would furrow slightly, and her gaze would turn inward. Her fingers came to rest over her heart. Her lips parted, drawing a short breath before she remembered herself and returned to the task at hand.

In these moments, Savegre liked to believe she was thinking of him.

"You are distracted." Urales emerged from the shadows of the prince's tent, a somber figure in dark robes.

Savegre let Taesara's image vanish and wrapped his fist around the crystal sphere. Candles hissed and flickered on the table next to him. "Am I a child, that you find reason to reprimand me?"

Urales spread his hands in an appeasing gesture. "No, my Lord Prince. All I seek is to support you in your quest."

Savegre breathed a sigh of resignation and set the crystal sphere on the table. "She is...unexpected. I thought her beauty would make her haughty; her suffering, bitter. Yet she is neither. Instead, she is humble and gracious. And sad. Always sad.

Melancholy does not become her. Why would such a woman appear among her kind, at a time such as this?"

"The path of the Gods is fraught with the unexpected. They test us, even as we walk the straight path, in order to strengthen our resolve."

Savegre rose from his seat and paced a brief circle. "It puzzles me that the Mage King should have rejected a woman as fine as she."

"Perhaps he saw what you cannot. Taesara is stubborn and dismissive of our kind. There can be no future between a man of magic and a woman who rejects and disdains his gifts."

"Then why do the Gods draw me to her? Why plant the fires of *aen-lasati* between us?"

Restlessness had wrapped around Savegre's heart, like the sea foaming over the rocky shores of his beloved home. At night, he dreamed of Taesara dancing barefoot at the water's edge, her dress a cloud of sheer silk, her laughter free upon the wind.

Such visions had meaning, did they not?

"She has her own spark of magic, tenuous but persistent. Perhaps it could yet be coaxed into flame."

Urales drew close. "Go to her if *aen-lasati* so moves you, but do not fool yourself. The pleasure the Gods grant you will change nothing."

"What did you see of her in the visions that brought us here?"

"Of Taesara? Nothing. For this reason, I say she is not important."

Urales traced a slow arc above their heads. The canvas roof of the tent faded, revealing the evening stars, a glorious stream of white fire flickering across the black heart of the universe.

"The prophecies are clear," he said. "The signs are just as we anticipated. The wanderers have aligned: Aithne, Caradoc, and Dragon look down upon us as one. Caedmon hurries to meet them, with Lithia close by his side. Every promise made to our people is coming to pass. You know the poems, Savegre. You studied them as a child."

A maga shall rise from the dead.
A woman who wields the sword of shadows.

"We've seen the signs well enough," Savegre said, "and we've studied the verses left by our ancestors. But do we truly understand their meaning? If the Mountain Queen comes to Taesara's aid, the kingdoms of magic will be divided against themselves. How would you interpret this?"

Urales closed his eyes. "The maga warrior Ghemena will be deceived. Khelia seeks to rest beside the Queen of Moisehén. I have seen them sharing wine and laughter. I have watched them kiss each other as sisters in magic."

A chill took hold of Savegre's heart. "You are certain?"

Urales's cool gaze settled upon the prince. "Why do you doubt what is written?"

The queens of the East shall rise together.

"We should advise Taesara of the coming alliance."

"No."

"She and her people may yet turn back if they understand what awaits them."

"You forget our purpose, Savegre."

"That woman does not deserve this fate."

"Her fate is not for us to decide," Urales said, emphatic. "She is a Daughter of Thunder! There can be no peace between her kind and ours, no rest until she and all her people are gone from the face of this world. The teachings of our ancestors are clear on this. Indeed, all our history is a testimony to this truth."

"She has magic of her own. I have seen it."

"Of course she does! All her kind could have followed Dragon and received the blessings of the Gods in return. Yet they did not. They turned from the light then, as they do now. Do not be fooled by Taesara's affections, Savegre. What she feels toward you is a momentary fascination for that which she cannot understand. This confusion of her heart will pass, leaving fear and hatred in its wake. I have seen it before, many times. Among lesser people, it brings heartbreak. Among nobles and kings, it breeds war, a cycle that will not be broken until we eliminate all those who have turned from Dragon's path."

"Perhaps we have misinterpreted the signs," Savegre insisted. "Perhaps there is something we have yet to see and understand clearly."

Urales smiled, a mix of sympathy and compassion in his aged

219

face. He laid a hand upon his liege's chest.

"What we understand with our hearts will soon be clear to our eyes, Savegre. You know this, as well as I. The time is now. The task is ours. This destiny of Roenfyn is written in the stars, my Prince. And their doom will be your glory."

CHAPTER THIRTY-TWO

Justice

THE LIGHT OF PRE-DAWN PAINTED the buildings in muted shades of gray. Banners of House Vortingen hung from balconies, their silver and black dragons undulating in a light breeze. At the heart of the square, guards encircled the waiting scaffold and unlit pyre.

Accompanied by Jacquetta and Mage Echior, Mariel took a place in a stand set aside for practitioners of high rank. Before long, a crowd began to gather. The trickle of men and women, young and old, grew into steady streams that flowed from the streets toward the square. They greeted each other with muted voices and quiet embraces. Each found a place and then stood, grim-faced and silent, as they waited for Queen Eolyn to arrive.

Mariel had heard stories of executions in distant lands, in the cities of Antaria and the empire of the Syrnte. There, public deaths were said to be like festivals: loud, raucous, and cruel.

Moisehén's traditions were different. Aithne and Caradoc taught that humiliation of the walking dead only condemned one's own spirit. So firmly did Mariel's people hold this belief, that no one would dare throw refuse or hurl insults at a person sentenced to execution. Instead, they received prisoners in silence and watched without cowering as each was delivered to the will of the Gods.

Trumpets sounded from the fortress above, announcing the opening of the castle gates. Moments passed while the Queen's entourage completed their ritual descent down the winding road. By now, people had packed the square, but they parted to allow passage as the royal procession appeared. Mariel rose in salute,

221

along with the rest of the practitioners and nobles.

"All hail to the Queen!" they cried. "Hail to Prince Eoghan, heir to the throne of Vortingen!"

The shout was taken up and repeated, magnified to a deafening roar, not so much of joyous adulation, but as a plea for vengeance. Their unified chant rushed toward the Queen, broke like a wave upon her and left her cloaked in shadow.

Mariel's cry died upon her lips. A cold mist wrapped around her heart. She had never seen her tutor like this. Eolyn's beauty was terrible to behold, ominous and irresistible. At her side rode young Eoghan clothed as King, his countenance as stony as his father's had ever been. Behind them came members of the Council, each under the banners of the houses they represented.

Corey and Thelyn, dressed in the forest green robes of their station, parted from the procession as it turned toward the royal pavilion. The mages dismounted just outside the circle of guards, removed their shoes, and approached the scaffolds barefoot.

When Eolyn and her attendants had settled, the High Mages began their homage to the realms of Dragon. The chant was joined by all those present. Together they invoked a ward to seal the power of death inside the circle and protect the people of Moisehén from treacherous souls unleashed within.

Mist rose from the ground. The sky darkened above. As the mournful cadence reached its peak, Eolyn let go an anguished cry. The white fire of Aithne burst from her staff, searing the sky with blinding light. Silence followed, heavy and absolute, so thick it swallowed the plod of horses and the creak of carts behind them.

Markl was brought in, bound to a wicker hurdle. His arms were strained at odd angles; one leg hung limp. A guard threw water in the young man's face. He jerked to consciousness, took in his miserable circumstances, and cried out like an animal run through.

Mariel closed her eyes, fighting back unwelcome tears. The finality of this moment hit her full force. After today, nothing would be left of her youth in the highlands of Moehn, its wild landscape and fragrant flowers, its humble people and rich forests. The children who had once laughed and run free in the safe places of Mariel's youth were lost; some through death, others through betrayal, still others through Baedon's flaying of her soul.

Mariel saw them all, even herself, in the battered body of Markl, dragged through this harsh world to be hung and eviscerated, his fate sealed by powers and circumstances beyond comprehension.

Two guards untied Markl, dragged him to the scaffold, and held him upright as the executioner slipped a rope around his neck. Thelyn's smooth voice resonated across the square, announcing the young man's crimes and punishment. Markl was given leave to speak his last words, but he said nothing. Instead his eyes shifted, impossibly, to Mariel's place among the mages. She froze, desperate to look away, yet unable to break the hold of his haunting gaze. She heard his voice in her mind, hoarse and full of regret.

I'm sorry, Mariel.

The executioner covered Markl's face. Then he sliced open Markl's gut with a quick and brutal knife and turned the man loose. The taut jerk of the rope cut off Markl's anguished cry. Long arduous shudders coursed through his body as it swung. Blood and excrement dripped from his feet.

Mariel covered her face in horror. Her gut revolted, and she doubled over, struggling to stop the surge of bile.

Jacquetta placed an arm around her.

"We can go, Mariel," she murmured. "We do not have to stay here and watch this."

Mariel shook her head and recovered her composure. "I'm not going. Not until they are all dead."

Baedon was brought forward next. His sorcerer's staff had been replaced by a common walking stick. He huddled over it, downcast, as Corey and the guards escorted him to the pyre.

Thelyn announced Baedon's crimes and sentence while the old man was tied to the stake. Before they lit the pyre, Corey exchanged a few quiet words with the old wizard. When the mage retreated, Baedon's eyes were closed. His head and shoulders drooped forward as if he had already surrendered to death.

Twelve mages surrounded the pyre to summon the breath of Dragon. Shafts of red flame surged from their palms and into the pile of wood. Smoke masked the wizard's figure. Fire leapt toward the sky. Soon Mariel smelled the stench of bubbling skin. The fire progressed, consuming the old man in a pillar of light. Not once did he cry out or lift his head. Not once did his blackened body jerk under the searing heat.

Nearby, Lord Langerhaans sagged inside his cage. Terror curled like mist over his quivering body. Sobs wracked his ponderous frame. When they dragged him to the block, he cried for mercy in long, piteous howls. They forced him to his knees in front of the executioner and gave him leave to speak.

Unlike Markl and Baedon, Langerhaans wept his regrets. He begged the Queen for pardon, expressed love and loyalty for the people of Moisehén. None of this saved him from having his head pressed down to the block.

His sobs escalated to cries of terror.

The executioner placed an axe at the nape of Langerhaans' neck and then he raised the blade high against a gray and unforgiving sky.

Then the Queen's voice thundered across the square.

Ehekaht!

Naemu amon.

The executioner stopped short of completing his task. He stepped away from the prisoner and went down on bended knee.

Eolyn rose to descend from her dais. Flanked by her guard, she strode toward the circle, staff crackling in her grip. The crowd parted to make way. The mood of the onlookers tensed.

Langerhaans, still immobilized by the guards, strained to see what was happening.

At the edge of the circle, Mage Corey stepped into Eolyn's path. She did not waver under his silent challenge, but held his gaze, undaunted. After a few heartbeats, Corey bowed to his Queen and let her pass.

Eolyn stepped onto the scaffold and approached the prisoner.

"You took my husband from me." Though she spoke in low tones, her words echoed across the square.

Langerhaans whimpered and tried to hide his face.

"You put into motion forces that severed the magic protecting our kingdom and broke open the gates of the Underworld," Eolyn continued, each word soaked in venom. "Your foul ambition robbed our people of their sovereign king, left me a widow, and my children without a father. Heroic men, loyal women, and faithful servants were condemned to the Underworld because of you. How should I reward you, Cramon Langerhaans of New Linfeln? What sort of death does a traitor like you deserve?"

When he did not reply, she struck him with her staff. Mariel flinched at the sound of the blow. Langerhaans cried out in pain. Great sobs wracked his body; saliva and snot mingled with tears.

"Answer me!" Fire sprang from the crystal head of Eolyn's staff and threw Langerhaans flat against the ground. Cries of fear erupted from the crowd, accompanied by the long, torturous wail of Langerhaans's wife.

The Queen closed in on the lord's trembling figure and said in cold, compassionless tones, "Answer me."

Langerhaans remained prostrate. His words came choked and distorted. "No mercy, my Lady Queen. I deserve no mercy."

"No, you do not."

Eolyn's staff ignited with a white flame that consumed Langerhaans in a luminous net. Fire crackled over his body. He convulsed and screamed. When the smell of his singed garments began to mingle with the harsher stench of Baedon's pyre, the Queen cut short the curse and broke the stream of fire.

Langerhaans wheezed and sputtered, coughing up blood and soot. Smoke rose from his clothes and hair. His hands and feet were black with ash.

Eolyn approached his trembling form and knelt close. She reached out and touched Langerhaans's singed hair with a gentle sort of awe. An odd play of emotions twisted across her features; as if she had discovered a perverse pleasure in this suffering.

Then she blinked and withdrew.

"Rise, Lord Langerhaans," she said.

The man tried to obey, but his knees buckled.

Eolyn signaled the guards to assist him. "Look upon your queen."

His shoulders sagged and his head lolled, but Cramon Langerhaans managed to lift his eyes, his expression dazed and infused with terror. His lips were blistered; his eyebrows had been burned away.

"I pardon you, Cramon Langerhaans."

The crowd roared in surprise. Consternation passed through

225

the ranks of nobles and mages. Thelyn and Corey exchanged a careful glance.

The Queen lifted her staff to quiet them all. "I pardon you on the condition that you swear allegiance to me and to my son, Prince Eoghan, the sole legitimate heir to the Throne of Vortingen. I pardon you on the condition that you never betray the House of our Lord King again."

Langerhaans' eyes became suddenly alert. They darted from the Queen to the dais where members of the Council stood.

Eolyn struck her staff upon the ground, snapping the lord's attention back to her. "What is your answer, Cramon Langerhaans of New Linfeln?"

He wheezed and croaked, then managed a shaking nod.

Eolyn signaled the guards to let him go. The lord fell to his knees. Convulsions wracked his body. Weeping in relief and gratitude, he crawled on all fours toward the Queen. Then Cramon Langerhaans, Lord and Patriarch of New Linfeln, took the hem of Eolyn's skirt and covered its embroidered cloth with feverish, blood-stained kisses.

Chapter Thirty-Three

Regret

EOLYN RETREATED DEEP INTO HER QUARTERS, seeking refuge from her troubled soul and the clamor of the outside world. Markl's miserable screams echoed inside her head. The stench of Baedon's burning flesh clung to her clothes. Pathetic images of Langerhaans groveling swarmed her inner vision.

"Get this dress off of me," she snapped. "I must find something else to wear."

"Yes, my Lady Queen." Talia stepped forward and began unlacing her bodice.

"And I would have a bath at once, before I meet with the Council."

A frown crossed Talia's dark brow, but she nodded and communicated the Queen's orders to the other attendants. As Talia worked to remove Eolyn's gown, the maga's stomach convulsed. She tore away from her maid and stumbled to the basin, finding it just as bile spewed forth.

Talia gave a sharp, urgent murmur that sent everyone away in a rustle of perfumed skirts.

Eolyn sagged over the basin, her breath coming in gasps. Sweat beaded her brow. Talia approached and pressed a cool damp cloth against Eolyn's forehead, then upon her neck. The tender touch brought comfort, followed by a sharp stab of pain.

Oh, Akmael! Why can't it be your touch that comforts me?

Eolyn's knees buckled. Talia caught her fall and guided her to a nearby chair. The lady knelt before Eolyn and, taking each hand in turn, refreshed her wrists with scented water.

"Perhaps it is a good sign, my Lady Queen," she said. "Perhaps our King left you a gift before he departed this world."

Eolyn closed her eyes as Talia's meaning dawned on her. "I'm afraid that's not very likely, Talia."

After all, she had taken customary measures to avoid pregnancy. Indeed, in the very last days, they had not made love at all.

If only I had known we had but a few nights left.

Talia set the cloth aside and finished assisting Eolyn in removing her dress, now damp with sweat. The lady's demeanor was submissive, her eyes downcast, as she brought forward a fresh robe.

They had not exchanged any words of consequence since the night the Naether Demons attacked, choosing instead to focus on the most mundane aspects of their daily routine. It was as if they had tacitly agreed on silencing all memory of the horrors they had witnessed.

The past is always with us, Doyenne Ghemena used to say, *and it grows more insidious when left unspoken.*

"Talia."

The woman paused and met Eolyn's gaze.

"You need not continue in my service if you do not wish to."

Surprise and fear crept into Talia's expression. "You would send me away?"

"No, that is not what I meant. It's just that…It must hard for you to continue here, after everything that has come to pass, after the way Rhaella died."

"She deserved the death the Gods chose for her."

"Oh." The conviction in Talia's voice caught Eolyn by surprise. "I see."

An awkward silence passed between them. For the first time in memory, Talia did not seem to know what to do with her hands. She glanced around the empty room and let go a shaky breath. "Forgive me, my Lady Queen. I spoke out of turn."

"I would have all the women of my court speak their mind. I have found that we hold our silence far too often."

"You do not resent Rhaella for what she did?"

"Rhaella was a pawn, like so many others of her station."

"Like me, you mean."

"That is not what I said."

"But you must know I was delivered into your service for the same purpose as she."

Eolyn drew a careful breath. *What do we have left between us now, save the truth?* "Yes, I know. There has never been a lady placed in my service who was not subject to the ambitions of her family."

"Yet, you have always treated us with kindness and respect. Friendship, even. Why?"

"You are not to blame for expectations forced upon you, and I never doubted the love of my King."

"Yet he had lovers, did he not?"

"Once in a great while, during the High Holidays, as befit his station and status."

"You felt no jealousy on those occasions?"

"I was raised as a maga, to humble myself before the will of the Gods and to honor the call of *aen-lasati*."

"Which means that you also...?" Talia's voice trailed off. Blood rushed to her cheeks. "Forgive me. I did not mean to imply...It's just, the teachings of Aithne and Caradoc...I have heard what they say about *aen-lasati*. I find it confusing at times."

"I suspect you understand quite well the teachings of Aithne and Caradoc. That is why you ask such bold questions."

Talia bit her lip and looked away.

Silence settled between them.

Winter winds whispered deep inside Eolyn's heart, igniting long-suppressed memories of East Selen: tall firs embraced by swirling snow, midnight cries of vengeful ghosts, the quiet call of Winter Fox.

"Tell me, Talia," she said quietly. "Would you have given yourself to another man, having known the love of our King?"

"No, my Lady Queen." Talia shook her head. "Never."

Then the lady drew a breath and added hesitantly, "My Lady Queen, do you believe a man could love me, and I him, as you and the King loved each other?"

"Of course." It seemed a strange question. "Why not?"

"Because there is so little love among our kind, my Lady Queen. Among the nobles, I mean. There is loyalty and duty, power

229

and advancement. But no love. That is why so many despise you and distrust you. They cannot understand how any union between a man and a woman can be built on love, just love and nothing more. There is always something to be gained, a prize to be won or lost. That's why so few of them recognized what I did, from the moment I first saw you with the King. What was obvious to me is inconceivable to them." Talia's voice lowered to a whisper. "I confess that I fear marriage, my Lady Queen. With all my heart."

"Why?"

"Because it will be thrust upon me according to my family's ambitions. But I dream of the sort of union that you found with our King. I would like to know what it means to love a man, and to be loved by him."

Eolyn stepped away, moved by this declaration yet at a loss for how to respond. She retreated to the window, where her eyes came to rest on a distant blue-green smudge that marked the border of her home in the highlands of Moehn.

She remembered the last morning she had shared with her coven, before the Syrnte invasion obliterated their happiness and drove her back into the arms of the Mage King. Faces lost in the war crystallized in her mind: sweet Tasha and prim Catarina, lithe Sirena and dour Renate. Her dearest friend, the passionate and beautiful Adiana. And Ghemena…little Ghemena. The youngest of them all, full of mischief and fire.

Only a few weeks had passed since she last wandered through the South Woods, yet its magic felt distant and unresponsive, fragile against the fatal games of Akmael's court.

I should return to Moehn and never look back. I should recognize Eliasara's claim and let Taesara assume this task for which she was bred, for I have little skill and no stomach for any of this.

But if she left, what would become of Eoghan? Either Taesara's assassins would find the prince, or others would use the boy's claim for their own advancement.

"What you ask for comes at a great price, Talia," Eolyn murmured.

"But surely love is worth any price that must be paid? Any sacrifice the Gods may demand?"

Eolyn turned the question over in her mind and came to the

troubling realization that she did not know the answer.

Still, she drew a quiet breath, said with steady voice, "Yes, dear Talia. It is."

CHAPTER THIRTY-FOUR

War Council

EOLYN TOOK HER PLACE at the head of the table. Upon her signal, the Council members resumed their seats in a rustle of robes and scraping chairs. Not one whisper escaped their lips, not one look was exchanged between them. The menacing hum of Eolyn's staff hung above their attentive silence.

I am their King.

The thought at once sickened and sustained her.

They know now that I will not hesitate to inflict suffering and death, and they respect me more because of it.

"Lords and Mages," she said, "let us begin. The days we have devoted to mourning our King and securing justice for the foul crimes committed against the Crown have given an advantage to our enemy. The armies of Roenfyn and Galia stand on the banks of the Furma River. We must set aside our grief and go forward to meet them without delay. I would hear the reports you have prepared, beginning with Lord Herensen."

The privilege granted to Langerhaans's chief rival had the desired effect. Herensen's sober face relaxed, exposing his gratitude. He spoke at length, detailing the levies gathered at his behest, as well as information brought back by his spies and scouts in Roenfyn. Eolyn called on young Lord Meryth of Selen next, and then Sir Turen, who sat in representation of Lord Borten of Moehn. From there she proceeded through the rest of the Council before returning to the lords of Selkynsen, where she began the rotation again.

Eolyn asked pointed questions and challenged any gaps she

found in their reports. She made note of those who underestimated her knowledge, and of anyone who allowed even a hint of condescension to creep into their tone. While she was not such a fool as to disregard the wisdom of her advisers, after two wars and ten years of Akmael's tutorship, Eolyn intended to hold her own in this conflict. She also intended it to be her last. Wearied by endless plots and renewed uprisings, she had begun to understand Kedehen's passion for crushing all those who opposed him.

The men finished their reports and deliberations. Silence settled over the gathering. The long oak table was covered with maps of Moisehén and Roenfyn, adorned with figures that represented troops at the disposition of each province and both kingdoms.

A dismal picture if there ever was one.

"It is not enough," Eolyn said.

No one dared agree or disagree, but she saw the grim acknowledgment of truth in their eyes.

"Roenfyn and Galia outnumber us, perhaps by thousands," she added. "Was our Lord King aware of this?"

"We knew Galia had responded to their call, my Lady Queen," Herensen replied, "but no one anticipated they would bring an army of this magnitude."

"Galian warriors are adept at magic. All of them," Eolyn said. "But only a small number of our own still command the traditions of Caedmon. The rest of our warriors are common knights and soldiers. This is another great disadvantage."

"My Lady Queen." Herensen bowed in respect. "You and our late King defeated the army of the Syrnte with odds little better than these. Cunning, skill, and courage are what decide a war, just as you demonstrated in the Battle of Rhiemsaven."

Akmael commanded that battle. All I did was finish it.

"Your words are well received, Lord Herensen," she replied. "If this is how we must meet our enemies, then this is how we will defeat them. Nonetheless, I would rest easier on the eve of battle, as I am certain would all of you, were the numbers more favorable than this. We should seek out our own allies."

"Messengers were sent by our Lord King to Antaria weeks ago," Thelyn said, "but they've no interest in the conflicts of the northern kingdoms. They will not come to our aid. As for the Syrnte, as I'm sure you well know, it would be folly to even consider—"

"I am not suggesting we invite the Syrnte back into our lands," Eolyn said. "What of the Mountain People? We share a common history, and they know much of our magic. Many of our sisters made a home among them following the purges."

"Made a home and never came back," Thelyn reminded her. "Save those who fought with the rebel Ernan against our King."

"Fought with my brother," Eolyn acknowledged. "Khelia was my ally once, and now she rules the mountain kingdoms. Her skills in battle are legendary. We would be hard pressed to find a better commander, or a more skilled army, to aid in defeating the Galians. And they are close, very close. The army of the Mountain Queen could meet us in Selkynsen if we sent our messengers at once, and if she heeded our call."

The Council sank into awkward silence. Several men shifted uncomfortably.

Herensen cleared his throat. "My Lady Queen, the magas who escaped to the mountain realms have nurtured hatred and resentment toward us for more than a generation. We cannot defend against one enemy by inviting another into our midst."

Corey chuckled just then. His quiet mirth spilled across the table, sending a crack through Eolyn's fragile foundation of power.

For the love of the Gods, Corey. Do not make a fool of me now.

"Mage Corey," she said evenly, "if you would be so kind as to share the source of your amusement?"

"Forgive me, my Lady Queen, but the mere thought of Khelia among us simply made me laugh. Were I, or any other man at this table, to ask the Mountain Queen for aid, she would march into the heart of Moisehén just to spit in our faces."

More laughter erupted from the Council, followed by stifled coughs. Energies were shifting, alliances already being reassessed. Before Eolyn could think how to grasp the reins slipping from her fingers, Corey spoke again.

"A summons from you, on the other hand..." His tone turned serious, and his unflinching silver-green gaze settled on Eolyn. "That would have an altogether different effect. Khelia will listen to

Eolyn, High Maga and Queen of Moisehén, because despite all that has come to pass, the sovereign of the Mountain Realms still considers our Queen her sister."

"I will not listen to this folly!" Herensen exclaimed. "We cannot invite Khelia into our realm."

"Enough," Eolyn said.

"Mage Corey brings poor counsel to this table, my Lady Queen," Herensen insisted. "Those mountain witches will tear us apart and feed us to the Galians. They are not to be trusted."

"I said *silence.*" Magic surged through Eolyn's staff and set its crystal head on fire.

Herensen's nostrils flared. Then he set his jaw and averted his gaze.

"We will send a delegation to the Paramen Mountains," Eolyn announced.

"Eldor and Gaeoryn might be appropriate for this task, my Lady Queen," Thelyn said. "Their flight is swift, and they are skilled diplomats."

"Your recommendation is well-taken, Thelyn, but our messengers must be maga warriors. I will appoint a delegation to depart at once, with a letter written in my own hand."

An awkward pause followed.

Thelyn spoke again, "My Lady Queen, some may question the wisdom of entrusting the magas with such a task so soon after their release from prison."

"Some may question my wisdom, High Mage Thelyn, but I am confident that you and the other members of this Council will not. As Mage Corey has already acknowledged, Khelia will not listen to the men of Moisehén. She certainly will not listen to our mages. So we will send my daughters in magic, and with them all our hope."

CHAPTER THIRTY-FIVE

Parley

TAESARA STUDIED HER DRESSES under the light of dawn, trying to decide which would send the strongest message of power, history, and destiny: The grassy sage of Roenfyn, or the ominous purple of Moisehén?

The celestial beauty of the fabric gifted to her by Savegre came to mind, a color that complimented her eyes rather than her allegiances. She let the thought go. The seamstresses were still at work on that dress. Even if they had finished, she would be inclined to reject it.

"My Lady Queen?" her attendant prompted.

Taesara indicated the purple gown.

Eliasara, unusually disposed toward the new day, had already sat down to breakfast. She ate with vigor and chattered about the Galian warriors and the graceful power of their dance.

"I have a new friend," she said between mouthfuls. "Her name is Nyella, and she's teaching Ireny and me Galian dances. I thought she was a servant, but mother says she's going to be a queen like me!"

Sonia scowled as she served girl fresh tea. "Those wizards are not to be trusted. It is unwise to call anyone among them a friend."

"Penamor calls them our allies. Why should I not call them our friends?"

"A king has no friends," Taesara said as the women laced up her gown. "A king has only allies and enemies."

"Penamor has no friends because he's too unpleasant," Eliasara retorted.

"His unpleasantness keeps this realm in order," Taesara replied. "It is the nature of his position and of our condition as royalty. You must become accustomed to it, Eliasara. When you are queen you will never have true friends. Only those who are loyal to you, and those who are not."

"Queen Eolyn has friends. She has her sisters in magic."

"Those sisters betrayed her and brought you to us."

Eliasara frowned and pushed her plate away.

"I'm not hungry anymore," she announced.

Taesara took a seat at the table. As she served herself fruit and cheese, one of the servants began plaiting her hair. "If you're finished with breakfast, you can go to the captain of the guard and tell him to ready my horse."

Eliasara glared at Taesara, then threw her napkin on the floor and departed.

Sonia approached and poured a cup of tea. "Are you certain of what you do, my Lady Queen?"

"You would question my intervention with my daughter?"

"That is not what I speak of." The lady's dark eyes were creased with worry. "I wish you would reconsider riding out with Penamor today."

"This is my duty, Sonia, to my daughter and her late father. Besides, I do not want to leave the parley with Selkynsen entirely in my uncle's hands."

Sonia opened her mouth as if to respond, but then bowed and retreated in silence.

Having finished her breakfast, Taesara rose. A thread of steel settled along the length of her spine. She washed her hands in a basin and demanded her cloak. Outside, Eliasara waited, head bowed beneath the slate gray sky. The girl's fists were clenched and her lower lip trembled.

"Why are you doing this?" she asked.

Taesara touched her cheek. "For you."

A sob escaped Eliasara's lips. "I hardly know you, and now you're going to get killed, too!"

Taesara caught her breath. "It's only a parley."

"I wish I knew a ward to protect you. Maga Eolyn tried to teach me, but I never had a gift for magic."

237

"Your concern for my safety is the greatest ward. That and the protocol that guides us this morning. You needn't worry, Eliasara. There will be no weapons, only words. You will watch us from the ridge, won't you?"

Eliasara nodded.

"That makes me glad, and gives me greater courage." Taesara drew her daughter into a tight embrace. "Don't fret. We will be together again soon."

Guards fell into place around Taesara as she mounted and rode from the camp. They followed a high ridge overlooking the valley of the Furma River. On the opposite bank, the red roofs and yellow walls of Selkynsen glinted under the rising sun. Smoke rose from blackened fields outside the city walls. Penamor's men and his Galian allies swarmed across the landscape, building siege engines and digging trenches just beyond the range of Selkynsen's archers.

This glittering city was the jewel of Akmael's kingdom, renowned for its art and commerce. The defenses were formidable, with two city walls, an inner fortress, and a keep. Without his Galian allies, Penamor might have decided to skirt Selkynsen altogether in favor of meeting the Witch Queen on the plains of Moisehén. But the Galians had promised to bring down the city walls with magic, and securing Selkynsen's surrender would put Roenfyn in a much stronger position to penetrate the heart of the kingdom.

Taesara's party descended a long, winding road to the river, the chink of metal and mail matching their gait. The Furma ran deep and strong, its waters lapping against the silty banks. Banners of Roenfyn hung along a wide stone bridge that Penamor's men had seized in recent days. The victory, small but hard-won, had saved them a much longer march toward New Linfeln in the south. The bulk of Roenfyn's army was now camped just south of the gates of Selkynsen, with a small garrison left on the western bank to protect Taesara and her daughter.

Penamor and Savegre greeted Taesara in full armor. The brilliance of Savegre's regalia eclipsed Penamor's more humble colors, and Taesara had to quell the impulse to greet the Galian prince first.

Penamor dismounted, strode forward, and took Taesara's hand

in his.

"My niece, Princess of Roenfyn and Queen of Moisehén!" His cheeks were flushed in excitement. "If war could be won by beauty, I would send all our men home in this moment."

"Flattery should not be wasted on old women, Uncle."

"Hah!" Penamor threw his head back in laughter. "Old, she says. You think her old, Savegre?"

"No." The Galian wizard bowed, dark eyes fixed on Taesara in a way that made her heart skip a beat. "Old she is not."

Penamor pulled Taesara close and lowered his voice. "I dare say the Sisters didn't do near as much damage as I'd feared. You still have some wiles left in you, niece. Don't think I haven't noticed."

"Uncle, I have not in any way encouraged—"

"Let's be off, then!" He released her, bowed with a flourish, and returned to his mount. "We have a city to conquer."

Taesara's stomach churned as they crossed the wide river into the territory that had once been her home. Penamor rode at her right hand, Savegre on her left. The traditional banners of Moisehén preceded them, silver dragons dancing against a purple night.

A cohort of knights and spear men followed. Most represented the noble houses of Roenfyn, though a handful of families from New Linfeln had already appeared to join their cause. It was rumored more levies were on the way. The port had once belonged to Taesara's father, and the loyalties of its families tended strongly toward her cause.

Along the banks, trees were being cut down. Trunks snapped. Verdant crowns wavered and fell. Leaves hissed as they rushed toward their end. Bare-chested men stripped foliage and branches off the trunks. They tied their quarry to beasts of burden and dragged the logs away, their progress feeding a network that led to different points outside the city wall, where siege engines were being mounted faster than Taesara would ever have imagined possible. High towers set upon wheels rose above a cacophony of hammering tools and shouting men. The great machines sat ready to hurl splintering rocks and blasts of fire at the enemy.

"You must have little faith in this parley," she said to her uncle, "to have put your men to work with such speed and vigor."

Penamor chuckled. "I merely seek to clarify the choice before them. Accept the beautiful and benevolent queen we have brought back home or suffer utter destruction. It seems an easy enough decision, but fools are known to be stubborn."

"I want them treated with mercy, no matter what the circumstances of their surrender."

Penamor cast her a sideways glance. "I imagined as much."

"I speak in earnest, uncle."

"As do I. This is war, Taesara, and we play by its rules. If the city resists, it will be plundered. There is nothing you or I or anyone else can do to stop that."

Taesara held her tongue, resolving to return to this discussion under more discrete circumstances. She would not have Eliasara's army enter Moisehén as a band of thieves, rapists, and murderers, destroying the very heritage the princess sought to reclaim. Penamor may desire vengeance, but what Eliasara needed was a kingdom, safe and whole. A prosperous land to rule over.

The Lord Regent signaled the party to stop.

Ahead of them stood the imposing gates of Selkynsen, great oaken doors elaborately carved with the crests of ruling families and protected by a heavy portcullis. Anxiety coursed through Taesara's veins as she scanned the high ramparts. She could see men on the battlements, arrows poised to sear through her chest. She felt the clarity of their gaze, tasted the salt of their deadly resolve.

Long ago, when Taesara was newly betrothed, the people of Selkynsen had greeted her with song and ceremony and countless fine gifts. Now they prepared a grim resistance. Along the ramparts a crowd of men and women had gathered. Taesara saw children on the shoulders of their parents; the fates of entire families chained to the tenacity of those who defended them.

Penamor leaned close. "We advance no more than thirty paces from this point, Taesara."

She nodded, throat dry though her pulse was steady. "I understand."

A suffocating silence flowed over the walls of the city and onto the blackened fields, swallowing the sounds of Penamor's camp, of metal upon wood and wood upon metal, of cries and shouts and steady chants, of trees that groaned and fell.

"I will ride at your side," Penamor said. "Savegre and his Galian advisers stay here. They must understand it is you and your daughter who return to assert a rightful claim. We can't have them thinking this is an invasion of foreign kings."

And what are you? Taesara bit her tongue and withheld the words.

A shout sounded from the wall, followed by the blast of trumpets. The portcullis rose and the gates opened. The strain of metal trappings and creaking wood grated upon Taesara's ears. For a moment the depths of the arched entrance remained shrouded in darkness. Then banners of gold and midnight blue appeared, fluttering over a procession of armed men. Taesara's heart sank when she saw the new sigil of Moisehén lifted high above the colors of Selkynsen: the black dragon of her husband intertwined with the silver dragon of his whore.

Penamor snorted. "Well. I would say their loyalties are clear. Let us not waste our time any further or risk your life with this mummer's show. Come, Taesara. I am quite ready to start pummeling these people into the ground."

"No." Taesara extended her hand. "Allow me to speak with them, Uncle. We must give the people of Selkynsen the opportunity to join us in peace."

As the procession approached, Taesara searched their ranks in hopes of finding someone she recognized.

The lord who led them halted at a prudent distance. He watched Taesara and her uncle with keen eyes. Thin grayish-blond hair framed a long and sober face marked by a prominent nose. In an instant his name came to mind.

"Remias Herensen!" Taesara exclaimed. "By the Gods, how you have grown."

The young lord's features relaxed, though he did not return her smile. "I would have hoped to have grown, these ten years past."

Taesara smiled. The last time she had seen Remias, he was hovering on the cusp of manhood, striving to assume the serious cast of his grandfather's house, yet still succumbing to occasional bouts of mischief.

"Well met, Remias of Selkynsen," she said. "It pleases me, truly, to see you so well appointed."

241

"Unfortunately I cannot share your joy in this encounter, Princess Taesara."

"Queen Taesara," Penamor interjected.

"I must ask you and your army to leave this territory." Remias kept his gaze fixed on Taesara. "You are not welcome."

"We come on behalf of my daughter Eliasara, who seeks not war, but justice."

Remias's eyes slid across the landscape. "This has all the appearance of war, my Lady."

"You would think my uncle a poor general indeed if he did not make some display of force to back my daughter's claim. Yet we are prepared to offer generous terms if you open your gates in peace."

"I will hear your terms, Taesara of Roenfyn, though I assure you they will not be accepted."

"Swear allegiance to my daughter, the true Queen of Moisehén," Taesara said. "Turn your army and levies over to her command. In exchange for these actions, you and your family and all those loyal to my daughter will retain their titles and status under her reign. No harm will come to your people; no damage will be done to your lands. We hold no grievance against Selkynsen. Indeed, we admire this city and wish to keep it whole. Join our cause. Together we can put an end to the reign of that peasant witch and her bastard son."

Remias regarded her a long and solemn moment. "You are well-remembered by our people as a kind and generous woman, Taesara of Roenfyn. There were many who questioned the King's decision when you were asked to leave our lands, but those voices have long since been silenced. From here to Rhiemsaven, from there to the King's City and beyond, to the forests of Selen and the highlands of Moehn, you will find no one who opposes our Prince or the Queen who protects his throne."

Taesara's smile faded.

"This is a long and bitter struggle you pursue," Remias added. "You would be wise to turn your back on Moisehén and depart these lands before Queen Eolyn's wrath falls upon you and your daughter."

"You would threaten my niece and the fruit of her womb?" Penamor barked. "You would reject these women of royal blood in

242

favor of a peasant whore and her bastard?"

One of the men of Selkynsen moved to draw his sword, but Remias stayed his hand. "Queen Eolyn is not a peasant. She is a High Maga, a woman of rare qualities and a worthy choice for the Mage King. For all your fair talk, Princess Taesara, you must understand it is impossible to assert the claim of any princess over a legitimate prince, especially a princess who is the treasonous daughter of a spurned woman."

"By the Gods of Thunder, I will destroy you for these insults!" Penamor drew his sword, face red with fury.

Remias responded in kind.

"Stop!" Taesara spurred her horse to stand between them.

The men paused, their mounts restless, their weapons shining in the sun. Deadly gazes sliced through Taesara like daggers, robbing her of breath. Never had she stood on such a precipice, where one false step could send her plunging into blood and violence.

"My liege and lords," she said, forcing calm into her voice. "We have not yet come to battle."

"Yet we have nothing more to say," Penamor replied in acid tones even as he sheathed his sword.

"Lord Remias." Taesara turned once more to Herensen's grandson. "Look what lays before you, what fate you might bring upon your people if you refuse the very generous peace we offer. The whole of Roenfyn has gathered here. Levies come from the territories of New Linfeln to defend our cause. Even the wizards of Galia fight at our sides. I know your province, its beauty and its strength. Yours are formidable soldiers, but they are not mages. That brand of magic was nurtured in the east, in Selen and Moehn and Moisehén. How will you defend this one city against all the forces we have at our disposal?"

"Do not underestimate our determination, Princess Taesara. Even if we should falter, Queen Eolyn and her mage warriors will soon come to our aid."

"Their march was delayed as they mourned the King. She will not arrive in time to save you."

Remias's eyes narrowed and he spurred his horse forward.

"Taesara," Penamor growled in warning, but she held her

243

ground.

The young lord of Selkynsen halted an arm's length away and studied her with open contempt. "Pray to your Gods that this city does not fall, Taesara of Selkynsen, for if it does, the blood of all my people will be on your fair and foolish hands."

CHAPTER THIRTY-SIX

Alliances

COREY WATCHED EOLYN bid farewell to her children as the rising sun spread golden light over the city gates. Members of the Council encircled the royal family. The army, ready for its march, was assembled on the vast fields below the city walls. A mass of people crowded this show of wealth and arms, lilies in hand, words of praise and encouragement on their lips.

The prince and princess of Moisehén bore the full regalia of their station. Silver circlets sat on their heads. Jeweled weapons adorned their belts. Brother and sister kept their heads high and their backs straight despite the weight of their riding cloaks. They did not fidget and they did not cry, though the trauma of recent days had shot dark arrows through their young auras.

They are the image of Briana and Kedehen, Corey realized. *As if my cousin and her King were recast in miniature and set anew before us all.*

Princess Briana's resemblance to her namesake had always unsettled Corey, but today the flash of those green eyes was particularly uncanny. The girl's gaze held maturity and purpose; a depth of experience that appeared wholly out of place in a girl of six summers.

Eolyn's voice faltered, a momentary lapse that belied the harsh emotions churning through her aura. Corey could imagine the tears she had shed in the privacy of her chambers a few hours before, when she was allowed to embrace and kiss her children for the last time. Here at the city gates, however, all the people saw was a public confirmation of their Queen's courage and resolve. Eolyn had learned much during her years with the stony Prince of

245

Vortingen. She had learned not to let anyone past the illusion of absolute power.

Thelyn and Echior would remain behind to watch over the prince and guide his stewardship of the city. They would be joined soon by Borten's lovely wife Vinelia, summoned to assist her husband in his recovery, and more importantly, to serve the Crown as a new member of the Council.

Corey had been appointed to ride at the Queen's side as they led the army toward Rhiemsaven. He might have interpreted this as an expression of renewed favor, but he knew better. Eolyn, like her late husband, preferred to keep those she least trusted close at hand.

The rites ended with Thelyn's invocation of Dragon's blessing. After exchanging a bow of respect with the prince and princess, Eolyn signaled her mount to begin the long ride west. Corey assumed his place at her side. The Queen's personal guard surrounded them. Banner men rode ahead, the colors of Akmael's house fluttering high over the procession. A shower of fragrant white petals fell on their path.

"Victory!" the people cried. "Victory to Queen Eolyn! Vengeance for her son, Prince Eoghan of Moisehén!"

Eolyn acknowledged their praise by unsheathing Kel'Barú and lifting it high. The blade shone silver-white against the rose gray sky. As her company rode from the city, a long snaking tail of infantry and cavalry, of carts and supplies, of craftsmen and whores, began to coalesce behind them.

Corey did not care for riding. Flight was more comfortable, though impractical unless one traveled alone or with others adept at High Magic. Imprudent, even, in times of war, when one's magic must be conserved for greater tasks. The tedious trod of a horse and all the aches it inspired could be assuaged somewhat with good conversation and bold laughter. Yet for the first time in memory, Corey found himself reluctant to violate the cloak of silence that had enveloped Eolyn.

Laughter is not the medicine she needs.

In recent days, Corey had grappled with the possibility that he had, at last, perhaps gone too far. For years, the mage had played the same game with Eolyn that he played with all the others, as if she were no more than another pawn inside a great game, as dispensable as any other.

That had changed the night of the Naether Demons' attack, when he almost lost Eolyn to the abyss. Afterwards, Corey berated himself for having allowed events to come to this, for having left himself with no choice beyond a ruthless and desperate curse that should have remained hidden until the end of time.

Well it worked, didn't it?

It was not in his nature to indulge in sentimental doubts, to wallow in what might have been. Had Eolyn perished, he would have found a way forward on his own, as he always had.

And yet...

Storm clouds were gathering over low hills ahead. Wind swept across the grass, buffeting Corey's senses with the aroma of fresh rain. A day would pass, perhaps two, before they hit that distant bank of misty gray. Poor weather would slow their progress, and with Selkynsen under siege, they could hardly afford another delay.

"What am I to do with your friendship, Mage Corey?"

Eolyn's question startled the mage out of his deliberations. He glanced at the maga, uncertain whether he had merely imagined her voice. "My Lady Queen?"

Her expression was one of puzzlement, as if contemplating a riddle that had no solution. Faint lines had begun to feather around Eolyn's eyes, and a crease had settled upon her brow. In the finest tradition of the magas, Eolyn was growing lovelier with age. Her face exemplified the beauty of wisdom shaped by loss; of inner strength defined by sorrows overcome.

"Your friendship," she said. "What am I to do with it?"

"I find it encouraging that you still call ours a friendship."

"What would you call it?"

Corey held her gaze. He remembered the first time Eolyn had come to East Selen, new and innocent among the members of his Circle. One walk with her through the woodland corridors, and all Corey's suspicions regarding the magical gifts of the peasant girl from Moehn had been confirmed. For a few brief and splendid days, he had envisioned a different sort of future. He had begun to believe the renewal promised by his cousin Brian might in fact be possible. Then the full truth of Eolyn's situation was revealed, and Corey was forced back onto a path of difficult choices.

247

"Ours is an alliance," he said. "One that has served us both well."

Eolyn blinked and looked away, focusing on the road that stretched ahead. Her fingers drifted to the Silver Web at her throat.

Understanding where her thoughts had gone, Corey returned to contemplating the landscape. The dark waters of the Furma River reflected a slate gray sky. In the reeds along the edge, a sleek silver heron stood still as a winter night, head tilted while it waited for a fish to pass within range.

"I have often wondered why my husband kept you in his counsel."

Twice now she had started a conversation. Corey could not help but think that was a good sign. "King Akmael knew I would not betray him."

"That is what I do not understand. What gave him that assurance?"

"We were kinsmen, Eolyn. Mages of East Selen, bound to each other by the blood in our veins"

"He was also Kedehen's son. You plotted against him and his father when you helped stage Ernan's rebellion."

"I made my true allegiances clear when I betrayed your brother."

"Did you? You delivered me to Ernan knowing we would confront Akmael in battle. It was a cunning move, Corey, ensuring a place for the Clan of East Selen in both camps, guaranteeing the survival of your people no matter what the outcome."

Corey let her words linger in the air. He drew a quiet breath. "I believe you have answered your own question, my Lady Queen. Though perhaps I should add, in my defense, that nothing is ever guaranteed."

Again silence fell between them. High on the opposite bank sat a lone fir, out of place in this landscape and twisted by exposure to the wind.

"I dream of him. Constantly." The words fell from her lips like pebbles dropped into a stream, gone almost before their passing was noted.

Corey glanced at the guards and invoked a sound ward.

"I would find it troubling if you did not," he said.

"During the day I hear him call my name. I turn around, expecting to see him, but all I find is emptiness. And at night…" Her gloved hands tightened around her reins. "To lose my Lord King in any moment would have been unbearable, but to endure his absence now with an army at our gates and treachery among our people…I keep thinking, tomorrow will be a better day. Tomorrow I will see the light somewhere in all of this. But it only gets worse. It's getting worse, Corey."

"It is not unusual for kings to die in times of war," Corey said, "and for queens to be left with the burden of defending the realm. You have done well, Eolyn. Moisehén might have fallen apart in a fortnight if you hadn't assumed power with such clarity and resolve. You have an army at your command. The people of Selkynsen defend their lands valiantly on the faith you will come to their aid."

"I don't think you understand." She looked at him with a haunted gaze. "A shadow is consuming my soul. The morning I spared Cramon Langerhaans…I *enjoyed* making him suffer. I drew power from his terror. Now there is a flame in my heart that longs for the same sordid fulfillment."

"It is a passing effect of the many great losses you have suffered. What you need is the breath of Dragon, a renewal of the Spirit of the Forest. Candles of sage and rose aithne, infusions of fresh herbs every night and every morning. I will make it my task to see you healed, Eolyn. I will give Jacquetta very specific instructions as to your care in the coming days."

"Then you have seen nothing? You have not noticed any breach in my aura?"

"No. I assure you, I have not."

"What if the Naether Demons find a way into this world again?"

"We would be fools not to prepare for the possibility, but the curse I cast bought us time. The portals the Naether Demons used in the fortress have been identified and sealed. Finding another path will not be easy for them."

"I did not want to leave the children alone, but nor could I risk bringing them on this campaign. What place is safe for them anymore? East Selen? The South Woods? Somewhere beyond this realm?"

249

"Hiding your children will never be the solution, Eolyn. If we fail in Selkynsen, the defense of the King's City will fall to your son and his advisors. He must be present to assume his reign."

"So much hate with so little reason." She shook her head. "When I do not dream of Akmael, I dream of his father. Kedehen comes to me and puts his sword in my hand. *Slay them*, he says. *Slay them all, for they will not be dissuaded from their bloody ambitions.* And I find myself inclined to agree."

"Yet you slay no one."

"I've slayed many. Mechnes, the Naether Demons, and now–"

"In the dream, Eolyn. In the dream you slay no one?"

She frowned. "I hold Kedehen's sword and I look with fury upon my enemies. I raise the blade and charge toward them, but then I wake up, troubled by the taste of their fear. By the promise of their blood."

The mage allowed himself a smile. "If there's one thing you should know of yourself by now, Eolyn, it's that you have a remarkable resistance to the desire for vengeance."

"I'm not so certain."

"You spared Langerhaans."

"Borten counseled me to do that. If I had executed Langerhaans, his entire family would have turned against us. If I had pardoned him without punishment, they would have scuttled away to join Roenfyn all the same. So I abused and shamed him publicly in a manner he and everyone else will never forget. Now, I suspect Langerhaans will play the same game you played. He will send some of his house to Roenfyn and the rest to me, hoping to preserve his blood no matter who triumphs. Not ideal, but more than we would have had otherwise."

She drew her lips in a thin white line.

"Once this war is over, I may yet find a way to rid myself of that troublesome lord from New Linfeln," she added. "And you, Corey? Why did you spare Baedon?"

The question caught him by surprise. "I do not understand your meaning, my Lady Queen. Baedon burned, by your command and by the will of the Council."

"Much good this alliance will serve us, Mage Corey, if we continue speaking to each other in half truths."

Corey held her gaze a long moment. Something released inside of him, then. The last barrier, perhaps, to the one path that had most eluded him.

"I am not certain, Eolyn. I knew Baedon in another time, when what he believed and did was seen in a different light. He and Tzeremond were not bad men, just a shade too rigid in their convictions. They taught me some formidable wizardry, and in that I owe them much. In spite of everything, I never ceased to admire their skill and knowledge. Baedon suffered in his own way, having witnessed the death of his closest friend, and having endured the restoration of all they fought to destroy. He was deeply repentant about unleashing the forces that killed Akmael. The man they brought to the pyre was miserable, exhausted and broken. I suppose I…I suppose I saw something of myself in him, what I might have been had history played out differently. It seemed a small mercy to put Baedon to sleep before the flames touched him. I do not regret it. I would do it again."

Eolyn studied him, her expression a mix of understanding and melancholy. "Would that someone had extended the same mercy to my mother, when she burned."

Corey looked across the river, toward the treeless landscape that led north to the wastes of Faernvorn. A cold and humid wind buffeted his face. "Who is to say no one did?"

CHAPTER THIRTY-SEVEN

Friends Made Enemies

MARIEL ALIGHTED ON A LOW BRANCH in the form of Mountain Hawk, ruffling her feathers as she secured a balance. Above the canopy, the last rays of twilight painted the mountains in subtle flames, but here the forest was shrouded in darkness. A soft beating of wings announced the arrival of her companions. Calling upon her human form, Mariel leapt silently to the ground. Knife in hand, she scanned their surroundings.

The chirp of crickets filled the night. The song of frogs indicated the presence of water nearby. Beyond that, no sound disturbed the sleeping forest or its thick carpet of dry leaves.

With the soft whistle of a midnight thrush, she called to Betania and Delavi. Her companions resumed their human forms in brief flashes of light and landed quietly next to her.

"Nice instinct, Mariel." Betania produced a glowing crystal. The flaxen-haired maga angled her light to illuminate a patch of willow fern. "We'll have soft beds tonight, and there's plenty of kindling here for a fire."

"I don't think we should build a fire," Delavi replied. "What if we're seen?"

"We want to be seen." Mariel went to the edge of the clearing and began harvesting willow fern with swift clean strokes of her knife. The fronds were feathery to the touch. The cut stems released a mild and soothing fragrance. "We are emissaries sent by the Queen of Moisehén, not renegades sneaking across the border."

"Then why are we acting like renegades?" Delavi asked. "We could have just gone up the pass of Selkynsen."

"It's faster this way."

"Not if we get lost, it isn't."

"We will not get lost," Mariel said. "These trees are kin to the South Woods. They are showing me the way. Come help with the bedding, will you?"

Delavi nodded and set to work, gathering armfuls of willow fern. She laid the fronds out near Betania, who stacked wood for a fire.

"I don't care whether the forests speak to you or not," Delavi said. "I would have much rather entered this territory openly, through a proper gate and tower."

"The forests are the gates of Khelia's realm," Mariel replied, "and the mountains her towers."

"Nonsense," Delavi said. "Even the Mountain People have proper roads. We just decided not to use them."

At Betania's quiet invocation, the pyramid of twigs ignited. The spark leapt into a bright yellow fire that chased away the shadows and the chill. Betania sat back on her heels to watch the flickering light.

"I'm hungry," she said. "I should have thought to catch a mouse along the way, or a bat. Did you see the swarm coming out of that cave at dusk?"

"You would have been stuck in Hawk's form all night if you did," Delavi said. "It takes forever to digest a bat."

Betania shrugged. "It's not such a bad way to sleep. Better, perhaps, than being vulnerable on the ground."

"I'll set a trap," Mariel offered. "We might yet snare a rabbit or two for supper."

"Breakfast, more like." Delavi rose and touched Mariel's arm. "I'll set the traps. You stay here and rest."

She vanished among the trees before Mariel could protest. The young maga looked at Betania. "Does it show that much?"

"Your fatigue?" Betania nodded. "Oh, yes."

Mariel sighed and took a place by the fire next to her companion. "I suppose there's no point in me insisting on taking the first watch then."

"Not a chance."

"I don't feel that tired, really. The forest awakens my senses."

253

"And your magic?"

Mariel shook her head. "Let's just say, I need a good night's sleep before shape shifting again."

Moon light broke through luminescent clouds, casting shadows of an altogether different nature from those of the city. Kinder, somehow. More inviting and less ominous. Trees beckoned toward sleep with their whispered song. Even the rocks called to Mariel, each revealing its name and place as if greeting an old friend.

Mariel picked up one of the whispering stones and held it in her hand, comforted by the feel of ancient magic seeping into her skin.

"I'm surprised Maga Eolyn sent you on this journey." Betania tossed a twig into the fire. "It seems too much to ask, given all you've been through."

"She didn't send me. She asked me if I would be willing to go, and I said yes." Mariel whispered to the stone and then put it back in its place, marking the position of its neighbors. "I wanted to see the forests and mountains again, to feel woodland magic in my spirit. And I'm curious about this realm ruled by women, about the warrior Maga Eolyn once called her friend."

"I've heard of Khelia's battles in Antaria and Galia," Betania said. "She slew hundreds in the Valley of Aerunden. She's ruthless and cunning, they say, with a thirst for blood that matches any man's. They also say she does not forget."

"That is why Eolyn hopes to secure her aid."

"Yet Maga Eolyn married the man who butchered Khelia's friend and ally; it's foolish to think she will come to Moisehén's aid now."

Mariel rolled her eyes, bone-weary from Betania's bickering. "You've been saying the same thing ever since we left the City. Don't you think you could let it rest for one night? The Queen has given us our orders. We must see her will done. That is all."

Betania shrugged and held her peace.

Mariel let her gaze rest upon the soothing dance of flame, grateful in her heart that Eolyn had decided to give her this charge. The mountain forests reminded her of happier days, when she and the other girls of Eolyn's *Aekelahr* danced around fires in a moonlit wood. There was majesty in those times, freedom and a sense of companionship she had never quite recaptured. None of the cynicism that characterized her sisters from the King's City had touched that quiet community in Moehn. Tonight the longing for the laughter of her youth was unusually strong, even painful.

Perhaps Maga Eolyn is right. Perhaps the best choice I can make is to return to Moehn.

A screech owl sounded nearby.

Mariel rose to her feet. The hair on the back of her neck pricked.

"Something's wrong," she said. "Where is Delavi? She should be back by now."

Leaves rattled in a passing breeze. Mariel caught the sound of muffled cries, of feet scuffling over the leaf litter, of blows on flesh. Just as she reached for her knife, Betania sprang at her from behind.

One arm closed hard around Mariel's chest. A blade flashed toward her throat. Mariel caught Betania's forearm with both hands, fingers digging into flesh as she strained to keep the knife at bay. They stumbled, rocks and leaves skidding underfoot, until at last Mariel found her footing. She flung back her head and felt the satisfying crunch of Betania's nose. The maga cried out and released her.

Naeom aenre!

Scarlet flame burst from Betania's palm and surged toward Mariel. She flung herself to the ground, palms skidding on hard earth. The stream of fire passed overhead and pummeled into a nearby tree. The trunk exploded into ashes and flame. Mariel clung breathless to the grass and turned her face from the scalding heat.

Gods help me! I have no magic left for this.

She forced herself to her feet. Betania circled the fire, eyes hard as stone as she stalked Mariel. Again she lunged, blade hissing past Mariel's face. Mariel dove to the ground and rolled into a crouch. Tearing her knife from its sheath, she flung it at her attacker. The blade hit its mark, sinking deep into Betania's chest. The maga warrior's eyes widened; her breath was reduced to short, hiccupping gasps. Blood pooled on Betania's lips. She fell to the earth, shuddered, and lay still.

Mariel stumbled toward the body, sank on her knees, and rested one hand on the bloodied tunic. Tears blurred her vision.

Her breath came hoarse and labored.

"What has happened?" she murmured in shock. "What have I done?"

The cold breath of steel grazed her throat. Mariel froze and lifted her eyes to see none other than Ghemena standing above her, sword in hand, a mocking smile on her face.

"What have you done, indeed?" she said. "Get away from her, Mariel."

Mariel scooted on her knees, conscious of the steel that kissed her skin. "How did you find us?"

"I had my sources." Ghemena cast a narrow-eyed glance at Betania's corpse. "Your knife was always quick, Mariel, but I didn't think you had it in you to kill one of your own sisters. Wasn't it Maga Eolyn who always said—?"

"Yet you ordered Betania to kill me!"

"She no longer considered you a sister."

Fury rose in Mariel's blood. "Gods take you, Ghemena, and everything you have unleashed upon our people!"

"I have unleashed nothing. It is your friends, the mages, who weave their dark plans and terrible spells. It is your weak and ineffectual tutor who does nothing but lie upon her back to please them."

"And Delavi?" Mariel nodded toward the dark wood. "Is she your spy, too?"

"Delavi had no eyes for the future. So now she is dead."

"Killing us will gain you nothing. If we don't reach Khelia on Maga Eolyn's behalf, someone else will."

"Khelia has no reason to come to Eolyn's aid. We have already spoken to her, Mariel. The Mountain Queen marches with her army to join Roenfyn and Galia. Together, they will destroy the Mage King's whore."

Dread gripped Mariel's heart. How could Moisehén hope to survive the attack of three kingdoms?

"I don't understand why you do this," she said quietly. "Why you hate her so?"

"Yes, well you were the one she saved, weren't you?" Ghemena shot back. "Had you been left behind like the rest of us, imprisoned, raped, tortured, and sacrificed, perhaps you would not be so blind to her deceptions."

"She loved us all equally. She may not have been able to defend the coven from the Syrnte, but she kept us safe as long as she could. And before all of that, she took us away from a life of poverty and abuse. She set us free through our magic. How could you forget that?"

"You call your life freedom? A servant of the Mage King, a slave to his mages? We did not learn magic because of Eolyn. We learned it through our own cunning and by the will of the Gods."

"So this is how it ends, then? You intend to slay me here, in a place not unlike the woods where we once played?"

Ghemena set her jaw. "You can still join us, Mariel. I would welcome you, and so would the others."

"To make war upon our own people?"

"Roenfyn's campaign is merely a means to an end. Once it is over, women will rule Moisehén. Magas will practice the ways of Aithne not as servants to the crown, but in true freedom. Join us, Mariel. I never wanted to leave you behind. There has always been a place for you among us."

Mariel turned Ghemena's offer over in her mind, attentive to the quiet thud of her heart, remarkably calm given the precipice on which she stood. High in the canopy, a mountain owl gave its quiet call. Leaves hissed in a passing breeze. Mariel's skin was damp and cool after the exertion with Betania. She tasted salt on her lips, felt the sticky residue of blood on her fingers. Beneath her knees, the damp earth exuded an aroma of sweet moss and young herbs. And the rocks...

The rocks continue to murmur.

Mariel followed their call back in time, remembering the warmth of Maga Eolyn's embrace, the provocative caress of her own lovers, the feel of a sword in her hand, the trials endured under the Syrnte invasion. At the end of this journey, she found the sweet smell of young Ghemena, a spirited girl of six summers recently arrived at the *Aekelahr*. Mariel had been the first to welcome the child. She had told Ghemena stories every night, filling her head with fantasies of the Magas of Old until she fell asleep.

"I would rather you kill me, Ghemena."

The maga warrior's brow furrowed. She pressed her blade

against Mariel's throat. "Why?"

"I do not care to live in a world where women are divided against men, and magas against each other."

"That's what I'm telling you, Mariel! We are putting an end to a conflict of generations. After this, we will all live in peace."

Mariel shook her head. She kept her eyes fixed on Ghemena as she extended her fingers toward the earth, beckoning the stones to do her bidding, sensing their ready tremor inside her magic.

"Your zealousness blinds you, Ghemena. It always has. The future of women's magic will never be secure if we keep laying our foundations with bloodshed. Slay me tonight and go your way. In truth you do me a favor. I am weary of this world and all its shadows."

Ghemena tightened the grip on her hilt. Determination settled in her jaw. As Ghemena drew back the blade, Mariel called to the stones. They responded, shooting toward Ghemena and slamming her in the forehead.

Stunned, Ghemena stumbled backwards. Blood spurted down her face. The sword slipped from her hands. She wavered for a moment and then collapsed without grace onto the grass.

Mariel rose and approached Ghemena's splayed form. Retrieving her sister's sword, she wrapped her hands around the hilt and set the blade against Ghemena's throat.

"Sweet Gods of Dragon," she prayed, "forgive me for what I am about to do."

CHAPTER THIRTY-EIGHT

Siege

FROM THE DARKNESS OF HER TENT, Taesara heard her uncle's weapons: the high arc as stones hissed toward the heavens, the deepening ring of their descent to the earth. Each impact sent a tremor through the ground.

Was it just her imagination, or at this distance could she hear the screams of those lacerated by splintering rock?

Unable to sleep, Taesara rose and donned her cloak. In the flickering candlelight, she paused at Eliasara's bedside. The calm of the girl's face hinted at some pleasant dream far removed from the chaos and death that ruled the night.

Another tremor shook the earth. Taesara donned her cloak and exited the tent, guards falling into place around her. With long and purposeful strides, she walked the short distance to a ridge overlooking the city of Selkynsen. The night was hazy and the stars muted by clouds. Across the river, stones shrouded in scarlet and purple flames flew toward Selkynsen, where they exploded in orange pillars of fire.

Every night the people of Selkynsen had endured this onslaught. Every morning the city had greeted the dawn beneath a haze of smoldering fires extinguished by deep wells, powerful magic, and sheer will. Whoever had not burned at night might be impaled, crushed, or dismembered by day. The shower of arrows from both sides had been non-stop; the occasional sallies from the gate brutal and bloody.

Penamor was collecting fallen bodies of the enemy. He let the corpses rot in rancid piles and then sent them, bloated and stinking, back over the city walls.

Whatever it takes to break their spirit, he had said.

All of it made Taesara sick to her stomach.

"They will not hold out much longer."

Taesara started at the gravelly voice of Savegre's advisor, Urales, who appeared beside her.

The wizard's dark robes blended into the night. A turban crowned his gaunt face. She had encountered Urales many times at this outlook in recent days, and still his presence unnerved her. His lean figure towered over every other member of her uncle's court, indeed over Savegre himself.

He caught her stare in a sideways glance and gave a slow nod of respect. "Forgive me, Queen Taesara. So accustomed have I become to meeting you in this place that I forget to extend the courtesy of a greeting."

Taesara allowed a sad smile to touch her lips. "Courtesies serve us little in times of war."

"On the contrary, my Lady Queen. Courtesy is all that illuminates the path out of these fields of death. Courtesy between allies, and even between enemies."

"I doubt much courtesy will be shown to Selkynsen, once their walls crumble."

"If Penamor chooses to punish the city, it will not be for lack of effort on your part to dissuade him."

The subtle acknowledgment of her will and her impotence made Taesara's heart ache. "I will try again tomorrow."

"That may be your last opportunity."

Urales extended his arm over the landscape, illuminating the fields beyond the river in a thin, gray twilight. The movement of soldiers became visible, at once frantic and well-ordered.

"Our moles have nearly finished their work along the outer wall," he said. "Tomorrow the fire of Uru'bai will be unleashed, and all will know the power of Galian wizardry."

"Is your Prince also bent on looting this city of dreams?"

"Savegre has heard your petition."

"That does not answer my question."

"Whatever the ambitions of our lieges, they will come to naught if rains arrive and extinguish the fires."

Taesara's gaze strayed north and east, where lightning illuminated the horizon. "Our rains usually come from the west."

"Those storms come for us."

"How can you be certain?"

He regarded her with a hooded gaze. "I am a Galian wizard. I know the winds and the rains, and the fires that race before them."

Taesara could think of nothing to say to this. She pulled her cloak tighter around her shoulders and stood the rest of the time with him in silence.

Hours later, Taesara returned to her tent, weary yet unable to sleep. Only when the assault paused briefly in the hours before dawn did she achieve a shallow state of rest. Soon she heard the movement of her ladies around the bed, followed by Sonia's gentle call to breakfast.

Taesara rose groggy and stiff. The women fussed over how best to conceal the dark circles under her eyes, and what color of dress might offset her pallor. Their chatter ignited Taesara's impatience. What did it matter, her appearance during war?

When at last they finished dressing her, the Queen sat down to her morning meal. She ate like an orphan starved for weeks, mystified by her own appetite. Eliasara drifted out of bed and took a place next to her mother.

"I want to cross the river today," the princess announced.

"We've already discussed that, Eliasara. It's too dangerous."

"It is torture to be this close to home and not even set foot on the land of my birth."

A greater torture it will be when you enter that corpse-littered field and look upon the ruin that was once Selkynsen. "We will cross the river together on the day Selkynsen surrenders, so that you can enter the city in triumph."

"It won't be my triumph."

"It will be a victory won by your uncle and his allies on your behalf."

"If I'm to be a true Queen of Vortingen, I have to do more than just sit around while others fight my battles."

"Soon you will be old enough to lead your own wars, though I pray to the Gods you never have to. Eat, Eliasara," Taesara added, anticipating her daughter's instinct to push away her plate. "Do not disdain this food. There is disease in the camp, and hardly enough to feed our soldiers. You must maintain your health."

Eliasara frowned but set herself to chewing on a piece of bread.

Having finished her own breakfast, Taesara rose and called for her horse.

Misty clouds hung low over the land, shutting out the rising sun. Accompanied by guards, Taesara descended the winding path to the river's edge, crossed the narrow stone bridge, and ascended the rise just south of the city.

The impact of Roenfyn's missiles thundered across the field, accompanied by cries and shouts of men pitted against each other in battle. Taesara wished not to look upon their struggle, but her gaze strayed toward the blackened landscape nonetheless.

Penamor's siege towers had not withstood the fires of Selkynsen's mage warriors. Their skeletal remains stood broken and burned near the walls of the city. Bodies of soldiers who had tried to scale the ramparts, only to be shot down by an unrelenting storm of arrows, littered the base of the western wall.

Taesara was uncertain as to where the Galian moles were at work. It was said they excavated tunnels with the same molten fire that carved through their mountains. Something about the thought of those orange flames illuminating the cold bowels of the earth unsettled Taesara, making her lips dry and her mouth water. Disconcerted, she turned away from the battle and urged her horse toward Penamor's tent.

The Lord Regent stood outside, fully armored and delivering orders to his officers in short, impatient barks. As Penamor's men dispersed, he signaled for his mount. Taesara quickened her pace.

"Uncle!" she called.

Penamor's sharp gaze settled on her. He grinned with pleasure. "Niece. To what do I owe this unexpected visit?"

"Please, Uncle." She reined her horse in next to him. "I would speak with you once more regarding the fate of the people of Selkynsen."

His smile did not spread to his eyes. "One would think you were born among them, so constant has been your plea for mercy."

"I only want you to consider—"

"I have considered everything, dear niece. Seven days we have borne hard upon them. Seven mornings they have refused to open their gates. We can no longer delay here, wasting men and arms on stubborn merchants. Our scouts and spies say the Witch Queen marches toward us from Rhiemsaven. It is time to lay waste to Selkynsen and seize your daughter's destiny."

He mounted his horse and accepted a helmet from his squire.

"Join us, Taesara," he said. "It will be a good show today. I daresay you will like the taste of victory."

Penamor spurred his horse forward. A company of guards fell into place around him, concealing his retreating figure.

The world closed in on Taesara. How could she feel suffocation in such open spaces, when all she ever felt in the close confines of the abbey was freedom of heart and spirit?

Tightening the grip on her reins, she followed her uncle and caught up with him at the peak of a low rise. Savegre greeted them there, expression grim and gaze fixed on the walls of the city. At his side, the ever-present Urales stood like a shadow stolen from the night.

The assault on the west wall had ceased. Catapults lay still as sleeping dragons. Soldiers had assembled along the length of the field, companies laid out in well-ordered rows. The flags of Roenfyn and Galia snapped overhead.

"Well?" Penamor's tone was sharp.

Savegre nodded. "Everything is ready."

Penamor drew his sword and held it high. Accompanied by a select number of his guard, the regent trotted downhill toward the gates of the city. He stopped short of the range of the archers and shouted toward the ramparts. "People of Selkynsen, hear me! Eliasara, Queen of Moisehén, declares that her patience runs thin. At her command, we have placed Galian magic under your walls, the feared breath of Uru'bai. Lay down your weapons, or all will perish."

Only a handful of sounds strayed into the silence that followed. A hawk keened high overhead. Ravens cawed in a nearby tree. A man coughed. A horse snorted. Thunder rumbled from distant and menacing clouds.

Then an unexpected rustle caught Taesara's ear, the soft slither of cloth unfurling against stone. A white flag descended over the gates of Selkynsen. Painted upon its face was a pale yellow diamond.

Taesara's heart leapt with joy. She urged the horse forward, but Savegre caught the bridle.

"Let me go," she said, indignant. "They have asked for parley."

"What they ask has not been granted."

"But Penamor will grant it." She looked toward her uncle. Doubt surged in her breast. "He must."

The regent held his sword high. His mount reared and pranced. Taesara could not see Penamor's face from this distance, but she could well imagine the hard glint in her uncle's eyes, the sardonic grin that crept across his face.

Breaking free of Savegre's grip, she spurred her horse and sped down slope toward Penamor, hooves pounding against the hard earth. Savegre shouted after her. Just as she reached the front lines, the Galian Prince cut her off.

"You will go no further!" Anger colored his every gesture. Even the black beast he rode was restless with rage.

"You know what he plans to do." Taesara tried to navigate around horse and rider, but without success. "If you will not let me stop him, then you must stop him yourself."

"I cannot."

"The men who control the fire of *Uru'bai* are under your command. Tell them they cannot invoke this weapon."

"That command has been given to your uncle. They watch him, not me."

"Then make them—"

Penamor let go a battle cry and brought down his sword.

Trumpets sounded. The earth shook. Thin pillars of sulfur-laden steam erupted along the battle field. Taesara heard screams of agony and realized with horror that some of their own men were caught in the scalding baths.

A geyser hissed to the surface a few paces away, like the breath of some long-buried monster billowing toward the sky. Taesara's horse panicked and reared. She lost her balance and tumbled to the ground. Pain shot through her shoulder and ribs. Stars flashed across her vision.

Savegre dismounted and hauled Taesara to her feet, causing her to wince.

"We must go," he said. "Now."

Officers harried their ranks to hold position as the muted explosions advanced toward the walls. Taesara's horse ran off, Savegre's black stallion following close on its heels.

Then the steam died out and the restless earth quieted.

Taesara turned toward the walls of Selkynsen, heart beating against a cloak of silence. Five times. Fifteen. Thirty.

Moments extended into minutes, yet the fire of *Uru-bai* did not ignite.

Shouts of relief sounded from the ramparts. The defenders of Selkynsen laughed and jeered and brandished their weapons, hope blossoming among their ranks.

Then the earth groaned beneath them and unleashed its bowels. Flames of scarlet and ebony burst from the ground and roared toward the heavens, piercing low clouds, shrouding the world in thick smoke.

Savegre took Taesara in his arms and threw her to the ground, covering her with his body just as the blast reached them. Wind screamed past Taesara's ears. Rocks and debris fell from the sky. Choking on hot air, Taesara writhed inside Savegre's steely hold.

At last the rain of fire and stone ended. Savegre loosened his embrace.

Taesara scrambled away and stood, legs trembling from shock. Amidst a gray haze she saw the shadows of her uncle's men stumbling and wheezing. Disarray had overtaken their ranks.

As the smoke cleared, Penamor came into view. By the grace of the Gods he was still mounted. Sword in hand, the regent took in what remained of the defenses of Selkynsen. The outer walls had crumbled; countless bodies were crushed between the stones. The roofs beyond were alight with orange flames.

Penamor laughed in triumph.

"Have at it, men," he shouted. "The city is ours."

The horns of Roenfyn sounded, and its army flowed over the ruined walls, provoking screams of panic and lament from the city beyond.

CHAPTER THIRTY-NINE

Seduction

RAIN DRUMMED AGAINST THE CANVAS, a merciful deluge that had begun shortly after the fall of Selkynsen's outer wall. The downpour had extinguished the fires ravaging the city but did little to stop the brutality and bloodshed.

Taesara paced restless inside her tent. Her temples throbbed. Lord Remias's curse echoed inside her head.

The blood of my people will be on your hands.

She clamped her hands on her ears to shut him out.

"This is the way of war," she said to the silence. "We have invented nothing on this day!"

From the time Thunder had descended to earth to protect her people from the followers of Dragon, men had slaughtered each other in pursuit of justice and power. Why should this generation, these struggles, be any different?

Yet she felt as if her own soul had been dragged through the streets of Selkynsen. Her throat ached as if it had endured the screams of Selkynsen's women. Her palms felt warm and sticky as if covered with the blood of its children. What peace she had found during her short years of service among the Sisters of the Poor had been obliterated by this campaign. Every life she had saved, every soul she had comforted paled against the countless victims falling under the swords of Roenfyn.

This burden is not yours to carry.

Taesara jumped at the sound of Savegre's voice, at once distant and intimate, like an echo inside her heart. She turned abruptly, searching the dim corners of the tent.

266

All the servants and ladies had long since been sent away. Most of the candles were extinguished. Eliasara slept soundly in her bed, her soft snore muffled by the insistent rain. Lightning illuminated the rim of the canvas, thunder sounded in the heavens.

A mist gathered over the floor, slipping under the hem of Taesara's dress, caressing her ankles. She bent low to touch it, fascinated by the cool, soft tendrils sifting through her fingers.

"Savegre," she murmured. A name that inspired heartbreak.

The mist billowed upward and fell away to reveal the Galian Prince.

Taesara rose to meet his gaze. "How well you blend with the shadows."

"You heard my words," he said.

"Yes. They are of little comfort."

"I did not come to comfort you."

Taesara would have asked, *why then did you come?* But she could feel the heat of his intentions, and she loathed burdening conversations with the obvious.

"What word do you have of Selkynsen?" she asked.

"The inner wall has held, and many escaped to its refuge. But the quarters exposed by the outer walls are in ruins."

"They would have been the poorest, the most destitute of Selkynsen's people." Taesara knew well the layout of the city. "So little in their possession when this day began, and now they have nothing at all."

Savegre took a step toward her. Taesara backed away.

"You brought down the walls, and yet your people did not participate in the sack," she said. "Why?"

"It was not our place to destroy the city."

"Yet it was your place to bring down the walls?"

"One promise was made to your uncle, another to our Gods."

"I see." Though in truth, she did not. Whatever the thread of Galian intent was in this war, it still escaped her grasp.

Again he closed the distance between them. This time she did not retreat. His war-roughened hand touched her cheek. Taesara close her eyes against the sting of tears.

"Go," she said quietly. "I cannot give what you seek."

"Lend me your magic, Taesara of Roenfyn."

"I am a Daughter of Thunder. I have no magic."

"Lend me your magic, and your desire will be granted."

"You know nothing of my..." She faltered, wanting with all her heart to believe in this illusion, in his promise of intimacy.

"You think I cannot see what you covet, Taesara of Roenfyn? You desire his power with every fiber of your spirit. You hope to use his crown for good."

Covet. A forbidden word in Taesara's training. A dangerous one.

She leaned into the heat of Savegre's body, inhaled his aroma of summer earth and salt-laden seas, interlaced with blood and fire and deep, abiding passion.

"Go," she said weakly, but she found Savegre's lips instead.

His embrace was the touch of the sun itself, warm and sensual. His kisses fell like flames upon her tongue and traced a burning river down her neck.

Taesara pulled away, heart pounding. A choked sob escaped her lips. "I said, go."

"I do not understand." He regarded her with a puzzled expression. "Why are you afraid of me? Why do you reject this gift, this spell that has touched your heart and mine? It is a blessing from the Gods."

"Not my Gods!" The rebuke came harsher than she intended.

Silence followed.

Taesara felt the sting of the lance she had just sent through his heart.

"I see," he said quietly. "I will not trouble you again, Taesara of Roenfyn."

Sorrow constricted her throat as he turned away; she felt the wounds of a fifteen-year-old bride still raw upon her soul.

"Savegre," she whispered.

It was enough to halt his retreat.

"I...I cannot please a wizard." Her voice shook. "That is why I send you away. Three years I tried. I gave him every gift at my disposal, yet I could not thaw his heart, nor even feel pleasure at his touch. With every day that passed, he grew colder, more indifferent, until he cast me out in anger and turned instead to his woman of magic. Now look."

She gestured in the direction of Selkynsen. "Look what my failure has wrought. Bloodshed and war, the suffering of countless souls. And you...You come to me with the fires of Galia in the palm of your hand. I would be a hypocrite, a liar to claim I am not flattered by your attentions, but I cannot bear to see the disappointment in your eyes that I saw in his. I would rather live to the end of my days imagining what might have been, than to unveil the bitter truth of my inadequacy once more."

For what seemed an endless moment, Savegre said nothing. Then a bemused smile touched his lips. "Taesara, Princess of Roenfyn, how is it possible that no one has honored you with this the most important of all truths?"

"I don't understand what you're saying."

"A mage must please the women entrusted to him, else his magic is worth nothing in the eyes of the Gods. It was not your failure that angered the Mage King. It was his own."

Taesara stared at Savegre in confusion. Then something shifted inside of her. The weight of a decade, of all her miserable failures, began to slip from her shoulders.

She reached out to touch his face. He responded with a sensual caress, a gentle but insistent tug on each fingertip that robbed her of breath and ignited an unbearable tension in the pit of her stomach.

Wrapping her arms around his neck, she set her mouth upon his. Images filled her mind's eye, of dark cliffs descending into white-tipped waves. Of moody clouds racing over thick forests. A humid breeze, loosening the tresses of her hair.

"Savegre," she murmured.

He lifted her up and carried her toward the bed.

"My daughter..." Taesara cast an anxious glance toward Eliasara's sleeping figure.

"She will not wake." Savegre laid her upon the soft cushions, slipped his hand beneath the loosened folds of her dress. "None of them will wake tonight."

Taesara gasped as he found her breasts and teased them into taut awareness. The gown seemed to dissolve at his touch, until she lay naked and glorious in his arms. A sea of fiery kisses coursed over her skin and down her abdomen before searing the landscape

269

of her thighs. Then his tongue found a place of terrifying intimacy, and Taesara cried out, possessed by an ecstasy so intense she feared she would come undone like the walls of Selkynsen, bursting from within and crumbling into formless waste.

Yet her body did not break, but was held together by some bright and miraculous thread. Waves of pleasure broke over her, each stronger than the last. With trembling hands she took hold of him, caressed his head as he delved deeper into that place of mystery. Taesara closed her eyes, disappearing inside sensation. A primal rhythm united their breath, their pulse, their dance of untold intimacies, until she succumbed to an explosion of light within.

She opened her eyes breathless, skin damp with sweat, overcome with awe and reverence. Outside the storm still raged, but the howling winds had faded against the clamor of this newly discovered need.

Savegre moved over her, a heat-filled shadow of weight and substance. The unfamiliar spice of her womanhood mingled with the salt of his sweat.

"My Queen is pleased?" He murmured in her ear.

Taesara let go a shaky laugh, thinking *pleased* an insipid word for the sensations that pounded through her. He could have asked anything of her in that moment, and she would have given it freely.

Savegre kissed her tenderly as he adjusted his weight. She felt the tip of his phallus probing a place of molten heat, teasing open a gate that until this night had guarded a barren landscape of stark duty. The first penetration evoked a gasp as her muscles accommodated his unfamiliar presence.

"My Lady Queen?" he said, concern in his tone.

"It is all right." She touched his face and gave him a tender kiss. "I am all right."

He moved inside of her then, gently at first though each thrust returned with greater vigor. Taesara laid her hands upon his back, ran her palms down its muscular, undulating surface. Reveling in the power of his desire, she pulled Savegre closer.

Breaths mingling, fingers intertwined, they laid open the pulse of the earth and followed its river of dark secrets toward destinations unknown. Taesara's spirit unfolded in a thousand colors inside his embrace. She let go of this world, of the perils that lay ahead and the regrets that lingered behind, wanting only this moment, this man, and this magic.

Forever.

CHAPTER FORTY

Lessons

MOUSE CROUCHED BEHIND A HALF-EMPTY CUP, whiskers trembling as she sniffed the air. The smell of stale wine pinched her nose. She shied away, keeping to the shadows as she scuttled from one shelter to another across the table. Pausing next to a clay pitcher, she lifted her head and listened.

Rain drummed on the tent. The muffled sound of men and movement drifted through the canvas. Yet within, nothing stirred. No thunder of footsteps against the floor, not even the shallow breath of a watchful giant.

Still she trembled, shivers coursing through small shoulders into tiny paws. Nervously she groomed herself, uncertain as to why she had come or whether she should stay.

The aroma of fresh bread and aged cheese pulled her forward. Step by cautious step she approached, sniffing and listening along the way. The plate was abandoned but dangerously exposed, cast in golden light beneath a burning candle. Mouse glanced once more around the dark tent. Satisfied by the insistent quiet, she scampered toward the meal. Her paws wrapped around a chunk of bread, and she nibbled. The sudden urgency of hunger overtook all other senses.

Without warning, darkness enveloped her, shutting out scent and light.

Dropping the food, she ran, only to be hampered by a soft barrier in every direction. A giant paw came down upon her, stifling all movement in a cup of bone and muscle. Mouse let out a frightened squeak, feeling herself lifted and manipulated beneath heavy cloth.

Light blinded her senses, and she froze beneath her captor's gaze. A quizzical expression marked his flat face. His eyes were oddly pale, his teeth large yet blunt. Giants did not eat her kind, but they had cats that did. Mouse squeaked and squirmed in his grasp.

Quiet little one. He spoke in her language. *I am not going to hurt you.*

She stilled, and he set her gently down on a stool. After a moment of hesitation, Mouse crawled out from beneath the cloth that had trapped her. Cautiously she groomed herself, watching him watching her. His eyes sparked with hidden threats. An amused smile touched his lips.

"You have grown bold, Mariel," he said, "to undertake spying on me."

Mariel allowed magic to spark through her. Shedding the shape of Mouse, she resumed her human form. "I'm not spying. I'm hungry."

Mage Corey lifted his brow but said nothing. He prepared a plate and brought it to her. Mariel devoured the simple meal and washed it down with wine.

"Maga Eolyn does not know you are here." Not a question, but a statement.

"No." Mariel shook her head. "I thought our army would have advanced further by now."

"These accursed rains have slowed our progress. Why did you come to me first?"

Mariel's stomach clenched. She set aside the plate and covered her face with her hands. "I don't know! I don't know what to do or where to go anymore. Oh, Corey! I have failed so miserably in everything."

"You mean Khelia will not come to our aid?"

"She marches to join Roenfyn."

The mage let go a long, low whistle. "And your companions?"

"Dead. Delavi by Ghemena's hand, Betania by my own. Ghemena ambushed us on the way to the Mountain Realm. Betania was one of her spies."

"Yet you escaped."

A lump rose in Mariel's throat. "Ghemena spared me. I don't

273

know why. She could have killed me. She should have, but all she did was knock me unconscious and abandon me in the forest."

"Did she spare you, or did she convert you to her cause?"

Mariel lifted her chin. "Bind my magic if you will. Lock me up again. I don't care! Gods know I would do less harm that way. I should have never been let out of the dungeon in the first place."

"Tell me what really happened, Mariel."

Mariel felt tears welling up. She cursed herself for not being able to hold a lie. "I know I should have brought her back. I should have cut off her head and delivered it to the Queen. But I couldn't, Corey. I had my blade upon her throat, and I just couldn't do it. So I left her. I don't know how long she was out, or where she might be by now."

"You've grown into a troublesome reflection of your tutor, Mariel."

"Are you going to arrest me?"

"I should have you burned according the edict signed by our late King, but no. I don't believe I will. Nor will Maga Eolyn. We know you, Mariel. You're not a traitor. You're simply an honest woman beset by an extraordinary run of bad luck. Augmented, I might add, by a touch of poor judgement. You are certain of what you say about Khelia?"

"I saw the army myself, coming down the pass of Selkynsen. I thought to seek out the Mountain Queen and plead our case, but I feared they would arrest me, or worse. Someone had to warn Maga Eolyn."

"You did well by coming here. Do you have a detailed account of their forces?"

"Yes. Of course."

"Well. That is something. Can you identify any more of Ghemena's spies among our own?"

Mariel shook her head.

Corey clucked his tongue and rose. He poured himself a cup of wine and refreshed Mariel's. "The mountain forests have returned color to your cheeks, and magic to your aura."

Mariel lowered her eyes, shamed by the memory of having broken under Baedon's curse. "It doesn't matter. Everything's falling apart because of me."

Corey took her chin in hand and lifted her face to his. "You must not blame yourself for these conflicts. They began long before you were born."

She jerked away, anger surging in her blood.

Corey took in her reaction, a thoughtful look on his face. Then he let go a slow breath and sat down in front of her. "There's something you wish to discuss with me, isn't there?"

Mariel clenched her jaw and looked away.

"Out with it, Mariel. I know what has been on your mind since Baedon took you. I will not have this silence between us anymore."

"You were his servant, weren't you? Baedon and Tzeremond trained you in their ways, and you used their curses against the magas."

"Those were different times."

"It does not matter!"

"Yes it does. It mattered a great deal. I made an oath to my cousin, Briana of East Selen. To fulfill that oath, I had to earn Tzeremond's favor, his absolute trust, no matter what the cost."

"How many magas perished because of your oath?"

Corey let her question linger in the air.

"Do you really wish to know?" he asked quietly.

"I don't know who to trust anymore! Sometimes I think Ghemena is right, that all mages are the same, and that you're the worst of them all. Yet you were the one who came to my aid, while my own sisters put blades to my throat. And Markl...Gods, Markl. I thought he was my friend. Why on earth did he turn me over to that wizard? How did I not see the evil in his heart?"

"Are you certain you did not see it?"

Mariel frowned. "Why did I not let myself recognize what was right in front of my eyes?"

"Ah." Corey smiled. "There is the question. Answer that question, and you will not be caught unawares again."

"And you? Who are you, Corey? Baedon's apprentice? Tzeremond's heir? Or something else entirely?"

Corey swirled the wine in his cup and eyed her as he drank.

"It's Maga Eolyn, isn't it?" Mariel said. "Something about her made you change your ways."

"Oh, I wouldn't give her that much credit. Though it is fair to

275

say her appearance was part of a fortunate set of circumstances."

"You could have betrayed her and gained much by doing so. Why didn't you?"

"She saved my life. Haven't you heard that story?"

Mariel rolled her eyes. "Such a debt would secure the loyalty of many, but not you."

"Your cynicism disheartens me, Mariel."

"*My* cynicism?"

"I saw something in her." He swirled his wine. "Something Briana of East Selen promised me when I was a boy."

"What? What did you see?"

Corey set his silver-green gaze on Mariel. "The future."

Mariel sat back, bewildered. She blew a wisp of hair out of her face. "Some future we're looking at now."

"Indeed...This may be my last and greatest lesson: how to remain on the losing side of a battle." Setting aside his wine, Corey rose and extended a hand to the maga. "Come, then, Mariel. We have delayed long enough. You have brought news which must be delivered with all haste to our Queen."

CHAPTER FORTY-ONE

High Waters

TAESARA DRIFTED SLOWLY OUT OF SLEEP, as if washed up on the calm shores of a warm sea. Daylight filled the tent, though the soft drizzle of rain could be heard. Beyond the curtains of the bed, her ladies conversed in hushed tones under Sonia's quiet reprimands.

The Queen snuggled more deeply inside the covers. A delicious ache filled her muscles. That place so wholly hers, and now also his, persisted in a slow heated throb, as if still wrapped around him, as if making love to his spirit.

She had a vague memory of Savegre's departure in the predawn hours, and wondered even now if it had all been a strange, vivid dream. She had heard of such nighttime visions, from sisters who claimed the Gods descended to their chambers and introduced them to pleasures untold. Stories whispered in awe outside of the presence of the Good Mother, who wielded a harsh punishment whenever such gossip reached her ears.

The Gods of Thunder do not debase themselves with crude folly, she often said. *It is Dragon who seduces you and turns you from the path of light.*

Taesara ran her hand over the place Savegre had occupied after their lovemaking ended, while she drifted toward sleep in his embrace. His aroma of summer earth and salt-laden seas impregnated the sheets, together with the sweet spice of her womanhood. She flushed at the thought that Sonia or one of the ladies might notice, not because the act shamed her — last night she had journeyed far beyond shame — but because any knowledge of a liaison with the Galian Prince would threaten her position in court.

Harlot, they would say. *A whore of wizards.*

"Gods of Thunder forgive me," she whispered, "but I would succumb to his spell a thousand times."

As these words fell from her lips, her fingers happened upon a smooth round object, cool to the touch and hard as stone. Curiously, she pulled it out from under the covers. Her eyes widened when she recognized the small crystal sphere.

"My Lady Queen."

Taesara started at Sonia's voice. She tucked the object under the covers just as her lady-in-waiting drew back the bed curtains.

"Forgive me for disturbing your sleep, but the hour grows late and we have joyous news. Selkynsen has surrendered. They open their inner gates to receive Eliasara as their liege today. The siege has ended."

Taesara sat up, alert. "In truth?"

Sonia smiled. "Our Lord Regent is anxious to undertake your triumph into Selkynsen."

"Oh, thank you, Sonia. And thank the Gods! This is great news indeed." Taesara clutched the sheets to cover her naked body. She caught Sonia's questioning glance as it settled upon her disheveled hair. "The damp heat from the storm last night was unbearable. I took my shift off in my sleep. Perhaps you found it?"

Sonia did not respond at first, but fixed a curious gaze on the space just above Taesara's head. A slight frown furrowed her brow.

"Sonia?"

The lady started. "Forgive my distraction, my Lady Queen. Yes, we found your shift and your dress in sorry states on the floor. I've sent both to be cleaned. You should have called for our assistance when you were ready to sleep."

"It was very late. My ladies, too, need their rest, and their well-being is worth more than any of my dresses."

A servant brought her robe. Taesara managed to slip the crystal sphere in a pocket unseen. She ordered a bath to be drawn and sat down to eat. One of the ladies began working through the knots in her hair. Sonia brought forward a parade of richly embroidered gowns, but Taesara waved them all away.

"I want the pale blue, the one we had made from the gift of the Galian Prince," she said.

Sonia stiffened. "My Lady Queen, it would be more appropriate to wear the colors of Moisehén or Roenfyn on this day."

"I would wear the blue."

"But your uncle—"

"Gods take my uncle! Must he dictate even my dress?"

Sonia subdued her shock and gave an apologetic bow.

As the gown was laid out and brushed, Taesara took her bath, luxuriating in the cool rose-scented water that they poured over her limbs and back. Servants dried the damp from her skin and braided her hair with jewels. She slipped into the dress and allowed her ladies to fuss with the lacing.

The fabric was feather-light and soft upon her skin, like a whisper of his caress. Heat rose to her cheeks and a now-familiar ache flared between her legs. As Taesara tried to steady her pulse, a servant picked up the breakfast robe.

"Stop." Her order caught the woman in mid-step. "Don't take that away. Leave it on the bed."

Taesara discretely retrieved the crystal sphere from the discarded robe and hid it in the pocket of her new dress. A few short weeks ago, she would have avoided such a dangerous object, but now she burned with an exhilarating mix of curiosity and dread. She longed for the moment when she could send them all away to be alone with Savegre's gift.

Eliasara was summoned. Taesara inspected every detail of her daughter's attire. While she herself had decided to wear whatever she pleased, on this day Eliasara had to look her part as Queen of Moisehén. Her gown was deep purple embroidered with silver dragons; her golden hair piled in an elaborate braid. Jewels adorned the girl's fingers and throat; a silver diadem rested upon her young forehead. They brought a magnificent riding cloak that sparkled with gold and amethyst and set it upon her small shoulders. Eliasara appeared lost and uncertain beneath all the regalia. Taesara touched her chin and bade her to straighten her back.

"Today is the day you have dreamed of, my love," she said tenderly. "Today we return to Moisehén as victors."

"Can I leave this cloak behind?" Eliasara asked. "I feel like I'm drowning in this thing."

On another day, Taesara might have insisted Eliasara dress according to her status, but on this morning, she simply nodded to the servants, who took away the burdensome brocade.

By the time they arrived at the shores of the Furma, the rain had stopped and sun was peeking through misty clouds. Overnight the river had risen. Branches and other debris rolled in a swift, muddy current that threatened to flow over the bridge. In places the water peaked in frothy, white-tipped waves.

Penamor met them in good spirits, surrounded by the men of his guard. Trumpets sounded, and the banner men assembled ahead of them. Eliasara took her place at Penamor's side. Taesara rode just behind. A company of guards and nobles followed.

On the opposite bank, Savegre waited with his retinue, bare-breasted beneath brilliantly colored cloaks.

Taesara's stomach clenched. Her throat went dry and her fingers turned cold. She let one hand drift to the pocket where she had hidden the crystal sphere, and found it warm to the touch. Perhaps beneath Savegre's ambitions there was some truth to his affections. She wanted to believe this, that she had moved him as deeply as he moved her.

As they crossed the river, Taesara's thoughts became occupied with what she would say to Savegre. The formal greetings of their station seemed too little. Yet any words she could think to add seemed too much.

Beneath the clatter of the horses' hooves, the river choked and gurgled. An uprooted tree groaned as it was forced beneath the bridge, branches snapping against the stone arch.

Taesara's horse became skittish. Taking firm hold of the reins, she brought the animal to a halt and leaned forward to stroke its soft neck. A deep groan sounded underfoot, reminiscent of the strain of the earth before the walls of Selkynsen fell.

The bridge began to list.

Taesara cried out to her daughter.

Eliasara spun on her mount, terror filling her face. The structure of wood and stone sagged beneath the girl and then crumbled altogether. Eliasara, Penamor, and their screaming horses fell into the river. The dark waters swallowed them whole.

"No!" Taesara cried.

She dismounted and ran toward the breach in the bridge. An arm of steel encircled her waist, stopping her momentum. Taesara struggled against the guard who dragged her back. "Let me go!"

"My Lady Queen," he urged. "We must retreat. The rest of the bridge might fail."

"Release me!" With inhuman strength she broke free of his hold. Charging toward the rail, she leaned over the river and searched for some sign of Eliasara. Unbearable loss gripped her heart. Tears blurred her vision. "Gods, no. Not this. Of all punishments, not this."

Eliasara's golden head bobbed above the waters, impossibly far downstream. On either side of the banks, men on horseback raced down river. Savegre and Urales outstripped them all. Coming to a halt ahead of Eliasara's position, the Galian Prince dismounted, abandoned his cloak, and dove into the churning waters.

Taesara assessed the damage to the bridge. The deck had collapsed entirely beneath Penamor and Eliasara, but one rail held steady. The breach might just be narrow enough to jump. She started toward it.

"Wait." The guard caught her again. "Wait, my Lady Queen. Let us help."

A large plank was brought and laid across the hole. One of the men-at-arms on the other side extended an arm toward her. "With care, my Lady Queen."

Gripping the outstretched hand, she inched over the slab of wood. Swirling and hissing waters threatened to make her dizzy.

"Look at me!" the guard said.

Taesara obeyed, keeping her gaze fixed on his weathered face. When at last she reached the other side, she demanded the first horse within reach.

Soon she passed the point where Savegre had dismounted. She continued down river, at once anxious and wary of what waited around the bend.

At last she caught site of Urales's mount standing alone on the bank. Spurring the mare to a gallop, she arrived at a place where the river widened into muddy riffles gurgling over smooth rocks. Savegre and Urales trudged toward shore. Eliasara sagged between them like a wilted flower.

Jumping from her horse, Taesara plunged into the low waters. The river soaked her skirts and threatened her progress. At last she reached Eliasara. Together, they stumbled back to shore. Clinging to each other, they fell to their knees on the silty bank.

Taesara wept and covered her daughter's face with kisses. Eliasara sputtered and coughed.

"He held me up, Mama," she said, shivering inside Taesara's embrace. "He held me up and would not let me drown."

CHAPTER FORTY-TWO

Succession

GHEMENA FOUND IRENY in the crowd gathered outside Taesara's pavilion. Smoke hung thick over Selkynsen, tainting rays of sun that broke through gray clouds. The outer rim of the city lay in ruin. The stench of blood and death impregnated the air. Roenfyn's victory could not have been more absolute, and yet a grim mood had taken hold of the people. They stood silent and wary, engaged in quiet conversation, alert for any movement from the guards that kept watch over the entrance to the tent.

"What has happened here?" Ghemena asked.

Ireny started at the sound of her voice, and then flung her arms around Ghemena in a tight hug.

"Gods, I was beginning to think you'd never return!" She glanced past Ghemena's shoulder. "Where's Nicola?"

"She decided to remain with the Mountain Queen. They'll join us soon."

"You've convinced her, then? Khelia's coming to our aid?"

"Yes." Ghemena averted her gaze, nodding toward the smoking ruins of Selkynsen. "Nicola will be sorry she missed this."

"Perhaps it's best she's not here to see it. That city was her home."

"A just punishment for the crimes they committed against the magas. This was a glorious victory, Ireny. Why is everyone so glum?"

Ireny took Ghemena's hand and pulled her away to a place of solitude. There, she invoked a sound ward.

"Penamor is dead," she said quietly.

Ghemena stared at her in surprise and then laughed out loud. "Well, that's good news! Convenient, too. I won't have to take care of him myself, then."

"Hush!" Ireny glanced around. "I swear to the Gods, Ghemena, your tongue will get us into more trouble—"

"Tell me how it happened. Did someone poison him? I hope not. Poisoning is such a mundane way to die. I hope he was disemboweled and given the opportunity to watch his guts spill forth before the Gods called him home."

"A bridge collapsed and the water carried him under. They haven't found his body, but it's been days now, and Roenfyn is anxious to continue this war." Ireny paused a moment before adding, "We almost lost Eliasara as well. Savegre went into the river after her. He's the only reason she's alive."

Ghemena whistled through her teeth. "At least he's proven useful for something. And Taesara?"

"Poised to take command of this army. The nobles swear allegiance to her as regent today. Tomorrow, we continue the march east."

As Ghemena absorbed these words, a weight lifted from her shoulders. She looked to the sky, half expecting Dragon to sail overhead, its silvery scales reflecting the smoky light.

"It is done, then," she said. "The Gods have heard and answered our prayers. We will have a new realm ruled by women, and a royal house that eschews all magic."

"We haven't won yet."

"No, but we will. This is a sign if there ever was one."

"The people don't entirely trust Taesara. She's been gone from their presence a long time. Her daughter is a foreigner, brought to them from the land of the Mage King. Some suspect them of witchcraft."

"Those two? That's a laugh. There's never been a woman more devoted to the stark traditions of Thunder than Taesara, and her daughter has no aptitude for magic whatsoever."

"You and I know that, but these people see magic in the works every time something bad happens. Some say Taesara cursed Penamor the morning he died, and that Eliasara foresaw the drowning."

284

"Well, there's no logic in that at all! Eliasara nearly drowned herself."

"You know I don't believe their silly rumors. I'm just telling you what's being said. It's apparently common knowledge in Roenfyn that water rejects a witch, even though they've never had any witches to speak of."

"Oh, for the love of the Gods!" Ghemena shook her head. "For a people that so despise magic, they certainly take morbid pleasure in believing it permeates their lives. Don't worry, Ireny. Like you said, these are all just silly rumors. The talk will fade once they get to know the fiber of their new ruler."

Ireny bit her lip. "There's something else you should know."

"What?"

"It's Savegre. He's been with Taesara."

"When?"

"The night before Penamor drowned."

"Curse you, Ireny! I told you to watch over her."

"What was I supposed to do? Hide under her bed? Knife him as he disrobed?"

"If that's what it took, yes! I told you, whatever was necessary."

"A fine fate that would have bought me, killing a Galian Prince."

"Castrating him would have been enough. Besides, it would have been an honorable death for you. We are here to give our lives for our people, after all."

"Castrate him yourself, if you think that's the answer."

"How many people know?"

"No one, as far as I can tell. Well, maybe the Galians, if they read auras."

Ghemena tapped her fingers on the hilt of her sword. "Perhaps it's a good sign Taesara's being discrete. There's shame at play there, or distrust. Maybe both. Whatever the wedge is, we must find it and use it to break them apart."

Ireny rubbed her forehead. "I'm sorry, Ghemena. Things happened so quickly while you were gone, and then I thought...I mean, she was happy with him, you know? I don't believe she'd ever experienced *aen-lasati* before. Not like she did with him."

"Ireny, you've a kind heart but war is not the time for sentimentality. Once this is all over, we can find a mindless suitor to please Taesara in a thousand ways. But Savegre cannot return to her bed. If he does, we must find a way to eliminate him."

"This is a Prince of Galia we are talking about. Eliminating him will be no easy task. Besides, we've no proof of his intentions, good or bad."

"He's a man, a wizard, and a prince. That's all the proof I need. Why would he bed her if not to marry her and take all three kingdoms for himself?"

"Not all men are vile power mongers, Ghemena. Some of them can be kind once in a while. Even fall in love. There was Caradoc, after all. And Caedmon—"

"Who drove Lithia mad."

"All I'm saying is that maybe you should watch Savegre for a moment before judging him. He cherishes his daughter and treats his people with generosity. And whenever he sets eyes on Taesara, it's obvious…" Ireny's voice trailed off.

"What?"

"This is more than simple ambition, Ghemena. I think he truly loves her."

"Love is the word men use to imprison us."

"Oh, Ghemena."

"Whose side are you on, Ireny? Are you with us in this, or have you become a servant of mages as well?"

"Of course I am with you! I have always been with you, and I won't disappoint you again. All I'm saying is that we give Savegre a chance to demonstrate what kind of wizard he is."

"There's only one kind of wizard: the rotten kind, the untrustworthy kind. The kind that stops at nothing until all power belongs to him. For the good of us and all our people, Savegre is not to touch Taesara again, Ireny. If he does, he will die, whether by your hand or by mine."

CHAPTER FORTY-THREE

Messenger

LORD HERENSEN'S FIST hit the table. The impact reverberated through maps, cups, and flagons. His face was flushed with anger; veins bulged at his temples. Eolyn half expected to see smoke-tipped flames escape from his flared nostrils.

"We've delayed too long." The lord dragged his clenched fist across the wood. "We have been robbed of our King and ravaged by our enemies. Ours was once a great people, but now we are broken and ragged, cursed by the Gods for all we have done and failed to do, abandoned to the doomed reign of this woman who understands nothing of the task appointed to her!"

Tension took hold of the Council. No one dared meet the lord's accusatory gaze, nor lift their eyes to the Queen.

Eolyn kept her shoulders straight, fingers spread upon the oak table. She could not condone Herensen's outburst, yet she understood his frustration. While they delayed and deliberated, unable to progress due to ceaseless rain, word had arrived of Selkynsen's terrible fate. Herensen's reliable calm had been stripped away, detail by brutal detail, until only this raw untested rage remained.

"Lord Herensen," she began.

He threw up his hands and abandoned their presence.

Eolyn drew a slow breath and collected her thoughts. She heard the shuffling of feet, the rustle of robes. One of the men muffled a cough.

"This news changes nothing," she said, "save to strengthen our resolve. We depart at dawn to take advantage of the recent break in the weather. Let us hope the Gods have finished their weeping. Depending on the speed of our progress, we will meet the enemy at one of the two passes Tibald has recommended. There we will defeat the army of Roenfyn and drive them out Moisehén. The families of Selkynsen will be avenged."

With this, she dismissed them. The men did not linger, but departed with purpose, all save Corey who had made it his habit to remain behind.

Eolyn sat down on a nearby chair. The full horror of Selkynsen's fall pressed down upon her. Remorse gripped her heart. She felt the terror of all those lost to the sack, even heard their screams as the city was ravaged.

Her head sank into her hands.

Oh, Adiana. I failed you long ago. Now I have failed your beloved city.

Outside the tent, mud sloshed underfoot as men and beasts went about their business. Shouts pierced the air. The officers had begun advising their soldiers of the coming march. Burying the cloud of despair that threatened to consume her, Eolyn dried her eyes and rose. Corey looked up from the maps.

"If it pleases you, my Lady Queen," he said, "I would speak to Lord Herensen."

"No." Eolyn called for Talia to bring her cloak. "This burden is mine to bear, Corey. I accepted it when I married our King."

"You need not bear it alone."

"At the moment, yours is a different task. Gather the mages and mage warriors, and send a message at once to Thelyn. We must find some magic that we can use against this Galian blight. I will not have our army roasted alive on the day we meet Roenfyn in battle."

Corey bowed. "Shall I call upon the magas as well?"

"Yes, just as we have discussed. You must include them in every conversation. Advise me the moment you or your spies observe anything suspicious. Make whatever arrests you deem necessary."

It pained her to speak of her own daughters in this way, but the ambush of Mariel had at last extinguished all doubt. There were traitors among the magas, and Eolyn did not intend to lose anyone or anything else to their schemes.

Afternoon light was breaking through the clouds when Eolyn

emerged from the tent. She paused to lift her face to the warm rays. The sweet song of a Tenolin sparrow rose frail and clear above the sounds of the camp. A momentary vision of the sun-flecked South Woods filled her mind. She felt Akmael's breath upon her ear, heard him murmur her name. The tingle of his magic graced her palm.

Eolyn had discovered that if she focused her attention, she could almost hear his steady gait, sense the brush of his lips upon hers, convince herself that she was falling asleep in his embrace. It seemed a dangerous game to play, given all the warnings of Aithne and Caradoc against invoking the dead. Yet she could not resist the pull of his memory. The need to have him close – the desperate belief that she could still somehow be with him – was driving her toward a reckless form of magic.

"My Lady Queen?"

A guard called her back to the moment at hand. He watched her, worry plain on his weathered face. A mage warrior of old, this man was one of a handful who remained from Drostan's generation. Had he observed the odd flicker of her aura? Was the shadow of the Underworld weaving its tendrils through her colors?

Despite the warm day, a chill passed through Eolyn's shoulders. She adjusted her cloak and bade him and his companion to follow.

Eolyn traversed the camp in an unhurried fashion, pausing to speak with men and women along the way, giving them words of encouragement. Many soldiers spoke of friends and family in Selkynsen, their fates for the most part unknown and now horribly imagined. Ignoring the protocols of her status, Eolyn embraced them in their grief. She used her magic to strengthen their courage and resolve.

At last she reached Herensen's pavilion, marked by flags bearing the rich colors of his province. Upon entering, she found the lord well-accompanied by several members of her Council. A troubled murmur passed through the group as they bowed to greet her. Eolyn made quiet note of each person present, names she would pass on to Corey, that he might exercise his subtle vigilance.

She dismissed everyone save Herensen, who did not meet her gaze but kept his head bent, one hand resting upon a small table.

His expression was hardened, yet his eyes were red and swollen. Unbearable loss writhed through his aura.

Eolyn approached and laid a hand upon his arm.

"Do you come to arrest me, my Lady Queen?" His voice was hoarse. His aged shoulders shook.

For the first time, Eolyn noticed how the years had caught up with him. Herensen's hair had grown thin; the lines on his face had deepened. Days would pass, perhaps weeks and months, before he knew just how many of his own had perished during the siege.

"I share your grief more than you can know," she said. "Were I in your place, I would have spoken and acted just as you did."

"I insulted my Queen. For that, there can be no pardon."

"A heart that cannot pardon is a heart doomed to torment. Caradoc taught us this by his example, Lithia through her tragedy. I would not be a High Maga if I did not ascribe to their creed."

"You are first and foremost a Queen, sole defender of the Crown of Vortingen. It is not my place to doubt you."

"Those words you said today," she insisted quietly, "were not without truth."

Herensen set a wary gaze upon her.

"Your loyalty to the Crown has always been steadfast," she continued. "I accept what disappointment you might harbor toward me, because I know and have always known that I was not bred to be a warrior, much less a queen. Still my King chose me, and so here we are. I must rise to this task, whether I understand it or not. I must succeed, for the sake of my Prince and all our people. Their future is in my hands, Lord Herensen, and I cannot secure it without your wisdom and advice. If this means I must also on occasion suffer your honest rage, then that is a sacrifice I am more than willing to make."

A reluctant smile crept into his expression. He looked away. "I thought the King an accursed fool when he banished the Princess of Roenfyn to wed you."

Eolyn frowned. How much honesty did he expect her to accept in one day?

"Anyone can fall in love," Herensen continued, "but a man of noble lineage does not favor his heart over his duty. This is the first law of our class and one to which we are bound from the day we are born. I believed King Akmael would bring us to ruin, and yet even this conviction could not sway me from my loyalty to the Crown. After all these years, despite all our losses, I understand now the choice he made, and I am glad for it. You gave him a son, my Lady Queen. A mage and a prince. We have prospered under your rule and at least for a time, enjoyed a peace we had not known for generations. Taesara was a good and gracious woman, but you are a true Daughter of Moisehén. No one would dare challenge this kingdom as long as mage and maga were united on the throne, as long as Aithne and Caradoc ruled as one. Prince Akmael saw this before any of the rest of us understood. It was a fortunate coincidence that he loved you as well. With or without that affection, having found the last of the High Magas, he was bound by duty to wed you."

Somewhere in this interpretation of her history, Eolyn recognized that Herensen meant to compliment her. Certainly the softening of his expression and the warming of his aura indicated as much. Yet it disturbed her, this conviction that Akmael would have made her his queen no matter what the circumstance, whether by love or by force.

"In order to defeat this army, Lord Herensen," she said, "I need you on my Council."

"You have me, my Lady Queen." He bowed. "Me and all my family. What is left of them, at any rate."

"It is very likely your sons and daughters who endured the siege still survive. The city surrendered before the keep fell."

"Those with honor will have fought to the death."

Eolyn held his gaze. "There is honor to be had in acting to save the people entrusted to your protection. Selkynsen was not prepared for the fires of Galia. Had they not surrendered, the entire city would have burned. All would have perished. I will remember this, Lord Herensen, when your sons and daughters are returned to our fold."

"If…" He choked back his words and covered his eyes.

Eolyn realized in horror what the old patriarch feared: that the invading forces of Roenfyn would massacre Selkynsen's ruling house, just as the Syrnte did when they took Moehn.

"Surely, they will not be so cruel," she whispered.

"Sylus Penamor was as cruel as they come," Herensen said bitterly. "I would expect no less of his—"

A sudden commotion outside interrupted their conversation. Mariel burst into their presence, agitated and breathless.

"A herald!" she announced, eyes bright and wary with excitement. "A herald has arrived, from the Mountain Queen."

CHAPTER FORTY-FOUR

Khelia

EOLYN CALLED FOR A SUMMER CLOAK, light but richly embroidered, and donned her late husband's crown, a simple circlet of silver adorned with the jeweled image of Dragon. Kel'Barú hummed against her hip. Her staff crackled inside her palm.

The excitement she felt ran much deeper than the hope of securing a badly needed ally. The very thought of Khelia's return answered some deep and forgotten hunger, the need for the sort of womanly kinship she had not enjoyed since losing her beloved Adiana. No student of hers, no woman of the court, had ever filled that vacancy in her heart. She remembered Khelia's companionship with great fondness, perhaps in brighter shades than it deserved, and now she dearly wished to see that friendship rekindled.

Yet she recognized this as a dangerous vulnerability.

I must listen to my advisors and be mindful of my own instincts.

Lord Herensen and Mage Corey waited outside her tent, along with the rest of the council members. Together they rode past the edge of the camp, to a small rise where other members of the court had assembled under the spreading branches of a large beech. Eolyn dismounted. Protocol demanded that she sit to receive their visitor, but agitation kept her on her feet. She scanned the ridge where Khelia's entourage descended a gentle slope. The bright sun drank up the earth's moisture, casting all of them in a steamy mist.

Herensen drew near. "My Lady Queen, there is yet time for you to retire to the heart of the camp. Let us meet with this woman first, gauge her sincerity before allowing her and her warriors into your presence."

293

"This is what we agreed upon," Eolyn replied, "and I am one to keep my word. Khelia will speak with no one but the Queen of Moisehén."

He nodded and stepped away, though his aspect remained wary.

The people of Moisehén stirred with curiosity as the Mountain Queen approached. She rode beneath billowing banners of snow white and ice blue, a single yellow orb at the center of each flag. Men and women in polished armor made up Khelia's formidable guard. Their gazes were sharp and unyielding.

A pack of snow tigers surrounded the soldiers on horseback. The great striped cats stood almost to the shoulder of the horses they flanked. Heads and tails slung low, they sauntered without hurry, each heavy step falling silently upon the earth. Eolyn detected the flicker of auras over their shoulders, revealing the animals as shape shifters.

A brief command from Eolyn's captain, and the mage warriors fanned out before her own party, magic poised for deadly use. Eolyn understood this was a ritual display of power between the two kingdoms. Still, she found herself praying the events of this day did not disintegrate into a bloody brawl between tigers and bears.

Khelia halted her company and dismounted. Flanked by two of her guards, she approached Eolyn with long, confident strides. The line of mage warriors parted briefly to allow them through.

Eolyn remembered the night she first met this enigmatic woman, daughter of a mountain prince and a maga who had fled the purges under Kedehen. Eolyn had been a peasant girl new to Corey's Circle; Khelia one of his finest singers. The mountain warrior had kept the truth of her origins well hidden beneath humble dress and clever conversation.

Then again, so had they all.

"Hail, Eolyn, High Maga and Queen of all Moisehén!" Khelia announced, spreading her feet in a warrior's stance.

She wore the robes of a man, as had often been her custom. Her short-cropped hair had grown whiter with the years. Fine lines feathered her pale blue eyes. She grinned, a familiar and disarming expression that had charmed Eolyn from the start.

"I must admit," the Mountain Queen added, "this is something

I wanted to see for myself."

Eolyn bowed. "We are most happy to receive you, Khelia, Queen of the Mountain Realms. I hope you will stay, you and all your party, and dine with us. We have much to discuss."

"We do indeed." She scanned the men who accompanied Eolyn. "These are your advisors, I presume?"

Eolyn nodded, and began to present each one by name. As she spoke, Khelia's eyes settled on Mage Corey. Eolyn's introductions died on her lips as she watched the Mountain Queen's demeanor change to one of predatory intensity.

Khelia approached the mage and dragged his name through her teeth. "Corey of East Selen."

Silence descended upon those assembled. Leaves rustled in the wind. Laughter could be heard, incongruous and distant, from somewhere inside the camp.

Corey met Khelia's piercing gaze.

"Welcome back," he said.

She spat in his face.

With remarkable reserve, Corey produced a cloth and cleansed himself. "It is good to see you too, dear Khelia."

"I cannot believe you keep this snake in your counsel!" Khelia said to Eolyn.

"It is not your place to question whom I choose as my advisors."

"I do not question your judgment. I merely express my surprise. After all, I am a queen myself. As such, I know snakes can have their uses. Indeed, if one is going to allow a snake to live, one had best keep it close."

Khelia snapped a signal to her guards. Two of them dragged a woman forward, her head bowed and hands bound. Wheat blond hair fell unkempt over her face. They brought the prisoner to Khelia's side and forced her to her knees.

"My gift to you, Queen Eolyn." Khelia touched the woman's chin and lifted it.

Eolyn quelled the gasp that rose in her throat. Remembering the lessons of her husband, she assumed a stony mask as she assessed Nicola's bruised and battered features.

"It was not our intention to hurt her so." Khelia spoke as if sensing Eolyn's distress. "But she resisted, as might be expected, when her fate became clear. At one point I thought it would be easier, kinder really, to simply kill the wench and deliver her head. But knowing the woman who now commands Moisehén — or at least, having known her at one time — I decided it better to bring the maga back alive. Her magic has been bound according to the protocol of your mages. I release her to you."

"Thank you, Khelia." Eolyn swallowed and found her throat was dry. "You must understand we receive this visit with some trepidation. We have had word that you agreed to assist the cause of Roenfyn."

"Your spies are good, but not good enough. I told that spitfire Ghemena that I'd be happy to support Penamor's war, and sent her dancing back into his fold with false news. A fine crop of students you've raised, Eolyn. Rebels like you, all of them. Though not nearly as smart."

"Khelia," Eolyn said evenly. "Why have you come to us?"

A smile touched Khelia's lips. "Because we are sisters, Eolyn, in magic and in war. I have not forgotten our friendship, and unlike some of the fickle women who now spurn you, I do not abandon my sisters. I might have taken up arms against your husband, at the appropriate time and under the right circumstances, but I would never take up arms against you. So let us fight together, Eolyn, Queen of Moisehén. Let us go to war as we once did, fed by dreams of victory. And this time, let us *win*."

Excitement rose in Eolyn's blood. She wanted to step forward and embrace Khelia, but prudence held her back.

On seeing Eolyn's guarded response, Khelia arched her brow. She took hold of Nicola's hair, unsheathed her knife, and set the blade upon the maga's throat. "If you need proof of my oath, then I am willing to slay this traitor at your command."

Moments passed. The court held its breath.

Eolyn studied Khelia's face and aura for any sign of deception. Corey, she knew, was engaged in the same task. Later they would speak of this. Already she could hear his rebuke.

You should have let Nicola die under Khelia's blade. Then there would be no doubt.

Eolyn turned to her captain. "Tibald, see that Nicola is placed under sufficient guard. Mage Corey, I would have you or one of your mages speak with this maga, to see what information she has that may be of use to us."

Corey bowed. "As you wish, my Lady Queen."

Khelia released Nicola from her grip. The prisoner was hauled to her feet.

"I want to go with them!" Mariel announced.

Her outburst brought all eyes to the young maga warrior, who stood somewhat hidden among the onlookers.

"What's this?" Khelia asked in amusement. "Another rebel of your making, Eolyn?"

Mariel flushed and dropped to one knee. "Please, my Lady Queen. By your leave, I would accompany Maga Nicola, and be present for any inquiry made of her."

Eolyn faltered, uncertain what to make of this request. She glanced at Corey, who shrugged.

"I see no conflict, my Lady Queen," the mage said. "If Mariel wishes to assist in our conversation with this maga, then let it be so. She might bring some useful insights to the process."

"Very well." Eolyn nodded.

Committing Mariel to such a task troubled Eolyn for more reasons than she cared to consider. Yet Mariel had asked, and Corey no doubt saw it as an opportunity to keep a close eye on her.

Perhaps Mariel could keep a close eye on him, as well.

"You have my leave, Mariel. I suggest you start by informing Nicola of the fate of her home in Selkynsen. It would do well for her to reflect upon that massacre, and to consider the valor of the allies she has chosen."

CHAPTER FORTY-FIVE

Sisters in Magic

KHELIA WARMED THE HEARTS of almost every noble attending the banquet given on her behalf. Even Herensen managed a smile in her presence. Eolyn offered the best food at her disposal: sausage and venison, aged cheese and roasted vegetables. Wine and ale were served in generous portions. Khelia brought musicians and dancers, whose entertainments tipped the mood from somber to merry.

The Mountain Queen refused to linger in the place assigned to her, but rose and worked her way around the tables, engaging each attendant in lively conversation.

Watching Khelia's grace reminded Eolyn of a certain Winter Solstice long past, when she visited East Selen for the first time as a member of Corey's Circle. Corey and Khelia had commanded the head table then, while Eolyn had occupied a modest corner that befit her rank among his people. That night had been filled with mystery and magic, music and passion.

How much had changed since then, and yet how very little.

"It is a remarkable gift of Khelia's," Mage Corey observed, "that even in her condescension she is utterly charming."

Eolyn allowed herself a guarded smile.

"I suppose I do not have to warn you to take care with her," Corey added.

"No, you do not."

The hour was growing late. The courtiers had sunk deep into their drink. Many had already taken their leave, some discretely and alone, others with newfound partners.

Khelia left a table roaring in laughter to resume her place at

Eolyn's side. With rosy cheeks and a broad smile, the Mountain Queen refreshed their wine.

"You have become rather attached to protocol," Khelia said.

"I have always behaved prudently when under the watch of others," Eolyn replied.

"A wise habit for a woman of Moisehén, now as ever." Khelia lifted her cup and winked at Corey.

Eolyn scanned the guards on duty, noting with satisfaction that none of them had been pulled into the revelry. "You have brought a summer festival upon us, Khelia."

"You speak as if that's worse than war."

"It seems out of place, somehow."

"We have to celebrate, Eolyn, and enjoy what life is given to us. We might all be dead in a few days' time."

"A grievous prediction. I thought it was your plan to win."

Khelia laughed. "It's always my plan to win, but sometimes the Gods have other ideas." She leaned close and lowered her voice. "Our people are duly occupied, Queen Eolyn. That has been my only purpose this evening. I propose we take advantage of their distraction to retire to a quiet place of your choosing. I have much to share with you, but I would do it away from the ears of all these men."

Eolyn's caution wavered under a deeper need to recapture the friendship they had once enjoyed. She nodded, and they rose in unison. The musicians paused, but on the command of both queens continued their sweet and lively melodies. The dancers twirled once more; the people laughed and filled their cups. Eolyn did not bother to signal Corey; she knew he would follow in one form or another.

Khelia tucked Eolyn's hand into her arm, an expression of intimacy that felt natural and right. When they arrived at Eolyn's tent, Tibald cleared his throat and asked Khelia to surrender her weapons. Eolyn suspected the Mountain Queen could slay just as easily without a weapon as with one, but there was no reason to dissuade the guard from his duty. Khelia handed over her sword and produced several knives from hidden places.

"You may search my person if you like." She spread her arms and legs, amusement in her tone. "I'd never say no to a handsome guard like you."

Tibald studied her for a moment with a stern expression, and then shook his head.

"You've good men watching over you," Khelia said as they entered the tent. "A disciplined lot, though it seems I am putting them all to the test."

Eolyn had the servants bring more wine and a modest plate of food. Khelia took a handful of grapes and popped one into her mouth. She paced the tent, running a hand over a finely carved chair, sifting through the maps that covered the long oak table, pausing to study the canopied bed toward the back of the pavilion.

"Your brother would be very proud of you, you know," she said.

Eolyn arched her brow. "I think Ernan would claim I've betrayed him and everything he stood for."

"No. He'd say you were the clever one, because you've accomplished through love what he intended to achieve through war. The Mage King is gone, and here you are, Ernan's little sister, High Maga and Queen of all of Moisehén."

"My marriage was not a conquest."

"Not in the conventional sense."

"I loved Akmael."

"Yes." Khelia nodded. "By all accounts you did, and looking at you now, I believe it's true. Still, that does not change the path the Gods opened up for you, a path that has given you sovereignty over the realm of the Mage Kings."

"I did not want this crown, Khelia. I did not ask for it."

"Of course you did not want it. To have *wanted* it would have been treason. Yet to have found it is still a victory. Wasn't it you who said the Gods interpret our acts across a grander scale of time and consequence?"

"I was speaking to a very different set of circumstances."

"Indeed you were. You've got good men on your counsel, by the way. I like them…But there's a problem."

"What problem?"

"They're all men."

Eolyn laughed. "Not all. My physician Jacquetta sits on the Council. Everyone thinks that she is a temporary presence, filling the place of her tutor Echior who remained in the City, but in truth

Jacquetta's appointment is permanent. This will be made clear as soon as the war has ended. I've also summoned my good friend Vinelia from Moehn. It's a lot to ask of her right now, as she just bore another child, but she is well-respected. As a daughter of Selkynsen, her appointment will have the support of Lord Herensen. For this reason I hope her presence on the Council will meet with little protest, even from those well-entrenched in the old ways. Two appointments may not seem like much, Khelia, but it is a significant change given what this kingdom has known in the past."

"And there will be more to follow?"

"Of course. Once this war has ended, there will be many changes."

Khelia nodded in satisfaction. "What about the one who spoke up today, who asked to follow Nicola? She seems to act with exceptional confidence."

"You mean Mariel." Eolyn refreshed their wine and bade Khelia to take a seat. "She would be a solid member of the Council, no doubt. But this is not the life I want for her. I want Mariel to relinquish the path of the warrior and return to Moehn; to build an *Aekelahr* of her own and finish what I tried to start so long ago."

"That is a lot to ask of a warrior," Khelia said, "to lay down her arms."

"I've never believed Mariel had a true calling as a follower of Caedmon. She's able enough with knife and sword, but she took up weaponry in the aftermath of the Syrnte invasion. Perhaps she thought blades would keep her safe. That faith has been challenged in recent times. Still, this must be Mariel's choice. If she remains in the City as a part of the Queen's guard, she will have a place on my Council. But I am waiting until it becomes clear where her heart is leading her."

"She was among your first, then."

"Yes, she was."

Eolyn met Khelia's gaze. A moment of mutual understanding passed between them: mothers, teachers, and leaders who cared deeply for her own.

"Tell me about your *Aekelahr*," Khelia said. "I want to hear everything."

So the stories began. Eolyn told Khelia of the community of

301

women she had built in the highlands of Moehn, before the Syrnte invasion tore that world apart, before love for the Mage King compelled her toward a different path. All her sisters came back to life in a dance of words: stern Renate and passionate Adiana; beautiful Sirena and quiet Mariel; the innocents Catarina and Tasha, still children when they were sacrificed to the Underworld. And Ghemena, whose rage had never found rest.

Khelia, for her part, related countless adventures from the Paramen Mountains, and spoke of the clever and sometimes cruel fashion by which she had united that fragmented realm into a single kingdom. She also shared stories of Eolyn's brother, retrieved from the battles of their youth. Some of these were heroic, others troubling, but each one a gift, a small piece of Eolyn's family returned to her heart.

Friendship wrapped around them like a warm and familiar cloak. The air sparked with humor and memories. Fresh flasks of wine were brought, emptied, and brought again. The sounds of the camp faded. The candles burned low.

At last even their conversation trickled to a halt, and they sank, satiated, into companionable silence. Eolyn reclined against the pillows of her bed and stared at the flickering candles. Khelia sat cross-legged nearby, studying her cup.

"I have not had a night like this since the days of my *Aekelahr*," Eolyn said.

"I know of what you speak. With leadership comes isolation. This is just as true for a woman as it is for a man."

"I never understood fully until now what it meant for Akmael to be king. All of this has given me another perspective on him." Eolyn gestured to the trappings around them. "I see now why it was so important for Akmael to have me at his side, why he lived in such fear of losing his family. Our love was the only barrier between him and utter solitude. No one knew him as long or as well as I did. No one could give him companionship in the same way."

"Spoken like a true spouse. You've a noble heart, Eolyn, but in my estimation, you gave up a lot to meet that man's needs."

Eolyn sighed. "He gave me much in return, Khelia. Akmael completed my magic in so many ways. I confess that at times I have wondered whether I made the wrong choice in marrying him, but what good would such regrets do me now? I made the decisions I thought best under the circumstances, and I have survived to see the consequences. That is all."

A chuckle escaped Khelia's lips. "Words stolen from Mage Corey. Not a standard I would aspire to, if I were you."

"Your resentment of him is well-founded, given everything that happened with my brother. Yet there is one thing I can say for Corey: he's been a constant companion in all the years since. Somehow, he is always there to support me."

"In his own devious and self-serving way, I imagine."

Eolyn smiled and emptied her cup. "In his own devious and self-serving way."

"I would have liked to have known the home you shared with Adiana and Renate in Moehn." Khelia drew close to refill their wine. "I miss them both dearly. Who would have thought, when we first met in the Circle, that our destinies would take such turns?"

Eolyn caught Khelia's hand and held her ice-blue gaze. "Khelia, why did you come back?"

"I told you why."

"You truly mean to join my cause?"

"Oh yes." She took a drink from her cup. "We are women of magic, and rulers besides. We must stand together."

Eolyn felt a quiet release inside. The tension of her muscles was receding. For the first time since Akmael's death, she began to believe she could do this. She could lead her people into this conflict and emerge triumphant.

"The very first time I saw you in Corey's Circle," Khelia said, "I wanted to kiss you."

Eolyn looked up, startled. Then she laughed. "I wanted to kiss you too."

Khelia tossed a pillow at Eolyn. "Now you're just making fun of me."

"It's no jest. I thought you were beautiful."

"Yet you bedded that mindless charmer, Tahmir, instead."

"As I recall, that was the same night you bedded that treacherous snake, Mage Corey."

Khelia threw her head back in laughter. "Yes, well, we were all young fools back then, weren't we? I hope Tahmir pleased you,

Eolyn. You deserved that much from him, at least."

"He did." The memory of her first lover subdued Eolyn. How many names had surfaced tonight of friends now counted among the dead? "And you, Khelia of the Mountain Realms? Did Mage Corey please you?"

"Oh, yes. He's a fine lover. Among the best I've had. And I'm not just saying that because I suspect he may be listening." Khelia raised her voice with these last words, glancing pointedly around the tent. Then she set aside her cup and reclined next to Eolyn. "I'm surprised you haven't discovered Corey's more intimate talents for yourself by now."

Eolyn flushed and averted her gaze. "I wedded a king, Khelia."

"Yet you are a maga. You cannot be bound to one man."

"Perhaps I became less of a maga when I married Akmael."

"No." She hovered close now. Her aroma of brisk air and mountain forests at once soothed and awakened Eolyn's senses. "I don't believe so."

Their lips met, an unexpected yet natural union that tasted of sweet wine and shared experience. Eolyn drew Khelia in to her, compelled by a new sort of magic, one fed by snowfall on high mountains, by crystalline lakes in deep and verdant valleys, by fresh herbs and resplendent wildflowers. Here was a light that could fill the void in her heart, that could chase away the persistent shadow of loss and grief.

She ran her fingers through Khelia's fine blond hair, arched as the mountain warrior's kisses fell like spring rain down her throat. A sigh of release escaped Eolyn's lips. Khelia's hand drifted to her bodice. Eolyn's breasts rose in anticipation, but in that moment, a shadow passed over the sun-warmed grass. War-roughened hands caressed her skin. The spirit of a dead king murmured in her ear.

Eolyn.

She broke away, heart pounding, and lifted her hand to stay Khelia's advance.

Oh, Akmael...

He was near. So very near. If she would just glance up. If she could just reach beyond the thin curtain of this world...

"What is it, Eolyn?" Concern mingled with disappointment in Khelia's voice.

"I'm sorry." Eolyn could not meet her friend's gaze. "It is too soon. The pain runs so deep. I cannot...I cannot do this, Khelia. Not with you, not with anyone. We would not be together, you see. Even as you and I embraced, I would be with him. Only with him."

After a long moment, the mountain warrior withdrew and stood. "I am the one who should beg pardon, Eolyn, for having violated the path of your mourning."

Frustration stung Eolyn's eyes. She had wanted this magic. She needed it. Why was she sending Khelia away?

"Your kiss did not displease me," she said.

"But the timing did." Khelia stepped away from the bed and bowed. "I will take my leave. The hour grows late, and we must be assured of our rest. We have battles to plan and a war to win. No more festivals until this is over, Eolyn. On that you have my word."

She turned to depart.

"Khelia," Eolyn said, halting the mountain warrior's retreat. "I am honored to have you here, as my sister in magic and my companion in war."

Khelia grinned and bowed with a flourish. "And I am honored to be reunited with you, Eolyn, Queen of all Moisehén. I am proud to be counted among your allies."

CHAPTER FORTY-SIX

Exile

AT NIGHT, TAESARA DREAMED of Penamor pinned beneath debris at the bottom of the river. A free arm undulated with the current. Floating hair framed his face. His skin was blue with rot, and fish pecked at his cheeks. He looked upon her with white eyes, mouth opening in a chasm that threatened to swallow her whole.

She woke shivering, his accusation echoing in her ears.

"It wasn't me," she whispered. "I didn't ask for this."

The words fell from her lips in a prayerful cadence. If Taesara repeated them enough, maybe they would assume the shape of truth.

Penamor's body had not been found. Perhaps for this reason the nobles had been so quick to accept Taesara in his place. Her uncle might yet reappear. The current was swift. He could have been carried far down stream before catching hold of a strong root along the bank and dragging himself to shore. He might have collapsed, exhausted, and been rescued by peasants, nurtured back to health on their meager broth. Even now he could be making his way toward them on foot, determined to finish the war he started.

"My Lady Queen."

Taesara jumped at the sound of Sonia's voice, and found herself sitting at the breakfast table, her meal untouched. Eliasara watched her mother with a curious frown.

How long have I been lost in my thoughts?

"You should eat more, my Lady Queen." Sonia spoke in gentle tones. "We've a long day ahead of us."

Dawn had not yet broken across the landscape, yet already the camp was alive with activity. Men shouted. Oxen lowed. Tents were being brought down in a clatter of wood and canvas. Servants packed Taesara's belongings even as she ate. They would march east today, toward Rhiemsaven and the army of the Witch Queen.

"Your tea." Sonia set a cup in front of her. Steam rose from its dark interior.

Taesara pushed the drink away. "It's too bitter."

"It will give you strength for the ride."

Their exchange disturbed Taesara, as if she were caught in some Syrnte spell where past and future converged upon the present. Everything seemed unreal, yet exceedingly vivid. A memory moved beneath the surface of her thoughts, but slipped away before Taesara could capture its essence.

She rose abruptly. "We're finished here. Bring my cloak. The only remedy for a long day's journey is to begin."

A sliver of light marked the eastern horizon. Stars still graced the western sky. The breeze was mild and humid, a sign of the warm day to come. Her guard waited outside the tent, along with several members of the Council.

Savegre stood by his horse. Urales, tall and grim-faced, kept vigil nearby. The Galian Prince took Taesara's hand and brought her fingers to his forehead. Taesara wanted to linger in the warmth of this touch, to confirm the tenderness she thought she saw, but she withdrew.

Savegre had not returned to her bed since their first night. At times when he was near, anger flared in her heart and she burned to demand why, though in truth she felt relieved by his absence. The Gods almost took her daughter the first time she slept with Savegre. What would they demand if she surrendered to him again?

Did he cast the spell that killed my uncle? Did he make the river rise?

Trumpets sounded across the camp as she and Eliasara mounted.

"To victory!" Three times the captain of her guard repeated his call; three times the army took up his cry, each round more belligerent than the last.

Taesara urged her horse forward, and the march toward the heart of Moisehén began.

She spoke with each member of the Council as they rode,

307

sharing the longest conversation with Penamor's foremost adviser, Lord Tobias of House Velander. Advanced in years and balding, Velander's soft-spoken manner seemed incongruous with the stories Taesara had heard of him in battle. She could see why her uncle valued the man; he must have provided a constant foil to Penamor's fiery impulse.

She, of course, faced the opposite challenge. Taesara would have to identify the boldest among her officers and listen to them, no matter how reckless their counsel appeared. How she would balance their opinions with her own cautious instincts she had yet to imagine. She knew so little of war. She prayed the Gods would provide her guidance.

The sun hovered low above the western horizon when at last they stopped to set up a new camp. Taesara's muscles ached. Fatigue sallowed Eliasara's face. After they ate, the princess retired to her bed and fell fast asleep.

"My Lady Queen." Sonia offered a tea that smelled of mint and chamomile, along with some other sweet ingredient Taesara could not place. She accepted the steaming cup gratefully. Sonia moved as if to sit next to her, but Taesara waved her away.

"You've done enough for today, Sonia. I have all I need. Go and rest, all of you."

The ladies and servants departed, leaving Taesara alone with her thoughts. The sounds of the camp were fading. She suspected that even the most raucous of her soldiers would retire early. Penamor's unexpected death had subdued them all.

The tea grew cold, forgotten in her hands. Setting aside the cup, Taesara let go a long and weary sigh. Her gaze lingered on a flickering candle before descending to the swept dirt floor. She waited in silent hope, but the mist did not gather and Savegre did not appear.

Dismissing her own disappointment, Taesara rose and extinguished all the candles save one that illuminated her bed. She shed her outer garments and snuggled beneath the covers. Glancing around the room to make certain she was alone, Taesara brought out the crystal sphere Savegre had given her.

She had found a strange sense of companionship in this odd device. Pale light emanated from the crystal's heart, a play of color

308

and shadow that coalesced into people, places, and events. Every night, she hoped to catch a glimpse of Savegre, but instead she saw herself, young and full of hope, a royal bride newly delivered to the Kingdom of Moisehén.

She witnessed the day she first met King Akmael amidst flowers, music, and ceremony. She relived the sumptuous feast of her wedding, the painful and glorious birth of her daughter. She heard Sonia's whisper the first time the lady leaned close and said, *that is the one he loves, the Witch of Moehn.*

The visions made her heart ache, and yet she could not look away. Gods, she had been little more than a child when they delivered her to the Mage King's bed. And he, through this crystal window, appeared surprisingly young as well. Deeply uncertain. At times, even afraid. She had never glimpsed this vulnerability when she lived under Akmael's command. She had seen only anger, distraction, indomitable power, and stubborn cruelty.

The nighttime hours slipped by. The candle burned low. Still Taesara watched the smoky crystal, though her eyes grew weary and the images began to blur.

Then she saw something she did not expect to see.

Taesara sat up, alert. As the scene replayed inside the crystal, a familiar, bitter taste settled upon her tongue. The cold dread of deception curled around her heart. She enclosed the crystal in her fist and hid it under the covers.

The candle sputtered. The flame went out. Still Taesara did not sleep, but stared brooding into the darkness until the gray light of predawn slipped beneath the tent.

During the morning meal, Taesara could not wrest her gaze from Sonia. Every task, every gesture of their daily routine seemed cast in amber light. She studied the care Sonia put into measuring herbs, the manner in which the lady demanded a precise temperature before pouring the water. This subtle exactness had always been there, and Taesara had long admired it as a defining aspect of Sonia's nature.

Today's brew had a heady aroma of fruit and spices that almost masked the bitter thread beneath. Sonia set the cups down on the table. Eliasara reached for hers, but Taesara caught the girl's hand and shook her head.

309

"I would have a word with Lady Sonia," she said. "Alone."

Eliasara frowned but obeyed, taking a piece of bread and some fruit with her. The other ladies filed out in a rustle of skirts and quiet murmurs. Sonia stood before her Queen, head bowed.

Taesara rose. Her hands trembled, and her heart pounded. Words lodged painfully in her throat. She paced a short circle and then stopped to face her lady-in-waiting, gripping the chair between them, knuckles white against the carved wooden back.

"Sonia," Taesara said evenly, "did you kill my son?"

The lady's eyes widened. Her lips compressed in a thin white line. "My Lady Queen, I don't understand."

"It is a simple question."

Sonia frowned and looked away.

In that moment, Taesara understood she had her answer.

"And my brother?" she whispered. "Did you do that too?"

"You must understand, my Lady Queen." Sonia's voice shook. "Kahrl was weak of heart and mind. He would have never held this kingdom together, much less led us into war against Moisehén."

"So you cursed him?"

"I put him out of his torment, and this at the behest of your uncle."

The words hit Taesara like a blow the stomach. Stunned, she sank into her chair. "So you are one of them. A maga."

"I am not a true maga." Sonia spoke quickly, hands clenching and unclenching. "I never completed my training. My mother fled the purges when I was a girl. We brought nothing with us save the cloaks on our backs. We sought to cross Roenfyn in hopes of escaping to Galia, but Mother perished from a fever. A family took pity on me and gave me a place in their home."

"And Penamor found you there?"

"My adoptive father served him. When he heard of your pending betrothal, he saw an opportunity to rise in your uncle's favor. He told Penamor of my gifts. Judging that I might prove useful, your uncle brought me to court and placed me in your service."

"To render me infertile?"

"No! All Penamor wanted was someone to watch over you, someone who knew their ways of magic."

"What, then, incited you to murder?"

"Not murder." Tears brimmed on Sonia's eyes. "Justice. The day my mother died, she begged me to put an end to the line of Mage Kings. I accepted the oath because I wanted her to enter the Afterlife in peace. But how could I, an orphan in exile, ever hope to learn the craft, much less confront the Mage King? Then one day, your uncle appeared in his fine robes and on his magnificent horse. He told me of his plans for you, and of my purpose within those plans. I knew the Gods had opened a path."

"All this time, I thought you a friend," Taesara murmured in disbelief, "when you are nothing but a spy and an assassin."

"My Lady Queen, I stood by your side long after all your other ladies begged to return to Roenfyn. I supported you against the Mage King's wrath and comforted you through his infidelities. I protected you from bearing his son."

"He was my son, too!" Taesara's voice shook with fury. "The blood of my womb, the love of my heart. You had no right to—"

"I had every right!" Sonia thumped her fist on her chest. "I had the sanction of the Gods. You too are part of their plan, though you refuse to recognize it."

"You killed an innocent child!"

"Innocent? There is no such thing as innocence in an unborn prince. There is only legacy and duty. His fathers forfeited their duty, so their prince had to die."

"And Eliasara? Do you mean to kill her too?"

"No." Sonia knelt at Taesara's feet. Her face shone with feverish intensity. "No, my Lady Queen. Don't you see? Eliasara has reaffirmed the will of the Gods. She is a true Princess of Vortingen. She will put an end to the rule of Mage Kings."

Taesara studied her in contempt. "Get out."

"My Lady Queen." Desperation invaded Sonia's voice. "I am but an instrument of the Gods."

"Get out!" Taesara roared.

Tears streamed down Sonia's cheeks. "I only want what is best for you and your daughter, what is best for all of us. I love you, my Lady Queen!"

Taesara struck Sonia, leaving a red welt on her cheek. "I spare you today because I cannot bear the thought of one more life upon my hands in this ghastly war! But I will not spare you tomorrow. As Thunder is my witness, if I ever see you among my people again, I will have you tortured, disemboweled, and hung. I will see your remains scattered to the wolves and left to rot on open fields. Leave me, Sonia, and do not ever come back."

The lady fled, sobbing, from Taesara's presence.

Tremors coursed through Taesara. Rage rose from deep within, rending her soul and tearing open her throat in an anguished cry. She swept her arms across the table, sending cups and plates crashing to the floor. Then she sank to the ground, covered her face with her hands, and wept. She heard the footsteps of her ladies, accompanied by agitated voices as they surrounded their wilted queen.

"Mama." Eliasara slipped an arm around her shoulders. "Mama, what has happened?"

The unexpected compassion in her daughter's voice ignited another wave of excruciating grief.

"What happened, Mama? Why are you crying?"

"Oh, Eliasara." Taesara gathered her surviving daughter in her arms and held tight onto her precious life.

I weep for my beloved son, who never saw the light of this difficult and beautiful world.

For him, and for all the children who would have perished in my womb, had the Mage King kept me at his side and Sonia remained in my service.

CHAPTER FORTY-SEVEN

Prisoner

AS EOLYN AND COREY stepped into the dim tent, Mariel rose to greet them. Behind her lay Nicola on a makeshift cot. A thin blanket covered the sleeping figure.

"You watch over your sister?" Eolyn asked.

Mariel nodded. "Mage Corey gave me permission. I know what she did was wrong, Maga Eolyn, but I can't...I don't want her to feel like she's alone."

"Compassion is the mark of a true maga," Eolyn said. "Ours is a better world, Mariel, because you remember that."

Nicola slept soundly, chest rising and falling in an even rhythm. Her hands and feet had been bound.

"You have her under a spell?" Eolyn asked Corey.

"Yes," he replied. "It was the easiest way to subdue her."

"And her magic is securely bound?"

"We made certain of that."

"Wake her, then."

Corey stepped forward, laid his palm upon Nicola's forehead, and murmured a brief invocation.

Nicola stirred and moaned. She opened her eyes and took in the stark surroundings. Recognition passed through her features. She focused on the mage who watched her.

"What is in store for me now?" she demanded in bitter tones. "Torture? Possession?"

"I'd rather skip those pleasantries and send you straight to the pyre," Corey replied evenly. "Yet ours is a merciful queen, and she seems to have taken it into her head to delay your sentence."

"Enough, Mage Corey," Eolyn said.

The mage took the young woman's arm and helped her to a sitting position. "Come, Nicola. Queen Eolyn wishes to speak with you."

Nicola hung her head, refusing to meet Eolyn's gaze.

"Leave us, Mage Corey. Mariel, you too."

"But I want to—"

"You heard me."

Mariel looked to Corey, who frowned and gave a slight shake of his head. The young maga bowed and left, disappointment plain upon her face.

"I would caution you against being alone with his woman, my Lady Queen," Corey said.

"I understand, Mage Corey. Even so, I bid you to go. Though I do ask that you not wander far."

As Corey departed, Eolyn took a seat on the stool Mariel had left behind. She invoked a glow in the crystal head of her staff, casting a bluish light over herself and her prisoner. Nicola flinched, and then was still again. Her hair hung lank and unkempt over her face. Her proud shoulders were bent, her strong hands clasped tightly.

What sort of leader have I become, that my own daughter in magic should be delivered to me like this?

"I expected you to march today." Nicola broke the silence with spite in her voice.

"The army of Roenfyn drives fast toward the heart of Moisehén," Eolyn replied. "Perhaps it was a mistake to delay again, but the arrival of our ally from the Paramen Mountains demanded a reassessment of our strategies."

"Khelia's decision changes nothing. You will lose this war. It is the will of the Gods."

"How many lives must be sacrificed in pursuit of what you call the will of the Gods? Was the destruction of Selkynsen their will? The suffering of its men, women, and children?"

Nicola clenched her jaw.

Eolyn felt Akmael's spirit materialize at her side. His breath upon her ear. His touch against her cheek.

The ever-present ache in her heart intensified.

"Nicola," she said quietly, "have you ever loved someone so much that you followed that person down a path all others considered folly?"

Nicola jerked up her head. Fire leapt in her gaze. "Don't you dare compare our bond to yours."

"You are right. The similarity ends there, because the path I chose brought our people a decade of peace. Not much, perhaps, in the great expanse of history, but precious nonetheless to all those who remember the War of the Magas and the purges that followed. Your choice, on the other hand, has dragged us into war. Innocents have died; a proud and beautiful city was lost. And by all estimates, this conflict has only just begun. My Council says you should burn. What do you say, Nicola? What would be just punishment for all the blood that has been and will be shed because of you?"

"You twist the truth to serve your own ends!"

"I speak only what I know, what I have seen and heard since the day you took Eliasara away and delivered her to a man who used her to further his own ambitions."

Nicola lowered her gaze.

"Some say love leads us toward foolish decisions," Eolyn continued. "I suppose in some cases this is true. Yet I hold fast to Aithne's teaching that on the whole, love tempers us toward better judgment."

"I grow weary of your platitudes. Tell me my fate, and be done with it."

"Your fate is yours to choose, Nicola. You may live among us, or you may live in exile."

Nicola lifted her eyes. "Live?"

"If you remain in Moisehén, you must renounce High Magic. The part of your magic that is now bound will be stripped away entirely. You will lay down your arms and swear an oath that what gifts you have will, for the rest of your life, be dedicated to serving our people in humility. If you break your oath, or attempt to petition for another staff of High Magic, you will be imprisoned; caged and forgotten in the darkest depths of the Fortress of Vortingen. Kept there without company until the day you die."

"And if I choose exile?"

"Then you may keep your staff, and I will pray that you find a

315

home where you can dedicate your gifts to a better purpose." Eolyn rose, having said what she wanted to say. "Tomorrow we march west. You will be taken back to Rhiemsaven, where you will remain a prisoner until this war has ended. Mariel will go as your guard and companion. I suspect you will have much time, Nicola, to reflect upon your path."

"Why don't you just burn me?"

Eolyn released a slow breath. "These have been troubled times. I've learned in recent days that I am capable of great anger and great cruelty. But this one thing I will not do: I will not execute my own daughters, no matter what their crime against me or my people."

With this, Eolyn turned to go.

"The Mage King would not have hesitated to see me burn," Nicola called after her.

Eolyn halted mid-step and met her student's gaze. "No, he would not have. But as I hope you come to see, Nicola, I am not the Mage King."

CHAPTER FORTY-EIGHT

Fields of Conflict

THE SUN SHONE HIGH OVERHEAD as Eolyn and her escort topped a low hill. Open grassland greeted them, marked by scattered groves of trees. The invading army had camped just beyond a ridge on the far side of this wide valley. Flags of sage and gold fluttered among banners of silver and purple, colors that defied Queen Eolyn and the claim of Akmael's only son. The camp itself could not be seen clearly, making it difficult to tell how many of Taesara's forces had amassed there. The ridge descended in a grassy slope that curved around the valley, reaching toward them with an earthen embrace. Northward, the terrain ended in sharp white cliffs over the Furma River.

"I recognize this strategy," Eolyn said. "My husband made use of similar circumstances when we prepared for the final battle against the Syrnte."

Shadows undulated over the field, precursors to tides of aggression and death.

"Except I'll wager that your husband had the high ground." Khelia reined in next to Eolyn. She clucked her tongue as she scanned the landscape. "With Mechnes and his army down below."

Eolyn nodded. "The ridge was also lower, and there were no trees, save for a small woodland well off the battleground. There were very few options for archers to hide, unlike here."

"That experience will serve you well, now that the disadvantage is ours. We risk giving Taesara's army easy access to our flanks when we move up that hill, and we can rest assured every one of those copses will have a small company of warriors. We have to plan carefully, protect our flanks while our forces move against the center. Their warriors must be driven back with every step we advance up that hill. And we should hold some cavalry in reserve. They're planning more than a victory here, Eolyn. They are hoping for a blood bath."

War is always a blood bath.

Eolyn let go a weary sigh. "I suppose we can expect no less."

"Taesara may have spent years among the poor," Khelia said, "but she conserved her instinct for battle, not to mention a healthy thirst for vengeance."

"I imagine it was her advisors who chose this terrain, not her."

"Don't underestimate that woman any more than she would underestimate you, Eolyn. She made the decision to accept their counsel. It's clear they hope to leave no survivors. You say the Galians cannot shape shift?"

"As far as we know, that magic is not part of their traditions."

"Well, at least we've got that trick on our side. I'll wager the Galians won't flinch at the sight of a few ivory fangs, but those superstitious rabbits from Roenfyn will scatter the moment our warriors turn into wild beasts."

"Bears and Snow Tigers may do us little good. Nothing strikes fear in the heart of a wild animal like fire, and the Galians are unsurpassed in their ability to wield it. By now their wizards will have dug tunnels below these fields and filled them with the breath of their volcanoes. Not only can they send our shapeshifted warriors into panic, they might tear our army asunder in flames just as they destroyed the walls of Selkynsen."

"Aren't Corey and his friends preparing magic to counter that?"

"We have some tricks up our sleeves, but those counter spells will do little good if our mage warriors are burned before they have a chance to invoke them." Eolyn nodded to a group of mages down slope, toward the river. "They are also mapping out the magic that runs under this valley. If the disturbance left by the Galians is great enough, we may be able to locate any existing trenches. But the Galians will have been clever in the placement and concealment of their work. Still, by the end of the day Corey should be able tell us what locations would be most conducive to Galian fire magic."

"Well, that's something." Khelia turned her horse around. "On to the task at hand, then. Let's call our officers together. We've some work to do before the games begin."

Eolyn.

Akmael's voice wove through the breeze, achingly distant, impossibly close.

Eolyn shut her eyes and lifted her face to the sun. She imagined herself slipping off her horse and wrapping herself in the cloak of Akmael's presence.

The trappings of war faded from the landscape. Eolyn walked barefoot through the field, the rich robes of her station replaced by the simple russet gown she had always preferred. A basket made from the bark of a tallow sapling was strapped to her back. Laughter floated over the hills. She recognized in that sweet melody the voices of Tasha and Catarina, the exquisite song of Adiana, the stern call of Renate.

She set her basket down and found it filled with seedlings of oak, birch, alder, and fir. Akmael appeared next to her carrying his own burden of burgeoning life. Together they planted the young trees, one after another. Hundreds, then thousands gifted to the dark earth.

In the wake of their passing, a forest grew, tall and verdant. When they had finished, they looked back upon their work and saw a tightly woven net of life, death, and renewal.

This too will pass, her companion said.

Eolyn turned and saw not Akmael at her side, but her beloved tutor, Doyenne Ghemena. The old woman watched her just as she had on the first day they met, with keen gray eyes and an amused smile. Eolyn's heart contracted painfully at the site of her mother in magic. She reached out for an embrace, but Ghemena stepped away, shimmering like a mirage a hot summer day.

All wars end, she said.

Eolyn shook her head. *Wars end only to begin again.*

A serpent cannot eat its own tail indefinitely, Ghemena insisted. *The cycle will be broken. Trust your instinct, and remember: Your path is made by walking.*

Eolyn opened her eyes, heard flags snapping overhead, smelled the fragrant grass as it bent beneath a constant wind.

Khelia waited along with Eolyn's other advisors and allies. Their polished breastplates shone brilliantly under the midday sun. Their expectant stance was marked by grim determination.

Her men and women.

Her warriors.

Her war.

"Come, then," Eolyn said, urging her horse back toward their camp. "Let us make this a battle to end all battles."

CHAPTER FORTY-NINE

Counsel

As soon as Taesara was advised of the situation, she summoned Ghemena and Ireny. They came willingly, only to be disarmed and bound upon arrival. Forced to their knees, they now knelt before the Queen and Eliasara. Guards held blades to their throats. Taesara's advisors, including Savegre and Urales, were assembled around them.

"I swear on the breath of Dragon, I did not foresee this!" Ghemena's voice shook with rage and frustration. "Khelia promised us her army. I had no reason to doubt her word."

"A maga's word is always false," Taesara said. "And now I must ask myself: Was it Khelia that lied to you, or you who have lied to us in order to lay a clever trap?"

"You think I would have left Nicola in their company if I had for one moment believed—"

"Of course you would have. Nicola, no doubt, has given them much useful information. They know the numbers of our infantry, spearmen, and cavalry. They know what magic we have at our disposal, our strengths and our weaknesses. Everything they need to win this battle was handed to them inside of her fair head."

"She will have died before betraying our cause!"

Ghemena drew a sharp breath at her own declaration. She looked away, her voice reduced to a whisper. "Indeed, she must already be dead."

Taesara nodded to one of the guards. He adjusted his stance and readied his blade.

"Treason can only be met with one punishment," Taesara said.

"But I would have you know, before you meet your Gods, that I am grateful for this at least: that you delivered my daughter to me."

The guard swung his blade.

Ghemena emitted an ear-piercing curse.

Light blinded Taesara. She heard feral grunts followed by the sound of metal tearing open flesh. Before Taesara could recover her sight, Ghemena caught the Queen's arm and twisted it behind her back. Pain shot through Taesara's shoulder, and she felt the kiss of steel at her throat.

"Mother!" Eliasara cried.

Taesara's vision cleared. Guards and nobles had frozen in their places. Savegre had his sword drawn, and Urales held Eliasara, one arm wrapped protectively around the girl's shoulders. Their gazes were fixed on the Queen, immobilized with Ghemena at her back.

Taesara became aware of a warm drip on her throat, and realized it was the blood of a guard at her feet, slain by the same blade that now threatened her.

Ghemena hissed in her ear. "Kill me, and you destroy your last, best hope."

Red flames sprang from Ghemena's hand to the roof of the tent. The canvas curled back in a smoke-rimmed circle. Wind and feathers beat at Taesara's face as the maga warrior changed shape. Ghemena soared through the opening with an eagle's cry. A guard sent arrows in her wake, but it was too late. The winged form became a small black shadow against the sky and then disappeared.

Taesara choked on the taste of ash and sulfur, on the stench of her own terror. Blinking back the sting of smoke, she looked to her daughter, and then followed Eliasara's worried gaze to where Ireny still knelt with hands bound and head bowed.

"Finish her!" Taesara said to the guard still standing.

"No!" Eliasara tore away from Urales and flung herself between Ireny and the guard.

Taesara lunged to separate Eliasara from the witch, but Savegre caught her arm and gave a slight shake of his head.

"Why did you not run, Ireny?" Eliasara asked, kneeling beside the prisoner. "Why did you stay while she escaped?"

A sad smile touched Ireny's lips. "My Lady and Liege, where would I go?"

"Get away from her, Eliasara," Taesara said.

"I need her, Mama. I must have a maga warrior to protect me, and she's the only one left to us."

"She is a traitor."

"She had nothing to do with the Mountain Queen! She's always been with us, guarding me. She's my friend."

"I've learned through bitter experience what sort of friend a maga makes."

"If she were a traitor, she would have run away!"

Taesara looked to the guards. "You heard my command."

Eliasara screamed and kicked as they dragged her from Ireny.

"Taesara," Savegre said quietly. "Think before you do this."

Angered, Taesara jerked away from him. "What would you say in that woman's defense? Even if she were innocent, we have no way to control a creature such as this. No protection against her schemes."

"Urales," Savegre said to his advisor, "bind this woman's magic and see that she is placed under adequate guard, pending her trial."

"I have not given you permission to assume custody of this woman."

"No you have not. But you know in your heart, Taesara, that this is what we must do."

My heart.

Something fractured inside her resolve.

What do you understand of my heart?

Taesara blinked and turned away.

"Do as he commands," she said.

Urales took hold of Ireny, who went without protest, surrounded by Galian guards. Eliasara followed close behind.

"Leave me," Taesara said to the others. "All of you. I would have a word alone with Prince Savegre."

Her attendants shuffled away in troubled silence.

Taesara drifted toward to the shaft of light beneath the hole left by Ghemena. She closed her eyes and lifted her face to the sun.

Savegre's approach was felt rather than heard, a wave of warmth that emerged from the shadows and wrapped itself around her.

"You think Ireny is innocent?" she asked.

"I think her death, had you carried it out in this moment, would have haunted you the rest of your life. And it would have earned you the lasting resentment of your daughter."

"There will be an inquiry and a trial. I may yet decide to execute her."

"That is your right and your duty. But execution should be a deliberate action with due process. Not a murder committed in the heat of the moment."

He embraced her from behind. She leaned into him, thinking this moment of sustenance worth all the sacrifice and uncertainty of recent weeks.

"I must send my daughter away from this place."

"Selkynsen should be secure enough until we are certain of the tide of the war," Savegre replied.

"Even there, she may be hunted by mages and magas. Ireny must remain under custody, and I don't have anyone else who—"

"I will appoint some of my own guard to watch over her, men and women well-trained in the ways of magic."

Relief flooded through Taesara. "Thank you, Savegre."

The Galian Prince pressed his lips against Taesara's temple. He murmured her name, a tender expression that revived the ache in her heart.

"Why did you not return?" The question was beneath her, but she could no longer hold it within.

"There were rumors of witchcraft following your uncle's death. It would have done you no good to have them discover a Galian wizard in your bed."

The sounds of the camp became muffled. There was a slight echo to his words, as if they bounced off some invisible barrier.

"Was it?" she whispered, fearful of the answer. "Sorcery?"

Savegre turned Taesara around and set his hands upon her shoulders. "A weakened bridge killed your uncle. A swollen river, caused by heavy rains. Death comes to us all, Taesara. My ancestors learned long ago that spells cannot hasten the ultimate will of the Gods."

"Yet there was magic between us, the night before he died."

"Yes, my beloved Queen." Savegre bent to kiss her. "But that was not the sort of magic that breeds death."

She pulled him closer, inhaling his aroma of fire, earth, and salt. He responded with ardor, lips leaving a trail of sparks down her neck. His manhood hardened against her abdomen. Damp heat flooded her loins. That her humble embrace could ignite such power seemed nothing short of miraculous.

"Come to me tonight," she murmured.

"No."

She ceased her kisses. "Why?"

"This is no place for our love."

"If not here and now, then when?"

"I do not know." Melancholy showed in his face, a disturbing expression that reached well beyond these words and this moment.

He stepped away, blending with the shadows that surrounded her circle of light.

"Turn back from this path, Taesara."

She blinked in confusion. "I don't understand."

"Abandon this campaign before it is too late."

"After having marched my people this far, after having won Selkynsen? I am to simply give up and go home?"

"It would be best for you and for all your people."

"*Best* for us? Why?"

He did not respond.

Taesara stepped out of the shaft of light, letting her eyes adjust so that she might better read his features. What she saw left a knot in her gut. "You believe we cannot win tomorrow."

"Victory or defeat is irrelevant. War is not your place."

"Yet it is my destiny."

"Not your destiny. Not this war."

"I have no choice but to stand and fight! Were I to call for a retreat, the Witch Queen would harry us all the way to the border. The losses would be catastrophic. If I do not win tomorrow, and the day after, and the day after, if I do not take this campaign to the gates of the King's City and bring those walls down once and for all, Eolyn and her bastard son will hunt my daughter unto her death."

"You cannot be certain of that."

"Yes I can," she said vehemently. "This is the way of princes and kings, and of the women who seduce them."

"You have seduced a prince, Taesara. Is this your way as well?"

Taesara lifted a hand to strike him, then clenched her fist and let it drop by her side. She trembled with rage and humiliation. "I have nothing in common with that whore. How dare you suggest otherwise."

He let go a slow breath and retreated a few paces, one hand working the tension on his brow. "Forgive me. I meant no insult."

Taesara swallowed, but her throat was dry. Panic was threading its way through heart and spirit. "Do you intend to withdraw your support? Is that what this is about? Your advisors are telling you we have no hope against the combined forces of Moisehén and the Mountain Queen?"

He took too long to consider his words.

"Answer me, Savegre."

A shudder ran through his shoulders, as if he were ridding himself of some terrible burden. The Galian Prince turned to meet Taesara's gaze. He approached and enfolded her icy hands in his.

"Beloved Taesara," he said, "I swear to you by the Gods of my ancestors, no matter what happens tomorrow, you and your daughter will have my protection. Always."

It should not have seemed such a weak promise, and yet Taesara sensed a shadow looming beneath his words.

"What is happening?" she whispered.

Savegre set his hand upon her cheek and pressed his lips against her forehead.

"Destiny," he said. "Destiny and war."

CHAPTER FIFTY

Prophecy

STARS HUNG IN THE FIRMAMENT, the faint breath of Dragon illuminating the night. A faint and refreshing breeze whispered over tall grass. The lonely call of a night heron floated from the shores of the Furma.

On the far side of the valley, the ridge glowed with fires of the enemy's camp. The sight was oddly warm and inviting, as if Eolyn and her companions had reached the end of a long and weary journey, as if Roenfyn were calling them home.

Three times I have stood on the threshold of battle, Eolyn thought, *and always it has been like this.*

Quiet. Expectant. A soothing cadence that preceded the terror.

Flames leapt from the heart of a sacred circle cast by Mage Corey. Aromas of juniper, rosemary, and winter sage filled the air. Officers and advisors gathered close, Khelia and her people among them. The spirit of the Mage King coalesced at Eolyn's side, his touch tingling upon her palm, his resolute strength feeding hers. Kel'Barú hummed on her hip, content inside dreams of battles long past, steady in its anticipation of the bloodshed to come. Tendrils of magic fell from the blade, snaking beyond the circle toward Roenfyn's camp.

In keeping with the traditions of their people, Corey oversaw the sacred ceremonies that had, since the time of Caedmon, marked the eve of battle. He knelt before each warrior and painted their hands and feet with dyes prepared from night berries and blue iris root, symbols designed to ward off enemies in this world and beyond. When he had finished with all the others, he knelt before

Eolyn, High Maga and Queen of all Moisehén.

The maga paid homage to east, south, west, and north, calling on the memory of their ancestors. Then she drew back her skirt, and Mage Corey placed warm hands upon her bare feet. Murmuring his own invocation to the Gods, he began quick practiced strokes with his brush. Their magic intermingled, spirits flowing toward each other in a way that had marked their relationship from the very beginning; a daunting sensation that inspired a mix of caution and curiosity in Eolyn's heart.

Here we are still: He the Orphan of East Selen, and I, the last Daughter of the Magas. What strange intention of fate feeds this union?

"Eolyn." Khelia's sharp call snapped Eolyn out of her reverie.

Corey paused in his task and looked up.

Metal rang in its sheath as the Mountain Queen drew her sword. She nodded toward a place beyond the circle where a mist was gathering along the ground.

"It follows the threads of Kel'Barú's magic," Eolyn realized.

More swords hissed as they were released from their sheaths. Corey rose and invoked an additional ward around Eolyn.

"Cast away your weapon," he said.

"No."

"That is a Galian sword." Anger filled Corey's voice as he gestured toward the mist. "And that is Galian wizardry."

The fog spread on the edge of their sacred circle, billowing upward as if testing the integrity of the barrier.

Faeom dumae!

The crystal head of Corey's staff ignited in a threatening, virescent glow.

Eolyn laid a hand upon the hilt of her sword, captivated by the deep calm she sensed in the blade. Kel'Barú lay quiet as the forest on a cold winter's night. Beneath this silence she felt anticipation, along with another emotion she struggled to identify...

Wonder.

The mist fell away, revealing a tall, gaunt man with dark robes and an ebony staff. For one startling moment, Eolyn thought she looked upon Tzeremond.

The old wizard's gaze slid across her companions and settled on the Queen. He bowed low, his movement stiff. "Eolyn, Queen and High Maga of Moisehén. I am Urales, High Wizard of Galia. I come to pay homage to you, and to the weapon you wield."

Eolyn caught Khelia's sideways glance. The mountain warrior shook her head.

"You have a message for us, Urales?" Eolyn demanded. "A petition from our enemy?"

"Show me the Sword of Shadows."

Sword of Shadows?

Eolyn guessed he referred to Kel'Barú, though she had never heard this name used in reference to her weapon. She gripped the hilt, reaching deep into the spirit of the sword for any warning it might give. Sensing none, she unsheathed the weapon and leveled the blade at Urales. Gathering the moonlight into itself, Kel'Barú took on an otherworldly glow.

Urales drew a ragged breath and went to his knees, eyes damp with zealous joy. He pointed a bony finger toward the heavens. "See how it is written in the stars. The wanderers have aligned. Aithne, Caradoc, Dragon. Caedmon with Lithia at his side. They stand as one above us on this night, to look upon the woman who wields this blade. So it was foretold. So it has come to pass. You, Eolyn of Moisehén, will end the War of a Thousand Years."

Eolyn frowned. "What are these riddles you speak?"

"No riddles. Three armies of Dragon in this place, under these stars, are destined to end the grief that Thunder brought upon us all."

Urales rose with some effort, leaning on his staff. He made a long sweeping motion across the field of battle. Eolyn saw the valley cast in an odd grayish light. Armies writhed in a dance of death, an illusion of the struggle to come.

"When Moisehén and the Mountain Warriors make their charge," Urales said, "Galia will attack Roenfyn from the flanks. Their soldiers will be trapped. None will be spared."

Eolyn blinked, stunned. "You intend to betray your allies?"

"Not our allies. Our enemy of a thousand years, delivered to this fate by the will of the Gods."

Fury and indignation rose in Eolyn's blood. "If Galia wanted to make war on Roenfyn, you could have done so without dragging the conflict into our territory."

"No." He beat his staff upon the ground. "It is written thus: Three armies of Dragon, five wanderers, and the woman who wields the Sword of Shadows. This is the path we have followed. The path revealed to us. Here, under these signs, all conflict will end."

"In slaughter?"

Urales set his jaw. "I come not to defend the will of the Gods, only to communicate it."

"Prophecy is meaningless to our people," Eolyn said. "We have no reason to trust you."

"Trust is irrelevant. Action will reveal the truth."

"You destroyed the walls of Selkynsen with Galian magic, and now you expect us to believe—"

Urales did not deign to receive her challenge. The mist folded over him, and he disappeared.

For a moment, no one spoke.

"Well." The Mountain Queen snorted. "You all know what I think about trusting a wizard."

"This changes nothing," Eolyn agreed. "Except to make us more wary of what they have planned for tomorrow. Khelia, Lord Herensen, call together our officers and inform them of what has happened. We must anticipate any sort of trap the Galians intend to lay with this ruse. I will join you shortly, once Mage Corey and I have finished our petition to the Gods."

Khelia and Herensen departed, along with other attendants.

Eolyn rested Kel'Barú's blade on her sleeve and listened carefully to its song, stubbornly tranquil despite these strange events.

"What do you make of that man and his words?" she asked Corey.

The mage shook his head. "I can tell you little more than what you saw for yourself. Urales seems part of the same generation that spawned Tzeremond and Baedon. Zealous wizards, all of them. Convinced they understood and served the will of the Gods."

"He makes no sense. How could they support the conquest of Selkynsen and then expect us to believe they intend to fight on our side?"

"A man convinced he is an instrument of the Gods can

330

assume many contradictions. Selkynsen was not entirely destroyed; perhaps the Galians had some role in that. And though they brought down the outer walls, by all accounts, they did not take part in pillaging the exposed quarters."

"That does not absolve Galia of what happened."

"Not in our eyes, but a man like Urales sees such casualties from a different perspective."

"You think he might be telling us the truth?"

"I think you are wise to consider all possibilities."

Kel'Barú hummed in her grip.

"What should I do?" Eolyn asked.

Here was the ultimate burden of a king: hundreds, perhaps thousands, of lives in the palm of her hand. *To arms, to battle, to the portals of the Underworld.*

Eolyn looked up at her companion. "Mage Corey, according to the tradition of our people I should at this time surrender my blade to you and ask you to commend it to the Gods. I hope that you will not take insult, should I wish to invoke their blessing myself."

The mage bowed and stepped aside, offering her his place in front of the fire.

"Thank you. You may join Khelia and the others. I'm sure they will have need of your insights."

Corey cocked his brow. "If you think, my Lady Queen, that I would leave you alone on this night, with Galian wizards prowling these hills, then you are quite mistaken."

The declaration made her smile. "My guards are still here, Mage Corey."

"As am I."

Eolyn nodded, stepped toward the center of the circle, and knelt before the flame. The grass felt cool beneath her knees; heat from the fire bathed her face. She offered Kel'Barú to the heavens and then, setting the sword on her lap, began her invocation.

Ehekaht, Ehekahtu
Naeom cohmae
Faeom denae
Naeom dumae...

She repeated the cadence again and again, a prayer for protection, wisdom, and calm in the face of death. The chant carried Eolyn deep into herself. Beneath its soothing stream, she contemplated the burning question of her heart.

Who is my enemy?

Faces of the past surged in her mind's eye. Tzeremond and Doyenne Ghemena. Kedehen and Briana. Kaie and Ernan and Tahmir and Rishona. Drostan slain in the pass of Aerunden. Mechnes charred on the fields of Rhiemsaven. Adiana lost to slavery. Eliasara opposed to her brother.

Who is our enemy?

The tide of the Magas rising against their King. The Clan of East Selen slaughtered in one night. The burning of Eolyn's mother, the destruction of Berlingen.

Kel'Barú took up her song, weaving its own memory through the melody, of battles won and violence forgotten, of unceasing struggle reaching back to the beginning of time, to the People of Thunder who rose with implacable fury against the followers of Dragon.

Who is our enemy?

Inside the voice of the Galian blade, Eolyn at last found the answer she sought.

War is our enemy, Kel'Barú whispered.

War is the enemy of us all.

CHAPTER FIFTY-ONE

Visitor

TAESARA WAS STARTLED from her sleep by a hand clamped over her mouth. For the second time in a turn of the sun, she felt the cold kiss of steel at her throat. The night was dark, her tent quiet as death. Unable to cry out, she lay immobilized by fear, trying to discern a face inside the shadow that loomed over her.

Naeom aenli.

A candle next to Taesara's bed flickered to life and illuminated her attacker. Again, she cried out, her call stifled by the witch's hold. Taesara tried to pull away, only to realize in horror that her limbs were heavy as lead.

Have I been poisoned?

The knife bit her skin.

"No one will hear you." The witch spoke with deadly calm.

Taesara's heart pounded inside her chest. Had the army of Moisehén taken their camp by night, attacking them in their sleep like thieves without honor? She craned her neck to see where her daughter slept, and remembered with infinite relief that Eliasara had been sent back to Selkynsen earlier that day.

"No one knows I am here," Eolyn, the Witch Queen of Moisehén, murmured. "Your soldiers sleep. Our battle has not yet begun."

Tension left Taesara's muscles. The weight came off her body, and feeling returned to her limbs.

"I did not come to slay you, Taesara of Roenfyn," the woman continued. "I merely want to speak with you, away from all the others."

Taesara shuddered at this strange request. The Witch Queen was not at all as she remembered. Her stature was small, her aspect unassuming. She wore a simple linen shift, and her throat was unadorned by jewels or symbols of power. Disheveled hair flowed freely about her shoulders. The face seemed older; indeed it was, though witches were not supposed to age.

"All our lives we have been at the mercy of their games of power." Eolyn nodded toward the camp outside. "Now you and I stand at the head of these armies of men. I thought perhaps we could endeavor to imagine the world differently. Will you hear me out, Taesara of Roenfyn? If not, simply shake your head. I will be gone, swift as an arrow flies, and we will settle our differences as they have always been settled since the time of Caedmon and Vortingen: On the battlefield, in currencies of blood."

Taesara studied her opponent, trying to discern what deception lay behind these words, but all she could read was calm determination, an absolute trust in this moment.

If she wanted me dead, she would have killed me by now.

She gave a slight nod.

The witch released her hold.

Taesara sat up, rubbing the place where the blade had offended her throat. "What do you want?"

"Peace. An end to war. An agreement that settles this conflict once and for all."

"You expect me to surrender?"

"No. Not surrender. A dialogue. A treaty that satisfies us both."

"Why?" Taesara demanded. "By all accounts, our forces are equally matched. Why would you beg me to turn away from this battle?"

"I do not beg. If you refuse, I will meet you at dawn with all the powers at my command. I will win this war, Taesara. Nothing will stop me until I do. Nothing save for the fact that we are all defeated in war, whether we attain victory or not."

The Good Mother might have said the same.

Taesara shoved away the thought in anger.

"By what witchcraft do you speak to me tonight?" she said. "You invade my thoughts and try to turn them against me, but your spells are cast in vain. I fight for my daughter and the future of her people. You cannot weaken my resolve."

Eolyn bit her lip, a gesture so familiar Taesara wanted to slap it off the witch's face.

"I am sorry," the witch said quietly. "Sorry for whatever suffering my path has caused you. I…I want you to know that. I loved Akmael. That was all."

"How dare you! You are nothing but a peasant and a whore, and you have no right to—"

"Why should something as simple as love cost so much blood?" Desperation overtook the witch's voice. Her plea was cast beyond Taesara, a cry delivered to the Gods themselves. "Why should love demand a thousand lives?"

Taesara could think of no response for this. She studied her rival a long moment, allowing her heart to harden with the memory of all the pain and humiliation wrought by this ruthless woman.

"Leave me," she growled. "Get out of this place at once, or I will call my guard and have your head delivered to your pathetic allies on the morrow."

Eolyn looked away. A shadow descended upon her brow. "As you wish, Taesara of Roenfyn. Tomorrow, we will bathe our hands in blood. May the Gods forgive us all."

Light flashed through the maga, and in a swirl of shadows and feathers, she was gone, a creature of imagination vanishing into the night.

Heart pounding inside her chest, Taesara shrank beneath the covers, already wondering whether this strange apparition had been nothing more than a dream.

CHAPTER FIFTY-TWO

Four Armies

EOLYN CHAFED UNDER THE CUIRASS as her attendants tightened buckles and tucked away leather straps. Gifted to her by Akmael, the breast plate was a beautiful piece of craftsmanship, its polished metal engraved with images of Dragon. The armor fit well, the bulk of the weight resting on Eolyn's hips and the interior padded to accommodate her breasts. Even so, she had worn it only on the rarest of occasions, mostly for ceremonial purposes.

By the end of the day, the polished metal would be spattered with blood. Eolyn's magic would be spent and her stomach heaving from forces of destruction channeled through her body. In her heart, she believed she would live, though she would be altered irrevocably, another piece of her spirit splintered off and delivered to the Underworld.

Outside Eolyn's pavilion, Khelia, Herensen, and the others waited beneath billowing banners that lent color to a pale dawn. All knelt as Mage Corey blessed them with the fragrant smoke of winter sage. Once again, he called on the protection of the Gods. Eolyn felt a familiar stirring in her heart, and Akmael's spirit materialized at her side.

I will be with you, he whispered. *Do not be afraid.*

Corey's chant drew to a close. Eolyn's commanders rose, grim in aspect and quiet in their determination. They exchanged hearty embraces before mounting their horses and riding forth to meet Taesara of Roenfyn.

The four armies had taken up their positions on the battlefield. Eolyn counted six companies of infantry under Taesara's command.

336

Flags of Roenfyn flew over the soldiers in the center, while Galia held the flanks. Behind them waited two companies of horse, with archers arrayed along the ridges. Eolyn had no way of telling how many soldiers were hidden in the trees, much less on the other side of that ridge.

"They are tempting us to drive a wedge into the center." Khelia's voice brimmed with enthusiasm. "We will take them up on the challenge, but not with cavalry. Harry them first with archers. Then send foot soldiers toward the center, mage warriors and shape shifters among them. We'll have a company of horse to the south and another on the north to keep those Galian scoundrels under watch. The others we will hold in reserve, including your guard, Eolyn. Be prepared to charge wherever their line breaks first. This promises to be a fine battle. A very fine battle indeed."

A tight formation of horses crested the opposite ridge. The head banner bore the old sigil of Vortingen, a silver dragon against a purple night. Colors of Roenfyn and Galia flew just behind. Amid the cluster of guards and officers, Eolyn caught sight of Taesara, regal in bearing and dressed in a sky blue gown. Her golden hair was piled in an elegant braid and she, like Eolyn, wore a cuirass that shone under the rising sun.

With a nod to her guard, the Eolyn of Moisehén rode forward to meet her opponent. The two parties drew to a halt at a prudent distance from one another. Next to Taesara, Eolyn noted a dark-skinned man, handsome in aspect. His bearing and dress marked him as a Prince of Galia. He reminded Eolyn, oddly enough, of Akmael, in the stony set of his face and the rich colors of his aura. Behind him, the wizard Urales watched with a zealous glint in his hawkish eyes.

Eolyn's eyes settled on Taesara, who watched her in turn with a wary gaze.

"Taesara of Roenfyn," Eolyn said. "You have heard my offer. I have nothing more to say."

This provoked an exchange of puzzled glances between officers and advisors from both parties. Taesara's eyes widened and her nostrils flared. Then her gaze disconnected from Eolyn and focused inward. After a moment she lifted her chin.

"On behalf of my daughter, Eliasara, Princess of Moisehén and

337

Heiress to the Throne of Vortingen, I command that you and all your army…"

Taesara paused and looked past Eolyn, scanning the companies arrayed behind her: thousands of men and women ready to die for the cause of two children.

A frown furrowed Taesara's fair brow.

"I command that you…" She faltered and bit her lip.

Then from one moment to the next, her expression relaxed. She smiled as if remembering some private joke. Leaning forward, Taesara patted her horse's neck and dismounted.

"My Lady Queen!" The cry went up from all of her company.

In an instant the Galian Prince was off his mount and at Taesara's side, sword leveled at the company of Moisehén.

"Taesara," he said. "What are you doing?"

She made no response, but stood next to her horse, petting the animal's soft neck until it gave a satisfied whinny.

Taesara lifted her face to Eolyn.

"Walk with me," she said.

Against the protest of her own guard, Eolyn dismounted.

Khelia jumped off her horse and caught Eolyn by the arm. "Don't be a fool."

Eolyn looked to Taesara. "We will walk alone, just you and I?"

Taesara nodded and gave her company the order to remain behind.

"All it would take to kill you is one archer from that copse of trees." Khelia nodded uphill.

"I'll be all right." Eolyn set a steady hand on Khelia's shoulder. "She and I wish to talk, Khelia. That is all. We need to talk, away from all these men."

Khelia's reprimand showed in the set of her jaw and the angry flush of her cheeks. "That was a different circumstance, Eolyn."

"No…No, it wasn't different at all. Trust me, Khelia. I know what I am doing."

Eolyn stepped away to meet Taesara, woman to woman and eye to eye. The rival queens held each other in a discerning gaze before turning as one toward the river.

When they had gone far enough to be out of ear shot, Taesara said, "Tell me your proposal, Eolyn of Moisehén."

Eolyn's heart skipped a beat. The next few moments would decide the fate of them all. War or peace now turned on a handful of words.

Please, Gods, let me choose them well.

"Both our kingdoms restored to their former states," she began. "Selkynsen must be returned to Moisehén. We will demand tribute to fund the reconstruction of the outer wall and to compensate for the lives and property lost when it fell."

Taesara shook her head. "Selkynsen was won with our own blood, by the men under my uncle's command. We cannot simply hand it back."

"I know. As part of the bargain, I am prepared to consider returning New Linfeln to the Kingdom of Roenfyn."

"New Linfeln?" Surprise flickered across Taesara's expression.

"The port was part of your dowry." Eolyn spoke quickly, hoping to drive the offer home before Taesara began to doubt. "Akmael, my Lord King, should have returned it when he dissolved the marriage contract. Understand, however, that we must reach an acceptable and binding agreement on port tariffs before that city or any of its territories are signed back to you."

"And my daughter?"

"Eliasara remains with you in Roenfyn. No grievance will be held against her, nor will there be retribution for her part in this war. However, she must renounce all claims to the throne of Moisehén, for her and all her descendants. There can be no question of my son's legitimate and exclusive right to the Crown of Vortingen." Eolyn paused before adding, "This is non-negotiable. In return, however, Eoghan and I will make our oath to protect your claim, and your daughter's claim, to the throne of Roenfyn. If you encounter any threat to your rule, internal or external, Moisehén will come to your aid."

Taesara nodded and resumed her walk.

Eolyn fell into step beside her, studying the woman's face, yet unable to discern whether anything she offered would be of sufficient value to avert this war.

Ahead of them, the Furma swirled in its winding path toward the sea. The waters were taking on a deeper hue of blue as the sun rose in the east.

"How am I to trust you, Eolyn of Moisehén?" Taesara asked. "How do I know you and your son will honor these agreements?"

"I can only give you my word, and ask that you grant me the opportunity to prove myself worthy of your confidence."

Eolyn felt the eyes of four kingdoms at their backs. Tension wrapped around her heart and descended to the pit of her stomach. Her skin itched inside her armor. She did not want go back to killing, to the sickening sound of metal rending flesh, to the stench of blood filling her nostrils.

Taesara's silence grew long and uncomfortable.

Unable to withstand the uncertainty, Eolyn decided to play her last card. "I am also willing to consider, as a guarantee of our agreement, a marriage contract between Eoghan and Eliasara."

A jolt ran through Taesara. She stopped walking and set her clear blue gaze on Eolyn. "My daughter with your son?"

"The match would reunite the line of Vortingen." Eolyn quelled all instincts that warned against this union. This was the way of nobility, wasn't it? They sealed their treaties with marriage. "There would be no questions anymore, no conflict for the next generation of heirs. When Eoghan and Eliasara come of age, our kingdoms will be as one."

Taesara frowned and looked eastward along the river. A flux in her aura revealed that Eliasara had been sent away not long ago, and that Taesara longed for the girl's presence more than life itself.

"My uncle would have been most pleased by that offer," Taesara said, her tone one of bitter amusement.

"A marriage contract is not a necessary condition. I only mention it because—"

"Because you anticipated I would think like Sylus Penamor?" A subtle smile undercut the challenge in Taesara's voice. "I suppose that's only fair. I rather expected you to think like the Mage King."

Eolyn averted her gaze, uncertain how to interpret this response.

"Last night," Taesara continued, "you asked me to imagine the world differently from the men who held power before us. I've decided to accept your challenge, Eolyn of Moisehén. For this reason, Eliasara will not be given away in marriage, not to the Mage Prince nor to anyone else. When the time comes, she will choose her own consort, and that man, whoever he may be, will never wear the crown of Roenfyn."

Eolyn could not help but smile, for she saw in Taesara's conviction a spirit not unlike her own.

"I think, Taesara of Roenfyn," she said, "that under different circumstances, you and I might have been friends."

"Friends?" Taesara arched her brow. "No, Eolyn of Moisehén. Friendship would be too much to ask under any circumstance. We might, however, succeed at being allies. That much I am willing to try."

CHAPTER FIFTY-THREE

A Gift

TAESARA AND EOLYN BADE FAREWELL to each other on the shores of the Furma River south of Selkynsen, where the waters were broad and shallow. The day's warmth was undercut by a chilly breeze, the first subtle sign that autumn would soon color the landscape in shades of rust and gold.

Taesara watched with mixed feelings as Eolyn, her former enemy and untested ally, embraced her daughter, Eliasara.

"I wanted to see Briana and Eoghan." Eliasara's eyes were damp with emotion. "I had hoped to make my peace with them before this all ended."

Eolyn touched the girl's cheek. "Your mother and I have made your peace for you."

"That peace is my exile."

"You are not exiled, Eliasara. You are free. A Princess of Roenfyn, heiress to a fine kingdom. At the moment, your duty calls you home to serve your mother and your people, but you will always be welcome among us. Just as you and Eoghan are brother and sister, so it is with Roenfyn and Moisehén. We are one family now. We will not be divided."

"But I wanted to see them."

"You will." Eolyn kissed her forehead. "Sooner, perhaps, than you realize. I've suggested to your mother that we commemorate our treaty with a new festival, here on the border between our kingdoms, every summer. She is amenable to the idea. And you?"

A smile brightened Eliasara's face. She removed the necklace Savegre had given her, the silver dragon suspended on a purple ribbon, and pressed it into Eolyn's hands. "This is for my sister Briana. I fear I have nothing to give to my brother, save my love and my wishes for a happy and prosperous future."

"Those words will bring more joy to his heart than any gift of this world," Eolyn said.

Eliasara flung her arms around the maga's neck and kissed her cheek. Then she returned to Taesara's side and took her hand.

"I am ready," she said.

Having spoken at length in recent days, Taesara and Eolyn exchanged no more words, but embraced as an expression of common purpose. Their negotiations had proved lengthy, and the question of port tariffs in New Linfeln had yet to be settled. Yet both women were confident a solution could be found, and ready to trust their ambassadors with finishing the task.

Taesara mounted and directed her horse across the river. Waters that had been turbid and high a fortnight ago now flowed in crystalline riffles over smooth rocks. When Taesara reached the opposite shore, she looked east one more time.

Queen Eolyn raised her arm in salutation.

Taesara responded in kind. Then she turned her back on Moisehén. The realm of the Mage Kings receded, taking with it all the grief she had known there.

Eliasara rode at her side, Taesara's advisors close behind. Savegre accompanied them, along with his daughter, Nyella, and a small company of Galian warriors.

Ireny, after due consideration, had been reappointed to Eliasara's guard. Watching Eliasara, Nyella, and Ireny now, Taesara understood what an error it would have been to execute the young maga. These three young women were forming an important bond of friendship, one Taesara hoped would serve them long after she and all those of her generation had entered into the Afterlife.

The bulk of Savegre's army had been sent south with Urales to New Linfeln, where they would return to Galia by boat over the Sea of Rabeln.

This had been Queen Eolyn's suggestion, not to allow the Galian army to cross Roenfyn twice, so as to avoid unnecessary burden to the fragile harvests of her farmers. Taesara had worried Savegre might take insult at the request. Yet he had acquiesced, asking only that he and his daughter be allowed to accompany her on the journey home. He had also, very generously, left three coffers of gold with the Maga Queen, as payment toward the tribute owed for Selkynsen.

News of peace and victory preceded them. Peasants and nobles came out to declare their allegiance and throw wildflowers in Taesara's path. Taesara responded graciously, delaying their progress to stop in scattered villages and share in the joy of her people.

Having shed the grim cloak of warfare, her men-at-arms began turning their attention to other matters. Busy months lay ahead. Fields would be harvested, sheep sheared. The coming migrations would demand long days of hunting game for down, feathers, fur, and meats. By the time Taesara reached Adelrod, half the army had dispersed, levies and soldiers eager to return home and begin preparations for winter.

Taesara entrusted the fortress to the care of Lord Tobias and continued west with her guest Savegre, their daughters, and the guards that protected them. More than a fortnight had passed when at last they reached the low-lying woodlands that marked the border between Roenfyn and Galia.

They set up camp in a clearing near the forest edge. As stars appeared in the sky, Savegre and Taesara sat next to each other for the evening meal. They ate roasted meats and vegetables, drank sweet wine, and conversed as if the war and all its trappings had never existed. Taesara was discovering a new sort of intimacy with him, one that did not depend on mystery or magic, but that flourished on shared memories and hopes for the future. They had much in common, she and this wizard from Galia. Taesara felt grateful to count him as her friend.

On the morning of Savegre's departure, Taesara woke before dawn to find a mist covering the floor of her tent. Moving as if in a dream, she drew a cloak around her nightshift and wandered outside.

The camp was immersed in other-worldly silence. Guards lay on the ground snoring. Fires had died in the night. Not even the animals stirred. Mist flowed thick from the forest depths, billowing around tree trunks and rolling between the tents.

Taesara caught sight of Savegre on the edge of the forest. His broad back was turned to her as he contemplated the woodland beyond. The sight of his proud figure beneath those spreading branches ignited a familiar ache in her heart. As if sensing her presence, the prince turned around. A grin spread across his face, and he extended his arm in invitation.

They walked in silence for a long while, enthralled by the majesty of this moss-covered world. Tiny splashes of color adorned a palette of deep green and dark brown. Flowers of purple, yellow, and rose sprang up on rocks and old trunks. A bird flitted quietly through the branches and then disappeared. Squirrels chattered in the distance.

Savegre led Taesara up through a terrain of ancient trees and large boulders. A stream gurgled and laughed nearby, tripping over stones on its way downhill. At times the ground was slick, but Savegre did not let Taesara's footing falter.

They came to a place where the forest opened into a wide grove. Sunlight sliced through mist-shrouded trees. A waterfall descended into a wide crystalline pool. A nameless desire moved Taesara's spirit, and tears stung her eyes.

"My Queen is pleased." Savegre regarded her with warmth.

"Yes. This place is a treasure above all treasures. Thank you for sharing it with me."

"I do not share," he said. "I give. I give this to you."

Taesara blinked in surprise. "I don't understand."

"This woodland, north to the Surmaeg Mountains, south to the Sea of Rabeln, and west to the Aerbel River, will belong to Roenfyn."

"Why?"

"Recompense."

"You owe us no debt. If anything, the expense of taking your army across Roenfyn to Moisehén without even—"

"Why is your first response to every gift refusal?"

His stance and quizzical expression reminded Taesara of their first meeting. She allowed herself a smile. Indeed, laughter bubbled up through her spirit and broke full upon her lips. Taesara could not remember ever having laughed like this, as if she were a young girl free of all cares, innocent of the difficult future ahead. Her ribs began to ache, and she sought a tree to lean against.

Savegre drew close and brought her fingers to his lips.

"The grasslands and marshes of Roenfyn have a magic of their own," he said. "You understand this, Taesara. I believe you have always felt it in your heart, even when you did not call it 'magic.' This connection between your spirit and your land can make Roenfyn a great kingdom. Yet without forest, Roenfyn will always be incomplete. So I give you this, that you might gather strength from this place. All I ask is that you care for this woodland as you care for your own daughter. If this forest suffers under the stewardship of Roenfyn, Galia will reclaim it."

Taesara shook her head, dizzy from Savegre's declaration, from the intensity of his presence, from the fragrance of flowers and moss that had saturated her senses.

"It is too much," she whispered, suddenly shy of meeting his gaze. "I cannot accept such a gift."

"Accept." He took her chin in hand and brought her eyes to his. "Accept this gift, Taesara, Jewel of Roenfyn."

Savegre's lips met hers, fanning the fires of their passion. Taesara wrapped her arms around his neck, inviting the rich pleasure of his embrace. He removed his cloak and laid it upon a bed of ferns; she loosened the laces of her shift and let it slip from her shoulders. They met as one and sank to earth, making love among the sun-dappled herbs.

The rhythm of the waterfall intertwined with their dance of intimacy. Taesara felt the very spirit of the forest embrace her and enter her, bringing her to such ecstasies as she had never imagined. Afterwards, they lay satiated in each other's arms, his breath warm and tender upon her forehead.

Taesara found herself wondering whether it had been like this for Eolyn and the Mage King. *If this was what they discovered with each other, then I was wrong. I was wrong to ever think it my place to stand between them.*

"I have not treated you with honor, Taesara of Roenfyn," Savegre said, interrupting her thoughts.

"This is no dishonor among your people." Taesara touched his face and traced the line of his jaw. "Nor, I think, will I allow it to be called a dishonor among my own."

346

"I do not speak of the pleasures we have shared. I speak of the words I have withheld." Savegre's tone was subdued. He shifted his position and gently released Taesara from his embrace.

As they readied themselves to return to camp, the Galian Prince unveiled his truth, a tale of conflict that had accompanied him from the moment they joined Roenfyn's cause. He told Taesara about the prophecies of his people, the charge that had been given him by the High Wizards, and the uncertainty he had encountered in coming to know her.

Taesara could hardly believe Savegre's words, and she looked with renewed confusion upon the bond that had grown between them. How to interpret this intimacy with a man who might have been her assassin? Who might have massacred her people?

"And you would have done it?" she asked, fearful of the answer, yet needing to know. "Would have slaughtered my own on the fields of Moisehén, had I not made peace with the maga?"

Savegre paused. They had reached the edge of the woods. The mist was taking on a golden hue under the breaking dawn.

"In Galia, we do not speak of what might have been," he said, "only what was or what was not. And yet Taesara, I can assure you that I would have given my own life before letting any harm come to you or your daughter."

Yet in destroying my people, you would have destroyed me.

"Urales was humbled by this turn of history," Savegre continued. "He wanted you to know that. He has gone home a sober and repentant man. We knew this war was meant to bring peace, to build bridges where so many had been destroyed. What we failed to understand, until all had been said and done, was how."

Taesara absorbed this in troubled silence. What could she say? What could she possibly say to this disturbing revelation?

"You see now why we offer you this gift?" He gestured back toward the forest.

"Yes." Taesara nodded. "And I accept, Prince Savegre of Galia. Though I do not know if I can forgive."

The answer seemed to satisfy him. He took her hand. To Taesara's surprise, she did not resist. Fingers intertwined, they walked out of the forest together, faces lifted toward the morning sun.

CHAPTER FIFTY-FOUR

Choice

FIELD SPARROW SLIPPED THROUGH a barred window and alighted on the floor. Predawn cast a pale square across the swept dirt. At the edge of the small room lay a figure curled on a straw mat. Shedding the form of Sparrow, Ghemena crept to Nicola's side and touched her shoulder.

Nicola started from her sleep; her cry was silenced by Ghemena's hand over her mouth. Recognition and joy filled Nicola's expression. She sat up and enveloped Ghemena in a warm embrace.

"You found me," she whispered.

"I'm sorry I took so long. I thought for sure they had killed you." Ghemena touched a fading bruise on Nicola's face.

"This was from the fight I put up at the beginning." Nicola managed a smile. "But they haven't mistreated me since. What has happened, Ghemena? What news do you bring?"

"Roenfyn surrendered," Ghemena said bitterly. "Taesara capitulated before they even met in battle. She's renounced Eliasara's claim and has taken her simpering daughter back to the sodden plains that spawned them both."

"By the Gods," Nicola murmured. "No blood was shed between them?"

"Not a drop. Pathetic, isn't it?"

"It's remarkable."

"Come on." Ghemena helped Nicola to her feet. "I'm getting you out of here."

"Where will we go?"

"To the King's City, to put an end to this once and for all."

"What do you mean?"

"You know what I mean."

Nicola stiffened and pulled away. They held each other's gaze a long moment.

Then Nicola said quietly, "I am not a killer of children."

"You were quite ready to let Roenfyn kill those bastards for you."

"That was different. Or at least, I thought so at the time."

"Gods, Nicola! We have to do this. There's no other choice now. Eoghan and Briana must die before their magic matures and it is too late."

"No."

The word hit Ghemena like a slap across the face.

"I've made my choice," Nicola continued. "I am laying down my arms and letting go of High Magic. I will journey with Mariel to Moehn, where we will start a new *Aekelahr*. There, I will dedicate my skills and knowledge to teaching and healing."

"You?" Ghemena snorted. "A healer?"

"I've made my choice."

"Don't you dare take the coward's road."

"Don't you dare call me a coward."

"Nicola, I cannot do this without you!"

"Then don't do it at all."

"Curse it all! We have a calling. We made a *vow*. Would you defy the will of the Gods?"

"What do we know of the will of the Gods?" Nicola shot back. "I do not hear their voices; I cannot claim to interpret their words from wind and stars. I can only choose what is right in my heart."

"Not long ago, your heart told you the Mage Prince must die."

"I believed Eliasara had to be returned to her mother, and was willing to follow that act wherever it led. Don't you see, Ghemena? The moment we delivered Eliasara to Roenfyn, the Gods took this war out of our hands. The fate of our kingdoms was given not to us, but to Taesara and Eolyn. And they have made their choice. Now it's done. It's over, Ghemena. We are at peace."

Furious, Ghemena turned her back on Nicola. Her fists were clenched at her side; her breath came in short, fiery gasps. From the time she was young, she had suffered all manner of betrayals, but this...This was too much to bear.

Anchoring her spirit to the earth, she spun back around, knife in hand and leveled at the woman she loved.

Nicola watched her like a lynx. "Now you would slay me?"

Tears stung Ghemena's eyes. The hilt burned in her grasp. "I can't let you live if you don't come with me. You will tell them I've been here. You'll reveal my intentions."

Sadness filled Nicola's expression. "So many years we have spent together, and yet how little you know me. I could have alerted them by now, if I wanted to betray you."

"Don't make me do this, Nicola."

"I'm not the one holding the blade."

"Come with me!"

"If the Gods have blessed your path, then they will give you the help you need. Nothing I say or do will make any difference. So I will stay here, Ghemena of Moehn, and I will hold my tongue. Not because I fear death at your hands, but because I love you. Whether or not you succeed, I want you to live. And if they are expecting you in the King's City, then you will surely die."

Ghemena studied Nicola's subtle aura, the smooth lines of her beautiful face. She etched every detail into her memory, knowing she would never see her sister in magic again.

Then she sheathed her knife and stepped away.

Through the barred window, the day was growing brighter. The skies invited her toward flight.

"Farewell, friend and sister," she murmured, heart clenching in grief. "May Dragon protect you, now and always."

Ghemena invoked the shape of Field Sparrow. Her body fell in upon itself. Bones shrank and reshaped, feathers sprouted across her skin. Transformed, she fluttered her wings and alighted on the windowsill.

Nervous chirps escaped her throat as she scanned the alleyway. Seeing no one that might recognize her aura, she leapt into the air. The town of Rhiemsaven fell away and was soon replaced by a rolling green landscape.

In the days that followed, Ghemena kept close to the river, pausing amid swaying reeds, eating seeds and insects along the way.

Rarely did she shed her animal form, though she knew what it might cost to recuperate her magic once she reached her destination.

At last, the King's City came into view, purple banners of Vortingen fluttering high over gray walls and slate-covered roofs. Ghemena found a perch in a low lying tree. There she recovered her breath, eyes fixed on the high towers where she knew Eolyn's children slept.

I must wait, she told herself.

For as long as it might take.

Wait, until the surest path to my destiny is revealed.

CHAPTER FIFTY-FIVE

Friendship

COREY AND NICOLA SAT facing each other, sheltered by the spreading branches of an ancient oak. The day had dawned cool and breezy; the sun shone brilliant in a turquoise sky. Whispers of an autumn not yet manifest crept through grass and leaves. High overhead, a flock of geese engaged in merry banter as they headed south.

Enaem

Maeneh ukaht, maeneh semtue

The last time Corey had invoked this spell, the purges were at their height. Renate had sat before him, her fear well concealed beneath a hardened heart.

Dear Renate.

One of the truest companions he had ever had.

Turning her back on her sisters, Renate had surrendered High Magic in exchange for her life. The decision would haunt her to the end of her days, though it had allowed her to see a new dawn, to help lay the foundation for a time when the Daughters of Aithne would be reborn.

We have, every one of us, surrendered a part of our souls in this struggle.

Has it been worth the price?

The invocation flowed from Corey's memory like water from a spring.

Reghebe Amschenke.

Aen. Maen. Dauwean. Umaen.

Reghebe semtue

Pelau, urturm, eom.

352

As he repeated the spell, Nicola's magic parted from her grasp like finely spun silver and gold. The threads fell from Nicola's aura as if she were shedding her skin. The earth absorbed the waterfall of light, which was then drawn up through the oak tree and dispersed on the wind in a rustle of leaves.

Corey opened his eyes and saw Nicola watching him, her gaze clear and honest.

"That is all?" she asked.

"That is all." Corey released her hands.

"I felt nothing, no pain. Just a slipping away..." Nicola's brow furrowed in confusion.

"The rite was not invented to induce suffering," Corey said. "The surrendering of High Magic has been with us almost since the time of Aithne and Caradoc. Throughout the ages, many of our brothers and sisters have chosen to lay down their staffs, for the burdens and temptations of Dragon's gift are many, and there are other paths to serving our people. You must not consider this a punishment, Nicola. It is merely an initiation into the next stage of your journey."

Corey rose to his feet.

A shudder ran through Nicola. Tears began to flow down her cheeks. Mariel, who had stood nearby during the invocation, knelt next to Nicola and embraced her. Corey turned away, leaving the burden of solace to Mariel, whom he judged more appropriate for the task.

Nicola's staff in hand, he walked back toward camp. Much of the army had dispersed by now. The bulk of Khelia's troops had departed for the Paramen Mountains, and the forces of Moehn had begun their march from Rhiemsaven toward Aerunden that very morning.

Still, the Mage King's army, now Eolyn's army, occupied a vast stretch of open fields. Corey wondered what would happen to all these soldiers, now that peace was the new project of the realm.

Of course, peace between neighbors did not mean an end to war. There were Syrnte ambitions to keep an eye on, unidentified threats from Antaria and beyond, not to mention the restless ambitions of the noble families of Moisehén. All sparks that might in any moment fan into flames, if not in their lifetime, then to the grief of their descendants. He would speak to Eolyn about this. He would make certain she was not too quick or too careless in dismantling her military.

Corey arrived at the Queen's pavilion and entered into her presence unannounced. Khelia's laughter filled the tent. The Mountain Queen was dressed for travel, with a simple linen tunic, dark pants, and a cloak. Only the quality of her sword and satchel belied her status.

"The next time you summon me to war, Maga Eolyn," she was saying, "I will remember to leave my army at home."

Eolyn had also dressed modestly, wearing a simple russet gown in the style that had so become her when they first met in the highlands of Moehn. Her hair was unbound, and she smiled at Khelia's jest.

"Gods willing," she said, "I will not have reason to summon you to war again."

"We shall see." Khelia gave Eolyn a hearty embrace. "There are still many dogs in the world that can cause us problems. Don't forget my advice to you. And don't hesitate to call upon me, should you ever be in need."

"Thank you, Khelia. I will miss you."

"Yes, I should hope so." Khelia set her eyes on Corey. "I thought we wouldn't have the opportunity to say good-bye, Mage Corey."

He bowed in respect. In truth, he was glad to see Khelia go. It needled him, in a way it never had before, to imagine Eolyn in the arms of another.

Perhaps he was growing rigid with age.

"Safe travels, Khelia," he said. "Thank you for all you have done for us."

"So formal." She stood before him now, arms folded, a broad grin on her face. "I still remember our days of wine and dance, Corey. I'll wager they live inside of you, too. Somewhere. Don't let politics make you stodgy."

He allowed himself a smile and acquiesced to her embrace.

"I see now that you are loyal to someone besides yourself," Khelia murmured in his ear. "Take good care of her, Corey, or you'll have me to contend with."

"You needn't worry, Khelia. I know my purpose."

She withdrew, looked from Eolyn to Corey and back again. "I believe we've lived this moment before: the three of us in a tent, the future hidden from our eyes. The last time I left you two to your own devices, you changed the course of history. Good record, that. Keep it up."

Khelia sauntered toward the exit and paused as if caught by an important thought.

"Don't you forget, Corey," she added. "I'm the one who told you to hire her in the first place. You owe me that."

Eolyn's smile deepened after Khelia departed, and her gaze turned inward for a moment. Then she nodded to Corey and bade him to approach.

"My Lady Queen." He laid Nicola's staff on the table before her. "It is done."

The smile drained from Eolyn's face. She ran her fingers over the polished wood.

During the purges, only mages had the authority to destroy a staff, but in the highest tradition of Aithne and Caradoc, this task fell to the tutor of the person who had surrendered her magic.

Eolyn signaled the guards and servants to depart. Once they were alone, she asked, "Is Nicola all right?"

"Your daughter in magic is fine. Saddened, but she understands her choice and believes in it. Mariel comforts her even as we speak."

"I am happy for them both. Relieved and glad for what they set out to do. Moehn will be blessed by their presence, by the *Aekelahr* they plan to build."

So it is that in our daughters, we long to see the fulfillment of our own dreams.

"Ireny in Roenfyn," Eolyn continued. "Nicola in Moehn. Only Ghemena remains unaccounted for. That worries me, Corey. It worries me to no end."

"Thelyn and Borten have been informed. They will have doubled the guard for the Prince and Princess by now."

"She won't harm the children. Ghemena's capable of much mischief, but the murder of innocents? No."

"That's an assumption we cannot afford to make."

355

"She is a maga, Corey. My daughter in magic. If she's found, I want her brought to me alive. We must seek reconciliation. I would give her another chance, just as I did with Nicola."

Eolyn had repeated these words on many occasions in recent days. Corey knew that even now she hoped Ghemena was listening.

"We have no choice but to be vigilant," he said. "Time will reveal whether she can be counted among our own again."

With any luck, Ghemena had fled south to Antaria or beyond. Wherever she was, Corey hoped to have word of her soon. Given the chance, he would have her eliminated without Eolyn's knowledge. Better that than to spend the rest of his days watching their backs because of one treacherous maga.

"There is the other threat we have not discussed since setting out for Selkynsen," Eolyn said. "The Naether Demons."

Corey nodded. "That too is a question of vigilance, my Lady Queen. Vigilance and further study. Though I am confident that the immediate danger has been abated, for reasons already discussed."

"Still, there are countless places across the kingdom where the curtain between this world and the next has worn thin. We must do what we can to prevent the Naether Demons from crossing over again. Once we have returned to the City, I would ask that you appoint a group of practitioners to travel to the wastes of Faernvorn and reinforce the barrier of stone that blocks that gate to their realm."

"As you wish, my Lady Queen."

Eolyn opened her mouth again to speak, but then hesitated. Her eyes settled upon her hands.

The silence between them lengthened.

Corey cleared his throat. "If that be all, my Lady Queen, I would ask to take my leave. We have an early start tomorrow, and I have much to prepare for the journey."

She nodded.

He turned to go.

"Corey."

The gravity of her tone gave him pause. "My Lady Queen?"

"I just wondered...If you would..." Flustered, she looked away. Her voice fell to a whisper. "Stay with me."

Before Corey could respond, Eolyn hastened to add, "I know

East Selen calls you. I can feel the longing in your heart, how you yearn for those forests just as I yearn for the South Woods. Always, always I have sensed this bond between you and the place of your ancestors, but now I have noticed something different wrapping around your aura. I'm afraid, Corey. Afraid that if you journey to East Selen now, you will not return to court."

The declaration moved him more deeply than she could know.

"I must go home, Eolyn," he said, nonetheless. "My magic is spent, my spirit most weary. No place restores my powers like the forests of my people. I will depart the City as soon as I finish the tasks appointed to me, hopefully by Samhaen. If not, shortly thereafter."

Eolyn nodded, thought disappointment flickered through her aura. "You must do as your heart directs, of course. It would be wrong of me to stand between you and the source of your magic."

He admired the firm set of her shoulders, the determination in her jaw that belied the tremor beneath her breath. Many might have assumed Eolyn had at last reached the end of her struggles, when in truth she stood on the threshold of the greatest challenge the Gods had yet demanded of her.

It was a lonely task, running a kingdom.

And magas were not meant to be alone.

Corey took Eolyn's chin in hand and brought her gaze back to his. "I will depart for East Selen before the maples shed their leaves. There, I will spend the winter and perhaps the greater part of spring. But this is not the end of our time together, Maga Eolyn. I made a promise to you long ago, and I do not intend to break it."

Eolyn's eyes turned damp. A gracious smile touched her lips. "Very well, Mage Corey. Gods help me, but it seems I'm at last inclined to trust you at your word."

Smiling, he drew her into his embrace, hand gentle upon her hair as she laid her head against his chest. They stood together like that a long while, paying silent homage to a friendship that had weathered countless storms.

CHAPTER FIFTY-SIX

Seedlings

COREY JOURNEYED BACK to the King's City after winter's end, in the days before Bel-Aethne. He enjoyed travel this time of year, when warm winds chased away the snow and painted the landscape in fresh shades of green. Flowers graced the fields with gold, crimson, and purple. Birds flitted from tree to tree, engaged in fierce rivalries of the mating season. Insects buzzed an incessant and happy song.

The King' City, reflecting the landscape, was alight with color and activity. Banners had been hung for the upcoming festival. Vendors crowded the alleyways offering an array of richly embroidered masks. Lilies and fir branches graced balconies and windows. Laughter rolled easily through the streets.

Corey brought with him oxcarts bearing fruits from his forest: bushels of seed gathered by children of East Selen, along with sprouted seedlings of fir, oak, beech, and other sacred trees carefully cultivated by his own hand. They would grow well, he believed, in the foothills of the Surmaeg Mountains. He intended to bring more every spring to support Eolyn's efforts to strengthen the barrier between the worlds of the living and the dead.

Thelyn and I have come to the same conclusion, Eolyn had written over Winter Solstice. *The pattern is clear to our eyes though, remarkably, not noted by historians of the time.*

According to all the annals, the creatures we now call Naether Demons first appeared during the conquest of the provinces, when the Princes of Vortingen broke open the iron mines of the Surmaeg and destroyed the surrounding forests. Back then, they were creatures of flesh and blood. We eliminated their home and forced them south, where they began to feed on our people.

Thelyn believes, as do I, that in addition to the stone monoliths that mark the edge of the wastes, we must erect a living barrier to protect our land from further incursions of the Underworld, just as the garden protected you and me and the children on the night the demons attacked.

Can you imagine, Corey? The northern reaches of our kingdom covered once again in woodland! I must see it done, for reasons that go well beyond the question of the Naether Demons. I understand now that this, too, is part of my purpose, part of weaving magic back into our land.

Later, she had written in a separate letter:

I have read in the fourth volume of Eranon, which Thelyn kindly lent me though he fears he will meet Tzeremond's wrath in the Afterlife, that the threads between this life and the next are not in fact separate but intertwined, so that every action we take in this world affects the spirits who populate the next.

And so I like to believe, dear Corey, that perhaps the Naether Demons are not entirely lost as the great teachers thought. Perhaps every tree we plant in this world will contribute to their healing in the next.

I am anxious for spring to arrive, so that we may begin our work.

Dear Corey, she had written.

He had rather liked that.

Eolyn greeted Corey in the outer courtyard of the castle. She clapped her hands in delight at his gift and ran her fingers over the seedlings, murmuring welcome in their language, registering the name of each one.

Though Corey maintained his residence in the Mages Quarter, Eolyn had set aside apartments for him in the fortress. After some consideration, he accepted her invitation.

The days before Bel-Aethne proved festive and full of activity, a refreshing change from his hermit's retreat in East Selen. Mornings were spent with fellow mages and old friends, afternoons devoted to music, dancers, and poetry in the taverns along the piers.

In the evenings, he would return to the castle to dine with the Queen and her court. In the tradition of the season, Eolyn had brought the best musicians, bards, and dancers from near and far. Some of these Corey recognized as former members of his Circle, talented artists who still graced the kingdom with their mastery of Primitive Magic.

On the first evening of Bel-Aethne, Eolyn descended from the dais to dance. Corey saw in the faces of the onlookers how the people of Moisehén had come to admire their Queen. He had never witnessed Eolyn quite like this, brimming with joy and confident in her hope for the future, though on occasion the shadow of her husband's absence passed over her, dimming the colors of her aura.

Briana, who had grown half a head since Corey last saw her, sat on his lap, though she was nearly too big to do so. She leaned her head on the mage's shoulder and watched her mother with wide, attentive eyes.

"You should dance too, Briana," Corey said. "It is the duty of every maga to dance during a high holiday."

"I would rather just sit here with you," she replied. "You've been away for so long. Maybe I will dance tomorrow."

Not inclined to argue, Corey pressed his lips to Briana's hair, inhaling her sweet aroma of pine and wild flowers.

Perhaps I will dance tomorrow, too, he thought. *Perhaps tomorrow, I will dance with Eolyn.*

The evening passed, and the hour grew late. Though the revelry continued, Briana began to nod off. Even Eoghan, sitting tall in his kingly chair, let his eyes close and his chin drop.

Sensitive to the needs of the children, Eolyn rose to take her leave and bade Eoghan and Briana to follow.

"I want Uncle Corey to come, too," Briana said, hanging back. "I want a story, Mama, before we go to sleep."

Eolyn cast a questioning glance toward Corey, permission to refuse clearly expressed in her deep brown eyes. She knew from long experience that there were many things a mage would rather do on the nights of Bel-Aethne than tell stories to children.

Corey nodded his assent. Taking Briana in hand, he followed Eolyn and her son to the children's apartments.

The moment they arrived, Eoghan's and Briana's enthusiasm was renewed. They begged permission to stay awake and play in front of the hearth, a petition Eolyn flatly refused, herding them instead into the bedroom.

Corey lingered behind, intrigued by the lively exchange of childish pleas and motherly scolding that marked their bedtime ritual, yet hesitant to enter until the children were settled and ready for their tale.

He stood by a window listening to the sounds of the festival that drifted up from the city below. He found the distance from all that noise unexpectedly soothing. For the first time in memory, a sense of true peace settled in his heart.

This is my Clan.

Corey had known this all along, of course. Yet somehow tonight he felt the bond to Eolyn and her children – indeed, to the fortress of Vortingen – more keenly than ever.

This is the end of everything that happened before, and the beginning of all that is yet to come.

Eolyn's scream shattered his thoughts.

Corey rushed into the bedroom, the heavy footsteps of guards on his heels.

They found Eolyn sinking against the stone wall. Her face was ashen. In her arms lay her son, Eoghan, his eyes glassy with shock.

On the other side of the room, Briana scrambled up a chair and onto a high table. Beneath her lay a large viper, coiled and ready to strike.

Faeom dumae!

Corey's curse flung the serpent against the wall. It fell to the floor, writhing in fury.

"Your sword!" Corey demanded.

One the guards gave him a weapon. The mage approached, wary of the serpent's reach. The swiftest way to kill a viper, he knew, was to cut off its head. But Corey was not inclined to honor her with a rapid death.

Renemen eh!

The snake froze beneath his curse, and Corey drove the blade home. Pinned against the floor, she thumped and hissed. Light flashed through her, but the shape held.

Corey repeated his curse. The serpent's skin dissolved in a wash of colors, revealing the maga within.

Ghemena looked up at him, the sword embedded in her chest. Blood pooled upon her lips, and her eyes shone with zealous fervor.

"It is done," she whispered. "I go to meet my Gods."

Raw anger overtook Corey. He twisted the blade and drove it deep. Ghemena shuddered and lay still.

Sobs broke the silence that followed.

"Corey." Eolyn's plea came choked with fear. "Help me. I'm losing him."

As Corey returned the blade to its owner, Briana began to scramble down from the table.

"No!" Corey raised his hand to stop the girl and nodded to one of the guards. "Watch her. The rest of you, search these apartments. Make certain there are no more vermin about."

They hastened to see his will done.

Corey approached Eolyn and knelt before her.

She cradled Eoghan in her arms, one hand upon his chest. The sacred words of Dragon fell from her lips in a desperate cadence, as if she were invoking every spell known to her heart. Their auras intertwined, mother and son, hers bright and full of color, his fading fast into the world beyond. Night streamed from Eoghan's chest into Eolyn's palm.

Corey realized with alarm that she was trying to draw the venom out with her own spirit. Gently he took her hand, finding Eolyn's fingers as cold as ice.

"That is not the way," he murmured, breaking the connection.

Carefully, he opened Eoghan's blood-stained shirt and examined the wounds. The viper had struck twice, once at the shoulder and again on the chest. Where the fangs had penetrated, a bluish rot had already taken hold. By now, the venom would have reached Eoghan's heart. The prince's skin had turned a translucent gray. The light in his eyes was fading.

Corey searched for the boy's pulse and found none.

"Eolyn," he said, and then he could speak no more.

Why did it always fall to him to deliver such tidings?

Why did the Gods always demand the highest possible sacrifice for her triumphs?

Anger flared in Eolyn's aura. "No! Don't say it. Don't you dare! Eoghan, hear me."

The boy stirred. His chest rose and fell in a sudden breath. His eyes cleared and focused on his mother.

"Eoghan," she murmured. Hope flickered in her voice. She gathered his hand in hers and held it to her heart.

"Mama," the boy said. A smile touched his lips. "I've seen

Father, and the place he has prepared…It's beautiful."

Eoghan closed his eyes and drifted away.

"Stay with me, my love," Eolyn whispered, tightening her hold. "Stay with me."

The boy drew another breath and looked at his mother once more. "Father says to tell you…Do not to be afraid of your destiny. He says…Everything is as it should be…We will be waiting, Mama…We will wait together, by the river."

Then Eoghan, the last of the Princes of Vortingen, drew his final breath and departed the world of the living.

Eolyn stared in disbelief at her son, as if she could not reconcile the awful sight of his corpse with the living boy who had brought her so much joy only moments before. The fruit of her love, the flesh of her body, torn brutally and irrevocably from this world.

Gone.

Forever gone.

"Eoghan?"

Eolyn's hands shook as she gathered the child to her breast. She beat her head against the wall behind her, letting go a long, terrible wail. Then she covered her son's body with her own and clung to his lifeless form, consumed by wretched sobs.

CHAPTER FIFTY-SEVEN

Moon Over East Selen

THE TRADITION OF THE MAGAS included medicines that hastened one's passage into the Afterlife. Their use was strictly forbidden, save to assuage suffering in cases where death was already imminent. In the days following her son's murder, Eolyn contemplated using these herbs, when sleep eluded her and the darkness of night mirrored the emptiness of her soul. Just as the tentacles of grief threatened to pull Eolyn over the precipice, Briana, curled next to her mother, would shift and murmur in her sleep. As her daughter snuggled closer, Eolyn remembered there was yet life in this world; a young girl who needed her. She stroked Briana's hair and kissed her on the forehead. Then the maga wept a little more and drifted back to sleep.

Eoghan was burned according to the tradition of his fathers, his pyre laid on the sacred Foundation of Vortingen, his ashes scattered to the wind. During the twelve days of mourning that followed, friends arrived from distant provinces to provide comfort and support.

Mariel and Nicola warmed Eolyn's heart with stories of their new *Aekelahr*, its humble buildings and lush gardens; its vibrant young students. Lady Talia, recently wed to the man of her choice, young Meryth Baramon, chased away grim shadows with her glow of new love. Jacquetta ministered to Eolyn with fine teas and soothing words. Lady Vinelia held her Queen's hand whenever tears threatened to fall.

Conversation among the women often turned to Eoghan and Akmael. Their spoken word resurrected the noble and generous nature of the Princes of Vortingen. Much was made of Akmael's bravery in battle and his keen instinct for justice. Eoghan's dedication to his studies, and his emerging skills as a warrior, were lauded as if he had been the son of every woman present. Countless stories were related, moments in the lives of the men Eolyn loved, now laid at her feet like spring flowers, so she might see her husband and son in ways she never had before. Even the men's bouts of stubborn fury were cloaked in a brighter light of humor and affection.

At times, Eolyn sensed the presence of others who had already departed this world: Doyenne Ghemena, Renate, the girls Catarina and Tasha, and even, impossibly, Adiana. Despite her sorrow, Eolyn experienced a deep gratitude for the enduring presence of their friendship, for the comfort brought to her by this community of women that transcended the world of the living and the dead.

When the days of mourning had passed, the Council met to deliberate over the question of Akmael's succession. Jacquetta and Lady Vinelia, Lord Borten and Echior, Corey and Thelyn, and all Eolyn's other advisors withdrew from the Queen's presence to attend to their duties as Council members. Only Mariel, Nicola, and Talia remained, accompanying Eolyn and Briana as they awaited the Council's decision.

Since the death of her brother, Briana had spoken little. She sat at Eolyn's side, head resting upon her mother's shoulder. On rare occasions, she smiled at the more humorous anecdotes of Akmael and Eoghan. But mostly she kept to her own thoughts, quietly summoning creatures of light with her fingertips: butterflies and frogs and colorful beetles.

Whenever she crafted something of particular beauty, she nudged her mother for attention. A momentary spark of happiness shone in the girl's eyes as Eolyn kissed her forehead in approval. Then the princess let the creature dissolve with her smile and started all over again.

Hours passed as the Council debated. On the evening of the second day, Corey of East Selen appeared in Eolyn's apartments. The women rose to receive him, and though it was not required of her station, Eolyn did the same.

Briana left her mother's side to greet the mage. She did not run or skip into Corey's arms as had always been her habit, but stood grim-faced in front of him. Silent understanding passed between them. The mage drew Briana into a tender but brief embrace.

The bond between these two had always been strong, but Eolyn thought it uncanny how Briana had tightened her hold on Corey in the months since Akmael's death. It was as if she had conscientiously decided Corey would assume the place in her life once occupied by Akmael.

As if a part of her spirit understands.

"My Lady Queen," Corey announced. "I have come to inform you that the Council has made its decision."

The women took their leave. Mariel extended her hand toward Briana, but the princess held back.

"Mama," she said. "I want to stay."

"I know, my love," Eolyn replied, "but I must speak first with Mage Corey. Do not wander far. We will call you soon enough."

The servants departed behind them, and the guards closed the doors.

Corey drew a quiet breath.

"They recognize Briana as sole legitimate heiress to the throne of Moisehén," he said. "They have agreed to swear allegiance to her and no one else."

Eolyn let go a sigh of relief. "Thank you, Corey."

"We must now hope that Taesara respects the treaty she signed in Selkynsen."

"I believe she will."

Taesara's condolences had arrived by messenger the previous day. *It burdens my heart,* the Queen of Roenfyn had written, *that this, the most terrible of all griefs that a mother can suffer, should be visited upon you, my neighbor and ally. May all the Gods be with you and your daughter in this most difficult time. Know you have our support and sympathy.*

"But we will remain vigilant," Eolyn added, "in case she does not."

"I should also caution you that there is no small amount of self-interest in the Council's decision. I give the noble houses of Moisehén two months – at most, three – before they start putting their own sons forward as suitors."

"Briana will not be given away in marriage," Eolyn said. "When the time comes, she will choose her own consort. And that man, no matter who he is, will never wear the Crown of Vortingen."

Approval flickered through Corey's expression. "I think it prudent that Briana retain sole proprietorship over the Crown. As for letting her choose her own consort…Perhaps we could withhold that privilege until it becomes clear just what sort of consort she would choose."

Eolyn could not help but smile.

Spoken like a true father.

Laughter bubbled in her chest, incongruous with the moment, and soon stifled by a deeper burden. She frowned and looked away.

"Shall we call the Princess?" Corey asked.

"No…No, Corey, if you would just wait a moment, I…" She bit her lip and studied her hands.

What to say? How to say it?

"Have you ever noticed," she ventured, "how the great stories of our lives always seem to end like this?"

"Like what, my Lady Queen?"

"You and me." She lifted her eyes to meet his gaze. "Alone, with the truth."

Corey studied her a long moment. Eolyn felt the intensity of his presence in a way she had not for a very long time. The clarity of his silver-green gaze, his aroma of pine and winter winds, the magic of East Selen that coursed through his veins.

The mage drew close and invoked a sound ward.

"The truth?" His tone hovered between question and affirmation.

"Of my failure." Her voice shook. "To my brother in the Battle of Aerunden, to my sisters during the Syrnte invasion, and now, my failure to our King."

"You protected Akmael's throne and secured his kingdom. I see no failure in that."

"His son died in my arms."

"That was not your fault."

"I should have foreseen—"

"Do not start down that path, Eolyn. The burden of Eoghan's death is not yours to bear."

Eolyn's heart contracted painfully. "Even if Eoghan's fate was beyond my control, I could have given Akmael more. Another son, as many as he desired. If I had, there would be a prince now to—"

"Akmael's father, Kedehen, had three brothers. We all know how much grief that brought everyone."

"Let me finish!"

The rebuke came harsher than Eolyn intended, but Corey simply nodded and took a step back.

"I would have thought it comical," Eolyn continued, "had not the consequences been so grave, that anyone, *anyone* could question Eoghan's ancestry. All one needed to do was look upon his face. Every feature, every gesture, every mood, thought, and word branded him as a Prince of Vortingen. His magic, like his father's, was tied to this mountain, to its heart of stone and fire. He was Akmael's true son, and he would have made a great king."

"Briana will also be a worthy queen."

"Yes, but Briana…She is different." Eolyn retreated from the mage, putting distance between them until she reached the eastern window, where she rested her hand upon the sill.

A breeze refreshed her face. Outside the evening sky was streaked with purple and red. In the east, stars began to herald the coming night.

"Briana's magic is not tied to this mountain," Eolyn said. "Her spirit thrives on ancient forests and living creatures, on timeless mysteries and constant change. Briana, like her namesake, is a true Daughter of East Selen."

Eolyn closed her eyes. The forests of Corey's home rose in her mind. Wind roared through towering trees. Snow fell thick and blinding. Voices howled through the night, the angry cries of a clan betrayed.

Winter Fox had called to her that night, its restless shape a warm refuge against the storm's fury. Snow crunched beneath her paws; moisture froze on the tips of her nose and ears. From one moment to the next, Eolyn had lost her way inside that blizzard. She had panicked and run in blind circles until she stumbled up a snow drift to scrabble desperately at a closed window.

When at last the shutters opened and she leapt into the bright warmth of that humble chamber, it took a moment for her to recognize where she was and what it would mean.

Seven days they had been trapped by the snow storm in East Selen, with the King's royal progress delayed in its efforts to join them for Winter Solstice.

Seven days that had changed the destiny of a kingdom.

Eolyn drew a shaky breath and released the burden of her heart.

"Briana is yours," she whispered. "Corey, my daughter, Briana, is also yours."

In the silence that followed, Eolyn heard the beat of her own heart. Corey's robes rustled as he approached. She felt the touch of his hand, warm upon her cheek.

"Eolyn," he murmured. "You think I did not know?"

Her eyes flew open. "You never said anything. You never asked—"

"That night was not to be spoken of again. It was not even to be remembered...Though I must admit, I have had a very hard time forgetting."

"I dreamed of her, Corey. The night we made love, I saw who she would be. Not this, of course." Eolyn gestured to the room around them, to the bitter circumstances at hand. "I did not foresee any of this. But I saw Briana's light and love, her joy and magic. Though I had it in my power to extinguish her spark, I could not bring myself to do it."

"It was a grave risk you took, bringing her into this world. I myself might have counseled you against it."

"I would not have listened to you."

"No." A smile touched his lips. "And I'm grateful for that. Grateful for our daughter and for the courage you had, delivering her to this world."

"And if I'd let go of her in the moment she was conceived? What then, Corey? Where would we be now? This is the question I've asked myself a thousand times since Eoghan's death. Have I done right, or have I done wrong?"

"We made our choices, nothing more. And we survived to see the consequences."

"I loved Akmael."

"I know."

"I promised him—"

369

"An eternity?" Resignation filled Corey's expression. "I thought you might have done something like that."

Eolyn looked away, uncertain. "And so I betrayed you both."

"You are a maga, Eolyn. You cannot be bound to one man."

"I bound myself to him."

"In the eyes of the kingdom, perhaps. But in the eyes of the Gods, never."

"And now I pretend to put a girl on the throne who—"

"Who will grow into a fine maga and a formidable queen."

"A false queen."

"False in what sense?" Impatience colored Corey's tone. "Did not the Kings of Vortingen violate their charge? Did they not murder your sisters and massacre my clan? In spite of this, we forgave them, served them, *loved* them, even. Can we not imagine for a moment that this child, a true born Maga of the Clan of East Selen, is the Gods' reward for our patience and perseverance? That our daughter will be their instrument, meant to guide our people to a brighter future?"

Eolyn frowned and shook her head. "I don't think it's our place to judge the will of the Gods."

"Whose place is it, then? The Council's?" Corey gestured toward the chamber outside. "Would you share this truth with anyone beyond those doors? You know the consequences, Eolyn. For us and most of all, for our daughter."

She sank into troubled silence.

Corey stepped close and took her hands in his.

"Our charge has been given to us," he said. "This is not a duty that we can set aside."

"I know," she murmured.

"I've long wanted to tell you how honored I was, the night you came to me. Honored and quite frankly, relieved. Not every man of this court would have understood or respected the magic that moved you. I hope that, if there have been others, you have chosen them with equal care and discretion."

"Others?" The comment surprised her. "No, there haven't been any others. Only you and that night, when winter bore down on East Selen with the breath of death, and the voices of the forest would not be silenced."

Corey furrowed his brow and withdrew. He paced the room, hands folded behind his back and gaze focused inward. When he returned to Eolyn, his expression was calm and resolute.

"Eolyn, I understand it may be too soon to think about such things, but when the time comes, there's something I would like for you to consider. Before you embark upon your eternity with Akmael, I thought you might perhaps spare a few short years of the life that remains to us, in this world, for me."

Fire sparked inside Eolyn's heart, warm and steady like a candle in the night.

She drew a quiet breath and offered him a tentative nod. "I will consider it, Mage Corey. When the time comes."

A smile illuminated his face. He kissed her then, an embrace that neither demanded nor imposed, but fed the light inside Eolyn's heart, chasing back shadows of recent days and months. Eolyn sensed a great magic stirring between them. A past left behind, a future as yet unrevealed.

As Corey withdrew, something behind her caught his eye. He nodded toward the window.

"Look, Eolyn."

Outside, the moon was rising, full and buoyant, over the distant forests of East Selen. In the shadows on its face, Eolyn saw the image of Dragon in flight.

"It's beautiful," she said.

Corey raised Eolyn's fingers to his lips. "So it begins."

Acknowledgements

The completion of *The Silver Web* trilogy has been a decade-long journey made possible by many people and places along the way. *Daughter of Aithne* owes its inspiration to all the amazing women who have been my mentors, friends, and colleagues over the years.

Special thanks go to my editor, Terri-Lynne DeFino, who never stopped believing in me or my work. Terri, you are and always will be the Sparkle Queen.

Thomas Vandenberg has been wonderful to work with, and I am forever indebted to him for capturing the heart and soul of Eolyn's world with his beautiful cover art.

Two writers groups have been with me from the very beginning: the Dead Horse Society and the Next Big Writer. Special mention goes to Charles Brass and Bill Slack for sticking with me all the way to the end of *Daughter of Aithne*. Thank you both for your excellent critiques and encouragement.

Dollbabies: I love you! I hope you see your beauty, strength, and courage reflected in these pages.

Many thanks to my family, who have been steadfast in their support of this time-consuming "hobby," and to all my readers, who waited with patience and enthusiasm for the release of this third novel.

Finally, for my muse: I am blessed by your presence in my life and forever grateful for this journey of imagination. May I always have the courage to write as you inspire.

This novel is my prayer for peace. The future is in all our hands. Love is the only path to victory. Let compassion guide your footsteps. Never forget that magic is within our reach.

About the Author

Karin Rita Gastreich lives in Kansas City, Missouri, where she is part of the biology faculty at Avila University. An ecologist by vocation, she has wandered forests and wildlands all over the world. Many of her stories are inspired by these experiences. Her pastimes include camping, hiking, music, and flamenco dance. In addition to *The Silver Web* trilogy, Karin has published short stories in *World Jumping*, *Zahir*, *Adventures for the Average Woman*, and *69 Flavors of Paranoia*. She is a recipient of the Andrews Forest Writers Residency.

Karin is starting a new collection of paranormal thrillers entitled *Path of Souls*. Look for the first book of this series in 2018.

You can visit Karin at krgastreich.com.

CPSIA information can be obtained
at www.ICGtesting.com
Printed in the USA
LVOW11s1939090817
544392LV00005B/903/P